Finding the Pieces

For the Heart Series Book Two

Jane Hayes

First Edition April 2025

Copyediting by Paisley McNab, Perfectly Write Editing Services

Beta Reading Service provided by E&A Editing Services

Cover Design by Melissa Doughty - Mel D. Designs at melissadoughty.com

ISBN 979-8-9904140-3-7 (paperback)

ISBN 979-8-9904140-2-0 (e-book)

Contents

Author's Note

Finding the Pieces is the second novel in the *For the Heart* series. While you can read any novel on its own, as the plot of each story stands alone, it is not recommended. There is a prominent found family component to the series, and reading the books in order will enhance the connection to the many side characters in this novel and build upon the foundation from book one. For the best reader experience—and to avoid spoilers—I strongly recommend you read them in order, starting with *Winning the Nightcap*.

If you have triggers that affect your reading choices, especially related to conceiving, pregnancy, labor, birth, postpartum, and parenthood-related topics, I encourage you to take a look at the content warnings before reading this novel. Your health and wellness are important to me and should absolutely always come first.

This story focuses first and foremost on love. The love between Ellie and Dominic as a married couple, and the love they have for their son, Luca. However, there are detailed descriptions of birth trauma and the mental health impact of the event on both parents. If this is not something you can consume safely, I kindly ask that you enjoy another book at this time.

I could not have read this book immediately after my birthing and postpartum experience. Today, it would reassure me that I was never alone in feeling and thinking a lot of really scary things during a transformational time. Maybe someday that'll be the same for you, and if not, that's completely okay. Don't be afraid to walk away if you're not ready. It's brave to acknowledge if this isn't for you. Please honor what you need.

I wouldn't be the person I am today if I didn't find help. If you are a parent struggling with mental health needs, there are resources available. Please reach out to your doctor, your local crisis center, or Postpartum Support International (PSI) - https://www.postpartum.net to find what would be most helpful for you. It takes a strong person to ask for help; you deserve it.

Sending all my love to you and yours.

Content Warnings

On-page sex scenes (intended for 18+ years of age, or legal age of adulthood);

Descriptions of pregnancy, deciding to attempt conception, and trying to conceive a child;

Descriptions of birth trauma and medical trauma;

Descriptions of postpartum mental health conditions, including postpartum depression, postpartum anxiety, post-traumatic stress disorder from a traumatic birthing experience, and intrusive thoughts (including thoughts of death and dying of the parent and child—this does **not** occur); and

Discussion of body image insecurities.

For my son and my husband. You make me feel more joy than I imagined was possible. You bring out the life in me. Thank you for loving me through it all, exactly as I am.

For my family. Thank you for being our village. For loving us, for taking care of us, and for making us laugh when it was all too much. Our lives mean more with you in it.

And for Rachel, who held my hand while I struggled to find myself on this side of motherhood. You taught me that becoming a parent is like "jumping into the deep end of the vulnerability pool." Here I am, treading water, thanks to you.

Prologue

SEVEN YEARS AGO

Ellie

"You're a pain in the ass, you know that?" I hiss, giving the printer a sharp slap on the side. I hit it again and yank on the paper wedged between the printer spindles with a grunt, shifting my body weight as I lean away from the stupid machine, trying to free the paper from the jam. "Listen here, you piece of—"

"Am I interrupting?"

I freeze, biting my lips as my mind and body race to decide what to do being caught mid-altercation with the third-floor printer in the University of Columbus student library.

When I took this job a few weeks ago, at the start of my junior year, I imagined helping students find the books they need, checking out rentals, shelving returns, and filling the time in between reading and drinking tea at the front desk. No one told me how much time I'd spend fighting this goddamn printer.

What's worse? Being caught mid-fight as I berate the damn thing...but I'm no quitter.

"If you just give me a second," I say as I tug again on the paper without success. "You may want to reprint whatever you're waiting for. Send it to printer 0895 on the second floor."

I hear a muffled chuckle behind me, like whoever finds me amusing is trying to mask it. Awfully polite, but unfortunately for them, I'm already irritated, so it's not enough to keep me from snapping my stare toward them, making them the lucky new focus of my aggravation.

"Something funny?" I ask before blowing the hair out of my face in a huff, my body angled toward the printer, fingers still gripping the paper trapped in this bitch printer's claws.

"No. Nope. Nothing amusing at all." Mystery man has the nerve to smirk at me, giving me a noticeable once-over. I roll my eyes and return my focus to the battle in front of me.

"Want me to give it a try?"

"Listen, Romeo, I do not need rescued right now. I...got...it." I give one final tug, turning the internal spindle at the same time—which is supposed to make this easier, but decided to wait until now to be helpful. "Aha, see? Got it."

I turn to find the stranger leaning on the door frame, arms crossed and smiling at me. A warm, shiny smile that has me blushing instantly.

I return my focus to the printer, closing the door to the internal panel and clicking the same buttons I click at least a few times a week to put this brat back in commission. When I brave another look at stranger boy, I realize he's no stranger boy at all. He's all man, definitely not some freshman.

His genuine smile is framed by a neatly trimmed beard, forearms flexing underneath rolled sleeves of a white button-up shirt with navy slacks. *Maybe he has to give a presentation today or something.*

"Looks like I don't need to send my paper elsewhere after all."

"Lucky you," I say with a shrug.

"Yeah, I'd say so." His smile reaches his eyes. Actually, it's more like positivity radiates off his entire body, completely at ease. And he hasn't taken his eyes off me.

When the printer jolts to life with a loud mechanical whir, I startle, realizing I've been staring at mystery man.

"You should be good. It's rebooting now. It'll print a few test sheets, then you can enter your code, and it should print whatever you're waiting for. If not, try again, and—for the love of god—send it to the second-floor printer." I force the words out in a rush before allowing myself another glimpse in his direction.

He's still leaning against the door frame, shoulders relaxed, carefree smile in place, head tilted at me with a look of...curiosity?

Unsure what else to do, I take a step toward the doorway to sneak past him. He shifts, resting his back against the frame, turning to face his body toward mine as I pass him.

"What's your name?" he asks, his voice deep and rich. His question gives me pause, and I lean against the door frame opposite him, leaving little space between us.

"Ellie?" I say like it's a question.

"You sure?" he asks.

"Apparently not. Yours?"

"Dominic?" he asks, mirroring my tone.

I nod thoughtfully. "It fits."

"With some effort, sure."

"Damn, that was quick." I can't keep the smile off my face as I refocus my attention on the suddenly very important scrap paper still in my hand, attempting to hide my blush.

"Can I ask you for a favor, Ellie?"

"A favor..."

"Two, actually. First, can I take you out for coffee sometime? Second, I sort of need to borrow a printing passcode."

I ignore his first question. "Oh, are you new to campus? You just enter your student ID," I say, gesturing to the pin pad on the printer.

I'm pretty tall, but he's taller. Confident stance, strong build, but still emanating an approachable, easygoing energy.

He rubs the back of his neck, looking to his feet, showing the first sign of insecurity. "Ruth normally lets me print under her code," he says, gesturing to the brown paper bag in his hand. I hadn't noticed it before. The local cupcake shop—beloved by everyone on campus—logo printed on the side.

I raise my eyebrow in suspicion. "Why are you bribing the seventy-five-year-old librarian with cupcakes when you could enter your student ID to use the campus printers?"

"Come on, now, Ellie. Ruth is seventy-*one* years young, turning seventy-two in November. And technically, I *was* a student. Graduated last year. I'm in my first year of teaching high school history, and Ruth lets me swing by to print materials for my class every so often."

"A teacher," I say, giving him an appraising once-over, loving what I see, but I'm not telling him that. "Regardless of if you're telling the truth, I might have to report Ruth for this." I would *never*. Ruth is a saint. "Pretty egregious violation of librarian policy if you ask me. And you..." I shove an accusatory finger in his chest and he lifts his hands in surrender, his smile growing wider. "Taking advantage of sweet Ruth. How could you?"

"Taking advantage?" he asks in mock outrage. "Did you miss the cupcake bribe? It is a mutually beneficial arrangement. But since you're here and Ruth is inconveniently missing, what if this cupcake became *Ellie's* cupcake? Would that get me printing rights?" he asks, wiggling the bag between us.

"I assume you're always this persistent?" I try to hide my smile, but his is contagious and I'm helpless to fight it.

"Agree to get coffee with me and you'll see how much worse it gets."

"Just coffee..." I agree, hoping like hell it turns into more than just coffee.

His smile and subtle wink tell me he has anything but innocent intentions, but then again, neither do I. "Sure, Ellie. We'll start there."

CHAPTER ONE

Ellie

ALMOST TWO YEARS AGO

My hands won't stop shaking.

This doesn't feel real, but the four tests lying on the bathroom countertop all prove that it is.

I'm pregnant.

I hover shaking fingers over my lips with one hand while the other snakes around my belly, fingers stretching along my lower abdomen, feeling around for signs of life. Impossible this early, I know, but that doesn't stop me from searching anyway.

A few walls of muscle and tissue separate my palm from the little being that'll someday be a whole person. A smile explodes across my face and a breathless laugh escapes between my fingers.

Tears roll silently down my cheeks and my mind empties. You'd think I'd have this grand poetic thought about how I'm going to be a mother and what that means. How I'm already bonding and connecting with this little, soon-to-be baby, but no. My mind is *completely empty*, shock and disbelief stealing my ability to think a single coherent thought.

"Hi, baby," I whisper softly, my eyes closing as I picture the little ball of cells making a home so near my heart. "I'm your momma. Momma's here."

Knock, knock.

"Hey, babe, we're going to be late. You almost ready?" Dominic—Dom—my husband, calls from the other side of our bathroom door.

My eyes snap to the mirror, taking in my rattled appearance. I barely recognize myself, the shock and excitement practically glittering in my eyes.

I take a deep breath, failing to calm my racing heart before opening the door to find Dom leaning against the wall in front of me.

God, I love him. I'm so lucky we're doing this together.

"We're already late," I say with a hysteric giggle.

His brows furrow in confusion as he stretches, pulling the sleeve of his button-down shirt farther up his arm so he can check his watch.

"Not yet, but we have to leave now if we don't want to miss out on the apps. You know Marie's Diner has the best sampler. At this rate, Jake and Chris will be halfway done with it before we park the car."

"I'm telling you now, *we're already late*," I say, unable to contain my excitement, clumsily reaching behind me to grab a test from the counter and holding out my shaking hand in the space between us.

His entire body freezes. Like he can't risk moving even to take a breath. My husband-turned-statue stares for one...two...three of the longest seconds of my life before his shoulders crumple and he hinges forward at the waist, his palms covering his face as a sob escapes.

I sob in answer and laughter bubbles up, too, as tears of gratitude, fear, and uninhibited joy escape my heart through my tears.

He stands from his crouched position after a moment, blindly reaching for me until he's wrapped me tightly in his arms, his embrace shielding me and our baby from every force in the world. It's just us. Here and now, just the two...three of us.

"Oh my god, Ellie. I love you. I love you so fucking much. This is it." He takes a step back, holding the side of my face with one hand as the other gently moves to my stomach, the warmth of his touch registering through the shock. When my eyes lock with his, my heart stutters and our dopey smiles of disbelief must mirror one another's.

"Holy shit, we need to go to the store. What do we need for a baby's room? I don't know anything about breast pumps—we need one of those, right? What kind of clothes do they wear when they're that small? We need to...need to..." His glassy eyes flutter back and forth, lost and searching for something to bring him back to solid ground.

"Dominic, breathe," I say, running my hand over his, both of them now stretched across my stomach. "Breathe. We don't need to do anything right now...except get your pregnant wife to the place with the *food*." I wink and that seems to break him out of his shocked state. Our nervous laughter echoes through the hall as we rest our heads against one another, threading our fingers together over the space I'll be growing our little one until they're ready to meet us.

We've been wishing and waiting for this, yet I don't think anything could prepare us for how it'd feel to realize we've already been strapped into the seats of this roller coaster, departed the station, and are making our way up the hill before we even knew. No idea what the track ahead looks like. Where it'll dip, dive, climb, and curve. How fast we'll be careened from one twist to the next.

But I know I'm ready. *We're* ready.

I know more than anything that this man is the person I'm meant to be with. The man I'm meant to share this life with as we welcome this little one into our bubble of love.

Chapter Two

Ellie

Present Day

I'm sitting behind the wheel of my car, imagining all the ways I could get into a wreck while driving to my parent's house. We're only a city away from them, in the suburbs of Columbus, Ohio, but the fifteen-minute drive feels like hours as my mind starts to race with *what-ifs*.

My son, Luca, is buckled into his car seat in the back, babbling away, oblivious to the mindfuck that has his mom paralyzed, unable to shift the car into reverse.

"Babe." Dom reaches over to squeeze my thigh, shaking me out of my trance. "Want me to drive? It's okay if you aren't up for it."

The look he gives me turns my stomach sour. It isn't pity; it's compassion, but I hate it all the same. I don't want him to have to be compassionate. I want him to joke with me and make a sarcastic comment about how he's become an old man with saggy balls waiting for me to haul ass out of our driveway.

I want him to treat me how he used to, without kid gloves. But I know this is what I need, and I fucking hate that I need it.

"No, I got it. I'll be fine." I adjust my grip on the steering wheel, my knuckles white from the pressure. "We'll be fine...right?" My confidence sputters.

Dom grabs me behind the neck, turning me toward him, and leans his forehead against mine, taking a few deep breaths—in and out—loud enough for me to hear. My breaths sync with his for a few beats, my racing heart slowing.

"We will be fine. You are safe. We are safe," he whispers my mantra to me before kissing my forehead.

I repeat the thought throughout the drive, willing it to stay true.

I am safe. We are safe.

***

The trip home is less eventful. My mind too tired from socializing with our families at dinner tonight to spin through my usual pattern of worst-case scenario thinking.

We pull away from my parents' house, where they hosted dinner for Dom's parents, his brother Jake, Jake's husband Chris, Dom, Luca, and me. I watch from the passenger seat as Dom effortlessly navigates the roads to take us home.

Of course, Luca fell asleep in his car seat immediately, which means he'll be up for the next three hours. Bedtime is screwed, but I'm too tired to fight to keep him awake for the drive home.

"Your mom brought up Luca's birthday again tonight," Dom says, interrupting my near-constant thoughts of sleep schedules, wake windows, and desperate questions like *will I ever sleep again?*

"Yeah, she asked me about it too."

An uncomfortably long silence hangs in the air between us. My heart pounds in my chest, and my palms turn slick with sweat. I know he's going to ask. Part of me wants to stall him, but the other part just wants him to spit it out.

"What are you thinking?" he asks.

"I'm thinking...I don't want to think about it," I say quietly.

"El, I need you to talk to me. I need to know what's going on." Dom takes my hand and squeezes reassuringly.

"I just..." I pull my hand away from him, running it through my hair. I lean against the passenger door and close my eyes, fighting to keep my voice level and hold back the tears threatening to spill. "I want to focus on celebrating Luca, but every time I think about his birthday…" I whisper, letting the thought drift away.

"I thought the flashbacks were getting better. Practically gone," he says without judgment. Just a statement. A wish.

"They are. Or at least they *were*."

Things were getting better. I hadn't had any flashbacks to Luca's birth in at least a month, but a few days ago, they started again. My gut is telling me it's because Luca's birthday is coming up at the end of the month.

Now, I keep finding myself caught between a state of choking panic or hollow numbness; I don't know what's worse.

I know what *looks* worse. The panic. The tears. The near hysteria. But the numbness aches *inside*, like subfloors rotting away beneath new flooring. It looks pretty, but in reality, the smallest amount of pressure in the wrong spot would tear a hole straight through to the decrepit basement.

I wonder sometimes what people see when they look at me. Look at that mom pushing her baby in a stroller around the block. Look at that mom taking her son to the playground. Look at that mom at the grocery store with her child.

What do they think of me? Do they know I'm falling apart piece by piece, wishing that someday I'll feel like a good mom?

No matter what other people see on the outside, I have no fucking clue what I'm doing. I spend every minute anticipating every single thing that could possibly go wrong. The truly horrific hypotheticals stay stuck on a loop in my brain all damn day and it's all I can do to keep a smile on my face and kiss my sweet boy's forehead and tell him how much I love him while shoving those thoughts down deep in my wrecked mind.

"What do you need, Ellie? Please, I just want to help."

God, if he doesn't stop talking, I'm going to break down and I don't know how long it'll take to pull myself back together.

I pull at the frayed edges of my sanity and tug them into place, shutting everything down. I'd rather feel nothing than lose it right now in this car with Dom's gentle voice whittling away my limited control.

I ignore his question and refocus the conversation on the party we need to host. "What if we do something simple? Just invite family and close friends to our place. I don't know, maybe lunch and cake?"

"Yeah. Yeah, that sounds good. Want me to work out the food and the invites?" he offers.

I hate talking about this like we both don't know that Dom's walking on eggshells around me. Unsure if he should push me to talk about it or let me bury it and get through the decisions we need to get through.

Because what kind of mom doesn't get excited to plan their child's first birthday party?

Shame cuts sharply into my lungs, stealing my breath, and I force a deep inhale, trying to will it away.

"Yeah, that'd be great. Thanks, Dom."

When I cut a glance in his direction, his gaze is focused on the road ahead. That little wrinkle in his forehead pulled tight in...frustration? I used to poke at that wrinkle when we'd tease each other or when we'd bicker over small, stupid shit. It'd always make him laugh, and he'd tease me right back, poking my solo dimple on my left cheek. It made me laugh too.

Something close to grief burns in my stomach.

Those people we were *before*. They feel like strangers.

I don't think we'll ever find them again.

I don't think they exist anymore.

Chapter Three

Ellie

"Remind me, which one of you picked this book? Tell me right fucking now so I can kiss you." Dee pinches her fingers, pressing them to her lips and giving a dramatic *smack* of a kiss, followed by the flourish of her wrist. "The slow burn. The tension. The dirty talk. Utter sapphic perfection."

"You're welcome," Abby responds, raising her glass.

"Was that your first pick for book club? Home run, babe," Bec says.

"*Uuuuugh*, okay, Bec, we get it. Your hot-bodied, big-bat-swinging boy toy hits home runs. No need to rub it in," Dee says with a sarcastic whine.

"Oh please, like you've ever suffered a dry spell in your life. Go find your own," Bec retorts with a laugh.

"I'll have you know that I'm living in the desert right now. And let me warn you, I'm parched and pissy. Abby, Carrisa, please tell me we can go out this weekend? I need some single babes by my side while I go hunting. No offense, you two," Dee says to Bec and me.

Bec and Aiden started dating last year, making us the only two members of our book club in committed relationships. I met Dee and Carissa in college, and Abby started working with Bec last year.

"Count me in," Abby says.

"Count me out. I picked up extra shifts this week. I'll be too drained for even the most half-assed small talk," Carissa adds.

"The hospital is still short-staffed?" I ask.

"Yeah, we're going on the third month of *sort of* optional overtime. Can't complain about the money, but my body is a wreck when I get home. I have just enough energy to shower before scarfing down whatever leftovers I have in my fridge while watching trash TV." Carissa gives a halfhearted smile while tying up her auburn hair in a messy bun on top of her head.

I recognize her cover-up well. The *please don't look too close* placating smile. It's easy to see past the façade when I'm wearing my own.

"Why don't they hire more nurses?" Bec asks.

"They have, but it's not enough. Intake is way up, and we're still training the new staff, so they're not fully up to speed. It'll be a while till things calm down. Not too late for a career change if any of you are interested in helping out," Carissa teases.

"Major credit to you, but I could never work in an emergency room. You'd have to give me my own bed when I inevitably pass out at the sight of a protruding bone," Abby says with an apologetic look.

"I'd be up for a protruding bone right about now..." Dee sighs, leaning her elbow on the coffee table from her spot on the floor, staring into the distance.

"Oookay, on that note, who wants to start?" Bec asks. "Just kidding. I'll start because I can't *not* talk about chapter thirty-two when Jessica was feeling insecure about her body and Scarlett had her strip while she fed her praises the whole time from across the room. They were, like, ten feet from each other...why was that so hot?"

"Because she felt safe," I reply automatically. Heat rushes to my cheeks as they blush with embarrassment, and my palms begin to sweat.

"I like it," Bec says gently. "Say more?"

Keeping my focus on the edge of the throw pillow in my lap, I play with the satin tassel, my mind racing to find the right words.

Fuck. We just started talking about the book and already I can't contain my word vomit. I need to keep the focus on this story. I'm not in the mood to answer questions about myself tonight.

"I think the distance helped. Added tension. Threw gasoline on the desire they were already feeling from the day they spent together with small, innocent touches. And…I'm guessing Jessica liked that she didn't feel crowded, and Scarlett's words were enough to overpower her own negative thoughts about her imperfections and she could just…let go."

A few seconds pass before I look up to find the girls watching me. *Shit.*

"Makes sense to me," Abby says, throwing me a lifeline with a kind smile. "I loved watching their bond develop into something *more* in a slower, thoughtful way. It wasn't all grabbing hands and *gotta have you now* energy. Don't get me wrong, I eat that shit up too. But this was…intimate in a different way."

I nod, and the conversation slips into safer territory. The girls talk about their favorite scenes, and I'm left to process my thoughts. *Why did that question feel so personal?*

Dom and I don't have sex as much as we used to, but that's normal for parents with young kids, right?

The longer I listen to the girls and the carefree way they talk about the book's intimate scenes, the more I miss the old me. The *before* Ellie didn't have baggage. She wasn't overwhelmed with her responsibilities. She had a high sex drive and the energy to act on it. She felt sexy and desirable and wanted her partner to see every piece of her.

She didn't worry that sex could lead to a pregnancy. I'm in no way ready for that now…maybe not ever again. I got on birth control as soon as possible after Luca was born.

My stomach sours as guilt settles in. How could I miss the *before* Ellie? How could I miss the person I used to be when I have everything I dreamed of finding?

I've always wanted to have a family with the person I love, and that dream has come true. Here I am dreaming about the life I had before. *God, what is wrong with me?*

I jump back into the conversation here and there with small comments, but nothing of real substance, too afraid I'll blurt out what I can't stop thinking: I love my husband, but I have absolutely zero sex drive, and I don't know how to fix it.

Fictional intimacy doesn't scare me like real intimacy does. These stories are safe, I'm in control of what happens and what feels good to me. Anything more makes me feel out of control...again.

Not that Dom isn't the most giving, respectful, and not to mention enthusiastic partner I could ever hope to find. But it's been almost a year since I gave birth, and my body *still* doesn't feel like mine. I don't recognize myself in the mirror or even the way I feel in my clothes. Shit, I'm still breastfeeding. My body is *not* my own right now.

Sexy is the last word I'd use to describe how I feel. It's impossible to want sex when I feel this...disconnected from my body.

Dom deserves better than what I can give him.

The girls and I wrap up for the night and decide on the details for next month's get-together.

"Hey." Bec tugs my elbow before I shove my arm into the sleeve of my jacket in the entryway of Carissa's apartment. "You doing okay?" she asks quietly, just for my ears.

My chosen sister asking me that is unfair. She's known me for most of my life. I can't lie to her, but I also can't bring myself to do this right now.

I'm sick of talking about myself. And if *I'm* sick of it, then everyone else has to be sick of me and my issues too. It must be exhausting listening to me fixate on the same things over and over, but I can't turn off these intrusive thoughts cycling through my head on repeat. A broken cadence of fear, anxiety, and irrational musings.

Bec went through a lot this past year, working through her own issues and helping Aiden overcome his personal struggles too. I don't need to weigh her down with mine.

The shoulder to cry on. The confidant. The helper. Those are the roles I'd rather take on. I'm tired of being the one they have to keep an eye on.

"Of course, just tired. Luca had a rough night and I'm hoping I can catch up on some sleep tonight." She gives me a look that tells me I don't have her convinced, but she doesn't push me on it.

I give her a hug and feel the cover-up I wear slip back into place. The one I recognized on Carissa earlier tonight. The one I barely recognize myself without anymore.

CHAPTER FOUR

Dom

I roll my head from shoulder to shoulder, attempting to shake the unease creeping up my spine. I never know what I'll find when I step through the door from our garage into our home.

I kick off my shoes, finding the living room empty, and make my way to the kitchen, dropping my stuff on the counter. An echo of laughter reverberates down the hallway.

My heart skips.

Maybe today's a good day.

Following the sound of an upbeat melody, interrupted by raucous giggles, I find myself at the bathroom door left slightly ajar. I quietly press my palm against the door and slowly push. I cross my arms and lean against the doorway, my grin growing as the sight before me floods every atom of my heart with hope.

Ellie's sitting on the floor beside the tub, her back toward me, rocking her body from side to side, her arms moving dramatically as she sings an upbeat nursery rhyme Luca loves—one that I always seem to forget the words to causing me to fudge it a little bit every time I sing it. I catch glimpses of Luca's face as Ellie acts out the lyrics and dances from her seat on the floor, making sound effects, all to Luca's delight.

He's beaming at her. He loves his momma so damn much.

I knew she'd fucking rock this. *God, I wish she knew it too.*

Giggles burst from our infant—soon-to-be toddler—as he claps off-rhythm and reaches for Ellie.

This is one of those moments.

Those moments that I desperately wish I could catch and cement into memory. But there are so many of those now that Luca's in our life, I know I'll never be able to hold tight enough for them to outlast the passing of time.

I know it's a gift to feel this grateful, this happy that I want to remember everything with perfect clarity. But even my happiest memories from the last year are already blurred around the edges—whether from the fog of sleep deprivation or the normal fading of time, I can't be sure. Either way, it feels like I'm grieving the days as they hurry by, wishing with every pulse in my veins I could slow them down to have more time in the present.

I watch my small family. Observe every detail, soak in every sound, and hold the warmth of this soon-to-be faded memory close.

Luca spots me and squeals.

Yeah, that'll never get old.

Without hesitation, I storm into the bathroom, matching Luca's excited squeal with one of my own, reaching for my son and wife, eager to join in the moment before it's only another foggy memory.

***

"How was work?" Ellie asks as she puts laundry away in Luca's closet.

"It was fine," I say from my spot on the floor. Luca squirms as I attempt to dry him off with the towel and wrestle him into a diaper. Ever since he's become mobile, every diaper change is a battle of wills. If we walk away without getting pee everywhere, it's a win. "How was today for you two?"

"It was good. My mom came over for a bit. Neither of us could get Luca down for his nap."

I wince. *Shit.*

I love my son, but I know bedtime is about to be a fucking shit show since he hasn't napped today. I don't state the obvious and neither does Ellie.

Bedtime is a daily source of stress, each of us doing our best to soothe a fussing baby who desperately needs to sleep but only wants to sleep on *us* and not in his crib.

It's enough to make me feel insane some nights. And usually enough to cause Ellie and I to argue about one thing or another.

Lately, it feels like I can't do anything right. Luca only wants her, and if I do manage to get him asleep, the second I lay him down in the crib, he's crying out only for our cycle of attempts to start over again.

We're both exhausted, drained, and burned out, leaving us without any energy or patience, unable to shut down any resentment we feel. Resentment that isn't against each other—and certainly not against Luca—but toward the situation. We're trying our best, but it's hard to remember that at three in the morning when you haven't slept for more than an hour. It's been like this for almost a year.

"What do you want to do for dinner?" she asks, pulling me from my thoughts.

"I don't know."

Luca rolls over again, pulls himself onto all fours, and starts crawling toward Ellie's feet. I swiftly pick him up and lay him onto a clean diaper, quickly securing the sides before he flails with all his strength and ends up back on his stomach, crawling away again. The clothes can wait—at least he's got the diaper on.

"What do you feel like having?" I ask.

Her eyes flash to mine, and she huffs out an annoyed breath. *Uh...okay?*

"You good, El?"

"So do you just want me to figure it out?" She gives me her back while she stuffs more clothes into the closet.

"Uh, no. I was just asking if you wanted anything specific for dinner."

Why do I feel like I'm already fucked here?

"It's fine. I'll figure something out. Can you watch Luca while I get his food ready?"

"Ellie, I can take care of dinner. I wasn't trying to put that on you."

I hate this. Things between Ellie and I are...strained. It's never been like this between us. I've never worried about our relationship like I have these past few months.

Every time I feel like we fall into a good rhythm, something comes along to disrupt everything, leaving tension high, our stress levels peaking, and we fall into some stupid, bickering fuck fest and we're starting over.

I can't shake this feeling between me and the woman I love more than anything. We keep drifting further apart and I feel helpless to stop it.

The look Ellie's giving me now tells me that tonight is going to be another one full of passive comments where both of us are just trying to survive the sleep struggle so we can find a second to ourselves to recover from the exhaustion.

I need to fix what's cracked between us. I want to cross this divide, wrap her in my arms, kiss her, and tell her how much I love her. But every time I get close, Ellie puts even more distance between us. Emotionally and physically. I don't know what to do here, and while I love her endlessly, Ellie's not really making it any easier. She won't talk to me until everything is boiling over.

Like now.

"It's not about dinner, Dom. Your answers are so clipped, you might as well not even respond. *It's fine. I don't know.* Are you hearing me? Did you hear me say our son *didn't nap*?" She jerks her arms around as she struggles to hang a pair of corduroy overalls onto a clothes hanger before she gives up, tossing everything onto the closet floor and closing the door.

"Is this what our communication is going to be like now? Us coordinating and surviving one day-to-day task to the next with no real substance?" Her voice is pitchy, shaky as she crosses her arms over her stomach.

I want to calm the winds of this brewing storm, but I'm tired, work was a shit show this week, and I can't seem to pull any patience from my arsenal.

"Ellie, I just got home, and in case you haven't noticed, our son is a D1 wrestler now. It takes at least seventy-five percent of my brain power to Houdini him into a diaper before he pisses everywhere. Let's figure out what we're doing for dinner, and then we'll talk, I promise."

Wrong. Everything I just said was very wrong.

Ellie glares at me while she picks up the laundry basket and wordlessly leaves me and Luca alone in his room.

Fuck.

"Looks like Dad screwed up, my guy. Any advice for your old man?" Luca gives me a look that says, *psh, you're on your own* before blowing raspberries and spitting everywhere.

Yup, sounds about right.

***

Dinner could have gone better. Ellie mostly talked to Luca, only addressing me or looking at me when necessary.

My stomach sinks knowing it's only a matter of time before all this unresolved shit between us explodes, but I can't figure out what I need to do to fix any of it. I don't know what she needs from me and everything I say only seems to piss her off.

We're cleaning the kitchen while Luca crawls around his gated play area in the living room, babbling, shrieking, and playing with his toys.

"Hey, come here." I reach for her hand, hoping to pull her in for a hug, but she shakes off my attempt. "El, I want to apologize."

"For what?" she says, her voice soft and hollow, and her expectant eyes find mine, waiting for me to go on.

"For not...I mean, you wanted me to say more earlier and help plan dinner and I was focused on Luca. I'm sorry."

"You don't get it," she says, turning away to load another dish into the dishwasher. "I don't want to talk about this now. Not in front of Luca."

I get it. She doesn't want to argue in front of Luca. I don't want to argue, period. *Can't we just talk about this?*

We both know Luca isn't going to go down for bed easy tonight, and I can't wait that long to know what's bothering my wife.

"Just tell me what I don't get, please."

"I said not now. Please," she whispers, squeezing her eyes shut like she's holding back tears.

After a moment, I nod, picking up a rag to wipe the kitchen table and clean off Luca's high chair.

But the night comes and goes as it usually does, and we never get to talk about it or about us. It takes almost three hours to get an overtired Luca to bed and we both crash immediately afterward, only to be woken by him two hours later and start over.

The cycle repeats, and we shove our shit to the back burner...again.

I'm so fucking tired.

CHAPTER FIVE

Ellie

I press my palms to my eyes, willing the familiar ache to dissipate. That worn-out feeling from crying too hard for too long and the never-ending exhaustion from months of sleep deprivation.

Luca, my sweet almost-one-year-old, has been sleeping for forty-five minutes now. The nap he refused earlier today came too late and now bedtime will be way too late and another battle. My heart sinks and I feel desperate to just *rest*.

This built-up exhaustion is bone deep. Soul deep.

I can't remember the last time I woke up on my own, without being startled out of a restless sleep by Luca's cries.

Will it ever get better?

I lie in bed, trying to do as they say and *sleep when the baby sleeps*. What a load of shit. The times I do fall asleep, he wakes up shortly after I finally close my eyes, and when I don't, he sleeps like a dream.

When am I supposed to work? When am I supposed to clean? When am I supposed to take care of myself? When am I supposed to have a relationship with my husband? When am I supposed to catch up with friends and family?

It would take a two-week-long nap to recover from this never-ending fatigue.

I keep thinking I can strategize my way to more sleep. If Luca has a good night, I find myself trying to recreate every single detail of the routine only for it to fail miserably the next night, with him fighting sleep and then waking multiple times throughout the night.

If one more person tells me I need to try sleep training, I might fucking lose it. I have no judgment against the method or parents who decide to use it, but I had a panic attack fifteen minutes into our first and only attempt at doing so before I ran into his room and cradled a screaming Luca in my arms, swearing off Dom from ever bringing it up again.

My nervous system can't take it. It's simply not an option.

Soft steps sound on the carpeted stairs. I hold my breath, my head snapping toward the baby monitor. Luca doesn't seem to hear the steps like I do—or maybe he doesn't mind—because he doesn't stir.

I close my eyes and pretend to sleep before I hear Dom enter our room, home from work. His slow steps approach my side of the bed, pausing as he lingers for a moment before his steps begin again, retreating from our room, the sound of the monitor fading as he leaves, taking it with him.

Tears collect in the corners of my eyes. I feel them stream down my face and into my hair as I open my eyes and stare at the ceiling.

I can't talk to him. I feel like I don't know him anymore. I don't even recognize myself.

***

I finally fall asleep, waking to the sound of Luca's cries from his room down the hall. My head is foggy as I roll to my side, my slow steps dragging as I make my way to his room.

Dom beats me there. He already has Luca in his arms, patting his back, hushing, and speaking softly in his ear.

The sleep routine is an ever-changing puzzle, and lately Luca's been waking up from his afternoon nap *inconsolable* and it takes a solid five minutes to calm him.

"Go rest, babe. I got him." Dom smiles as he sways and rocks our sweet boy in his arms.

I nod numbly, wrapping myself in my arms, and return to our bedroom with unsure steps. I sink to our mattress, holding my middle like I'll split into two if I don't.

When I'm not the one taking care of Luca, I feel like I should intervene. Like no one can take care of him like I can. It's not rational, especially when the person holding him is my partner and Luca's very capable and loving father. But the thought still rattles around my head, untamed and uncontrollable.

When I'm in the thick of parenthood—endless dirty diapers, crying, fussing, meals, bathtime, cleaning, and near-constant redirecting of a toddler on the move—I desperately want a break. For someone to take over so I can get a minute to myself. A minute alone. A minute of peace. But when I finally get that moment, every part of me abhors it.

It's my job. My responsibility. Luca needs me to be better at this, and I'm failing him.

I wish I was the type of mom I always imagined I'd be. Patient and easygoing, who laughs all the time with a natural maternal instinct. Who isn't a mess of nerves and self-doubt.

I never expected to feel like I have to rediscover who I am after becoming a mother. It's as if the day he was born, my old self disappeared—the person left standing having no idea who she is.

Mom is a title I've always wanted, but I don't know how to fit into the role I dreamed of playing. The shoes I bought don't fit, and the unease I walk with leaves me blistered and hurting.

I change into a pair of leggings and one of Dom's old hoodies—basically, my postpartum uniform at this point. My pre-pregnancy sweaters still hug tightly across my stomach and they're not as comfortable as Dom's looser-fitting ones, so I opt for his most days.

Downstairs, I find Dom on the floor playing with a now calm and happy Luca.

I quickly scan the living room, making a mental list of everything I need to do. I notice several of the plants, both in here and the attached kitchen, are starting to wilt and make a mental note to water them later. The diaper stash I keep in the living room is running low; I'll need to grab more from the store this weekend. And that shirt is looking a little small on Luca; I need to go through his clothes again and size up. *Another growth spurt already?*

Dom is seated with his back resting against the side of our large sectional sofa that takes up most of the far wall of our living room across from the fireplace.

When we moved in, I chose vibrant, bold paint colors for the shared living spaces, and even today, feeling both exhausted and run down, the pops of color help brighten my mood. Our kitchen walls are warm, sunny yellow and the cabinets are teal. The backsplash tiles are large and patterned, each different yet cohesive. Our living room is painted an almost emerald green and our large sectional sofa is royal blue. The rust curtains and pillows pull it together.

My husband gives me a once-over, taking in my outfit, and his lips curl.

"I like that one on you," he says, nodding at my stolen sweatshirt.

"I think it's as old as our relationship," I say with a laugh as Luca crawls over to me as fast as he can, focused and grunting, until he reaches my ankles. I pick him up, holding him close and kissing his head, breathing him in.

My milk lets down.

Hot, right?

I plop onto the couch, placing a firm pillow underneath Luca, kissing his light brown hair—just as messy as his dad's darker hair—before getting us both comfortable. He doesn't nurse nearly as often now as he used to, but I'm not rushing the weaning process.

I don't miss the way Dom's gaze lingers on my chest before Luca latches. Dom coughs into his fist, strokes his beard, which is longer than normal and in need of a trim, and starts picking up Luca's toys scattered throughout the living room.

I hide my smirk and focus on Luca. The ladies have been *through it* after a year of breastfeeding, but that doesn't seem to stop Dom from appreciating them.

At least some things haven't changed.

"Older, actually. Pretty sure I got that one during orientation my freshman year," he says.

"Jesus, what'd they make this thing with?" The letters spelling out *University of Columbus* might be cracked and faded, but the fabric has that perfect softness that can only be achieved after years of wash and wear. Three things that only get better with time—sweatshirts, sweatpants, and Dom's laugh, which he shares with me now.

"With how much they charged us for tuition, it better last me the rest of my life."

"I think you mean *me*." I smile at him.

He straightens, leveling me with a serious look. His face turning serious, he practically growls at me. "No. Don't even think about it. It's one of my favorites."

"I'm sorry, babe. It's the natural life cycle of old hoodies. There's no use fighting it. Eventually, they all make their way to my side of the closet. You can say hi when I wear it."

He gives me an appraising look, and I have to fight not to roll my eyes. Only Dominic Moretti would ogle me in sweats, my hair a mess, one giant nursing nipple out in the wind, not to mention the permanent dark circles under my eyes from almost a year of the shittiest sleep imaginable.

"It's yours, Ellie...like everything else," he says, making his way to me. His eyes lock with mine as he brushes the flyaway hairs away from my forehead before placing a soft kiss there as well.

"Looks better on you anyway. Thanks for taking care of our boy, Mama."

Then he winks, and my stomach does the thing. That little flop, my heartbeat kicking in the base of my throat. That heat rising to my cheeks because he is looking at me *like that*.

Seven years together and he still looks at me *like that*.

A flicker of heat rekindles long enough for me to appreciate him appreciating me. But when I imagine taking things further later on tonight when we finally get a rare minute to ourselves, my gut wrenches.

No, not tonight.

The three of us settle into a comfortable silence, Dom tidying up while Luca finishes nursing. When I put him back down to play, he crawls as fast as his little body will take him to the bin of toys Dom just put away.

He rolls his eyes, before falling onto the couch next to me. Before, we would have snuggled up together, hands interlocked, me leaning into the space between his arm and side, head curled up against his chest.

The silence is screaming. Things are so different between us now. It's evident in every moment of our day. I see it—I feel it—all day long. *Does he feel it too?*

"I'm going to close my eyes and pretend our son isn't about to trash this room for the fifteenth time today," Dom says.

"I want to tell you it's going to get better, but with his birthday coming up, our friends and family will inevitably buy him gifts with ten thousand pieces. It's going to get so much worse."

"Fuck, you're right," he says, swiping a palm over his face on a deep exhale.

"We could ask that everyone skips the gifts," I suggest passively.

He looks at me, eyes wide with disbelief as he whispers in horror, "But it's his *birthday.*"

I giggle at his mortification. "He's *one*. He's not going to care."

"*I* care. I'll tidy up the new toys."

"Will you still complain?" I ask, raising my eyebrows at him, knowing the answer.

"I reserve the right, but that doesn't change my answer."

I smile to myself, loving that Dom wants to see his son spoiled, knowing he's the kind of man who never cares about getting gifts himself. Dom has always been generous, always thinking of others and how he can support them. How he can show his love. The biggest heart I've ever felt. The sweetest one I've ever known.

"We'll need a bigger toy basket," I say. "Or a small shelf or something for the living room."

"Consider it done."

Dom flips the TV on, changing the channel to Aiden's baseball game. The Columbus Aviators did well this season, earning them a spot in the playoffs. I move to sit on the floor, joining Luca while he plays.

"So, what seat are the Aviators in?" I ask, my focus split as I show Luca how to use the mallet on his toy xylophone.

"Say that again?" Dom asks.

"What seat are they in?" I repeat, nodding toward the game playing on TV. He gives me a look, and I tilt my head. "Why are you looking at me like that?"

He stands abruptly, then jogs into the kitchen. When he starts fumbling and digging through our junk drawer, I gasp.

"What are you doing?" I call out to him from my spot on the living room floor.

"Getting the notebook," he yells back, shooting a shit-eating grin my way before returning to his search. We need to clean out the junk drawer. It's bad, even by my standards.

"It better be for you," I say with conviction, crossing my arms over my chest and lifting my chin. "Sure as hell isn't for me."

He strides back into the living room, notebook jostling in his hand as he asks, "Ellie, what are baseball rankings called?"

"Umm...seats," I say with little-to-no confidence. *Shit.* He definitely got the notebook for me.

The *notebook* is almost as old as the sweater I'm wearing. Back when we first started dating, we were at dinner when Dom confused the saying it's a *dog-eat-dog world* and instead he said *doggy-dog-world.* I laughed so hard I snorted wine out of my nose.

Not even a week later, I *may* have accidentally said *nip it in the butt* instead of *nip it in the bud.* Before he could control his laughter, he was digging in my school tote, stealing one of my notebooks. He dated the first clean page, claiming the notebook was being repurposed so that we could document which one of us was more confused about sayings we should most definitely know by now.

The edges are worn and the inside cover has been divided into two columns, marked up with sloppy tally marks to track which one of us is "losing." Well, losing *worse*. There's no winner here. This happens way more than it should.

"I fucking knew it. God, I love you, Ellie. It's seed. What *seed* are the Aviators," he says, flipping to the front cover to give me another tally before writing down my slipup with today's date.

You'd think this couldn't happen often enough to warrant a notebook, but we're going to need a new one soon with just a few pages left to spare. Those first ten pages of Biology 101 notes are still there, even if a little faded.

"*Seed*? Why the fuck is it a seed?" I retort.

"Close your ears, Luca. Mommy's about to cuss up a storm," Dom says with glee.

I cover Luca's ears with my palms and he smiles up at me, a big, lopsided, toothy grin showing off his four adorable baby teeth. I smile back at him, my heart trying to burst free from my chest from how adorable he is.

"Yes, mommy is," I say with an exaggerated smile, which I keep on my face as I turn toward Dom. "Proof, Daddy. I want proof."

"Ooo, *Daddy*? I think I like it, Ellie. Say it again," he taunts.

"Ugh, you're impossible." I move my hands from Luca's ears to his belly, giving him a little squeeze before pulling out my phone to do a quick search.

"Goddammit," I mumble, the internet confirming Dom's not lying. "Well, they should change that. Sitting in a *seat* makes more sense."

"No, babe..." Dom says, trying, and failing, to keep from laughing at me. "They aren't sitting in a seed. They just...are."

"So, they become a *seed*? I'm supposed to ask what seed they are?" Dom covers his mouth with his hand, crossing his other across his chest and nodding. "Sports are so fucking weird."

I don't know how Bec handles this. She has to understand what's going on since baseball is Aiden's career and they're dating. Good luck to her.

"I love you," Dom says, trying to comfort me. "And that beautiful brain of yours. You're too creative for the English language."

"You're only trying to make me feel better about this because if there was a loser to this game, it'd definitely be me."

"Does that mean I'm...winning?" He points to his chest. "Oh right, I am," he says smugly. "Speaking of Aiden, he got us tickets to one of the playoff home games. The guys are all in. I'm sure you'll hear about it from Bec and the girls this week."

I stiffen, my shoulders hike up toward my chin, and I try to focus on Luca as I rub my thumb over his temple and he plays with the bracelet dangling from my wrist.

I keep waiting for this part of parenting to get easier. I know it's insane to think I should be with Luca all day, every day, but when I leave to do anything that isn't necessary—like choosing to be social for the sake of being social—guilt claws at my spine, working its way from base to skull.

The stress only worsens while I'm separated from him. I don't know how many times I've texted Dom, our family, our friends, or whoever was watching Luca while I wasn't there to check in on him. No one shames me for it, always saying they understand and that I'm an attentive mom, just missing her son.

I do miss him when I'm away, but my calls are never about that. What forces me to pick up the phone is some horrible thought that I can't turn off. Horrific images of the worst-case scenario—Luca getting hurt, graphic images of accidents happening, gut-clutching imaginary scenarios—flip through my mind like one of those old photo reels and I'm powerless to stop the track or turn away. Unable to stop it, unable to protect him.

I *need* to call and make sure that the situation I'm imagining isn't really happening. It never is. I know it's not real, but it feels fucking *real*.

What kind of mother am I if I can't keep my baby safe?

The first therapist I saw after Luca was born dismissed me entirely. Invalidated everything I was saying. I know how it sounds. Of course, I can't predict every possible dangerous outcome of a situation and prevent it. But shouldn't I try?

If Dom sees the shift in my body language, he doesn't comment on it. I wait to respond, trying to keep my voice even when I finally do.

"When?" I ask.

"Saturday night. My parents are free."

Immediately, my blood is boiling.

"What do you mean, Dom?"

"Huh? Oh, I texted my parents when Aiden mentioned the date. Wanted to make sure someone was free to watch Luca."

Fuck, why does that enrage me?

He's assuming I'm okay leaving Luca, and went ahead and made plans? Of course, I want to support Aiden. It's not every year his team makes it this far in post-season, but Dom didn't even talk to me about it first. It's not a question. It's an assumption, and I'm not involved in any of the planning.

It throws me back...like everything is happening *to me* and I have no say. No control.

Sometimes motherhood feels like one giant *fuck you*. Get pregnant, but don't complain about how difficult it is mentally or physically. Deliver the baby, but heal quickly so you can be productive. Spend months growing a baby, but your body better bounce back to its previous size. Become a parent, but act like nothing changed even though *everything* fucking changed.

"You should have asked me," slips out, my tone sounding unbelievably hurt, even to my own ears.

It catches Dom's attention immediately, and his brow furrows. That little wrinkle makes an appearance, but the sight of it isn't enough to distract me from the building pressure and panic in my chest.

"What's going on? You don't want to go?"

"You should have asked me first, Dom. The last time we went to a game, my parents struggled to get Luca to take a bottle and he wouldn't sleep. He was fussy and wanted to cluster feed when we got home because he refused the bottle. We were up half the night even though we got home after one in the morning. It was exhausting. Besides, our parents aren't getting younger, we can't ask them to watch him that late—"

"Ellie," Dom says, interrupting my spiral, and my chest heaves with heavy breaths.

I didn't notice Dom had knelt in front of me and Luca on the floor. His stare locks with mine and all I can see is pity in his eyes.

His sympathy makes me feel like shit. I'm tired of him acting like I'm crazy because I don't want to leave Luca. Isn't it a good thing that I want to spend as much time with him as I can? We won't get these years back. I can't miss a minute of it, and if anything happens to him, it'll be my fault. I'll never forgive myself.

"Ellie, look at me. Breathe, love. Slow it down for me."

The moment his forehead touches mine, my eyes fall closed, feeling so fucking heavy. Tears spring to my eyes and I don't fight to hold them in. There's only so much fight left in me.

"Nothing is decided. We were invited, and I asked our family if they were free to watch Luca to see what our options are. We'll figure it out together, okay?"

"Okay." I scoff, pulling back and wiping my cheeks dry. "So I can be the bitch who misses the game when everyone else is going? So I can be the big buzzkill? When you tell your parents I want to cancel, they'll question why and you'll tell them it's because I can't handle leaving Luca? Why do I always have to be the one to hold all the worry? I can't carry it alone."

Anger feels good. Anger feels better than falling apart.

Shitty thing about it is that Dom is the one it always seems to be directed at, and a guy can only take so much. He doesn't deserve any of it, but I can't seem to stop.

I watch him bristle, and he looks at me like he doesn't recognize me.

"Jesus, Ellie, how did we get here? We were having a great night," Dom asks, shoving his hand through his hair, ruffling the longer sections so they lay unevenly. Good, now we can both look frazzled.

Why does the rest of the world get to keep spinning while I'm fucking drowning?

Does he not see me? Does nobody see me?

"We got here because you forgot that I can't just *go* and *do things* like this. You just keep pushing, and pushing. One day, I'm going to fucking snap. You want to *fix* me. You want me to be the person I was before all of this, but I'm never going to be that person again, Dom," I yell, breaking my own rule against arguing in front of Luca.

I'm not in control. I need to get out of here.

"Ellie, I'm not trying to *fix* you. I'm just trying to *help* you. I'm trying to *love* you. You're not *fucking broken*," Dom snaps at me, throwing a teether into the toy bin with more force than necessary, finally letting his frustration breach the surface. A rare occurrence for Dom.

"Yes," I whisper, silent tears falling. "I am."

His face falls, heartbroken and so...so lost. I can't look at him for one more second knowing I'm the cause of that pain.

Things may not be easy between me and Dom right now, not like they used to be, but this is where I draw the line. We don't speak to each other like this in front of Luca.

This whole conversation started out so easy. How did it devolve into *this*?

I storm out of the room before I say more that I'll regret. Guilt sinks like a brick in my stomach. Tears burn my eyes before they fall. I've failed as a mom and a wife...again.

Chapter Six

Ellie

Luca's face ignites with joy as Dom pushes him in the swing. I listen to my favorite sound, his giggles, from my seat on a nearby wooden bench. The small playground near our home is nearly empty this early in the morning.

The leaves are beginning to change, some already starting to drift silently to the frosted grass. A chill lingers in the September morning air, but it'll be warm enough for T-shirts again in a few hours. We're in that confusing part of Ohio's autumn where you need to dress for early winter in the morning and late summer in the afternoon.

I snuggle my chin further into my scarf and cling to my travel mug, desperately willing the heat to warm my fingers. Damn that double insulation.

"Mind if I sit here?" a woman appearing to be in her early thirties asks, gesturing to the seat next to me.

"Of course, it's all yours," I say, scooting over to give her more room.

She plops her purse down next to my diaper bag.

"Stay where I can see you, Rose!" she calls out to the young girl hastily climbing up the rock wall.

"Okay, Mom!" Rose yells as she scrambles to the top.

I smile to myself, imagining the day when Luca is old enough to play independently without either me or Dom helicoptering over him. I can't picture it. I see five, six, seven-year-old kids with their parents. Little personalities blossoming, asking hilariously difficult—and valid—questions, becoming tiny versions of the adults they'll one day become. But all I can see is Luca at the stage he's in. So perfect.

"Wave to Momma," Dom says from the swings. I wave at my boys, and my heart swells with gratitude.

I'm not perfect. Not by a fucking mile. But those two smiles...I want to be worthy of those. I wake up every morning striving for that.

"So sweet," my new neighbor says, before taking a drink from her own travel mug. "How old?"

"He turns one in two weeks," I say, ignoring the confusing pang of giddiness and grief that hits me. I'm stuck in a loop of wanting Luca to stay little forever while also being enamored and fascinated with every new development.

"Awe, that's such a fun age," she says wistfully. "Fun and exhausting. Cheers to you, Mom." She raises her coffee, I presume. I smile, lifting my own in response.

"You would be right," I say with a laugh, taking another sip of the perfect cup of coffee Dom prepared for our little outing. He makes it best. I can never get the proportions quite right, even though I use the measurements listed. Dom goes based on vibes; I swear to god. The man never measures anything in the kitchen, yet everything he touches is perfect.

"Rose just turned seven last week, but I remember her at that age. The cuddles were the best, but I was a zombie most days. How you hanging in there?"

Wow...no one ever says that to me.

No one outside of my close family members and friends ever ask about *me.* Strangers mostly want to comment on Luca and how incredible babies and motherhood are and how grateful I should be. *Better enjoy every moment* and *isn't motherhood just the best?*

I'm grateful. Every day I'm grateful. But when someone reminds me to be thankful, it feels like they're really saying *better not complain, because this could all be taken away from you.*

Maybe it's the trauma talking, but I know toxic positivity is some shit too. A lot of people use it to make themselves feel more comfortable when things get too real or I'm too honest. It's easier to keep things superficial. Yet, here's a total stranger cutting through the surface level to ask about how I'm handling things. Acknowledging that parenting isn't all rainbows and sunshine. It's refreshing to hear another mom be real about how hard it can be too.

"Zombie is a pretty accurate description," I admit.

"I'm Isabel," she says. "We live over on Wooster, near the elementary school."

"I'm Ellie. That's my husband Dominic and my son Luca. We're just a few blocks away on Northview Drive."

"Well, since we're both close by, if you ever need a fellow mom-zombie to hang out with, I'm here," Isabell says, and we both laugh.

"I'd like that. I don't have any close friends with kids," I say.

Dom and I were ready to have kids, but it's lonelier than I expected it to be, being the first of our friends to have a child. All of our loved ones are above and beyond supportive, but sometimes I wish I could talk to someone who's going through the same thing as me. There are some experiences I can't explain.

"We went through the same thing when Rose was born. Now, all my friends have toddlers and look to me for advice." She grimaces. "It's quite the compliment, but god, I was as clueless as they are. None of us know what we're doing, right? Doesn't it blow your mind how we assumed adults had their shit together when we were kids, only to become parents and realize they were all full of shit? I'm winging this *hard*, and now my poor friends realize there are no easy answers to the questions they're asking me."

"So, what you're saying is that this *holy shit, what am I doing* approach to parenthood never goes away?" I ask jokingly.

"Afraid not. But you get more confident winging it. More comfortable sitting in the unknown. Following your gut gets easier. At least, that's how it felt for me. I was so frustrated and isolated in the first two years or so, thinking everything was black and white. That there was a right way and wrong way to do everything, and I needed to figure out what was right so I could strictly abide by that method. Took me a long time to realize that was all bullshit. I had to blend the black-and-white rules into a murky shade of gray, something between following my gut and making the best call I could with the information I had. Parenthood is a series of impossible decisions with minimal sleep, maximum overstimulation, and a million unwanted opinions from people who are *not* your child's parent."

"How did you do it? How'd you get to the other side of that?" I ask. Isabel is a stranger to me, but in just five minutes, she's put into words what I'm feeling better than I could in *weeks* of meeting with my last therapist. "I spend every moment of every day afraid that what I'm doing isn't enough. I'm not doing enough for my son, my husband..."

"What about you?" Isabel asks. "What do you do for *you*?"

That stops my thoughts from spiraling into another tangent of guilt.

"Well, I like to read...and I love my friends...I used to like doing yoga..." My voice fades with uncertainty.

"Yeah, and when is the last time you read?" she asks.

I struggled to finish last month's book club pick...and that was the only book I picked up all month.

"And when you see your girls, are you talking to them about what's going on? Or hiding in the background, content to let them lead the conversation and keep it all surface level in case you accidentally let them see what's going on underneath the perfect persona you're attempting to maintain," she continues.

"Fuck, are you a mind reader?"

She laughs, lifting her mug to take another sip before saying, "Nope, just another mom. One whose mind told her all the same things I'm willing to bet that yours is telling you. That you're going to hurt the baby, that something bad is going to happen, that you have to hurry home from your precious solo trip to the store because no one can care for the baby like you do. That even though you're running yourself into the ground trying to do everything perfectly, you never feel like you're reaching this *elite mom* benchmark. Like the mom you imagined you'd be is so far from the mom you actually are. No one seems to see it, so you keep up the front, keep doing what you're doing and try to hide what you're thinking and feeling. Because if they knew what was going on in your mind...I mean, fuck, we're already judged for every single decision we make as mothers—can you imagine if they heard our entire inner monologue? Shit can get dark up there."

"That's...exactly how it feels." My eyes stuck on Luca, I ask, "Does it get better?"

I realize I'm crying, tears rolling silently down my cheeks, and I work quickly, wiping them away as embarrassment rains over me.

"Yes," she says with conviction. My eyes lock on hers, and hers soften immediately. "Absolutely, yes. When sleep isn't quite as hard to find. When you start talking about what you're going through with the people who matter and love you. When you finally remember that you were a person before you became *Mom*, and you're allowed to be some version of that person again. When you allow yourself to ask for not just what you need but also what you *want*.

"When you take a drive by yourself and scream your favorite song at the top of your lungs. When you go out with your partner, and their hand brushes your thigh and gives you chills. When you put on clothes that feel good for your body as it exists today, and it boosts your confidence. When you go dancing with your girls, and don't give a fuck how you look while you're doing it. When you read that book you've been putting on the back burner, and it's so good you finish it in one sitting. When your baby hits that next milestone and looks up at you with eyes full of pride. When you make space for the bad and the good, but don't let either define your day. When you learn to live in the gray but still let yourself see other colors too. When you let yourself feel the bad shit instead of trying to shut it down, then it finally lessens and makes room for the good shit. You've got to let that toxicity burn away before you can put on the bandages. You can't stifle the hurt forever. You're just inviting it to stick around."

"Wow, you sound like a therapist." *Better than the last one I paid.*

She smiles wistfully. "Not a therapist. Just a big fan of them."

"I tried that already. It...didn't work out," I admit.

"Eh, therapist shopping is like trying to find a pair of jeans. Uncomfortable but necessary, and the right one puts some pep in your step. I know a good one, if you want her info. Here." She pulls out her business card and writes another number on the back.

"Here's my number and hers. If you need some informal bullshit like what I just fed you, or someone to sit next to at the playground, I'm your girl. But if you're ready to step into the fire, call her. I promise, she's the real deal."

CHAPTER SEVEN

Dom

"Aiden, I don't think I've ever seen you this uncomfortable before," Ellie says with a smirk.

"Of course, I'm uncomfortable. The last time I was here, Luca and Hopper conspired against me. It's only a matter of time before it happens again," Aiden says. He's leaning against the wall between the kitchen and living room, arms crossed, and a look on his face that says he's ready to run at the first sign of trouble. Apparently, a baby spitting up on your chest and your dog proceeding to lick it off is *scarring* or whatever.

"Babe, they can smell fear. You're making yourself an easy target. Where's that confidence from last night?" Bec says with a wink.

"Ah-ah-ah, not in front of young ears." Ellie laughs, holding her hands over Luca's tiny ears.

A blush finds its way to Aiden's face as he glares at Bec. Well, glaring as much as he can. The guy's fallen *hard* for Ellie's best friend; there's not much he wouldn't give her. Except a glare, I guess.

"Hey, don't lump my son into this. He's not even one. Isn't your dog supposed to be trained?" I ask.

"Don't blame the trainer," Bec, a professional dog trainer and Hopper's unofficial dog mom, singsongs from across the room where she and Ellie are seated on the floor. "Peek-aaaaaa-boo!" Luca giggles and babbles, eyes wide with wonder as he looks to Bec to do it again. Hopper lies on his side, his back flush against Bec's outstretched leg. She absentmindedly rubs her hand along his belly as Ellie pets his head.

Spoiled dog. Good for him.

"Well, if I can't blame the baby, the parents, the dog, or the trainer, who can I blame?"

"Yourself," we all say in unison, before Aiden rolls his eyes and mutters something about getting another drink before heading into the kitchen.

I let loose a chuckle as I finish my own beer, following him to the fridge. "You know we're right," I say.

He hands me the bottle opener and sighs.

"Yeah, which is why I'm begging you to remove me from the babysitting list. When Luca hits T-ball age, then you and Ellie can tap me back in for babysitting."

"Deal. But was it really *that* bad?"

"I swear to god, it was the grossest moment of my life," he says, a grimace taking over his face. *Is he turning green?*

"Gonna have to get over that squeamish shit when you and Bec have kids."

Aiden watches Bec as she plays with Luca, Ellie, and Hopper in the living room. Even from a distance, it's clear how different this is for him. How different he is because of her.

Aiden's been a great friend for as long as I've known him. He went through some heavy shit with his family growing up, but he never let it affect him. At least he made it appear that way. Everything came to a head a few weeks ago, but he started seeing my therapist and leaning on Bec and the rest of us for support instead of keeping it all inside his head. He seems to be doing a lot better.

He had to do the heavy lifting for himself—we couldn't do that for him. But still, I can see the way Bec has changed his life for the better. The same way Ellie and Luca have changed mine.

I know what's coming.

"Yeah, about that," he says, eyes still on Bec, a small, knowing grin tugging on the corner of his mouth.

Never mind, I didn't expect that. Guess we better save Luca's hand-me-downs.

"Shut the fuck up, you didn't..."

"Huh?" Aiden looks at me and must realize what he implied. "No, not *that*," he says, shoving me lightly on the shoulder before taking a sip of his beer. "No kids, yet. I'm going to do it, Dom. I'm going to ask her. I want Bec to be my wife," he says quietly, eyes returning to her.

The girls are singing "I'm a Little Teapot" to Luca, arm movements and all. Luca is *enraptured* with their performance, clapping and wiggling along, while Hop wags his tail and his tongue hangs out of his mouth.

This is another one of those moments I want to keep forever. Watching my wife laugh and act ridiculous with her best friend and our son.

I'm relieved to know Aiden is finally working through his past and doing better for it; enough that he knows he's ready to propose to the woman he loves.

I'm grateful that we're all here to see this, despite every obstacle. *Dammit, why are my thoughts going there?* Maybe Ellie isn't the only one rattled by the anniversary of all that happened when Luca was born.

"I'm excited for you. Both of you," I say, with a clap on Aiden's shoulder. "I like seeing you happy."

"Happy doesn't even cover it."

"So, what's the plan?" My mind immediately starts turning. *Bec likes big romantic gestures, right? Who doesn't? Maybe at a playoff game...on the field...Aiden could bring her out to throw the first pitch—Hop could come out with her—and I could give signs to a shit ton of fans in the stands, and when they hold them up, the signs would spell* WILL YOU MARRY—

"Aaaand that's enough of that," Aiden says, coming up behind me, slapping both hands on my shoulders, and pushing me into the front hall. "Had to get you out of there, your face was about to give me away."

"This face?"

Yeah, right. Me? Being obvious? Not a chance.

"Yes, *that* face. Your smile is about to crack your skull in half."

"I was just thinking—"

"Dom, I love you like a brother. I can't thank you or Ellie enough for being there for Bec and me when everything happened with my mom. And while I appreciate the *creative* thoughts I know are racing through your mind, I already know exactly how I'm going to propose. I got this."

"Okay, but if not me, then you should at least run it by the boss."

"Trust me. I plan to. Can you talk to Ellie for me? I'm too scared to text her and have Bec accidentally see the message, but I'm hoping she can come ring shopping with me to make sure I don't fuck this up."

"Oh, we'll be there."

"But I only need her—"

"*We'll* be there, it's really no trouble."

Aiden laughs and rolls his eyes. "Thanks, Dom...for everything."

"You haven't seen anything yet. I've got experience ring shopping. When do you need us?"

"I know schedules are tight with playoffs, and you guys are probably planning a birthday party for Luca, right?" Aiden asks.

Fuck, tonight is going so well. Ellie seems genuinely happy. I haven't seen a single line of stress stretch across her forehead all night. Her smile feels like the real one. I haven't caught her staring in that distant, lost sort of haze. I don't want that to end.

"Hey, do me a favor and don't mention Luca's birthday to Ellie," I say quietly.

"Uh...okay? Is his birthday a secret?"

"It's not. Ellie can't...she's having a hard time..."

How do I explain this?

I'm not in the habit of lying to my friends, but that's concerning *my* personal business. I'm not into broadcasting Ellie's struggles widely when I know that's the last thing she wants. Not that I really know what she wants anymore. Or if anything I do helps. Lately, it feels like I just make it worse.

"I was going to text you. We're having something small here a week from this Saturday. Think you guys can make it?"

"You know Bec will be here. Send me the time, and I'll check my schedule." The Columbus Aviators, the pro baseball team Aiden plays second baseman for, are still in the playoffs. When I met Aiden in college, he was a phenomenal player, but seeing what he's capable of on the field now? He's on an entirely different level.

"Great. Then we'll figure out a good time for Operation Happily Baiden After."

"Jesus, promise you'll work on the name for me, okay?"

"Not a fan? Okay." I shrug. "I'll come up with some options."

Maybe this is exactly what Ellie needs. A massive, happy, incredible surprise like this—helping my best friend propose to her best friend—might be enough to help her get through the next couple of weeks without sinking into *that* place. The one that moves like quicksand drowning us just when we think we've wriggled ourselves free.

I'll take all the help I can get to hold onto her as we trudge through it together.

CHAPTER EIGHT

Dom

Luca tears into the homemade birthday cake, smothering himself in bright green frosting as cake crumbles and sprinkles get caught in his rolls. Ellie kneels in front of his high chair, calling his name and singing for his attention as she captures several pictures and video clips.

We finally made it to Luca's birthday. Our families and our closest friends in our home to celebrate as we planned. Well, as Ellie asked me to plan.

I kept things simple. Just a handful of loved ones invited to our place for pizza, a homemade cake, baked by yours truly, and simple birthday decorations.

Over-the-top, celebratory fanfare is usually my specialty, but I wanted to be prepared for a last-minute plea from Ellie to cancel everything. If I planned anything too elaborate, the fallout and inevitable guilt Ellie might have felt would have been worse.

I checked in with her every day this week and several times already today, but she's doing...incredible. Better than I could have imagined. I've been hesitant to trust it.

Experience has taught me that my wife has the ability to hide her anxiety...until she doesn't. I've never minded, but I *have* learned. Sometimes Ellie needs me to reassure her of something she *knows* to be true. To dispel any doubt she has and reassure her she's doing the right thing and that everything is going to be okay. Sometimes she needs me to help quiet the voice in her head telling her the worst is going to happen. I've never resented her for it. What I struggle with is when she buries it, hides it from me, and when she finally lets me in, it's too late to cushion her fall.

"How has she been today?" Ellie's mom, Carolyn, asks as she steps beside me.

Ellie's family feels as much mine as hers. I met them shortly after we started dating, and asked her father and mother for permission to marry their daughter the day we met. I knew where our relationship was going, and how I wanted things to end between us, which was not at all.

"She's...okay?" I say, unable to hide the surprise and disbelief from my voice.

"Yeah, I thought the same. Felt the same way about it as you do, it seems. I wanted to check in with you in case she was putting on a brave face for me."

Guilt creeps up my spine. Carolyn assumes I'd know better than her. Truth is, Ellie can slip on the mask easily most days, fooling even me. But holding that mask wears on her. I can see how draining it is when the crash inevitably comes, always lurking not far in the future.

"This month has been hard, but she's been trying. There are moments when it seems like it comes easily, then others when..."

"I know," she says, resting her hand on my shoulder. "We're always here if you guys need us. I know how hard she is on herself, but then I watch her with Luca, and she's doing such a wonderful job. I wish she could see that," she says, her eyes brimming with tears.

"I promise, I'll call. I'm grateful to you and Gary for your help. We both are."

"Did I hear my name?" Ellie's father, Gary, joins us, a small plate with a slice of cake in one hand, the other coming to rest on his wife's waist as he pulls her into his side.

"Just reminding Dom that he can call us anytime. What? No cake for me?" she says with a sly smile while her husband smirks and feeds her a forkful from his own piece.

I look around the room and I'm reminded of how much support Ellie and I have. Everyone we love in one space, spoiling Luca, and showing up for us in more ways than that this past year.

I never understood why people said it takes a village. It's abundantly clear to me now. There's no way Ellie and I could do any of this on our own.

I watch Ellie, a stupid grin on my face, as she and Dee dance and sing to Luca, who giggles and waves his frosting-covered hands around, doing his own dance as much as he can in the confines of his high chair. Chris reaches over the crowd, handing Ellie a few damp towels to help with the cleanup. *Yeah, it's going to take a lot more than those towels. I might as well get the bath running.* Carissa is cutting the sheet cake while Jake and Dylan hand out slices to the rest of our friends and family. My parents are talking with Bec and Abby in the kitchen, most likely about the dog they keep saying they're going to get "one of these days."

Today is perfect.

Another moment in time I wish I could hold onto forever, but forever slips through my fingers again.

***

I peer into the darkness, willing my eyes to turn superhuman and give me sight into Luca's bedroom. After a minute, my eyes adjust to the low lighting, the soft glow from the sound machine in the corner of his room.

Ellie's still holding him in the rocker. I tiptoe closer, kneeling beside them, and see that Luca is well and truly passed out, lying limp on Ellie's chest, lips slightly parted, as she rubs his back and holds him close.

I don't speak, too afraid of waking him. It's difficult to see, but I can feel Ellie's stare. That innate knowing after spending years with someone. Knowing them inside and out, going through...all that we went through together.

There's so much left unsaid between us. Some of it because we're busy, moving from one task to the next, stuck in survival mode, but mostly because we don't have the words.

Words can't undo what happened.

Words can't fix whatever is breaking between us.

I lift my hand and place it on top of hers, where it's resting against the small of Luca's back. She continues to rock and hold our entire world in her arms.

The longer we stay like that, the better my eyes adjust, seeing her clearer than I have all night. I was naive to think the day had passed for her with ease. When her mask falls, the strong façade she displays for all to see melts away. She's sitting here, gorgeous, her blonde hair falling around her shoulders in loose waves, her soft curves gorgeously on display in a black nightgown with thin straps and shelf cutouts to make nursing easier. Tears glisten in her eyes and on her cheeks.

Luca stirs for a moment and lets out a deep sigh. After making sure he's still asleep, my eyes return to Ellie's to find her still watching me, deep in thought.

At this exact moment a year ago, we were recovering from the most terrifying moment of our lives. Not in too dissimilar of a position than this. Thankfully, the three of us came home.

What does it take to heal from something like that?

I need to figure it out before this breaks us entirely.

CHAPTER NINE

Ellie

"**W**hen will she be lucid?"

Dom? I lift my hand, attempting to find his, but I'm not sure it moves.

Someone responds, but it's muddled, distorted. I can't make sense of the words, my mind foggy under the surface of a sleep I can't shake.

I'm not sure how much time passes. I can't move. I can't speak. My thoughts flutter around too quickly for me to make sense of them. There was something I was supposed to do. Something important. I was with Dom, we were at the hospital, and then...then...

"We're going to place the little guy on her chest now. Would you like to hold him first?"

"No. No, she should hold him."

Our baby's here? Him?

My heart explodes at the feel of pressure concentrated in the center of my chest.

And then I feel it. Limbs stretching slowly across my skin. Hair tickling the crook of my neck. Soft skin, warm against mine. The light scratch of a diaper tab.

And then I hear it. A muffled cry, followed by fussing that settles quickly. A content sigh. Small squeaks.

I'm holding my baby...for the first time.

"Ellie, baby. You did it. He's here. I've got you both."

Dom.

His arms wrap around my shoulders, squeezing gently. I want to respond, to tell him I hear him, but I can't find my voice.

"Ellie. Open your eyes, honey. Ellie," he calls to me, louder this time.

"Ellie, are you listening?" I startle at my mother's voice. Something in her stare tells me she's been trying to get my attention for some time.

"Sorry, I got distracted. What were you saying?" I shake my head, willing away the memory and the accompanying ache buried in my chest, forcing it further down until all I feel is numb. I close my eyes trying to collect myself, but immediately open them when unwelcome images come flooding to the surface, unbidden and unwelcome.

Luca getting frequent checks and testing by the nurses after my surgery. Bec running into my hospital room, flustered and scared at the sight of me, clinging to me tightly while I sob. Dom and I alone in a quiet hospital room at three in the morning, my hand in his as he softly rubs his thumb over my knuckle before he drops a kiss to the same spot. My vacant stare reflecting back at me in the hospital mirror; my first look at myself after delivery. Dark, gray circles under the eyes, the adult diaper, numerous angry, purple stretchmarks, orderly stitches across the lower abdomen, a swollen but empty belly. *Who the fuck is she?*

"Come on, honey. Let's grab some tea," my mom insists, calling my attention back to the present as she stands, reaching for my hand.

I glance at my dad and Luca who are seated on the floor of my living room, playing with some of his new toys from his birthday party.

My dad offers me a warm smile, reassuring me. "I've got him, Ellie. I won't take my eyes off him."

My weak grin must show every anxious thought racing through my head. I thought I'd been that good at hiding it, but can you really hide those kinds of things from the people who raised you?

"Sit with me in the kitchen. We'll keep an eye on these two," Mom adds, reaching for me again since I'm still planted firmly on the couch.

I take her hand and join her in our attached kitchen. I sit when Mom insists that she'll put the kettle on the stove.

"Tension tamer or raspberry? What am I saying? Both. Always both," she adds, muttering to herself while she puts the water on and digs through my disaster of a pantry. Mom never uses one tea flavor. She digs into the depths of my stash to brew a new potion every time. It's always delicious.

She works quietly and I watch from a short distance as Luca giggles. Dad beams at every sound. It has to be true what they say. That strong, intergenerational relationships keep the grandparents young and do so much for baby's development too. It's beautiful to witness.

I want to fully appreciate these moments. Savor these memories. Except that I'm here, but I'm not. I'm partially stuck in the past even though I desperately want to move forward and live in the *now*.

I was doing better, but the last two months sent me spiraling back to the place I was a year ago. Now I'm left wondering…will it ever stop?

Will I ever be able to celebrate my son's birthday without fixating on all that went wrong the day we welcomed him into our arms and our hearts? Will I ever laugh without the fear that this will all be taken from me, because it almost was? Will I ever be able to drive past the hospital without crying? Will I always take the long way around to avoid driving by the place altogether? Will I forgive myself for what happened? For what I couldn't control when I was at my most vulnerable state?

The whistle of the kettle draws my attention back to Mom, who finishes her tinkering before bringing two mugs to the table for us, her sitting by my side to join me in watching over the grandfather-grandson playdate in the living room. After a minute or two, I drop my stare to the drink in my hands and wait.

Mom texted me this morning asking if Luca and I wanted some company. The timing seemed suspicious given it's Monday, Dom's first day back at work and my first day home alone with Luca since his birthday party. They always seem to sense when I don't want to be left alone.

I'm hardly ever truly alone these days, but still, motherhood surprised me with how isolating it can be. I rarely want to *talk* about my struggles, but being around the people I love helps quell the loneliness.

Mom and Dad practically bulldozed the front door down when I gave them the green light. Turns out, they were already in the driveway with breakfast in hand. Family and friends who bring parents hot meals are good people. And when they don't judge the shit show state the house is sure to be in? They're the *best* people. It's a fact.

"So," my mom begins. "Saturday was fun."

I nod. "It was. Luca had a great time."

She hums her agreement before sipping her tea. "And you?" she asks cautiously.

"It was nice to get everyone together." I shrug. When Luca woke up on his birthday, I shut down any part of me that wanted to spiral back to *that* time and place. I focused all my attention on Luca, worked so hard to see the day through his eyes only. Until he fell asleep in my arms, where Dom found us. A person can only fight for so long before they crash.

But throughout the day, I surprised even myself. I smiled, laughed, and shared the day with the people who mean the most to us. I'm grateful Dom organized everything, and to everyone who helped the party run smoothly and spoiled this kiddo with so many toys; it looks like we need to start some kind of a toy rotation.

"It seemed like you were having fun. But I..." Mom hesitates. Typically so steady and confident, it's rare to see her unsure. "I just worry that maybe you were trying to put on a brave face for us...and for Luca. Are you all right, sweetheart?"

I buy some time, taking a large gulp from my mug, the nearly too hot liquid burning on its way down. I nod vigorously. "I'm okay, Mom. I had a rough month, but things are getting better."

Lie.

Her eyes search mine, and it's clear she sees through my placating smile. I wonder if I'll be able to sniff out the bullshit Luca throws at me someday too. Is that a universal maternal gift or a Carolyn special?

"You know you can talk to me, right? To us?" She tilts her head toward my dad.

"I know, Mom." That's never been the problem. I know my loved ones would drop everything to be there for me if I asked. They would be loving, and they would listen. I've just never had the words. Never wanted to dig deep enough to find them.

I refused to let my issues ruin his birthday, but I gave myself my moment. It wasn't until I had finished his nighttime nurse, and held Luca in my arms, rocking him to sleep, that I finally let myself feel. Grief and shame, gratitude and relief, joy and sadness, all flooding me in rapid succession and cycles. Dom found us there, me unwilling to part with the baby I'd give *everything* for.

I could finally let my careful restraint slip without having to explain anything to anyone. I don't have any answers for them anyway. Except Dom did see. He slipped into Luca's room and held us, just like he had the day he was born.

Neither of us know what to say. Some things are just too hard to push past. It's better to bury it and try to move forward as much as possible, even with these goddamn flashbacks and intrusive thoughts hammering inside my mind.

"I love you," she says, her eyes watery with defeat.

"Love you too," I say, resting my head on her shoulder as she pulls me in close. We watch Luca and Dad play and laugh with ease.

I won't put my problems on my family. I can handle whatever this is. I just need a bit more time.

Lie.

CHAPTER TEN

Dom

"Dom. Dom, wake up," Ellie says, pushing my shoulder as I slowly surface from sleep.

"What's going on?"

"He's up. It's your turn," she says, a sense of urgency in her voice. She gets anxious when he cries, but I can't leap out of a dead sleep into a sprint. I'm a heavy-ass sleeper and my body doesn't work like that. My brain needs a second to catch up.

"Huh? Yeah. Okay, I'm...I'm up," I mumble, voice hoarse. I rub my eyes and pinch the bridge of my nose with one hand, checking the time with the other. "Holy fuck, El. It's two forty-five in the morning."

She flops onto her back and glares at me. "Yeah, well, I was up with him from twelve-thirty to two. Like I said, *you're up*." She rolls back to her side.

"Fuck," I mumble as I make my way into Luca's room. Only a forty-five-minute stretch of sleep. *What the fuck is going on tonight?*

Luca's never been one to sleep through the night, but since his birthday party a few days ago, he's been giving us longer stretches of uninterrupted sleep. Guess he was still recovering from the excitement of the party. Seems like that's over now.

"Hey, hey, shhhhhh. Little man, it's okay. You're just crying because you're tired, right? I say, taking a screaming Luca into my arms, holding his head against my chest, and trying to soothe him as best I can.

Fuck, he's inconsolable.

Time drags on and I try everything in my arsenal. I shush, I sing, I hum. I rock, I pat, I sway. I sit, I stand—shit, I even lie down on the ground next to his crib at one point holding his panicked hand as he reaches through the slats in the crib.

"Goddammit," I huff. I'm running out of ideas, but the idea of calling Ellie in for help isn't appealing either. We both know nursing gets him to sleep faster, but she was just up with him for an hour and a half while I slept. But I have to work tomorrow and she's home with Luca. He might nap for her, and she can rest. I'm sure she'll understand.

I try to calm him down for a few more minutes, but nothing's working.

"Ellie?" I call out cautiously, stepping into our room with Luca still crying in my arms.

"Yes?" she hisses from underneath the covers, frustration evident in her tone.

"I've tried everything. I can't get him back down," I say, admitting defeat and bracing myself for a different storm. One of the Ellie variety.

"Did you try singing? Humming? Changing your hold?"

"Yes, yes, and yes. Still no luck."

"And you checked his diaper, right?"

Fuuuuuck. I'm so fucking exhausted; I forgot to check. I'm not thinking clearly.

"Shit. I'll do that now," I say before quickly dodging out of our room and into Luca's nursery before Ellie can respond.

Wouldn't you know it? The damn diaper was wet.

So, I try again. Still, more tears from Luca, but I do my best, cycling through all my methods again, each attempt seeming to piss him off even more. Putting him in his swing. Rocking him in the glider. Singing, bouncing, everything. A guy can only handle so much screaming, and I'm about to hit my limit.

"I got him changed and still…nothing. Do you think you can take a turn?" I ask Ellie, daring to venture back into our bedroom.

"Do you know how long you've been in there?" she asks, sitting up straight, hair a mess, eyes cold enough to cut through my insides and leave me burning afterward.

"Noooooo?" I draw out the question, afraid to hear the answer.

I'm operating on maybe three hours of interrupted sleep. I know this is a bad idea, but with Luca screaming in my ear, Ellie attempting to kill me with her thoughts alone it seems, and the desperation I feel to get some decent sleep before I have to get to work in a couple of hours, I can't seem to avoid the obvious trap.

"Twenty minutes. *Twenty minutes, Dominic.* I gave it an hour and a half, and you can't give it more than twenty minutes?"

"You know he just wants to nurse. There's no point in me trying."

"Of course he wants to nurse. He's fucking *teething*. Weren't you listening to me earlier when you got home from work? He was cluster feeding all day even though it seemed like he was weaning last week."

I shove my free hand through my hair, letting it fall to my side in a tight fist before shaking it out.

"I can't take in information right when I walk in the door from work. I'm usually still caught up in my thoughts brainstorming for class."

"Right, so your job is more important than listening to me talk about our son. I'm just supposed to handle everything while you *wind down* from your day, even though you just had an entire commute home to do so. Guess what, Dom? *I don't get a commute.* I'm in the thick of things with Luca all day. There was no one clawing at you and gnawing on your chest while you went about your day. Excuse me for being touched out. I know he wants to nurse, but—spoiler alert—my nipples are fucking raw. He is *hurting* me and I need you to put him back to bed so I don't have to sit there in pain while you sleep peacefully a wall—might as well be a whole fucking world—away!" Her chest rises and falls rapidly. Despite her disheveled appearance, her stance is assertive.

I don't argue. It's impossible to when I know she's right. I tell her as much and make my way back to Luca's room to try again.

Another twenty minutes, and I finally get Luca calm. Thirty minutes after that, he's finally out. I hold my breath as I try to hover out of his room, avoiding stepping on the one spot in the flooring that I know will creek if I put any weight on it.

I hurry to our bedroom, turn the monitor on, and breathe a huge sigh of relief finding Luca still asleep. Without wasting any time, I plug the monitor into the charger and jump into bed, ready to pass out.

"His body is out of the camera shot," Ellie says, voice uneasy as she stares at the baby monitor. "How did that happen?"

"I don't know," I say, getting comfortable and rolling onto my side before closing my eyes.

"Dom, I can't see if he's breathing when he's out of the frame." The panic building in her tone has my body going rigid.

Don't say it, Ellie.

"We have to fix the camera."

"Ellie, no. He *just* fell asleep. There's no goddamn way we're stepping foot in there. He is *fine.*"

"Are you fucking kidding me?" she hisses with disbelief, as if I'm the unreasonable one right now.

"No, I'm really not." I sit up to find she's already upright. She looks like she's about to leap out of bed and storm into Luca's room, and I cannot deal with what we both know will happen if she does. "I don't know what your mind is telling you right now, but Luca is safe. He's asleep. He's breathing. Okay?" I flop back onto my pillows, hoping with every bone in my body that's the end of it.

Tomorrow—well, today—is already going to be impossible. I've gotten basically no sleep, it's four in the morning, and I can't deal with another hour and a half of fighting to get an overtired Luca back to bed. At that point, it'll be time for me to get ready for work anyway, any chance at getting some much-needed rest evaporating.

"You're being kind of insensitive," she volleys.

"And you're being incredibly paranoid," I mutter, unthinking.

Like a fucking idiot.

"Now you're just an asshole," she says, voice thick with tears. Instantly, what I've said registers in my stupid, sleep-deprived brain, but before I can stop her and apologize for being a jerk, Ellie's already out the door. I hear her soft steps on the baby monitor as she makes her way to the camera and watch as she adjusts the view. I see Luca's body come into the frame and I hold my breath, waiting for the smallest noise to disturb his sleep.

But I was wrong. She escapes without incident, comes back into our room, grabs the monitor, and hurries out. I hear the soft click of the guest room door closing.

Fuck me. I am an asshole.

***

"You okay, Mr. D?" Joey asks from his seat in the back row.

"Yeah, you look like shit," Hunter pipes in, unhelpfully, might I add.

"Shut up, Hunt. You're being rude," Tiffany reprimands her twin brother as she doodles in her notebook.

"It might be rude, but at least I'm honest," he retorts.

"You kind of look like you did a few weeks ago. No sleep for the mini-Moretti?" Gabrielle asks.

Ungrateful. That's what this class is. I gift them the ultimate prize as a student...a movie day. No expectations, no discussion, no homework. A no-strings-attached, all-too-precious *movie day*—all because I'm a fucking zombie—and *this* is my reward? A good old-fashioned roast, compliments of my third-period freshmen class.

"How about a thank-you for the free period?" I ask, taking a sip of jet fuel—sorry, I mean coffee. Mabel is the sixty-three-year-old school secretary, and basically the boss of all us teachers. She only knows how to make her coffee like this, a shot of adrenaline in a ceramic mug. I've clung to her breakroom brew every morning since Luca was born like the gift of life that it is.

Unfortunately for me, even the strongest cup of coffee can't clear up the gray clouds hanging over me today. Because I wasn't just up late with a toddler who wouldn't sleep; I was up late fucking up my marriage.

I just keep making things worse.

Of course, I didn't mean the stupid shit I said. I was burned out, touched out, and fucking exhausted. The thought of risking my last chance at sleep only to adjust the baby monitor camera felt insane to me in the moment. Now, with some distance and some caffeine, I can recognize that while Ellie's anxiety doesn't always make sense to me, it's very real to her, and I was the opposite of a supportive partner last night.

No, I made things infinitely worse.

I'm not perfect, never claimed to be, but now I have some serious damage control to do. I'm already trying to figure out where I'll be stopping on my way home to pick up flowers and something with a whole lot of chocolate for Ellie when my class decides to offer more...feedback.

"Uh-oh. You messed up, didn't you?" Bethany chimes in.

"Crap, you're right. Look at him. Remorse is written all over his face," Jerry adds smugly, like my pain and suffering are hilarious.

"Hey. Movie. Focus," I call out, gesturing to the screen and dropping my head into my hands as my elbows rest on my desk.

"Relationship problems. Clear as day. Look at him practically pouting," Joey agrees with all the seriousness of a surgeon being asked for a second opinion on a serious case of the husband fuckups.

"I've lost all control. Subjects are becoming too aware," I mumble into my palms, loud enough for Jerry to hear, little shit.

They're actually a great class—a fun and intelligent group of kids—but I don't need their above-average observation skills today.

"Whatever you did, you need to buy her something nice," Hunter says confidently, making his sister roll her eyes.

"You can't undo stupid with gifts," she says in a reprimand.

"Hey," I say defensively. Who says I was stupid?" Tiffany gives me a knowing look and laughs. Fucking laughs. "Okay. So, if I was stupid, *hypothetically*, what would you recommend?"

Am I asking fourteen-year-olds for advice? Shit, I guess I am.

"Apologize, take her to dinner, and spend some time together. Show her she's appreciated," Tiffany says.

"Yeah, and do something special that tells her you're thinking about her when you're not with her," Gabrielle adds.

The guys look at each other, dumbfounded. Yeah, we still have some work to do to catch up my half of the population when it comes to relationship competence. I mean, look at me...Exhibit A.

"I'll take these recommendations under advisement. Now...movie," I say, gesturing back to the screen. My class might be invasive, but even in my fuzzy state of mind, I know they're not wrong. A night out would do Mom and Dad some good. Let's see if I can work some magic.

CHAPTER ELEVEN

Dom

It took some planning, but we finally made it happen. It had been weeks. Months? Shit, I don't know, but too fucking long since Ellie and I had a night to ourselves. An honest to god date night.

Babysitters? Check.

Nice restaurant? Check.

Good food and drinks? Check and check.

We finally took a second to breathe and enjoy each other's company and a meal that wasn't interrupted by our son screaming for one of us to scoop his food faster or flinging it onto the floor.

After our fight, I apologized profusely, gave Ellie an intense amount of chocolate-covered pretzels and flowers, and proposed we take a step back and make time for a date together, just the two of us. Turns out, regardless of the fight, we needed this anyway.

It only took about two weeks to get the details worked out, my brother Jake and his husband Chris agreeing to babysit. *Agreeing* might not be the right word. They all but screamed at us to *get out* and told us to plan another date night soon.

Ellie and I still talked about Luca, of course; impossible not to—he's perfect. But we also reminisced on our dating life when we first met and gossiped about our friends because I don't care what anyone says—when you're married, you gossip. I somehow managed to not spill the beans about how Aiden plans to propose to Bec quite yet; I need to hang onto that secret for now.

We joked and laughed like things were easy. Like we did this all the time.

I love being a father. Luca is curious, silly, determined, intelligent, and my everything. But Ellie was my everything first and I can't wait months to get another night like this with her. We can't maintain a relationship with one good night every few weeks or even months.

After we arrive home and catch up with Chris and Jake for a bit, I watch Ellie wave goodbye from our front door. She locks it and turns toward me, leaning back against the frame.

Fuck. She's a knockout, and my dick swells at the sight of her popping her hips to the side, sliding her shoes off her feet, all the while keeping her eyes on mine.

"Come here," I say. She crosses the entryway, stopping only inches from me. I brush her hair back from her shoulder, watching the blonde curls fall away. I palm her neck and lean my forehead against hers.

Relief fills my lungs when I feel the weight of her forehead pressing against mine in return. We stay like that for a minute, leaning on each other, breathing together. It's been so long since I've gotten a taste of Ellie and I almost groan at the thought. This woman means everything to me and all I want is to hear her gasping and moaning my name while I take care of her.

Intimacy is still understandably difficult for Ellie. I always want her to be honest with herself—and with me—about what she needs, what she wants, and what she doesn't. I would be sick if she ever tried to push herself into doing more than what she's comfortable with, and right now, she's not comfortable with much happening between us physically very often.

Sure, we've had sex since Luca was born, but it's rare. That spark from before is buried. We just have to find a way to bring it back when she's ready.

I've talked to my therapist about it, even though I know Ellie would probably be embarrassed knowing that I've asked a professional for advice about our sex life. But I'll be fucking damned if I'm going to unknowingly cause my wife more hurt. I can't control the way life hurts us, but I can spend every last shred of my energy protecting her from what I can control.

I need Ellie to know that she's always safe with me. With her body and her heart. But that doesn't mean I don't crave her just as badly as I did when we met.

When I married Ellie, I vowed to spend my life making her happy. During this stage of life, that looks different than it used to. Less sex and more support.

Do I get to taste her as often as I wish? No. Do I fill her ridiculously giant water bottle every night before bed to find she only took a few sips before morning? You fuckin' bet. Because she's my everything, and when we promised to be each other's partner, I knew that meant we would evolve and our relationship would have to evolve too.

This is a season, and I'm going to celebrate every milestone I can, even if they look different than they used to. Wouldn't life be fucking boring if we didn't find something new to celebrate? New wins to remind us we're alive? This is going to be a win for us someday.

And I can be very, very patient.

"Well, this was fun, but I got an early morning tomorrow," I say, lips pressed to her cheek before running my nose along her hair, breathing in her shampoo and perfume. She laughs, reassuring me my joke hit like I wanted it to.

Ellie relaxes into my hold, her cheek pressing lightly against my chest and her palms running across my lower back.

"Funny, I was about to say the same. My boss likes to get the day started at the ass crack of dawn. Sometimes he even calls me in the middle of the night if he shits the bed on a project."

"Talk about the toughest job in the world. I hope your boss pays you overtime."

"Truthfully, I volunteer. No pay, but the benefits are exactly what I dreamed of. He's the best. I wouldn't change it for anything."

My world stops and quiets. I'm enraptured entirely by the gorgeous smile lighting up my wife's face. She's radiant. Pride and love and joy flowing from her with love for our small family.

Her playfulness tells me that we'll wrap up this night in the usual way. We'll get ready for bed, side by side. I'll fill the giant water bottle while she sets up the monitor the way she likes—at full volume, and the screen on so she can keep a close eye on Luca.

I'm caught off guard when I pull back and meet Ellie's stare to find her looking at me like she used to. Her eyes glazed with hunger, dipping to my lips.

It's the briefest moment, but it's something more. I know Ellie, and I know that look.

I swallow, running my palms up her back from her hips to her shoulders before pulling her in close, my lips grazing hers before placing a light kiss to her soft lips. She pulls away for a moment, her eyes closed, before she presses her lips to mine again, more forcefully. She slips her tongue in my mouth and I'm fucking gone.

I reach into her coat to push it from her shoulders, letting it fall to the floor before backing her against the door and trailing kisses down her neck. Her nails trace lines up the back of my skull before she grips my hair, keeping my attention on her neck, where I lightly nip at her skin.

"More," she whispers, and my body responds instantly. I lean in, pressing my cock against her. I grip her knee and hitch her leg around my hip. I grab her ass before palming her thigh, wishing I could rip the clothes off her body and have her here.

I groan into her neck at the feel of her warm heat.

"Upstairs," she demands.

She ducks under my arms and races for the stairs. I swat her ass as she passes me, before following the sound of her flirty giggle as she climbs the stairs.

I can't look away, entranced by the sight of her delicious curves swaying with every step, but when I catch up with her in our bedroom, I immediately sense the shift. It's subtle, but her eyes find mine, wide and unsure. Like what she did and said a moment ago and the implication of where this is leading and what she's asking for are hitting her all at once.

Fuck. She doesn't want this.

She opens her mouth, her hands fiddling and wringing in front of her stomach like she can expel the nervousness and anxiety out of her body through her fingertips.

"Ellie, it's okay...nothing has to happen, sweetheart," I say softly, keeping my distance so she knows I mean it.

"But you went to all this trouble setting up a fun date and—"

"Ellie, look at me." I wait, only continuing when her glossy eyes meet mine right before a tear falls down her cheek. "Let me stop you right there. You're breaking my heart with this," I say, pulling her into my arms and wiping at her tears softly with my thumb.

"*Nothing* about us is transactional," I reassure her. "Our marriage is a bond, not an exchange. I don't spend time with you so you'll give me this."

"But don't you miss it?"

Of course, I fucking miss it.

Ellie's gorgeous. She always has been. Sure, sex is part of it, but it's more than that. More than anything, I miss *her*. I miss *us*.

Day in and day out, I find myself looking at Ellie and wanting to touch her, wanting to hold her in my arms. Our chemistry hasn't changed, but there's distance between us now that's more than physical.

I miss the emotional intimacy. For almost a year, things have been tense, strained by exhaustion and a thousand competing priorities, and if I'm honest, we're both still working through what happened when Luca was born. That shit doesn't happen without changing a person, and it's no surprise the experience impacted every facet of our lives.

"Ellie, I need you to hear me," I say softly, but keeping my hold on her firm as I palm the back of her head, before dropping a kiss there too. "I need you to stop thinking about what you think I want. If you want to know, you ask me, okay? The most important thing to me is that you're okay. That we're okay. We can't give anything to each other when we're struggling on our own. What I miss is you talking to me like you did tonight. What I miss is giving each other our time. It's not our fault; this past year has been a lot. It's been *incredible*, but so fucking hard too. Do I *want* to have sex with you? Always. Twenty-four seven, three hundred sixty-five, babe. But what I *need* is for you to take care of yourself so that we can take care of each other."

My heart breaks again as she sniffles against my chest, my shirt damp where she presses her cheek against me, and her hands wrap tightly around my back.

"Don't you miss who I used to be? Wasn't she easier to be around? Wasn't she easier to love?"

"The woman I met when I was twenty-two? She was fucking phenomenal. The woman I married? My fucking soul mate. But the woman you are today? There is no end to my love for her. There aren't words to explain this knowing in my heart that we were meant to spend every minute of our lives side by side. Fighting our demons, sharing our successes, and making each other laugh. It's not just easy to love you, it's impossible not to."

"I'm tired of feeling like this. I want to feel like me again," she whispers, her voice cracking.

"You will, Ellie. I promise. Give it time. Give yourself time. I'm not going anywhere."

***

"Morning," Ellie mumbles, rubbing her eyes as she makes her way into the kitchen.

I meet her at the kitchen island, dropping a kiss on her lips before putting a cup of coffee in front of her. She leans back on the bar stool, wrapping her hands around the warm mug, her eyes watching me as she takes her first sip. She melts a little, relaxing into her seat, and licks her lips before smiling at me.

"Morning, gorgeous," I say. She pulls the baby monitor in front of her, huffing out a breath as she stares in disbelief.

"Okay, but what the actual fuck? Chris and Jake babysit and Luca sleeps in for the first time in his entire life?"

"Did you hear Jake say it only took them ten minutes to get him to sleep?"

"Are you fucking kidding? Call them. They have to move in," she says, face serious for only a second before she breaks into a smile, giggling at her own joke. *There's my girl.*

"As his brother, I reserve every right to tell you, you don't want to live with Jake."

"I will trade you for him in five seconds if it means Luca sleeps like this every night," she deadpans.

"You'd miss me too much." I wink at her. "Besides, you guys don't like the same shows. Do you really want to spend the rest of your life fighting for the remote in exchange for just a couple of hours of decent sleep?"

"First of all, that wasn't *decent* sleep. That was life-changing, soul-reviving, dark-eye-circle-healing sleep. And hun, I love you, but we only have, maybe, two shows we both like to watch, so if that's what we're basing this off of, fine. Then Chris can move in and you can have Jake. Chris and I share *every* show."

"I hope you two will be very happy together." I cross my ankles and lean against the counter.

"Eh, I think I'll take my chances on bad sleep and hang onto you a little longer. You make the best coffee." Ellie smiles at me as a comfortable silence stretches between us, both sipping on warm drinks in an unhurried morning. Hot coffee, quiet house, and the woman of my dreams sharing it with me.

Unable to wait any longer, I dive in, hoping she'll hear me out.

"Hey, I've been thinking," I say. *From approximately one to three in the morning*, I don't add. Figures the first good night of sleep we get from Luca in who knows how long, and I was stuck awake, tossing and turning, trying to figure out how I wanted to approach this conversation with Ellie. "I want you to know that I love you. I love you so much, Ellie. But last night—"

"I'm sorry," she rushes out, placing her hand on mine. Her grip tightens, her fingers digging into my palm. Her eyes close and she shakes her head slightly as she says, "I've just been feeling insecure and touched out lately. I had a great time last night. I'm sorry I ruined it at the end."

My chest aches. Her words are another reminder that we still have so far to go. We have a lot of work to do to repair what we've neglected for months while we focused on other things. We can't afford to push *us* aside anymore or I'm afraid there won't be an *us* for much longer. How long can a relationship last on the path we're taking? We need to be our priority now.

"I'm going to need you to take that back," I say.

"What do you mean?"

"When exactly do you think you ruined our night? On our date, while we talked and laughed in what was probably the longest uninterrupted conversation we've had in months? When you kissed me and lit my insides on fire with your perfect body pressed to mine? When you fell asleep in my arms and hummed my name in your sleep?"

"I don't talk in my sleep," she says softly, her eyes glistening with amusement, even though her posture screams that she's feeling uncertain and vulnerable.

"Yes, sweetie, you do—always have—but that's not my point." I circle the counter and turn her seat until I'm standing in front of her. I lean down, dropping my hands to each armrest at her side, and bend so we're eye to eye.

"There is no part of last night that was in any way *ruined*. I was with you. If you asked me to change one thing about it, I wouldn't. It was exactly what we needed. Which brings me back to what I wanted to talk to you about." I pause, steeling myself for an uncertain reaction to what I'm about to suggest. "I think we need to put sex on the back burner right now."

I wasn't sure how best to approach the subject, but in the moment, it seems like I've decided to go with being direct. I hope I'm not fucking this up.

"You...don't want to have sex with me anymore? Are you not attracted to me?" The question is laced with unmistakable hurt.

I straighten, lifting her chin so her eyes stay on mine.

"I meant what I said last night, Ellie. I always want you. Twenty-four seven, three hundred and sixty-five. You're even more stunning today than you were the day I married you, but I want us to take some time to focus on other things without the pressure of sex lingering in the back of our minds. Every time it comes up, you apologize and talk about what you think *I* want. But I need to know what *you* want. I want more than anything to give it to you. It feels like it'd be easier if we could focus on taking care of ourselves and each other in the other ways that matter first. Then we'll put sex back on the table when we're ready."

When you're ready.

The hurt seems to dissipate as she absorbs what I'm saying. I know it'll take more than one conversation to reassure her that this is a good thing, but we have to try something different. What we're doing isn't working, and this is the best I can come up with. I just hope I'm not making things worse.

"So how will we decide when we're ready to put sex back on the table?" she asks, tucking her hair behind her ear as she stares into her coffee mug.

"Let's not set any time limits. Let's just feel it out."

"Feel it out?" She chokes, disbelief radiating off her.

Come on, babe. Trust me.

I nod, forcing confidence into my posture. Begging her silently to put her faith in me, to give me a chance to fix this.

She studies me, and she must find what she's looking for because she agrees. "Okay, I trust you."

"This will be good, I promise. Now, I have one more serious topic for this morning. Before Luca wakes up, we have *got* to work on it."

She rolls her eyes. "The second we sit down to work on it, he's going to wake up. It's like when we lie down to fall asleep...it's the loudest sound in the world, straight to his tiny ears like cymbals crashing in a high school band."

"Nah, Luca loves his dad too much to not give me an extra twenty minutes for this."

I pull Ellie from her seat, and she joins me at the dining table. It never gets used for dining. Its purpose is almost exclusively for *this*.

Several completed puzzles lie on the table, off to the side. The unfinished one is set up in front of where Ellie and I sit. Only the puzzle's outline is completed. Ellie takes a minute to tuck her feet underneath her, getting comfortable, surveying the pieces while she calculates her first move. I dive in, reaching for the first piece when we hear Luca's cry ring out over the monitor.

We lock eyes and Ellie giggles.

"I'll get our boy. You get some puzzle time in."

I grab her hand before she can get too far and pull her into me for a quick kiss.

"I love you, Ellie."

"And I love you."

She leaves to get Luca, and I hear her a few moments later on the monitor, still on the table in front of me. I watch the screen as she pulls him from his crib and listen as she sings and shushes, soothing him almost immediately. She's a natural, even if she always doubts it.

I knew Ellie would be a phenomenal parent. With her family and friends, she's always been a steady constant. The nurturer, capable of showing endless love and compassion for the people she cares about. Even still, seeing her become a mom, watching her grow into her own is one of the greatest privileges life has ever given me.

It's not her fault. I don't hold onto any resentment for the struggles she's battling right now. But I wish she could see herself like I do. If she did, she'd see bravery. Bravery to wake up every day and give everything she has to this tiny human, dependent on her for every need, even when I know she's second-guessing every move she makes. I close my hand in a fist, silently wishing I could explain to her—that I could show her—so she'd understand she doesn't need to be scared.

She deserves to walk with confidence and be proud of everything she's survived. I can't take away the hurt completely, but if I can help, then I'm going to give it my all. The puzzle piece in my hand pokes into my palm as my grip tightens in frustration, reminding me that I never found its place.

I open my palm to see one of the edges crinkled, a little worse for wear, but it will still fit into the bigger picture just fine. I find myself turning the piece over and over in my hand...and it makes me think. If Ellie won't listen to me when I try to tell her this...maybe I need to show her.

Chapter Twelve

Ellie

"What did you do to my brother?" Jake asks, appalled as he stares at Dom dancing at the end of the hallway before dashing back into the living room out of sight.

"You think *I* planned this?" I ask incredulously. "You know us both better than that. Get it together."

If anyone had to convince anyone to dress up like an ogre for Halloween, it was absolutely not me convincing Dom. I hold the door open as Jake and Chris step inside, then give them one-armed hugs, my other arm full of a wriggly Donkey, a.k.a. Luca, before they follow me into the living room.

Dom hugs them hello, his ogre ears practically poking them in the eye, much to Jake's horror. Dom and I are both covered in green body paint. When Luca first saw us in costume, he shrieked with joy. Could have gone the other way just as easily, so I'm relieved he's excited and not terrified. He was happy to hop into his furry donkey onesie and complete our trio.

Carissa, Dee, and Abby dressed as Charlie's Angels. Bec and Aiden dressed as Princess Leia and Hans Solo. They completed their ensemble with a rambunctious Hopper, dressed as Chewy, who's strolling around the room excitedly stealing pets anywhere he can find them and hoovering up crumbs from snacks

Luca's thrown around, abandoned to the forgotten corners of our floors. Dylan is dressed like Bob Ross, with his own paint palate, while Chris and Jake are dressed in full Aviators gear. Aiden laughs when he sees them.

"Hey, this is what you get for spoiling us with merch. We were set up with a free Halloween costume," Jake says.

"Plus, this might be my only opportunity to put Jake in baseball pants. Yummy," Chris adds.

"I second that yum." Dee smirks, slapping both Chris and Jake on the ass as she walks by.

"This is why you're my favorite," Jake says with a laugh.

"Okay, are we doing this or what?" Dylan asks.

"You can't be fucking serious. I thought that was a joke."

"What part of trick-or-treating is a joke to you, Deanna?" Dylan asks.

"The part where five grown men take a one-year-old who can't eat candy trick-or-treating. You know you're not actually supposed to steal candy from a baby, right?" Dee asks.

"It's not stealing," Dylan says defensively.

Dom wraps his arms around my waist, closing the space between us as he steps behind me. "You sure you don't want to come with?" he whispers in my ear.

"Nah, you guys knock yourselves out." Dom and I already hit a few houses with Luca before everyone arrived so we could both enjoy the memory of his first trick-or-treating, even if he is too young for it. Last year, we kept him home since he was only a month old at the time. "Show Luca how it's done. Bring home some sugar, Daddy."

He stills, turns my jaw to look at him, and I smirk.

What? We're not having sex, but a girl can still flirt with her husband, right? He looks me up and down.

"My ogre bod is doing it for you, isn't it?"

I snort a laugh. "Yeah, Dom. Had to be that. Save it for...you know..." I'm suddenly shy and embarrassed. "Later," I mumble.

The smile I get in return is genuine. Not a hint of resentment. "Oh, I will." His eyes dip to my green cleavage and back up.

"Okay, this is officially weird," Bec says, staring at us.

"Says the girl who asked for a taste of my lightsaber before we left the apartment," Aiden says.

"We need better boundaries," Carissa says with a sigh.

"No way. This is way entertaining." Abby laughs, unwrapping a KitKat from the candy bowl and propping her feet up on the coffee table.

The lamp in our living room flickers for several seconds and catches Luca's attention. It's been doing that for a few weeks and I keep forgetting to change the bulb.

Luca points, laughing at the light show, and then claps.

"What is he pointing at?" Dylan asks. The light flickers again and Dylan straightens. "Seriously, what's going on?"

Dom gives me a confused look, which I return.

"Uh, you mean the light? We need to replace the bulb. Dylan, why the fuck are you backing up?" Dom asks.

"I don't know, man. You got a lamp flickering on Halloween, and your son is laughing at it? Can't babies see into the aether and shit? What if Luca is seeing things we can't?"

The room falls quiet, everyone looking at Dylan to see if he's serious.

The lamp flickers and Luca laughs and points again, eyes fixated on the lamp.

"Dude, seriously, what's wrong with that lamp?" Dylan asks, before trying to shove a hand through his hair in frustration. He must have forgotten about the Bob Ross wig.

"Dylan, are you kidding me right now?" Chris asks. "Are you seriously spooked?"

It flickers again and Luca laughs and starts crawling toward it.

"No way, Luca. I've seen this movie. We're getting the fuck outta here." He scoops Luca up and turns to the door. "Let's go, boys. I'm sure the ladies can handle the ghost on their own since Dee's so brave."

"Buh-bye!" Dee shouts after them. "Look both ways before crossing the street, Dylan! Don't forget to hold Aiden's hand!"

The girls and I settle into the front room, just off the entryway of our home, with a few themed drinks—I couldn't help myself when I found the recipe online—and an obscene amount of Halloween candy. We take turns greeting the trick-or-treaters making their rounds through the neighborhood.

"Dee, why are you giving all the kids different amounts of candy? Are you using a scoring system or something?" Bec asks, eyeing Dee skeptically when she makes her way back to her chair after doling out the last few handfuls of candy.

"Of course. Aren't you?" Dee says with a shake of her head and shrug of her shoulders.

Bec laughs. "No, I'm just giving the kids candy."

"What's the criteria?" Carissa asks.

"Easy. Five-point system. Creativity. Execution. Enthusiasm. Etiquette. Trailblazer," Dee explains, ticking off the list on her fingers.

My brows hit my hairline. "You've given this a lot of thought," I say with a smile.

"Listen, candy isn't cheap anymore. If you want your five pieces when I'm on duty, you're going to need to deliver on all five."

"Okay, how many pieces of candy would we get?" Abby asks.

"Us? We're all tens, of course. A five-point system could never do us justice," Dee replies confidently, kicking her feet up on the coffee table and opening up some nerds before dumping the entire miniature box into her mouth.

"Luca was so happy in his costume. How have you three been lately?" Carissa asks. I don't miss the look in her eyes. The one that says she's hoping to get more than a surface-level answer from me.

Maybe it's because I'm still feeling a little raw after Luca's birthday last month, all that trauma rising to the surface, throwing my nervous system out of whack, but I choose to spill instead of keep it all in, at least for tonight.

"Things have been okay this last month. We made it through Luca's birthday party, which was the big hurdle. I didn't really want to talk about it at the time, but I was having some anxiety about the whole thing."

Bec sits up, her eyebrows drawn together in concern. "I had no idea. You didn't seem stressed at all."

I circle the rim of my glass with my finger, needing to keep my hands busy. "Dom planned everything. I know that's awful; I should have helped, but...flashbacks of what happened when Luca was born started up again and I couldn't think about it more than my mind already forced me to in the *worst* ways."

"It's *not* awful that you didn't plan the party," Bec insists. "Dom loves that shit; you know he's happy to do it."

"Do you want to tell us about it?" Carissa asks softly. "What happened?" Her eyes meet mine. Compassion and empathy practically pouring out of her with just one look. I've never told them. Even Bec, who came running to the hospital when I called her, hysterical after the surgery was finished. I was still coming out from the haze of medication. She held me, then Dom, and then Luca like the sister she is to me. She held my little family and tried to piece us back together with just her love, support, and hugs alone. She didn't force me to talk about it. I couldn't. They've *never* pushed me to talk about it, but every so often they ask me if I want to share. I always say...

"Not today," I whisper, forcing a half smile to my face.

"What about the party? Are you feeling better now that it's done?" Abby asks.

"Surprisingly, the party was...great. When I woke up, I told myself to focus on Luca. To see the day through his eyes and not my memories. I held onto that idea all day. I think it helped."

I may never be the same as I once was, but it'll kill me if my mental health impacts Luca as he grows. I have no idea how to prevent what happened to us—how we started our lives together—from changing the way I parent.

My anxiety, my need to control everything, my need to hover. I can't protect Luca from everything, but that doesn't stop this gut feeling that I need to try. It's slowly killing me.

Will he have anxiety like me because I inadvertently pass on all of my fear and worry to his sweet and carefree self?

"Maybe getting past the first anniversary will help the anxiousness subside," Dee suggests.

"Maybe." I nod, wanting to believe her. But I know all it takes is one moment to send my brain right back to that moment, tossing my body into that impossible split-second reaction...fight, flight, freeze, or fawn.

CHAPTER THIRTEEN

Dom

Dee's singing Christmas carols proudly, inserting perverted lyrics in place of the real ones, obviously, while hanging stockings on festive hooks above our fireplace.

I can't hold in my laughter and I struggle to keep my grip on the trunk of the artificial Christmas tree as I try—and fail—to secure it in the base.

"Dammit, Dom. Just shove it in." Aiden grunts, frustration evident in his tone as he holds the top of the tree steady.

"Babe, stop hitting on Dom," Bec calls from where she's placing garland and tiny string lights Ellie said we *needed* along the built-in bookshelves on both sides of the fireplace.

"I'm not hitting on him," Aiden mutters.

"What did I say about threesomes?" Bec asks.

"Uh...did we talk about threesomes?" Aiden responds hesitantly.

"No, but it seems like a good time to mention that Dom isn't invited to participate in one," Bec says.

"Excuse me, I'm giving the performance of a lifetime over here. You guys are really stealing my thunder with your bickering," Dee whines.

"Okay, little ears are returning to the room now, so if we could sing Christmas carols with the normal lyrics and stop talking about threesomes, that'd be great," Ellie says, Luca propped on one of her hips as she, Carissa, and Jake bring in a handful of Christmas ales and hand them out to everyone.

"I'd like to say that's going to be the worst thing he ever hears from me...but I have a hard time remembering to filter myself. Apologies in advance for when he starts school. You can tell his teacher it's my fault," Dee says, giving Ellie a salute. "I'll send them a bottle of wine to make up for it."

It's the first weekend in November, meaning it's officially Christmas season in Ellie's world. And since I live in Ellie's world, that means Christmas is about to throw up all over our home. Thankfully, our friends are always willing to help out, and everything will be in place weeks before our annual Friendsgiving party.

I finally slot the base of the tree into the stand and rise from my crouched position, giving my back a quick stretch.

Everyone is busy with their Ellie-assigned task, milling around the living room and kitchen.

Abby, Bec, and Ellie start pulling tree ornaments out of their protective packaging. Luca reaches across Ellie's chest trying to get his hands on the fragile bulbs.

"On second thought, maybe we only put durable ornaments on the bottom of the tree and a few fragile favorites near the top," Ellie says. Luca starts to fuss, frustrated his mom won't let him play with a glass snowman.

"You got a point there. Here, do you need a minute?" Abby asks, offering her arms to take Luca, which Ellie gratefully takes her up on, freeing both of her hands to grab several large, soft bows made of gold ribbon and place them along the base of the Christmas tree.

Those are about to become Luca's favorite toys. Should take about ten minutes before the bottom of the tree is bare and those are thrown to all different corners of the room.

Carissa, Dee, and Jake are at the kitchen table, arranging nine ceramic reindeer on a snowflake table runner.

Aiden joins Chris, and together they place small figurines of cottages, gaze-bos, snowmen, and fake snow along the mantel.

"Sorry, I'm late," Dylan calls as he enters the room from the front hallway, a bottle of wine and six-pack in hand.

"Ugh, gross," Dee says with a sigh.

"Good to see you, too, Deanna," Dylan says, shaking the snow from his shaggy blond hair as he shoots a smirk her way.

"The displeasure is mine, per usual. Please tell me we can kick these guys out so we can finally talk about the holiday novella," Dee begs the girls.

"Probably not a bad time for a break. Dom, can you order the pizza before we split?" Ellie asks me.

The guys and I have plans to catch the University of Columbus football game while the girls have their book club tonight. Obviously, Luca is joining the boys because my wife likes her books spicy, and therefore very not-child-friendly conversations are bound to take place.

You won't find me complaining. I owe a lot of memorable nights to those books.

***

"Damn, I need to join book club," Chris says as he exits the kitchen, eyes wide. "Babe, you would not believe the shit I just heard. I need a minute to process."

"You don't need them. You've got us. We'll start our own book club and it'll be a thousand times better than theirs," Dylan says, a bitter edge to his tone.

"That reminds me. What's going on with you and Dee? You two have never been at each other's throats like this. It's always seemed like good fun before, but now..." Jake's voice drifts off, waiting for Dylan to fill us in.

"Trust me, there's nothing more going on. Dee just...she's always got to..." Dylan's voice fades as he shoves his fingers through his hair.

"Uh-huh, sounds like a whole lot of nothing to me. Remind me to say I told you so when that *nothing* magically turns into *something* that pops out of *nowhere* and you finally admit you need our help. Don't pull an Aiden and wait years to do it," Jake says with a heavy dose of sarcasm.

"Hey, I got there eventually," Aiden says around a mouthful of pizza.

"Yeah, and we're still waiting for our thank-you card," Chris says.

"What? The Aviator's tickets and gear isn't enough?"

"I just want to hear the words *you were right.* It'll be the fuel I need to help Dylan when he finally admits he needs us." Chris laughs and Jake pulls him in closer to his side.

Dylan scoffs and sips his beer before throwing his head back against the couch, eyes closed. "Trust me, when I have something to say about it, I will."

I'm sitting on the floor with Luca, where he's happily playing with his barn and farm animals. Ellie puts a lot of effort into finding toys that seem to interest Luca and help him with whatever stage of development he's going through. She's overly thoughtful, and I wonder if she realizes how she naturally thinks three steps ahead. Or maybe it's not as effortless as it seems. Does her brain ever take a break?

I finally have the guys alone, and I don't know how long we'll have. I need to do this now.

We're not entirely out of earshot of the girls, since we're watching the game on the TV in our front room, so I keep my voice low. "I hate to derail an interrogation, especially on Dylan's account, but before you intervene in his personal life, I need your help. Did you bring the goods?"

They stare at me.

"The goods?" Chris asks, eyebrow raised.

"Yeah, you know...the *goods*," I reiterate.

"You're making it sound shady," Dylan says. "But yeah, I brought the *goods*," he says with mirth, taking an envelope out of his back pocket and throwing it on the table. Luca's eyes widen and he starts crawling in earnest to steal the exciting piece of paper. I swear, we have a thousand toys in this house, and he acts like he'd rather play with an envelope, a spatula, or a remote control. If we had known that, we could have saved some money. Thanks for nothing, Fisher-Price.

I quickly grab the envelope before Luca can swipe it and verify said goods are inside before holding out an expectant palm to the rest of the guys.

Chris, Jake, and Aiden slowly reach into whichever pocket they put the small pieces I need for this all to work.

God, I need this to work.

"Dom," Chris says, eyes locked on mine. "I need you to know that this might be the most romantic gesture I've ever witnessed."

"*Hey,*" Jake says defensively.

"And as your brother-in-law, I want to see you succeed," Chris continues. "But I also need you to be careful."

Huh? Be careful with what?

"Yeah, he's right," Aiden agrees. "You need to think about how you're going tell Ellie about this."

"Guys, I appreciate whatever it is you're trying to do here, because it seems like your hearts are in the right place, and I'm grateful for your help, but let me put your minds at ease. I know my wife. I've seen this woman at her lowest of lows and highest of highs. I know her fears, I know her dreams, and I make it my responsibility to memorize every shift in those as we walk through life together. I'm the man she's trusted to keep her safe. I'm the man who promised to love her and give her every bit of happiness she deserves in this life. I'm not going to stop doing those things until I stop breathing."

"Damn, can I get that engraved on a ring?" Aiden asks quietly.

"We're just saying," Dylan adds with an unusual softness in his voice. "That it might not go exactly how you expect."

"Ellie's been through a lot, Dominic," Jake says, full-naming me, for fuck's sake.

"You're acting as if I don't know that," I retort. *As if I wasn't fucking there.*

Now I'm annoyed. This is supposed to be a good thing. Why are they saying this shit like I'm about to hurt Ellie instead of help her? This is all supposed to help her. Help us too.

"I don't mean anything by it," Jake says, leaning back in his chair, worry evident in his expression. "But what you guys went through...you can't fix it with games and romantic gestures. It takes more than that."

"I know what it's going to take," I say, bile rising in my throat, because...*fuck,* they might be right. "Look, this is just something I need to try, okay?" Even I can hear the uncertainty as my voice breaks.

Am I doing what I always do? Using big gestures, plans, and gifts to try to fill the void of something bigger? Something that can't be fixed without burning it all down to the stumps first? Fuck, maybe I am.

"I'll be careful when I tell her. Now, if you're done trying to lecture me out of my great idea, I'll take the rest of your pieces now," I say with a grin, trying to will away the awkward concern reflected back at me with every bit of false confidence I can muster.

Because if I don't believe this will work, then it won't. And I refuse to sit by and watch my wife fade away. This is how I bring her back; I can feel it.

Chapter Fourteen

Ellie

"Baby's heart rate is..."

Baby's heart rate is what?

"Three, two, one, lift..."

FUCK. Pain, searing pain shoots from my pelvis, through my abdomen, and all I can do is scream.

"Ellie, I need you to breathe..."

I can't...I can't...I can't breathe...

Someone pulls my arms roughly, pressing them hard against the table beneath me, but I resist, pulling and screaming, unable to focus on anything other than the excruciating pain and panic sweeping over me, crashing against every inch of my body and mind. The urgency in the voices around me doesn't calm me, it has the opposite effect, and my fight response kicks in.

No one's looking at me. No one's talking to me. What the fuck is happening?

Help me...help us...please...

***

"Ellie...Ellie! Jesus Christ. Ellie, *wake up*," Dom pleads.

I slowly sink into reality, the blurred edges of my nightmare falling away like the autumn leaves of our willow tree out back. The memories of the hospital operating room recede into the dark recesses of my mind.

A sheen of sweat covers my body. The hum of the sound machine playing through Luca's baby monitor isn't loud enough to drown out the sound of my labored breathing. My heart pounds wildly, frantically in my chest—the aching, thrumming beat is powerful and the sensation only makes my panic worse, my entire body frozen. Our bedroom is dark, but a sliver of moonlight streams into our bedroom through a crack in the curtains. I see the outline of Dom's face as he hovers over me. He's pinned me to the bed, his thigh between my own and his body half covering mine. He's gripping my biceps tightly, as if he's trying to hold me together.

But my body isn't falling apart this time.

Everything else is.

"Ellie, I'm right here. You are safe. We are safe," his voice sounds just like it did that day as he parrots my mantra for the millionth time, trying to comfort my shattered sense of safety. A melody for a nightmare. Hearing that kind of terror in your loved one's voice. Feeling how hard they're trying to protect you, trying to comfort you, knowing they can't do either.

He throws his chest over mine, his familiar scent grounding me. I breathe in through my nose, attempting to slow my breathing and keep myself enveloped in his scent. I try to imagine his arms can hide me from the poison in my mind. My breath stutters as I exhale and the tears hit me like a sudden storm finally breaking past the paralyzing panic. I choke out a sob, and Dom wraps me in his arms tighter, pressing his head into my neck. I weakly place my shaking hands on his lower back.

"Fuck, Ellie. I'm here," I hear him say, voice unsteady. I can't tell if the tears falling are his or mine anymore.

It feels like you're getting better until you aren't.

It feels like you're making progress until you fall a thousand steps backward.

It feels like someday you'll find yourself again, until you realize that person is gone and you're not sure what's left.

CHAPTER FIFTEEN

Dom

After getting Luca down for his nap, I find Ellie in the living room, sitting in her favorite corner of the couch, leaned against a stack of pillows. Her legs are curled beneath her and her temple rests on her fist.

She's wearing my old college hoodie again, several strands of her blonde hair falling out of the messy bun she's thrown on top of her head. Our Christmas tree glows in the corner of the room, the only light she's turned on. The giant festive bow decorations Luca loves to pull off the tree are scattered on the floor, victims of today's playtime. Indie folk music is playing softly from Ellie's phone, tossed aside on the cushion next to her.

She's caught up in her e-book and hasn't noticed me yet. I use the opportunity to take her in. A flash of her wedding ring catches my eye, the stone glinting in the flickering glow from the fireplace.

I remember the moment I first saw her in her wedding dress. The moment I put her wedding band on her hand and promised to give her everything, because she is *my* everything. I promised in public and in private to hold her close, guard her heart, and love her with my every breath.

I asked her to trust me with her life. I promised to fill it with joy. I promised to be understanding and patient, and she promised the same.

So many promises whispered across intertwined fingers, a bouquet, a suit, and a beautiful dress. But what does any of that matter if they're just words? If I can't make good on the promises I made, where does that leave us?

The encroaching fear that I'm too late—that we're already headed over the cliff with no edge to grab hold of—shrouds my vision.

I asked Ellie several times over the last few months to try working with another mental health professional. I even invited her to my appointments with David, my therapist who I see once a month. She met with someone for a few weeks when she went back to work part time after her maternity leave ended. It all came to an abrupt end when it became clear it was a bad fit. A really bad fit. Since then, she hasn't *refused* to find someone new, more like she's made it her last priority.

I know it'll only make things worse if I push her—she needs to take a step like that for herself, not for me—so instead, I'm doing what I do best. I'm solving a puzzle...and Ellie is going to help me do it.

Her eyes, while stunning as always, have that lost look today. When she woke up from her nightmare last night, her eyes only held terror. It was like she was looking straight through me. She wasn't lost, she was *gone*, drowning in whatever horrible memories pulled her under.

She didn't want to talk about it as I held her in my arms and softly stroked my hand along her back. She didn't pull away, and I took long, slow breaths until her pace matched mine. Eventually, I felt her body soften in my arms and I knew that she had found sleep.

She didn't want to talk about it this morning either. She sat beside Luca and me on the floor while we played and listened to his favorite song—this mind-numbing monstrosity about toothpaste tasting like mint chocolate chip ice cream—the biggest lie I've ever heard. She slid her palm along the floor until her fingers found mine, holding on like I was her lifeline. The moment had me reeling—when was the last time we simply held each other's hand?

We're always holding Luca, or grabbing the groceries, or cleaning the kitchen, or swiping something out of Luca's reach, or doing something from our endless to-do list. All things that seem stupid to prioritize now...when I'm sitting in front of my wife realizing I don't know what she's thinking anymore.

I used to read her so easily. I used to *feel* her so easily. From the moment we met, we operated like two gears, interlocked and spinning together. When one of us stopped, the other did too. When someone shifted direction, the other followed in support. But now, we're so disconnected I can't feel her push or pull, and I know she can't feel mine either. I can't follow her lead, and instead, we've wound up so far apart that I can't see where she's going. We're on opposite ends of the room, both spinning off without anything left to ground us, connect us, or slow us when the brakes give way.

I shift, leaning against the wall, causing the contents of the box I'm holding to shift. The rustle catches Ellie's attention, and she smiles softly at me.

Fuck, this could be a disaster. But I have to do something. I have to try.

"Hey, handsome," she says, putting her e-reader on the arm of the couch.

"Hey, momma," I say. "How you feeling?"

She curls into her side, facing me and laying her cheek against the back couch cushion, tucking her chin in the neck of the sweatshirt. "I'm okay."

I wait, giving her space to say more. Her smile fades a bit when she realizes I'm not going to accept her answer. That I'm begging her for more. That I'm starving for her to fill the space between us with honesty and to finally let me help her carry the burden on her shoulders.

"Really, Dom. I'm okay, now. Last night was...an outlier. Things have been better and that came out of nowhere."

I join her on the couch, placing the box on the coffee table and keeping my eyes down so she can react to my words without the scrutiny of my stare. I want to be able to talk to her without her shutting down, getting defensive, or dismissing my idea altogether.

"Ellie, I love you. You know I want to help. Was there anything that happened yesterday that might have, I don't know, thrown you a bit?"

She's quiet, but her thoughts are loud.

"I guess there was this one thing...Carissa mentioned in passing that one of her coworkers recently had a baby. We only talked about it briefly, and I shouldn't have asked any more about it, but I couldn't help myself. I guess she had this beautiful birth story, and I...felt *everything*. I felt jealous because why did this stranger get to have the moment I'd been dreaming about for nine months—for my entire life—while we went through what we did. Then I felt equal parts guilty and relieved because I never want anyone to experience what happened to us. Then I felt suffocated by heart-stopping, gut-wrenching grief because I wanted *that*, and we'll never have it. We'll never get that moment back. We'll always be the parents who started this chapter of our life like *this*. I began my journey into motherhood hurt and confused and scared, and I want to know why. Why did this happen to us?"

I take her hand and rub small circles across her thumb with my own. "I don't know if there's an answer, Ellie. We might never know."

"Why does that break my heart?" she says, voice cracking and silent tears rolling down her rosy cheeks, wetting the strands of her hair that have fallen loose from the knot on top of her head.

"Honey, it's normal to want answers, but maybe there aren't any this time. Maybe we're just normal people who went through something awful. It's not fair, but there's nothing we could have done to avoid it. You didn't do anything wrong."

Her face falls and a small sob escapes. She covers her mouth with one hand while the other wipes at her tears. I'm immediately moving, pulling her to my chest. She leans against me and we stay like that for a few minutes.

God, this was so stupid. She needs more than what I can give her. More than some stupid fucking game. But she won't agree to finding a professional right now, so here goes nothing.

"Do you still love me?" she asks through shuddered breaths.

That catches me off guard and I take her by the shoulders and lower my face to hers, waiting for her to lock eyes with me. "Ellie, I could *never* stop loving you."

"But I'm a mess. I can't let this go. Crippling fear is controlling my every thought all day long. It's not fair for you to have to deal with things like last night."

"Last night wasn't your fault either." I keep my voice gentle, but hearing her break like this, because she's worried about *me*, makes me want to scream. "Can't you see that none of this is your fault? Let me try to help," I say, picking up the solid brown box, void of any decoration.

She eyes the box, then me, skeptically. "What's this?"

"I need you to keep an open mind while I show you. Can you do that for me, love?"

A small smile pulls at the corner of her lips. She's so beautiful.

"That's a dangerous question coming from a man like you, Dominic Moretti. Last time you asked me to keep an open mind, we were in contract on a house twenty-four hours later."

She's not wrong. I saw this house for sale and immediately pictured my wife in the front bay window reading her smutty books, on the porch watering her plants, and in the garage getting our bikes ready for the local trails.

You could say I'm impulsive, but I'm not. I'm decisive.

I saw this house and all I could see were my wife's smiles. All I could feel were her arms around me as we danced in the kitchen. All I could hear was our laughter filling the space between the walls. When it feels like that, you buy the fucking house.

"And that was great, right? But this is a little different." I lift the lid off the box.

"Seriously, another puzzle? Dom, there are five on our dining table as we speak. What is this?"

"This is *your* puzzle."

"I love that this is your hobby, babe, but I don't do puzzles."

"Well, that's not true. You help me with them all the time. Plus, you promised you'd keep an open mind, remember?" I say with a smirk.

Her fingers hover over the pieces as I begin to lay them on the coffee table upside down.

I'm surprised she doesn't comment on them facing the wrong direction, but she's focused on another issue. Her brow furrows in confusion. "There aren't enough pieces here for this to make anything..."

"That's because you'll only get a handful of pieces at a time," I say.

"Ooookay?"

"You're not convinced, that's fair. Let me show you." I begin to arrange the two dozen pieces or so on the table, looking for edges. "These pieces are all from the same section of a larger puzzle. You have what you need to finish a small section entirely. When you're ready, I'll give you another section to add to this one."

"I love you, but you've lost me."

"There are special pieces mixed in with the others," I say excitedly. "I'm calling them Ellie pieces."

"*Ellie* pieces," she says with a heavy dose of suspicion and disbelief.

Yup, she thinks I'm losing it. Shit, maybe I have.

"See? You got it. Ellie pieces. When you come across an Ellie piece—and this is where I'm going to need you to keep an open mind—you have to do what that piece says."

"Dom." She laughs incredulously, ready to shut me down.

"Please, I need you to trust me." The shift in my tone from playful to serious has her sarcastic smile fading, and she quietly nods, giving me space to continue. "I'd never do anything that would hurt you. This is all for you...everything I do is for you and Luca. I know things have been...*difficult* lately. This whole year has been the best year of my life and maybe the hardest too. I can't fully understand what you're going through, but it's killing me to watch you suffer. I don't like failing you—"

"Dom, you're not failing me."

"I am, Ellie. *Please* let me do this. Try this with me. If worse comes to worse, it's just a fun game you can tease me about later," I beg.

She pauses, eyeing me. A small smile breaks her expression and I release my breath in relief. This is going to work.

"It's *worst* comes to worst," she says with a smirk.

"Huh?"

"It's *worst* comes to worst, not *worse* comes to worse."

"Oh, honey," I say, much more confidently than I'm feeling. "I'm so sorry to do this in the middle of something so serious, but we have to add that to the list." I stand and jog to the kitchen, grabbing the notebook of fucked-up sayings and racing back to her as I say, "You are so very wrong."

Her laughter lights up the room. I toss the notebook on the table. I'm going to finish my pitch, but then I *will* be getting my points...I think.

"I'm *not* wrong, but stop changing the subject for a second." She swallows and wrings her hands in her lap before looking at me. "Dom, this is very thoughtful, but you are not *failing* me. You are my husband and my partner, but this is *not* your responsibility. This is mine. I need...I need more time to work through what happened, that's all."

"Honey, I love you," I reassure her. "But it's been over a year. I don't want you to think I'm not proud of you for how far you've come. You went through something terrible, and you're strong as hell for it. You're an incredible mother and wife, but you're not okay. You keep telling me time and time again, and I hear you. I want to help. Please let me help you."

"You went through it too," she says softly.

Fear, the ghost of terror that filled me that day, pulses in my temple at her reminder, but I shake my head, willing it away. This isn't about me.

"It's not the same, El. Please."

"So...*if* I agree to this," she says slowly. "What kind of activities are on these *Ellie* pieces?"

I smile like an idiot, knowing I've got her. My brave, wonderful wife is hiding in there somewhere, hidden by layers of self-doubt, anxiousness, and trauma. I'm going to dig her out with my bare hands if I have to.

"You'll get the first one soon. I also asked our family and friends to all take a turn, contributing their own pieces to the puzzle," I say with a smile. "You ready to play?" I ask, my heart pounding with pride as her shy smile lights up my chest with electricity.

She's got this.

"One more question. Why do I have to do this upside down? How am I going to complete an entire puzzle when I can't see the picture?"

"That's life. One piece at a time, we don't get the full picture until the end," I assure her.

We're going to do this together. We're going to find our way back to each other. We're going to find our way home.

CHAPTER SIXTEEN

Ellie

"You really shouldn't do that with candy canes," Carissa says, her face stuck in a grimace.

"Oh, you mean in chapter twenty-four when the three of them…wait. Why does your face look like that? Has someone come into the ER with a candy cane stuck in their…*unmentionables*?" Dee asks, wide eyed.

"What happens in the ER on Christmas Eve, stays in the ER. Trust me, it's for the best," Carissa says, before taking a long drink from her glass of wine.

"I have questions I'm sure I don't want answered, but I'm afraid I lack the self-control to hold back," Dee says, holding up her finger.

Abby's our lucky host for the December book club. What a way to start the festive review.

"Allow me to assist," I interrupt, in a plea to talk about anything else. "I have my own questions I need answered. So, did Dom include you all in his *plan*?"

They exchange glances like they were waiting for this conversation.

Bec cracks first. "I'm sorry we didn't tell you. He swore us to secrecy so he could explain it to you himself. He kept things light on the details and said he'd let you share it with us after he told you everything. Are you mad?" Bec asks with a wince.

I've thought a lot about this since Dom told me all about his puzzle last night and the fact that he had asked our family and friends to be involved.

Was I mad? No. Maybe a little ashamed that my problems are big enough to warrant this type of over-the-top intervention from my selfless, acts-of-service husband. Of course, it's incredibly thoughtful to have our loved ones help. There's a small piece of me that's embarrassed, but an even bigger part of me that's excited to see what they have planned.

My throat tightens and I force a swallow in an attempt to keep the emotions bursting in my chest from spilling over my cheeks as tears.

My husband, the man I love so much but can't seem to find my way back to, did this all for me. Calling on the ones who love me most to remind me of that love. That aching weight sitting on my chest that normally numbs the emotions I don't want to feel lightens just a bit, enough for me to remember how it feels to be cherished like this. I want to let it in, but a part of me doesn't feel like it's meant for me. Undeserving.

"I'm not mad. I was surprised and caught off guard. I know it's coming from a good place. Maybe something like this will help shake me out of this mindset I'm stuck in. I think I could get excited about it, when I'm not focused on how embarrassed I should probably feel."

"Wait, why would you be embarrassed?" Carissa asks, a genuine look of confusion on her face.

"Because isn't it sad that I need this? It's like everyone knows I'm falling apart all the time. You should have heard Dom explaining the whole thing. He was so excited to tell me his plan. Like he was proud that he'd figured out something helpful we can try together. Like he isn't ashamed of the kind of person I am right now."

"What do you mean the kind of person you are right now?" Abby asks gently.

Did I really say it like that?

"I guess I'm not sure. But this is the first thing Dom and I have shared in the last year that wasn't about Luca. God, I sound like such a *shitty* mom. What I mean is that Dom and I spend all our energy trying to give Luca everything he needs that we haven't really had time for *us*. We've been stuck in survival mode, and when things do finally calm down, we're crashing, clawing at scraps of free time, trying to squeeze in a minute to rest so we'll be ready for the next time we're needed. There's nothing left for us to give each other at the end of the day. Dealing with my issues doesn't make that easier on Dom either."

"Do you honestly feel that way?" Dee asks, a softness to her voice she doesn't usually use. "Dom *loves* you. Your mental health isn't an issue for him to *deal with* like a burden. It's something you both care about and take care of when you need to. Like when people get hungry and someone makes dinner. Or clothes inevitably get dirty and someone does the laundry. Meeting our physical health needs isn't more important than our mental health needs, babe."

"Dinner and laundry are smaller jobs than what I got going on up here…" I respond.

"Holiday dinners can take days to prepare. Laundry after a rainy, muddy day will take twice as long. How much time and effort we need to put into something doesn't make it worse. It just means it needs a little extra care. A little extra love," Abby says.

"Your poetic artist side is showing," Bec says with a smile, making Abby roll her eyes.

I consider what they're saying.

"He was so excited to tell me. It was like when we first met. He was the goofy guy who makes everyone smile. Who loves so fully without a care in the world and without hesitation. I'm afraid my apathy this past year has made him scared to be his peppy, carefree self. And because I'm struggling, all my gray clouds darken his skies along with mine. He's chasing me in this storm, desperately trying to catch up, reaching out to me to hold the umbrella over my head and bring me home."

I don't normally share this much with the girls. I barely talk about things with Dom—only when I fall apart after holding it in for so long, or the feeling of failing consumes me and I break apart despite my every attempt not to.

A hollow sort of numbness swept over me the moment everything spiraled out of control when Luca was born, and I've never fully wanted to feel anything since.

If I let myself feel that soul-igniting happiness, that heart-pumping desire, that exhilarating carefree eagerness, that lungs-on-fire laughter, then the other big emotions will follow.

I'm not ready to face them. The panic, fear, shame, guilt, incompetence, and lack of control. If I keep my feelings small, buried away, busy myself with anything and everything. Keep my mind and body focused on other people, other things, then none of it can catch up with me.

But sharing half of my heart isn't enough for Dom anymore. What if I lose him because I'm not ever willing to put in the work?

I know I need help. I know he'd do everything he could to make that happen if I told him I was ready. Every time I try to say the words, make the call, set up the appointment with a new therapist, something stops me. This voice in my head saying, *if you do this, then everyone will know.*

I'll have to give voice to everything, all the intrusive thoughts, and that makes them so fucking real.

I'm terrified that I'll never truly heal. That this is my forever. That I'll never get to be the mom I wanted to be, the wife I used to be, or the woman I was.

Becoming a mom added so much more than a title. It turned that *before* woman into a stranger and the *after* woman into a ghost. Here, but not really. Present, but hollow. Aware, but empty.

"What would be so wrong with letting him, El?" Bec asks, reaching over to take my hand in hers. "If you're right, then this game isn't just for you but also for him. Maybe he knows you need this, and doesn't realize he does too. There is no world where Dom considers you a burden. Your relationship isn't one side giving and the other taking. Sometimes you show love and need love differently. If this is something you want, I think you should trust that Dom wants it too. Just because it might bring you happiness doesn't automatically mean it's his burden. Why can't it mean happiness for you both?"

"Doesn't that make us a little codependent?" I ask.

"Making good memories together doesn't sound like codependency to me," Bec says.

It's hard to argue when she frames it like that. She smiles, sensing victory. "So, you're all in then?" I ask. "You all have puzzle pieces in Dom's secret stash?"

"We're all in," Dee agrees. "He didn't explain how it'll all work, just that we were all building a puzzle together. We all still have our puzzle pieces. Dom hasn't collected them from us yet, so we still have time to think of what we want ours to be."

"He also wanted you to be able to talk about it with us, without being biased by his explanation," Bec adds.

Fuck, that man is something else. He gave me this. This thoughtful gift, and then let me have this moment with my girls.

"So, tell us everything," Abby says with enthusiasm.

I allow myself a small smile, sharing everything Dom told me last night. The girls' excitement feels like permission to finally feel it too. Maybe I can let myself have this indulgent fun. Maybe I let Dom play this game and see where it gets us, for once not letting my anxiety make the decision for me.

CHAPTER SEVENTEEN

Ellie

"Sorry I'm late," Evie says in a rush, tugging her scarf from around her neck. Aiden's younger sister joins us at the jewelry counter before tossing her giant purse onto the floor. She sits in the vacant chair next to Aiden.

"Hey, Eves. No problem. I'm glad you could make it," Aiden says, before returning to his examination of several rings displayed in a velvet tray on the counter.

Stones, large and small, catch the light and sparkle in a variety of settings, from delicate, vintage pieces to bold statement rings.

Goddamn, my best friend is going to need to up her lifting to carry around a ring like this. Perks of dating a professional athlete.

"Think we could see a few more? None of these feel right," Aiden says. The woman assisting us, Joanie, smiles and nods, taking the tray.

Aiden is the most nervous I've seen him. Even when Dom and I were trying to talk him through a difficult time this past summer, this is completely different. He's hunched forward, elbows resting on his knees, both bouncing incessantly since he sat down fifteen minutes ago. His shoulders rise and fall before he looks to Evie, a hint of panic in his voice. "We just got started, but I'm worried that nothing will feel good enough for Bec."

"You know, you don't have to do this. Grandma's ring is still sitting at my place just *waiting* for you," she says cheerfully, bumping his shoulder with his.

"Evie, we've been over this. That ring is meant for *you*."

Her shoulders sag slightly with his declaration. "Bec would love it."

"Of course she would; it's beautiful. But it's *yours*."

"Single ladies do not need rings like that."

"You don't need to be in a relationship to deserve a ring like that. Besides, just because you haven't found someone to spend your days with, doesn't mean you won't. Mom wanted you to have Grandma's ring, and I do too."

I melt a little at the sweetness. Having no siblings myself, I sometimes find myself paying closer attention to the dynamics siblings share. I've been fortunate to have a family that loves me, and I've never felt like I was missing out, especially since I grew up only a few houses down the street from Bec and her three older siblings. I always felt like the fifth in their crew.

Bec's older sister Danny and her mom couldn't make it today, but Aiden promised to video chat with them to show them his final choice before he made the purchase.

I'm seated on Aiden's other side, Dom standing behind me with Luca on his chest in his baby carrier. His hands are resting on my shoulders, occasionally kneading the muscles. The casual contact probably appears natural to people around us, but it has me feeling giddy. Like I just met him and all this physical affection is brand new. In a way, it is.

Over the last year, our casual physical intimacy has...dwindled. Hands too busy, minds too tired, overstimulation and exhaustion controlling every aspect of our lives, emotionally and physically. It got to the point where showing physical affection was so infrequent it felt like if one of us initiated it, that it had to go somewhere...go all the way. So, instead, it kind of just...fizzled out.

But ever since Dom suggested we wait to have sex for a while, I've been able to focus on just being with him. I think it's helped me get out of my head. I know small touches won't give him the wrong idea and lead him to assume I want more, so I can touch him all I want.

It seems to have done the same for him, too, making him more relaxed. I welcome it, basking in the warmth of his hold, the deep pressure of his kneading fingers relaxing my muscles and relieving the stress I didn't realize had solidified there.

Joanie places a new set of rings on the counter in front of Aiden. I peek up at Dom to find him intently studying the next tray of rings, that wrinkle in his forehead making an appearance, causing the corner of my lips to turn up in a smile.

It's really not fair for him to be out here in the wild with his sexy dad bod on display, beard a little longer than usual, backwards Columbus Aviators baseball hat on, all while dissecting engagement rings like I imagine he did years ago for me.

My gaze rolls over him, and when I make my way back to his eyes, I find him staring at me with an eyebrow raised and a smirk on his face. Then he winks at me. *Goddamn winks* at me before looking back at the rings in question and responding to a question Aiden asked that I didn't hear. There's a direct line between a wink and my panties and after seven years, he fucking knows it.

"Ellie? You good?" Aiden asks, seemingly not asking me his question for the first time.

"Uh, yeah. All good. Sorry, what was the question?" I blush. My husband isn't supposed to distract me from something this important.

Focus, Ellie.

"How about these? Are any of these closer to the dream ring?" he asks, a vulnerability and nervousness on the edge of his voice.

The last tray had beautiful rings, but they weren't Bec's. She and I spent hours in our college dorm room dreaming about rings, sharing Pinterest boards with numerous styles, metals, cuts, and settings. It's been years, but I still have access to her page, and I skimmed through the pictures last night to remind myself what types of rings she was drawn to. But while Bec and I have talked a lot about rings, her favorites always changed, and that was years ago. The best I have to go off of is the similar characteristics and the feel of the design.

"I really feel drawn to one of these, but I want your opinion first," Aiden continues, wringing his hands, his eyes almost pleading.

I smile, biting my lips to keep from giggling at his nerves. Every day that passes only solidifies my confidence that Aiden will always protect Bec's heart, and that's all I want for the people I love.

"May I?" I ask Joanie, who nods before returning to her paperwork.

I pull the tray closer in front of me and study the four rings. Just like the ones before, all of them are stunning, with beautiful stones, cuts, and settings. I don't know anything about clarity, color, or the technical aspects of stones or settings.

Call it what you want, but I go with my gut. What *feels* more like Bec? What can I envision her shrieking in excitement over seeing for the first time, showing it off to her friends and family, smiling at it when she's alone at the reminder of the man who loves her more than anything.

I hold them one by one, twirling them in the light, not putting any of them on my own finger because that feels wrong for some reason. When I get to the last one, I know immediately this is the one I'd choose.

"Okay, if you asked me of all we've seen so far," I say. "My favorite is on this tray."

He sighs a breath of relief and gives me a knowing smile. "The last one, right?"

"The last one," I say with a nod, sliding the tray back toward him. He picks it up and studies it again.

A quick glance at Dom and Evie as they watch Aiden smile at the ring tells me we're all on the same page.

"It's perfect, Aiden. As radiant as Bec," Evie says.

"Twenty minutes, and you've got your ring." Dom sighs. "That's got to be a record."

Aiden's eyes stay glued to the ring as it sparkles in the showroom lighting. "It only took a few hours to know I wanted Bec in my life forever. It's fitting it should be that quick of a decision for this too."

To be so sure of something, someone. It's not lost on me what a gift that is. It's a gift to witness too.

"Well, glad I showed up for the good part," Evie says with a laugh. "Who's feeling lunch? There's an amazing place next door. You guys in for a celebration?"

The four of us spend the next two hours sharing great food and raising our glasses in cheers to the soon-to-be proposal, all while Luca babbles between me and Dom, throwing all the food we put in front of him across the table. We tip accordingly. What a mess.

I can't wait to see Bec wearing that ring soon, knowing she'll say yes before Aiden even has the chance to finish asking her.

CHAPTER EIGHTEEN

Dom

"Dom," Ellie sings. "Merry Christmas," she whispers in my ear, curling into my back, her body wrapping around mine, and her hand clinging to my stomach as she tugs herself flush against my back.

We used to cuddle every night and morning, but having her *big spoon* me right now is a reminder that we've stopped doing that. Luca's had a really good week of sleep, and I don't hear him fussing on the monitor, so we must be getting another day of him sleeping in.

A very Merry Christmas indeed.

"Merry Christmas, beautiful," I mumble, voice groggy. Our room is still dark with the curtains drawn. The exception being a vintage, one-foot mini-Christmas tree on our dresser with small rainbow-colored bulbs. Ellie found it at a thrift store last year.

Every single room of our house has at least a splash of festive decorations and cheer, thanks to her. Luca has his own mini tree in his nursery, too, even though we have to turn it off at night so it won't keep him awake. We don't need anything else working against us.

"Another good night," she says before placing a slow, lingering kiss on my bare shoulder. I sleep shirtless, and sure, the Dad bod thing is real. I've definitely softened around the middle and lost muscle tone since Luca was born a year ago. Working out becoming my last priority is to be expected at this point in my life. I'm not bothered by it when I see the way Ellie still looks at me when she thinks I don't notice.

Less time meal prepping and working out means more time with my family. More time to wind down when we finally get a precious minute to ourselves. Sometimes convenient comfort foods make more sense when meal prepping feels like too big a task to take on. None of that matters to me. As long as I feel good, can keep up with Luca, and Ellie still looks at me with fire in her eyes, then I don't give a fuck if I've softened up or lost a little muscle here or there.

And Ellie? Her body is something else. I've always loved every inch of her, but watching her go through pregnancy and birth? I'm in awe of all she's given to create this family of ours. I know she's still getting used to the changes...the stretch marks, the scar from the c-section, and other things I don't notice but she tells me *feel* different...like breastfeeding and all that comes with it. For the record...not a *single* complaint on my part. Every mark on her body is a reminder of how fucking strong my wife is, and yeah, it gets me hard. Because she is as stunning—if not more so—as the day I met her.

I always wanted to be a father. To have this family I have now. The physical evidence of her sacrifice to give that to me has never done anything but make me want her more. But she can't see that, so I have to tell her, and I have to show her...when she's ready.

I thread my fingers through hers before pulling her palm to my mouth to place a quick kiss there, reveling in the feel of her warm body against mine. Shit...shouldn't revel too much, I guess. The feeling of her tits against my back is hard to ignore. There won't be any hiding my growing erection if I don't get my shit together.

"Want me to start the coffee?" she asks, sleep still lingering in her voice.

"Not yet," I say, tightening my grip on her hand before turning to face her and pulling her into my chest, dropping a kiss on top of her head. I breathe in the familiar scent of her shampoo—the one she's used for years—and my entire body relaxes on impulse.

Ellie in my arms, content and well rested, on Christmas morning with our son sleeping peacefully, about to have a fucking blast while we spoil him with holiday magic. This is my dream come true.

My heart knows it's found home and beats alongside its match.

In moments this perfect, it's difficult to remember what stops us from playing on the same team sometimes. What makes us defensive, or speak more tersely than we should, forgetting ourselves and each other when we're exhausted. When things are this goddamn good, none of those things seem to matter. I want it to feel like this all the time. Easy, joyful, and loving.

We stay like this, using the time to talk about our excitement to see Luca's face as he takes in the site of brightly wrapped packages. We guess which book and toy he'll love most, and dream about what Christmas mornings will be like when he's older and he comes barreling into our room at five in the morning like Jake and I used to do to our parents when we were too impatient to wait for them to wake up to start opening gifts.

Luca gives us a solid fifteen minutes before waking up.

Way to go, little man.

Shockingly, he wakes up happy, singing, cooing, and giggling when we walk into his room together to get the day started. I make coffee while she changes Luca's diaper, and we share a lazy morning together. Christmas music plays softly in the background, the scent of Ellie's pine candles has me believing for a second that our tree is real. I throw a pack of cinnamon rolls in the oven and make mimosas for me and Ellie while she nurses Luca.

It's actual heaven on Earth. I know when I look back on my life and think about my best moments, days like this will be among them.

"Here," I say. Handing Ellie her stocking while she sits with Luca on the floor.

She hums in suspicion. "You and Luca up to no good together, conspiring against me this Christmas?" she asks.

I try to bite back a smile at her antics, and fail. "Yes, we *conspired* to get you a gift. Aren't we the worst?" I ask our son, who blows raspberries in sarcastic agreement, I'd guess.

Ellie pulls the small brown box tied with green ribbon out of her stocking and gives it a small shake.

"Ah-ah, careful," I warn her too late. "It's fragile." She freezes.

"It is?"

"Yes, slow down and try not to move the box too much. Hopefully it isn't already broken," I say with a grimace.

The worried look on her face almost has me feeling guilty for teasing her.

"Dom," she says, voice full of reprimand. She drops her hands to her lap, box included. "This is a box of puzzle pieces."

"Like I said, precious cargo."

"You said very fragile."

"Nope, gotta get your ears checked, love."

She rolls her eyes, before I catch a glimmer of excitement in them as she looks at the puzzle pieces.

She digs around, pulling one piece apart from the rest. "My first Ellie piece?" she asks, failing to mask her eagerness.

I grin and nod. "This one is from Luca."

She turns, gasping and smiling at him, tickling his belly. "You got this for Momma?" she squeals and he giggles, flailing his arms as he unsuccessfully tries to swipe the puzzle piece from her hand.

She turns the puzzle piece over to read it.

"Next year, it's Momma's turn." Her brow furrows in confusion. "I don't get it."

"I got Aiden's blessing to adopt his family's Christmas tradition," I say.

Aiden's mom started this tradition when he was younger. He and his mother and sister take turns choosing a new ornament for the tree each year, slowly building their collection, each with a special memory and meaning.

The whole thing is really sweet. And of course, something Ellie told me she loved when we heard about it. She's an absolute sucker for holiday cheer, magic, and decorations. But more than anything, she loved the sentiment behind the idea, and I loved the thought of incorporating the practice into our small family's future traditions.

"Luca picked the ornament this year," I point out. "But like the puzzle piece says, next year, it's your turn."

I hand her another box. "I promise this one is actually fragile."

Ellie slowly peels the paper away and bursts out laughing. "Babe, what is this?"

"What do you mean? It's the ornament your son picked."

"You didn't give him any direction at all?" she asks, disbelief heavy in her voice.

"Uh, no, then it wouldn't be *his* choice." Clearly, she's confused.

"Our son is just starting to walk. How did he even pick? I'd pay a million dollars to watch my eccentric husband and happy-go-lucky toddler in the holiday aisle. Please, paint me a word picture."

"Okay, so I took him to the craft store you like, where they have all the holiday aisles we're never allowed to skip."

"Great first step."

"Then I took him down every aisle so he could scan all his options. Let me fucking tell you, there are *a lot* of options. There was one I thought he might pick. It was a baby bottle. In the end, I'm sure he vetoed it because it's a little inaccurate in his case. A boob ornament would have been more realistic, but for some reason they didn't have one of those." She rolls her eyes, and I continue. "But this is where we ended up. In the festive animal aisle."

She lifts the glass ornament, admiring it thoughtfully, the corner of her mouth lifting.

My family doesn't live a perfectly curated, photo-album-ready type of life. Why would I want an ornament that didn't feel like us? This absolutely did. So, when Luca didn't want to see any other choices after he set his eyes on this one, I couldn't agree with his choice more.

"Well, a llama in a party hat is certainly a memorable first ornament to kick off the Moretti tradition," she says.

"The first of many," I say, dropping a kiss to her perfect lips. "Can't wait to see what you pick next year."

CHAPTER NINETEEN

Ellie

Dom pops his head into our closet, catching me in my shapewear. God-dammit. Nothing says sexy like nude shapewear I had to jump, shimmy, and shake my way into, but my dress for tonight calls for it, so here we are.

"Hey, Momma," Dom purrs, his body still hidden behind the door frame, and his eyes rove over my form. "Looking good."

"Stop," I say with an embarrassed laugh. Despite my brutal inner monologue about my body, Dom has always made sure I know how much he wants me.

"Couldn't if I tried. Hey, close your eyes for a second."

"We don't have time, babe. We're supposed to be there in forty-five minutes. I still have to get into my dress, and you know I like to give our parents a rundown of the latest bedtime routine before we go." Luca's routine changes all the time. A million small adjustments in a hopeless attempt to get longer stretches of sleep. I think at this point I've convinced myself that if we follow every step to a T, Luca will magically become a baby who loves to sleep. Dom's accepted his fate. He says he's learned to function as a caffeine-fueled zombie. I'm not giving up.

"I'll only take a minute," he says, striding into the small walk-in space with another small brown box in his hand, with a familiar rattle.

"Another one?"

He flashes me one of his perfect smiles, and I take the box and open it.

I'm still digging through the pieces, trying to find the one with his familiar—albeit almost illegible—handwriting.

Cheese. That's all it says.

"Dom, what does this mean?" I ask.

He reaches above me, grabbing a gift bag I hadn't noticed off the top shelf of our closet.

"This one requires some new tools."

"Are you giving me sex toys in our closet while our family is downstairs watching our son?"

"No, babe, you're a screamer. That would be poor planning on my part to give you something I couldn't use right away without traumatizing everyone."

I lightly slap his chest and he smirks in response.

Fucking smart-ass. Ugh, I love him.

"Open it."

Not one to turn down a present—sue me, a girl can enjoy being spoiled—I toss the tissue paper over my shoulder to find a...

"Oh my god," I whisper, hand coming to my mouth. I can't believe it.

I'm holding my dream camera, a Canon EOS R5.

"Aiden thought you could use the upgrade," Dom says, shoving both hands into his pockets and rolling back on his heels, an amused expression at my shock.

"Why? I can't accept this."

"Babe, he's a professional baseball player. Let's say thank you and take the camera. Besides, you've got a job to do tonight and he's offering that as payment for his investment."

"Okay, now I'm really lost," I say, shaking my head.

"He's asking her. Tonight."

"Holy shit...Aiden's proposing to Bec *tonight*? And you're just telling me this *now*? At the very last minute? What, does he not think I can keep the proposal plans a secret?" I say, with mock horror, because that's exactly what he should think.

"Uh, *yeah*. You and Bec have a hive mind. I tell you something and Aiden is texting me about it two seconds later because Bec's already running her mouth."

"You knew what this was when you married me," I say with a shrug. He wraps his arms around my waist, pulling me close and placing a kiss on my forehead.

"I'd do it all over again tomorrow. But unfortunately, this is why I was in full support, possibly even the mastermind behind keeping you in the dark about it. He's asking her tonight, and this is his puzzle piece for you."

I'm too distracted by the gorgeous camera I continue to turn over in my hands, in awe that Aiden would do something like this before what he says registers. "Wait, what?"

"He's hoping you'll take a few photos of the engagement tonight. You got a purse big enough to hide a camera that big?"

My heart beats wildly with excitement. Faded, in the hazy edges of my heart are memories of how much joy photography used to bring me. I'd taken a couple of classes throughout college—something to help with my marketing degree—but I fell in love with it. The afterthought, supplemental, elective course became my passion project that I inhaled until my lungs burned any chance I got. I took photos for the university, documented all the big events, even provided them with promotional material for the athletic programs. I never considered doing anything serious with it. Daydreams of being a photographer felt indulgent. Maybe a little unrealistic to think I was good enough to make a career with something I felt that passionate about. Wasn't a job supposed to be that? Just a job?

"I haven't taken photos like that in a long time," I say, a sharp spike of insecurity twisting my thoughts.

"What better way to dive back in? What do you say, Ellie? Ready to get back in the game?"

***

The shutter snaps in quick succession as I blink away tears. Aiden down on one knee, staring up at Bec as he whispers words of love and devotion, speaking of promises and gratitude.

My heart swells, thrumming with joy. Bec deserves this. Aiden deserves this.

They've shown each other, and themselves, that they can work through hard things together. But this isn't one of those moments. This is a new beginning. One I'm lucky enough to capture.

The space is gorgeous. Aiden rented out the entire rooftop bar of the hotel Dom and I got married at years ago—and the place where Bec and Aiden met. I move quietly, trying not to draw focus from the proposal. I adjust the lens, and angle so I can get good shots of both their expressions with the evening skyline in the background.

Bec's and Aiden's parents and siblings are huddled together. I take a few shots of their reactions, with Aiden and Bec still the forefront of the image.

When the big moment is over, and Bec hugs her mom, I continue snapping a few more photos. I capture celebratory cheers of congratulations, empty threats from two older brothers and older sister, if I had to guess, and a teary *welcome to the family* from both Mr. and Mrs. Miller. Evie squeals and grips Bec and Aiden in a firm, if discombobulated group hug, Aiden towering over both of them. Aiden speaks softly to his mother and holds her hand while she looks at him with a soft smile.

I pause to skim through the last few shots, looking up at the sound of heels clicking in a speedy approach. Bec's arms are tight around my neck before I catch a glimpse of her brown curly hair flying away from her face and into my mouth.

"Ellie, this is crazy. Did you know?" she asks, half giggles, half hysterics.

"Only for about an hour before you did. Can you believe Dom and Aiden? Those guys didn't think I could be trusted with a secret," I say with a laugh, spitting out her hair and returning her hug with a tight squeeze, careful of the camera in my hand. I mean, I know Aiden can afford to replace it, but she's too pretty to break and I've already named her. Stella and I are going to go a long way, finding beautiful images together. I can feel it.

"We've got a lifetime to make them pay for it," Bec replies with glee.

***

"I've been told I owe you an apology," Aiden jokes.

"I can keep a secret," I say defensively. *I can't keep a secret.* "Apology not accepted. How about another camera, instead?"

Aiden and I are standing on opposite ends of the corner of the rooftop bar—thank god for the space heaters—him leaning on the edge and me seated at the other.

"Dom told me to get that camera specifically."

"Oh, Stella's perfect," I assure him. "But you know, if you need more photos taken in the future, I *might* need a new lens or something."

He laughs before taking a sip of his drink, letting his eyes wander back to Bec as she laughs with Carissa and her sister, Danny, seated on a cushioned L-shaped couch surrounded by greenery and string lights.

"It's the least I can do to repay you," he says, his attention returning to me. I know it'll be about thirty seconds before he steals another glimpse of his fiancé. The man is infatuated.

"For what? Twenty minutes of me taking pictures does not equate with the cost of that camera, I promise you."

The playfulness disappears, and he drops his gaze to the bar, tapping his fingers against his glass.

"I don't know how long it would have taken me to come back to myself, Ellie. Without you and Dom, I'm afraid I would have lost Bec to my own idiocy before I managed to pull myself out of that place, if I ever did at all. I could have lost her." His voice sounds haunted. It was months ago, but nothing that painful is forgotten quickly.

"Aiden, promise me something. Let yourself enjoy this. Savor every moment of your life with my best friend. You don't owe Dom or me a single thing, but you and Bec owe everything to each other. You brought yourself back, but we will always be here for you both when you need help remembering who you are."

"You know that goes both ways, right?" His question catches me off guard, though I guess it shouldn't. Not with the way Dom has everyone in on his game for me.

"I'm okay, really. I'm grateful for everyone who agreed to...participate in what Dom has planned. But really, I'm okay."

"You know it'd be okay if you admitted you weren't."

An uneasiness settles into my lungs, making it difficult to take a full breath.

"You didn't ask me to explain myself," Aiden continues. "When I was struggling, you didn't dwell on all I could have done differently. You helped me pick myself up and move forward." He swipes a palm over his face. "I don't want you to think you have to minimize what you're going through with all of us."

All I can do is nod, biting my lip because all of a sudden, I feel like crying. This feels dangerously close to digging into my own wounds, and I'm not doing that tonight.

I bury it, shake it off, and force a smile.

"Thank you. I'm going to be okay."

He waits a moment, measuring the truth of my words before he nods. "I know. And like you said, we'll be here for you both when you need help remembering who you are. Thanks again, Ellie. I don't know if I can ever thank you enough, but I'm grateful all the same."

He takes off, heading toward his mom and Evie, who are speaking with Mr. Miller and one of Bec's brothers, leaving me feeling...vulnerable.

With only a few words—my own thrown back at me—all my doubt, all my insecurities are laid bare for everyone to see. I've been doing my best to hold myself together, desperately grasping at the seams to pretend I can do it all without falling apart.

When you need help remembering who you are.

It's a punch to the gut. By trying to reassure Aiden, I've only shaken my perception of myself. I don't remember who I was. That version of me feels so far away, like a stranger, an imaginary someone who never really existed. If I can't remember who I was, then who am I now?

CHAPTER TWENTY

Ellie

"This is weird, right? Why did Dom think I needed to do something like this?" I ask while Dee, Chris, and I put on safety gear at Ruby's Rage Retreat.

The infamous Ruby is a short, no-nonsense elderly woman with stark white hair cut close and wispy around her small face. Her eyes were cold and her smile was nonexistent as she showed us to our room and explained the setup and rules. The walls are covered with tools ranging from hammers to golf clubs. A cracked leather sofa is shoved against the opposite wall. Really cozies the place right up.

"Maybe the mastermind behind this plan didn't *think* you needed to do something like this, babe. He *knew*," Dee says, with a wink at Chris. She picks up a metal baseball bat, giving it a twirl before picking up a sledgehammer.

I scoff at the sight of her double fisting her weapons of choice and at the sentiment. "And you? Do you also think I need a rage retreat?" I ask Chris, who is suspiciously quiet.

Avoiding eye contact, Chris takes off his safety glasses, cleaning them as if we aren't about to wreck a room together with no real need for his sight to be *that* clear.

"Chris?" I ask again.

"Okay, I need to tell you something," he says so quickly I have to do that thing where I slow down what he said and replay it in my mind again to make sure I heard him correctly.

Chris shuffles his weight from one leg to the other and stares at his thumb while he picks the side of it. He huffs a deep breath, shoulders dropping as he straightens his spine, looking at me with determination and a flicker of hesitation.

"I picked it. This was my idea. Dom asked me to choose the next activity," he says.

"And here we are," Dee says with glee as she runs her palm up the side of a metal pipe.

Jesus, are we playing Clue? Dee in the rage room with the candlestick. No one would be surprised.

"Why didn't you want to tell me this piece was from you?" I ask.

"I don't know. I was nervous you wouldn't like my contribution to the whole puzzle thing," Chris says with a tight smile.

"It is quite the surprising pick from you," I say, trying to make light. Chris won't meet my gaze. "Are you all right? You're not acting like yourself..."

"I'm just worried about you. I remember how it felt. When I was at my lowest," he says. When his brown, glassy eyes lock on mine, I don't even think; I step closer and wrap my arms around his waist.

"Did you come to one of these before?" I ask softly, knowing he's had his own struggles. He nods. "Did it help?" He nods again.

"Jake brought me here back when we were working together and hadn't started..."

"Fucking each other's brains out?" Dee interjects casually, zipping up her neon yellow jumpsuit.

As usual, Dee cuts the tension from any situation with the most perfect timing, and my shoulders relax for the first time since I stepped into Ruby's lovely establishment.

"Yeah," Chris says, chuckling, the vibrations rolling off him in waves while he's holding me. "He could see I was going through something; I was having a really difficult day—a shitty month, really. My depression was the worst it had been in years and my meds needed adjusted. I was suffocating under the weight of it. He didn't ask me what was going on. He didn't make me talk, but he looked at me like he knew. He asked if he could take me somewhere, and he brought me here."

"What happened?" I ask, having never heard this story before. A rare occurrence. I've known Chris and Jake for years. They were already married when I met Dom. The four of us have been close ever since Dom and I started dating.

"We joked around and eye-fucked each other while we smashed some heavy shit. Afterward, we went our separate ways until work the following Monday."

I give him a look.

"At the time, I didn't have the words. I never did when I got that low. My brain felt so far from my body. I hadn't felt good for weeks. Jake could tell I had hit a wall and needed to release the energy. I wouldn't lie to you, sis...it helped. I can't explain why or how, but when we left, it was like so much of the shit floating around my head, mucking everything up, stayed in that room, torn to pieces, shattered on the floor. I didn't take it with me. And when Dom asked me what I wanted to do for my piece of the puzzle, I thought...I mean, I know it's different, but I thought it could help you too. To let some things stay here. To let some things go."

His words cause my stomach to lurch, because he described it perfectly. The disconnect between my mind and my body has been a riddle I can't solve. Probably another residual effect of trauma, my mind trying to protect me. Even though it's all over, I still have no idea how to find my way back to myself.

"If it helped you, then I'm willing to give it a try. Let's do this," I say with a smile.

"There's our girl," Dee says with a smile that screams trouble. She takes my hand and pulls me to a table with a binder that looks one rough turn away from falling apart. "Now that you're all in, I need you to make the two most important decisions of your entire life."

"Most important decisions of my entire life? Not who I'll spend my life with or whether or not I should have a child?"

"Eh." She shrugs. "Anyway, *focus*. I need you to pick your tool and your tunes."

"Oh...my...god," I whisper, and I can't hold back the huge grin overtaking my expression. "I get to pick a song?"

"Pick a song? We aren't half-assing anything today. I bribed Ruby. You get to DJ for all of the rooms for the next hour," Dee says, her eyebrows rising in challenge.

"Hand me the bat," I say, reaching out an open palm.

"With pleasure," Dee says, fitting the cool aluminum into my grip.

***

"Should we stop her?" Chris asks, concern evident in his tone.

"Hm? Nah, she's good. We still have eight minutes left of this glorious production."

Dee and Chris lean against the door to the rage room. There's glass, metal, wood, and who knows what other materials shattered and scattered on the concrete floor. A rainbow of fresh paint covers almost every surface, and I'm breathing heavily from the physical exertion.

God, it feels good to move.

"What do you think?" Dee calls out. "Something new or run it again?"

"Run it!" I shout before bringing the hammer down on a stack of dishes with a loud crash.

"Again, please, Ms. Ruby," Dee says, her finger holding down the intercom near the exit. Within seconds, the music picks up and I can hear the muffled cheering from the group of guys in the room next door, followed quickly by a series of loud thumps as they tear their own room apart.

I'm grateful they approve of my song choice.

Yes, I picked *one* song to play on repeat for the entire hour we were allotted to trash this room. Because in a movie, *this* is what I'd want to hear playing in a slow-motion montage while the three of us hop around this beat-up cinderblock of a room in our neon jumpsuits, headgear, gloves, and safety glasses, breaking it all into a million pieces.

The slow-paced staccato guitar run trickles through the speakers before the percussion picks up. Bosson's "One in a Million" has been the soundtrack—on repeat—to this epic battle between me and the dinnerware.

The song plays through one more time, and when it ends, I pull off the glasses and gloves and wipe my forehead with the back of my hand. Sweat is dripping down my body. I can't remember the last time I worked this hard. Even Chris has a sheen of sweat over his dark brown skin, and the short hairs around Dee's neck are damp and curling with sweat.

"So, what's the verdict?" Chris asks with a knowing smile.

"I think we should come back next week," I reply, grinning wide.

"Deal. Dibs on the sledgehammer," Dee says before turning and launching the door open. "Ruby, put us down for next Saturday. What are my other options here?" she asks, gesturing to the tools on the table. "You got anything special in the back?"

"I'm proud of you, Ellie," Chris says, still perched against the door frame.

I take a look around the room. Piles of broken pieces littered on the floor. It feels better to do the breaking for once, instead of feeling like I'm the one being broken.

"I'm proud of me too," I say, breathless. "Thank you."

The smile on his face is so loving, my heart warms at the reminder that my family could possibly be this wonderful.

Maybe I can leave a broken piece of myself here. Add it to the pile to be swept away at the end of the day. Maybe I don't have to carry it all with me. Not forever.

CHAPTER TWENTY-ONE

Ellie

I'm brushing my teeth when Dom joins me in our en-suite bathroom. He steps up to the counter and loads his own toothbrush with far too much toothpaste before he starts brushing alongside me, his eyes finding mine in the mirror before he flashes me a wink.

I can't help the clumsy smile that takes shape around my toothbrush, and I'm forced to spit the frothy bubbles into the sink. I start flossing, leaning my hip against the counter, turning to face him, and he does the same, still brushing.

I've learned to love the simple moments of two lives lived alongside each other, like this one. Quiet, seemingly unimportant moments, easily taken for granted.

But not by me. Not after what happened. Not when I thought there was a real possibility that I might not see any more of them. I wonder if everyone trying to make sense of some traumatic experience feels it. This weight of responsibility to appreciate all the little things, because now everything that used to feel small feels important, and everything I used to stress about feels small in comparison.

We finish getting cready for bed in comfortable silence before Dom turns down the forest-green duvet and beige sheets and I close the matching curtains.

Dom turns off the light on his nightstand and I check the baby monitor *one* more time to make sure Luca is okay before settling under the covers. My brain tells me he's fine before the intrusive thought jumps out like a fucking jack-in-the-box, and well...an obsessive habit is born.

"Did you finish your puzzle pieces today?" Dom asks. He'd given me about a dozen pieces earlier, my next batch. So far, I've been getting a handful of puzzle pieces every few weeks, but this time was different. I haven't seen any new pieces since Chris and Dee took me to the rage room at the end of January. It's the end of February now.

"I did, but there was no special piece. No Ellie piece this time?"

He boops my nose.

"Nice try. Here." He hands me another puzzle piece, based on the feel of it in my hand.

"In bed?" If he could see me—which I'm not confident he can, given how dark our room is—he'd see my eyebrow raised in question.

I thought we were still waiting on sex. We haven't talked about it lately. Is he bored? Is he tired of waiting? Is he feeling as affected by me as I have by him lately?

Something about sex being taken off the table has made me think more and more about how good it might feel to put it back on the table. Or folded over the table. Or on the edge of the table. Fuck, we should fuck on a table.

"Should have probably waited to turn off the light. Here," he says, flicking the small bedside lamp on his nightstand.

I turn the puzzle piece over in my hand to find his scribbles.

Talk pillow to me.

"I'm going to need some help here, sweetie," I say with a laugh, having no clue what this means.

"Ten minutes, Ellie. Every night before we fall asleep, I want ten minutes of pillow talk, without the sex, obviously."

"Without the sex...for now."

"For now," he affirms with a reassuring smile. "I was thinking the other day about all the little things we used to do all the time, like cuddling or even holding hands. I know we've both tried to give our relationship a little TLC when we can, when we think of it, but I want intentional time set aside every day, just the two of us. I'm craving this in-between stuff. The stolen moments buried in our too-busy day.

"I think we forgot how to slow down. I want us both to sink into the quieter, unhurried moments together. We've been so busy trying to make big, loud memories, I forgot how to listen for the soft ones.

"Then...Christmas morning happened. We only had fifteen minutes. Fifteen *uninterrupted* minutes together. It made me realize how much we might need that kind of time. So, I'm asking you to gift me ten minutes at the end of the night. Even when we're tired, even when we have to battle Luca at bedtime, even when your book just got good, or my video game kept me up too late."

"You'd interrupt my book boyfriend for pillow talk?"

"I would."

"Ballsy," I say with a giggle. "What do you want to talk about?"

"Anything. Everything. I just want to hear you. I'm going to make an effort to slow down wherever I can. I want this time for us to slow down together."

A lifetime ago, we would stay up late, into the early morning, talking on the phone or texting, filling the space between my college apartment and his in the city with banter, jokes, and love.

Then we moved in together and it was all sex and dates and sex and talking and more sex.

Then we got married and Dom found this home for us. Our focus shifted; nesting for our future, figuring out how to be real adults, talking, planning, dreaming, wishing, sharing, and loving.

Then we had Luca, and everything changed. He became our sun, and we orbit around him like two starstruck planets in awe of the force of gravity centering us around the most beautiful, joyful, and perfect little star.

The love between us is still there, but it's different, transformed into energy spent on critical things like learning to keep a baby alive, playing, singing lullabies, making crafts, tracking milestones, a thousand pediatrician appointments, cautiously introducing allergens, and cringing while your baby tries to learn how to eat solids without choking, and remembering to take pictures and capture memories.

Those little moments between Dom and I just…faded quietly into the background. Like I'm sitting in the front row of a theater, and those special rituals all stepped back, silently finding places to wait in the seats farthest from the stage, bordering the edges of the room, filling up the nosebleeds. Dom and I let these moments get pushed further away until neither of us realized they were missing. The seats next to me are the tasks I can't ignore, demanding all of my attention and energy.

"This may be my favorite piece yet," I say, my eyes filling with tears. This man is wholly, unapologetically, unfairly a pile of lovey, gooey, selfless affection. I find myself glowing as he focuses all that energy entirely on me. On *us*.

"I have one small stipulation I'd like to add, if you agree to it," I say.

"What's that, gorgeous?"

I'm almost embarrassed to say it out loud. Embarrassed in front of the man who watched me struggle through gross and way-to-real pregnancy moments, birth insanity, and then postpartum, which is just a science experiment on the human body while hormones have a fucking field day in your system. I force myself to ask anyway, knowing I'll regret it if I don't.

"I want you to hold me. I want us to hold each other for the ten minutes."

The grin that explodes on his face forces any lingering embarrassment to slip away, and I answer his smile with one of my own.

"I can't believe I didn't think of that. Of course, Ellie. Get over here," he demands, opening his arms wide across the bed.

He's lying on his back, so I throw my leg over one of his and snuggle my head to his chest, wrapping one arm over his waist. I breathe in his freshly showered scent. The smell of his body wash and the comforting scent of him underneath releases all the tension from my muscles as I melt against him. Our bodies taking the same position we've lied in together a thousand times over the years, but we're so different now. Our bodies a little worn, a little softer. Our minds a little scattered, a little tired.

"So, where do we start?" I ask.

"Well, you could start by telling me why I got a text from a rage room offering me a frequent customer card for repeat visitors."

I laugh, turning my face into his side to muffle the sound for fear of waking the sleeping babe in his room down the hall.

"Dee may have bonded with the owner of the *fine* establishment that Chris took us to last month, and now we're friends with her on social media. Dee was trying to help Ms. Ruby with her business page and one thing led to another. Now we're in a group chat working on how to help her market her business. Ruby doesn't like to text, so she ignores our messages and keeps calling one of us to fill her in on the conversation. I forgot to warn you that Dee was using all our phone numbers for the test messages."

"Hmm." The hum of his chest reverberates against my cheek pressed to his pec muscle. "Checks out. Count me in next time."

"While we're at it, why did I get an email confirmation that a package shipped to us from Silhouettes and Sapphire? I looked up the company and I know you're buying shit from a sex toy website, Dominic."

I peek at his face, my chin resting on his chest as Dom blushes...actually blushes, sweeping his arm over his face and hiding in the crook of his elbow.

"I'm gonna kill Aiden," he mutters. "He and Bec were reminiscing about the time Aiden sent a vibrator to her apartment, only for it to accidentally be delivered to her elderly neighbor instead. I might have asked him what website he used. I thought maybe, when we were ready—when you were ready—it wouldn't hurt to try a few new things. The computer must have auto-filled your email when I ordered...the things."

An embarrassed Dom is a rare sight, normally so full of confidence, but I love this sheepish version of him as much as the rest. My stomach drops when I realize what he's implying, a nervous but excited anticipation drawing up my thighs at the idea that Dom was shopping for sex toys.

"That could be fun," I say.

He peeks at me from beneath his elbow before lowering his arm entirely, his fingers beginning to slowly trail up and down my back in a comforting rhythm. "Really? I don't want to push you, which is why I wasn't going to mention it until later. We never have to open them if you're not interested in trying anything new."

"Dom," I say, sitting up and placing a palm on his chest over his heart. "I promise, I like the idea. When the time comes, if it's too much, I'll tell you."

We don't talk for ten minutes. We don't talk for thirty. It's well over an hour later I fall asleep in his arms, listening to the steady hum of his voice. I wake up the next day after a dreamless sleep to find Dom's already left for work, as usual. I squint in the darkness at the baby monitor on my nightstand. Luca is sleeping peacefully. In the light from the screen, I see the familiar shape of a puzzle piece resting on my nightstand, left behind for me.

Chapter Twenty-Two

Ellie

"I'd like Wild Meadows. Thank you." I point at the sage green nail color on the sample strip. It might not be the bright and bold green I usually go for this close to St. Patrick's Day, but I figure it's festive enough.

If I had known that Jake's contribution to Dom's puzzle was going to be a spa day to get manicures and pedicures, I might have accepted this whole idea with a bit more enthusiasm. Sitting here in a massage chair, my feet soaking in warm water while I'm soaking in one of the few truly relaxing moments since Luca was born, I think about how Dom stayed true to his promise.

All of these *Ellie pieces*, they've been...fun. It's been a breath of fresh air to step away from my responsibilities to do things that feel easy and a little self-indulgent. Things my pre-baby self would have loved.

My eccentric, thoughtful, generous husband and his never-ending sense of optimism and humor have always made him easy to love. Everything about this has been easy to enjoy too. I mean, fuck, getting a mani-pedi with my brother-in-law is no hardship.

The relaxing spa ambiance comes complete with low lighting, soft, ethereal music, and aromatherapy oils diffusing around us. Yeah, no hardship at all.

"So, when was the last time, Ellie?" Jake asks before sipping his champagne in the massage chair next to mine.

Heat floods my cheeks. "Ew, Jake," I say with a giggle, the second glass of champagne already making my head feel light and relaxed.

"Oh my god, Ellie, gross. When was the last time *you got a pedicure*?" he clarifies with an eye roll.

"Um...I don't know. I think with the girls the weekend of my baby shower?" I say absentmindedly, closing my eyes and resting my head onto the cushion as the nail technician rubs the arch of my foot. *Holy shit, that feels amazing.*

"That was like a year and a half ago," he says, voice heavy with disbelief.

I roll my head to the right to give him a look. "Yeah, life's busy, I guess. It hasn't exactly made it to the top of my priority list. Are you saying my feet are scary?"

"Wasn't going to say anything," he says with a smirk.

"Liar, you would." I laugh.

"Hey, what are big brothers for?"

"Free pedicures apparently."

He returns the look with a gentle smile. "Seriously, I'm sorry Chris and I didn't drag you here or anywhere else for a break. We would have if we had realized."

"No harm done. See? Look how great they're looking already," I say, gesturing to my feet.

"No harm done, huh? Before this whole plan of Dom's, when was the last time you did something for you? Doesn't have to be a pedicure. Just something for you."

"I do stuff for me all the time. I go to book club with my girls every month. And I decorate for the holidays. And..." *Shit. I do more than that, right?*

"Seeing your friends once a month? And creating a festive environment for your family for the holidays? No, Ellie. That's not what I mean. What do you do that's just for you? Something superfluous for any other reason other than it brings you joy. Not because it's on a list, not because someone says good parents need to do it, not because there's some unspoken expectation. What do you do for you and you alone on a consistent basis so you don't burn out?"

My fading smile must give him all the answer he needs.

"I don't know, I guess," I say, my voice barely above a whisper.

"Well, let's fix that. What do you want to do? What did you use to enjoy doing with your free time?"

I rack my brain. This shouldn't be a hard question. I was a person for almost three decades before I became a mom. That person is still in there, right? She had interests and hobbies. So why can't I think of a single one?

"Okay, I'll go first. I like to do at least one sudoku a day. I ride my bike on the trails between our houses. I play video games. Your turn. Give me three things you like to do simply because they bring you joy, and then promise me you'll do them this month. Then we'll check in and see what you're going to try next month if you don't like the ones you choose."

"I used to go for walks a lot. That sounds dumb, doesn't it?"

"Not at all. I love it, actually. What did you like about walking before?"

"Well, I'd listen to a podcast or an audiobook. I'd look at the houses in the neighborhood and be creepy deciding what I'd do with their landscaping if I lived there."

"Always the green thumb. Okay, so I think you should make time to go on walks alone then. No baby in the stroller, no husband, no company. Just you, your headphones, and your daydreams. Got it? Okay, next." He waves his hand in the air in a go-on motion.

"I miss my mornings. I don't think I have too much control over this one, though. Luca wakes up at unpredictable times, usually upset, so I have to hurry in to get him. But I used to love making time in the morning for a cup of coffee while I read in the front window of the house. I like the lighting in there in the morning and my plants are all around me. It was nice."

"Okay, tricker, I'll admit. Do you and Dom split weekend morning responsibilities? Maybe talk to him about every other Sunday, you give each other the morning off or something. That way, at least twice a month, you take your time, you get your hot coffee, a good blanket, and a good book, and you start your week off right."

Why hadn't I ever thought of that?

"I'm sure Dom would be on board," I say.

"Good. See? You got this. One more."

"Well, there's this new yoga studio that opened up near our house. I used to go a few years ago, and every time I drive past this place, I feel drawn to it."

He gives me a soft smile. "Hm…I'm sure an opportunity will come up soon for you to check it out. Let's prioritize the other two first and then we'll make sure you get to that yoga studio."

Excitement bubbles up knowing that there will be more moments like this. A little anxiety too. I already hate leaving Luca, but every time I do and nothing bad happens, I feel a little braver. It's good for him to play and have time with his family, who loves him. Maybe it's not so bad for me to take moments like this to feel more like…me.

Jake and I don't often get time alone. The four of us usually spend our time together, but it's nice to be able to talk with him without my attention split on our husbands or Luca. I genuinely have a problem paying attention to anything when I've got one eye on Luca.

My brain can finally close all the open tabs and focus on one. I know this break won't last forever, and I certainly don't want it to, since I'm already missing Luca, but I still enjoyed myself.

I'm thanking Jake again as we walk into the house. Listening closely, we give each other a look, concerned as we take off our shoes and coats. We walk down the hallway that connects to our kitchen, and the distinct sound of an Enya song plays through the living room speaker.

My hand flies to my mouth, and I gasp, giggling as I take in the sight of Dom and Chris on the couch, face masks on, cucumber slices on their eyes, and their toes drying with hot pink toe separators. Luca spots me from his spot between them on the couch as he plays with his own cucumber slices. The baby nail clippers and file are on the coffee table next to all the other adult nailcare supplies.

"What are you laughing at?" Dom asks, not even removing the vegetable slices from his eyes.

"What on Earth are you three doing?" Jake asks.

"It's spa day. Since *someone* didn't invite us along, we had to improvise. Don't judge us; We got jealous," Chris says.

Jake looks at me, rolls his eyes, and mutters, "He's been complaining all week because I said I wanted one-on-one time with you." He turns his attention back to Chris, who hasn't taken the veggies off his eyes either. "I said we could go next month, just us two," he says in a measured, placating tone.

I gasp, tapping Jake's shoulder with the back of my hand. "Am I so easily replaced? I see how it is."

"There is no winning in this family," Jake grumbles as he heads to the fridge.

Luca kneels next to Dom, pulling the cucumber slices from his eyes and slapping his pudgy hands onto Dom's cheeks. Dom smiles so brightly, I can't look away. And when both my boys look at me, Dom's face still smushed between Luca's chunky fingers, their similar features unmistakable, my heart feels like it's pulsing back to life.

CHAPTER TWENTY-THREE

Ellie

"Fuck," I mumble as I spill coffee on the counter, missing my cup completely. I yawn as I clean up the spill, then try again to fill up my cup, this time successfully, with the caffeine I desperately need. Luca had one of the worst night's sleep he's had in weeks. Of course it falls on a night before I have to work.

Half zombie mom, half employee reporting for duty.

What a joke.

I'd take a sick day, but I depleted them during my maternity leave, and when I finally accrued a few, we got hit with the flu and all three of us were down. Then the cycle repeats.

Taking care of an infant while also being sick is truly a special kind of torture. Especially because it makes my anxiety skyrocket watching Luca struggle. He even lost his tiny voice for a few days after his first illness. I felt helpless.

The nagging voices inside my head were screaming at me and blaming me for letting him get sick. The reasonable voices battled, knowing I can't prevent him from getting sick for his entire life.

It's draining, to say the least, to sit in the middle while your rational thoughts lose every fight against the incessant drone of anxious ones. The part of you that will never be satisfied with knowing *I tried my best*. That part of me that demands I be perfect.

Still, I'm grateful that Dom and I were lucky enough that I could drop my work hours to part time after Luca was born, and even luckier that my employer agreed to the change. It's not perfect, but for now, it works for us.

I've worked at this marketing company since I graduated from college, even interning here during my senior year. My coworkers are nice enough, the pay is fair, and at least the work is second nature to me now. But even the most supportive employer on paper is still an employer at the end of the day.

It doesn't matter that I didn't get more than three hours of sleep last night...interrupted, mind you. All that matters is that I show up today, looking professional—minus the dark bags under my eyes that no amount of makeup can conceal—and ready to work.

Being ready to work feels subjective in my case. Am I ready to give 100 percent of what I have? Sure. Do I only have 10 percent in the tank? Damn right. But Luca is with my mom for the day, and I'm here, so I'm going to give it every bit of that 10 percent.

I return to my desk with my coffee and continue working on my presentation for next week. I work from home one day a week and come into the office two days a week. My in-office days are difficult. Constantly checking in with whoever is watching Luca. Stealing glimpses of pictures of him and blinking away the tears at the ache of missing him and wishing I could be in two places at once. Fighting frustration with having to set up in the lactation room several times a day to pump, which isn't as big of a deal now that Luca is older, eating solids, and nursing less, but in the first few months back at the office, it was torture fitting a pumping schedule into the workday.

The rest of my day is a blur between calls, meetings, and emails, I'm left with little time to actually get my work done. By the time I'm packing up to go home, I'm ready to collapse in a heap on the elevator floor.

Then I remember that I'm a mom, and while I used to be able to go home and put myself to bed at 5:30 p.m. on days when I felt like this, the reality is that my second shift is about to begin.

***

"Here, boy. Hopper, watch Momma!" Bec stands behind me, calling, snapping, and making kissy noises in an attempt to keep Hopper's attention as he sits with several other therapy dogs in front of The Center for Faithful Companions building.

Therapy dog he may be, but Hopper's still a bundle of energy just waiting to be unleashed, his tail flopping wildly from side to side behind him as he pants, practically smiling at Bec from yards away.

I snap a few more photos of the dogs before Abby, Bec, and a few other employees leash them. I call out a few directions and capture the last photos I need, including one final shot of all the training facility staff and animals.

When I think I have what they need, I let Bec know and she dismisses everyone while I flip through my film to double-check that there's nothing we need to reshoot.

Bec and Abby sidle up beside me, peering over my shoulder, *oohing* and *aahing* and *awing* as I flip through the shots. This is my favorite part; hearing their reaction when they see what I see behind the lens.

"Thank you, Ellie. Our website is in serious need of an upgrade. These photos are the last piece of the rebrand the Center needs," Abby says, squeezing me in a warm hug.

"No thanks needed. It feels good to do this again. First, Bec's engagement, and now this? I wish I could do this more often," I say.

Bec gives me a thoughtful look. "Wait, that's a great idea. Weren't you just saying you wish you had a more flexible work schedule?"

"Uh, yeah? Where are you going with this?" I ask.

"Do more of *this*," she exclaims with unbridled enthusiasm. "You haven't taken photos in years, and just from our engagement and today, it's clear this is your calling. You should make this your career, Ellie. Would you enjoy that?"

I give it some thought before giving her a noncommittal shrug, beginning to pack away my things. March in Ohio is unpredictable at best, and my fingers are starting to freeze in the chilly breeze as we stand in the parking lot outside the Center. "I mean, have I thought about it before? Sure. But it's too risky. Definitely not as stable as my current job."

"Yeah, safe is good. I get it," Abby says with both understanding and longing in her voice. She has yet to show the girls and me any of her artwork, but I know it calls to her probably even more strongly than photography calls to me. But artist to artist—if you can even call me that—she gets it.

"Sure, safe is one thing. But happiness and fulfillment are another," Bec says with conviction. She means well, so I try not to let myself act on the defensiveness that flares in my chest from her words.

"I'm happy with my job," I say, most likely convincing no one, since the words taste like the lie they are coming out of my mouth.

"It's easy to dream but painful to admit that's what you want in case you don't ever get to see the dream become a reality," Abby says softly. "Have you considered if this is what you really want? Or if that's something you and Dom could ever make work?"

"I haven't thought about it since college. I started my internship when I was a senior, and sort of fell into a permanent position. I've been at the same company ever since. I guess I never dreamed beyond that. Then when we got pregnant, I was focused on other things, only really thinking of my job in a sense of financial practicality and logistics."

"There's nothing wrong with that, Ellie. I'm sorry, I don't mean to imply what you're doing is wrong. I just loved seeing you behind the camera today," Bec says, fiddling with Hopper's leash. "You should consider if it's something you'd want. If it is, mention it to Dom. Daydream about it together. It doesn't matter if it's in a year or ten. Maybe someday, it'll make sense for you to try."

"Which is why we want to give you this," Abby says, handing me an envelope.

"What exactly is this?" I ask.

"I know you said you'd do this for free, but we talked to our supervisor, Tonya, to see if there was any room in the budget to reimburse you for your time and talent. There are also a few employee donations in there, too, since everyone knows you'll be at New Hope next weekend to take photos for the shelter too.

We're excited to see the Center and New Hope websites both get a refresh. Especially with New Hope's new partnership with the Columbus Aviators, we want to be ready for this season," Bec explains.

Another point for Aiden. Of course, the man shows up in every way possible to support Bec in all that she cares about, which is why last year he worked with the Aviators' community engagement team to help facilitate a partnership between his professional baseball team and the local animal shelter Bec volunteers at, New Hope.

"I can't—" I start to say before Bec shoves a palm over my mouth and I startle in surprise, letting out a giggle behind her hand.

"No take backs," she yells, before grabbing Abby's hand, and the two run inside, Hopper prancing alongside them, leaving me in the middle of the parking lot with my camera around my neck, my bags and supplies around my feet, and an envelope stuffed with cash in my hand. I drop my head back, closing my eyes and letting out a sigh.

I'm not sure why I try to fight it, but I fail. A huge grin stretches across my face. Could this be a way forward? Could this be what I want?

There's no comparison between sitting at my desk in the office or at home working at my laptop and *this*. *This* ignites a fire in me that I can't describe. I shake my head and check the time on my phone. Time to go home and start the second shift.

Luca lets out a shriek of excitement when I join him and Dom in the living room. I bend down and wrap him in my arms, breathing him in. Dom kisses me on the forehead, another touch of affection long missing from our daily life that he's recently brought back, and I feel my face flush.

Later that night, I don't mention anything to Dom. But when Luca finally goes to sleep, and I can hear the rhythmic breathing of Dom next to me telling me he's asleep as well, I let my mind wander...and wander...and wander. Thinking through pretend logistics, imaginary budgets, and possible schedules to make something part time work. Me doing freelance photography instead of my current job. It's crazy and just pretend...right?

Chapter Twenty-Four

Ellie

"Wow. I didn't realize how much I needed that." My body feels like it just woke up from a year-long nap. A little sweaty, topped with a little ache. I'll be sore tomorrow.

"We should have done this sooner," Mom says, leaning back in her wrought iron chair as she peruses the menu. I don't know why she bothers. We both know she's getting the quiche and I'm getting the banana bread.

My favorite hidden gem in the city, Pat's Cats. The owner, Pat, believe it or not, loves cats, and the entire café is decorated with mismatched cat pieces. It's chaos, whimsy, humor, and cuteness wrapped into one historic home turned restaurant. In the cold months, they use multiple patio heaters so they don't lose the space to Ohio's cold winter and unpredictable spring seasons. The result is a secluded slice of heaven that feels like a fairy tale. Evergreen trees surround us, twinkle lights decorating their branches. Small, delicate chandeliers dangle above each of the four tables. Music drifts softly through the speakers, a classical piano soundtrack.

"Did you talk to Jake?" I ask, eyebrow raised in suspicion.

"A little birdy might have mentioned that someone was missing yoga class, and I might have borrowed the idea. I needed a little inspiration for my puzzle piece. It's been years since we've taken a class together, and I know you've been wanting to try the new studio since it's so close to your house."

"The instructor was incredible. I already want to go back," I say before taking a sip of my tea.

"We could make it a monthly mother-daughter date if you want? I'm not opposed to the post-yoga brunch, of course." She smiles and holds my hand while she keeps searching the menu.

My eyes fill with tears. It's impossible for me to hold myself together in front of my mom when I want to fall apart. Around anyone else, it's almost natural. But in front of her, all my strongest armor falls away and I feel like I'm nine years old again, stepping into her arms and asking her to keep me safe from the reality of the world. Coming out of class today has me feeling extra sensitive.

"I'd like that." She must hear the shake in my voice, thick with emotion.

"Honey, what's wrong?"

"Nothing." I giggle as tears fall. "This past year has felt like I've been stuck in a pattern of surviving. It was nice today to just...connect with my body like that. It made me realize how much I've been ignoring what it needed since...everything changed."

I have complicated feelings about my body. I've never been what you'd call skinny. I'd describe my pre-baby body as medium build or average. I gained weight, too much weight per my OB—fuck her very much—during my pregnancy.

I lost almost none of it.

My body looks nothing like it did before. It *feels* nothing like it did before.

Exercising and good nutrition are the last thing on my mind when my mental health is tanking and I haven't slept in a year. Plus, my body is a little busy making food for my son.

Between trying to work and be a good parent, wife, friend, and daughter, who has time to take care of themselves?

But today, having an hour to myself, my body untouched and unneeded, eyes closed, and breaths synced with the instructor's pacing, felt unreal. The calming scent of essential oils filled the air, and several salt rocks lining the room gave off just enough light to navigate the space while still making the whole experience feel almost dreamlike. Everything about the class felt like I had stepped into an alternate reality, and the splash from diving back into my daily struggle is going to be a stark contrast.

"You're a mom, so I know you understand sacrifice," Mom says. "You know what it means to choose to stay still, watching your child sleep on your chest when you could really use a good meal, a bathroom break, and a nap. You know what it means to give up sleep to comfort another and be everything that they need. You know the impossible struggle of trying to be everything to everyone, everywhere, all the time. If I could tell myself anything after you were born, it would be to trust myself, love myself, and find ways to take breaks when I can."

"Taking a break feels impossible most days."

"That's why I love that Dom and you are doing this. Maybe it's a good push to remind you that you *can* take time away. Plus, you know you can always call your father and me when you guys need a hand." She pauses, sliding her menu onto the table, giving me her full attention. "I hope these special moments give you time to focus on more than just *surviving*. Do you think it's helping?" my mom asks, her voice lifted with hope.

I know it hurts her to watch me struggle. The guilt that comes with knowing I'm causing her stress weighs on me. Add it to my mental health tab.

"I think so," I say, hesitant to get her hopes up. "I've had a lot of fun with everything so far. Everyone's put a lot of thought into it. I'm really grateful."

"And things are good at home?"

"Yeah, things are...good." *How much has Dom told her?* I know he would never talk about our sex life with my parents of all people, but it's clear she knows something about our relationship is off. If anyone could offer me insight about how to navigate marriage after kids, it'd be my mom, right?

"Did you and Dad ever go through a...roommate phase?" I ask tentatively. "In your marriage, I mean. A time when you were so focused on life that it just got in the way of feeling like a couple?"

"Oh, honey, of course we did," she says, sipping from her tea before pouring us both more from the pot.

"But you two always seemed so effortlessly in love. I always remember you being happy together."

My mom laughs. Hard. Literally wiping tears from her eyes.

"Oh, honey. I'm so relieved to hear that's what you remember. It takes a lot of work to keep love alive for as long as we have. A lot of messing it up too. We got so many things wrong. We argued, we didn't make time for each other, we got stuck in that survival rut too. It doesn't last forever, but that doesn't mean you don't deserve *more*. You two just need to figure out a way that works for you in this season of life. It doesn't look the same for every couple. And with a man like Dom, you know it's going to look like...well, like *this*." She gestures to her and me, sitting here today because my loving husband had to create an entire fucking game for me.

I love everything about that man. It used to be easy to show it.

"He doesn't know how to half-ass anything," I say.

"Neither of you do, Ellie. I know this last year has been hard on you, but I want you to be gentle with yourself. It's okay to have doubts. It's okay to feel insecure. But don't shut down, please. We're here for you, always."

"I love you, Mom."

"I love you with my whole heart, Ellie."

CHAPTER TWENTY-FIVE

Dom

"You're trying to make this difficult for me, aren't you?" I say, then let out a dramatic groan.

Ellie pauses, confusion flittering over her face, before she finishes putting her hair in a loose bun on top of her head, then plugs her phone into the charging cord and places it on her nightstand.

"That definitely sounds like me, but I'm going to need you to be more specific."

"You wore *the* pants," I say, gesturing to her bottom half.

She gives her head a small shake as a smirk threatens to appear at the corner of her lip. "Are you trying to tell me they're out of season?" she says, putting her hands on her hips and popping her weight to one leg.

Yes, it's April, but it's not the season that's throwing me off kilter.

"The *Halloween* pants, Ellie. You know they're my favorite."

"They're *leggings*, and yes, I know they're your favorite. They're mine, too, so you'll have to control yourself, Mr. Moretti. Let me live my most comfortable life, please, and celebrate Halloween whenever I want."

I don't know what it is about these fucking *leggings*. The print is insanely festive. A mess of bright orange, black, and purple littered with jack-o'-lanterns, witches, ghosts, monsters, and candy. Large text reads *TRICK OR TREAT* in bold, white lettering.

Treat. It's always a *goddamn treat* to see these make an off-season appearance.

I can't explain it. They're soft and they hug Ellie's every curve. The fabric's just thin enough I can catch the jiggle of her ass if I watch close enough as she walks. It's impossible to look anywhere *but* her ass when she wears these...and she *knows* it.

I helplessly watch her finish getting ready before she climbs into bed, fluffs her pillows, and checks the baby monitor before picking up her phone to scroll.

Shaking my head in an attempt to shake off the sight of Ellie's ass looking like *that*, I head to the restroom to finish getting ready for bed.

Well, two can play this game.

A few minutes later, I step out of the bathroom, only to cross my arms and ankles, leaning my side against the doorway.

Sensing my lingering presence, Ellie looks up from her phone to see what's keeping me from climbing into bed, and she giggles at the sight of me.

Backwards baseball hat, the shirt she got me for Father's Day—a dark gray tee that just says *DADDY* in all caps. She thought I'd be embarrassed, but jokes on her, I love it and I wear it all the time. I complete the look with black boxer briefs. See? Irresistible.

"Trying to fight fire with fire, I see." She laughs, rolling onto her side to lay her cheek on her folded hands as I stride closer to the bed.

"Just two attractive people, at their most attractive, appreciating each other's attractiveness, wouldn't you say?"

"Something like that. Get over here, Daddy," she says. "Though, I think you might need to ditch the hat to sleep."

"That's why you're the brains of the operation here," I say with a sigh, tossing my hat onto the nightstand and ridding myself of my shirt before joining her in bed. I don't miss the way her gaze coasts over my body before her eyes reach mine, blush coloring her cheeks.

"Pillow talk?" she asks.

"Been waiting all day. Come here, babe." I open my arms wide and she folds herself into my chest immediately, fitting her cheek against the dip in my collarbone. I pull her tightly against me and her thigh finds its way between mine, our legs interlocking.

Cuddling? Underrated. And over the last year, underappreciated by me. Never again.

I don't honestly know what the fuck I'm doing with Ellie. This whole game could blow up in my face, or it could make no difference at all. But over the last few weeks, during this time before we shut our eyes—our pillow talk—it feels like we're making progress, even if we only have a few minutes before we both pass out, it's helping somehow. And I'm not above trying fucking anything to make this work.

"What do you want to talk about tonight?" she asks, voice soft and content.

"I started last night. Your turn, wifey," I say, pressing a kiss to the top of her head.

After a minute or two of silence, I'm sure she's fallen asleep in my arms, too exhausted to talk. Which is why I'm caught off guard by her abrupt question cutting through the silence.

"What's your favorite time we've had sex?" she asks, the words flying out of her mouth so fast I almost miss them.

"What?" I ask, huffing a laugh. "Where did that come from?"

"I've been thinking about my favorite time for the last few days, and I want to know if yours is the same."

She can't see, but my eyebrows are sky high, and I try to keep my dick from swelling at the thought of Ellie ruminating over the history of our sex life and fixating on her favorite memory. Now I'm dying to know.

I've been trying to keep this cuddling strictly that, cuddling, without any implication that I want more. Yeah, I still ogle my wife and tell her how stunning she is as often as I can. But I meant what I said when I proposed we hold off on sex for a while. We need to give the foundation of our relationship a little TLC before we try fucking on the second story. I'm pretty sure that's a common figure of speech or something.

"You've had more time to think about it. You first," I say.

"Okay. Third day of our honeymoon."

I search my mind for the memory, which takes no time at all because... "*Fuck,* that...was a good time." My hand trails along her side, resting on her waist, my fingers dipping to her lower back.

We'd gone to some liquor-tasting event at the resort and done a bit too much tasting. We were both buzzed silly, absolutely no inhibitions. Both a little sunburnt, a little giddy, and very...vocal.

"Remember when our neighbor pounded on the wall and told us to shut up? They left a note under our door cursing us out because it was noon and I guess we were screaming?"

"*You* were screaming," I say.

"Objection, your honor. Hearsay," she says, slapping my chest lightly, pretending to be outraged by my claim.

"Hearsay? I was *there*, love, and you...were...screaming," I say, nuzzling into her neck and kissing her, slipping a bit of tongue to taste her. She arches her back and runs her hands down my chest, nails scraping lightly over my skin, making every nerve ending come alive at her touch. "What did you like about it?" I ask before laying more wet kisses on her neck, her collarbone, her shoulder, my fingers tensing and gripping her lower back harder, keeping her body flush with mine.

Ellie's breathing quickens and she can't hide how her body's reacting when I gently bite at her skin and she gasps in surprise, her hips unconsciously undulating in response.

"I liked when you surprised me in the shower," she says, breathless.

"Go on," I murmur, my lips grazing her ear, my hands drifting up and down her sides, the pads of my thumbs gliding over the sides of her breasts.

"I liked that you wrapped my hair around your fist and pulled me back against you," she says before swallowing audibly.

"Mmm, then what happened?"

"You let the water run over my chest while you played with my nipples, tugging and kneading. You whispered everything you were going to do to me in my ear."

"And did I do them all?"

"Every single one." She runs her hands down my chest again before lightly scraping her nails back and forth above the waistband of my briefs.

"What happened next?" I ask, my voice low and husky from her teasing.

"You bent me over in the shower and fucked me from behind."

"Then you got on your knees and sucked me clean."

Fuck. What are we doing?

I'm so fucking hard right now, and there's no way she hasn't noticed, but I can't seem to stop, and she doesn't seem to want to either.

"I stopped you before I could come down that pretty throat," I say, threading my fingers through her hair at the base of her skull and tugging gently at the roots.

"And then I dragged you to bed," she says. "Our bodies dripping wet, and I pushed you onto the mattress before climbing on top and straddling your waist. But before I could sink down on your hard cock—"

"I pulled your thighs up around my head and made you ride my face. *This* is where I remember the screaming."

"Well yeah, kind of hard not to. You were relentless."

"I was *hungry.*"

She laughs, before slapping her hands over her mouth as if she remembered our sleeping one-year-old down the hall.

"And you made me come." Her eyes lock with mine as she whispers in that voice that makes me want to strip her bare.

"God, your thighs were shaking so hard, I thought I'd have to carry you around the rest of the day."

"Then you flipped me on my back," she adds, glancing at my lips.

"And I pinned your hands above your head so I could eat my dessert in peace."

Ellie's writhing now, her hips circling, restlessly squirming with her center pressed against my upper thigh.

"You licked my tits for like ten minutes afterward. I almost came again from that alone."

"You would have if you didn't buck me off before climbing into my lap," I say.

"I wanted to ride you."

"And I let you," I say.

"But not before you pulled my arms behind my back and pinned them there," she says breathlessly, placing wet kisses of her own on my chest.

"I needed you arched just right so I could finish sucking on those perfect tits."

"I remember thinking there was no way you could be any deeper. You were so hard and thick, and the friction was unreal. I couldn't stop from screaming again."

"Now you admit it. Glad we both remember it that way," I say with a smirk, and she slaps playfully at my chest. "And when you were done, I flipped you onto your back."

"Threw my feet over your shoulders," she pants, her hands dropping dangerously low on my abdomen.

"And fucked into you hard, and deep," I growl.

"Your fingers digging into my thighs and my ass lifting up off the bed."

"Your tits bouncing with every stroke," I add.

Fuck, I can picture it now.

"Before you filled me to the brim with your cum until it spilled over and ran down my ass. We had to ask for new sheets from room service that night," she says.

"Then we got in the bath, our legs tangled together," I say in a soft voice. Our rushed cadence breaking in a pause to remember how sweet the afterglow was after that hot, messy sex.

"We talked about the wedding and how much fun it was," she says, with a dreamy look on her face. "We talked about how we wished we could extend our honeymoon by a month. We talked about how perfect everything felt, our future, and all that we wanted our life to look like."

By this point, we're both breathing heavy, in a comfortable quiet. I hold onto Ellie tightly, remembering that moment in time, knowing there's no memory I could think of to top that one. Sitting with her in my arms and talking through it all, hearing her recall every dirty detail, filling in the gaps between her perspective and mine, feels almost as arousing as the memory itself.

"I know the path was different than we may have envisioned in some parts, but this is exactly what I've always wanted my life to look like," I murmur.

"Promise?" she asks, holding me just as tightly.

"With my entire heart, Ellie. I'm exactly where I want to be." I don't see it, but I feel her smile against my chest, setting my skin on fire beneath her touch with electricity, warmth, and love.

"So...which memory is your favorite?" she asks.

"You win, Ellie. There's no topping that." I pull back to look at her. "Until you're ready for me to try again. Now I have a good idea of where the bar is...for now."

Then I kiss her until her lips are puffy and her hair is a tangled mess. We haven't made out without it leading to sex since college. It feels nostalgic. It feels like pieces of us are waking up and finding each other again. That flicker of hope in my chest ignites and burns brighter.

Chapter Twenty-Six

Ellie

"Bec, it's...incredible."

"Absolutely stunning."

"It's perfect."

"You look beautiful."

"Holy hotness. Aiden's going to come in his pants when he sees you."

Bec stands in front of the one-hundred-and-eighty-degree mirror in a wedding dress—soon to be *her* wedding dress—as the rest of us sing our praises because she looks *radiant*. Joy and giddiness fill the space as we all gush over the finer details of the dress and start talking about accessories.

Tears form in the corner of my eyes, and I blink quickly in an effort to hold them back. My best friend is getting married. I couldn't be happier for her and Aiden.

I smile, a fleeting memory quickly racing through my mind of Bec and me in opposite places, her helping me make a final choice about the wedding dress I would wear when I got married and she was my maid of honor. Danny, her older sister, and I are her maid and matron of honor. Yes, she'll have two, and I couldn't be more honored that she asked me.

Bec and Aiden set their wedding date for this December, ensuring that the Aviators' season will be over before the big day. They opted for the shorter engagement rather than wait for the following post-season since they aren't able to predict the progression of Aiden's mom's Alzheimer's disease. They want her to be able to enjoy the day with them as much as possible.

Bec's dress couldn't be more perfect for a winter wedding. I'm not a fashion expert, but I'd call it vintage boho. The A-line dress is completely lace and ivory with a champagne color underlay. The long sleeves billow slightly around her forearms and cinch in around her wrists in two lace cuffs. The V-neckline plunges low with tasteful cleavage, of course. You're welcome, Aiden.

"Thanks, guys. Mom, Danny, and I stopped in impulsively last week after we grabbed lunch. It was the first dress I tried on, but I wanted to show you all to be sure. I think I have my answer. Oh, and we also found a few dresses we loved for the bridal party. If you're up for trying on the different styles, they're here for you to look at."

The bridesmaids' dresses are beautiful. Several shades of purple, all complementing one another. The chiffon dresses are in an array of different styles, and I heave a sigh of relief.

I love my friends more than anything. They're beautiful inside and out. But my outsides have my insides feeling a little insecure lately, and if I have to stand next to them on Bec's big day, I'd like to at least have a smidgen of self-esteem by choosing a style that flatters my curves. It's not a big deal to them, but to me, I'd obsess about how I look compared to them if we were all in the same dress.

The girls and I start browsing, talking with Bec about what she envisions for the various wedding decisions—flowers, centerpieces, décor—when a dress catches my eye. It's a deep purple, A-line dress with soft, flowy sleeves that look like they'd fall just shy of my elbow. The back has a large cutout with a decorative bow that ties at the base of the neck. I pull the dress off the clothing rack and notice a long slit up one side. *That's a lot of thigh.*

I smile at the thought of Dom seeing me in this. Just that feeling alone, and how giddy it makes me, tells me I need to at least give this one a shot.

We all come out of our dressing rooms a few minutes later, having picked a range of styles and shades of purple. The confidence I had moments ago shrivels up when I see the other girls in their dresses. I felt amazing a second ago, until I let an ugly jealousy rule my mind completely.

"Oh my god, Ellie. That dress is perfect." Carissa beams. "I absolutely love the color and style on you."

Dee whistles and fans herself before yelling, "Hot momma."

I blush from the attention but know that my friends wouldn't lie to me. If they say the dress is flattering, I have to believe them. Especially since I don't really want to try on any more options with my confidence shaken. Even more so when the seamstress comes to take my measurements for alterations. I know they're just numbers, but god, sometimes it's hard to hear. I do my best to shake it off and not let the insecurities bouncing around my brain ruin a perfectly good afternoon with my girls. But like they say, easier said than done.

CHAPTER TWENTY-SEVEN

Ellie

With one hand on my chest and one on my stomach, I slow my breathing. *In for four, hold for four, out for four, hold for four.*

The steam from the shower billows around me and I do my best to keep focused on my breaths alone. *In, two, three, four…*Frustration takes over and I scrub my hands down my face, letting out an annoyed huff.

"Ellie, you okay in here?" Dom calls out.

Fuck, I don't want him to know I'm upset.

"Uh, yeah. All good. What's up, babe?" I fight to keep my voice even.

"I just thought I heard something. Hey, can you leave the water on? I want to hop in when you're done."

My body reacts immediately at the thought of him joining me. Sure, we're not having sex right now, but my thoughts go there regardless.

I'm grateful that Dom suggested we take a break, removing the pressure of sex from our relationship entirely. Slowly, I've been feeling this growing pull toward him physically. As if by taking the expectation for sex away, I could finally breathe. This desire I've been feeling now continues to build naturally instead of forcing it where I thought I needed to.

It really has done more than I thought it would to know that there's no expectation for any affection to go any further. Not that he's ever pressured me to. But I think I was pressuring myself, trying to force myself to feel what I thought I should.

Months. It's been months since we've had each other.

Guilt threatens to climb up my throat, but I shove it down. Maybe intimacy has to look different for us right now, and maybe that's okay. Maybe building up all these other pieces of our relationship has allowed for some of my sex drive to return.

Well, holy shit. Dom was actually onto something with this plan.

"Or you could...come in here? With me?" I offer hesitantly.

Dom doesn't say anything for a while. Long enough for me to wonder if he left the bathroom before I hear him say, "I don't want to intrude on your space."

I squeeze my eyes shut in a wince and drop my head back. Dom has seen every inch of my body, up close and *personal*. But things feel so awkward between us now.

I haven't asked Dom if he wants to put sex back on the table yet, but maybe we could slowly make our way back to...that.

Lately, every touch, every lingering look makes me feel...maybe a little sexy. And after today, when dress sizes and ugly comparisons I made up in my mind *shredded* my self-esteem, I want to feel sexy again. I want to feel beautiful and desirable.

Fuck, just because I'm a mom doesn't mean I don't want to feel good. Feel wanted.

Dom and I used to have great sex. I don't want that to be another thing my brain and never-ending anxiety steal from me. I miss my husband.

"You're not intruding, Dom. Please?"

Another pause.

I don't say anything—the cloud of rejection starting to swirl around my mind—but a moment later, Dom slides the shower curtain to the side, stepping in.

Dom's tall, but I'm not short either. He leans in close, still inches between our naked bodies, and presses a light kiss to my lips, pulling back quickly. He runs his palms from my elbows to my shoulders before turning me around so my back is to his chest, the spray from the shower head running down the front of my body. He steps into me, allowing our bodies to finally connect, and I close my eyes, resting my head back on his shoulder, turning my nose to tuck under his chin.

He wraps his arms around my middle, just above where the residual numbness from my c-section scar begins, and I do my best to tamp down the insecurities and dark memories that come roaring to the surface.

The skin on my breasts is softer after more than a year of nursing. My skin is painted with stretch marks regardless of how much oil and lotion I used during my pregnancy. My skin dips where they cut me, and my stomach hangs over the scar—the "c-section shelf." I'm sure there are exercises and things I could do to improve the appearance, but my scar is already difficult to look at without triggering more flashbacks. Touching it is too much for me to deal with right now. Once my body healed from the surgery, I left it alone and now I ignore it as much as possible.

What if I didn't? my mind screams at me. What if I could learn to love my body as it is now? What if I could someday accept, and even embrace, the fact that while it'll never look like it once did, it's still a damn good body?

I've tried to will away my resentment and bitterness. I've tried to be *grateful*, like everyone says.

You should start a gratitude journal...You'll bounce back...Your body knows what to do...At least you're both okay now...At least you didn't have to give birth naturally...At least...At least...At least...

I assume every comment was said with good intentions, but anything anyone said to me after Luca was born that started with the phrase *at least* was the kind of toxic positivity I had to block out to hold on to the last shred of my sanity.

I don't want an *at least* kind of life. I want the *most* out of every piece of it.

Including right now. With a man who loves me at my back. A man who does cute shit for me even when I don't do anything to deserve it. A man who sacrifices. A man who loves with no regard for what it can bring him but only for what he wants to give.

What if I just let him hold me for a minute, and I spent that minute enjoying the way it felt for the man I love to keep me close instead of worrying about what my body looks and feels like?

"I love you," he whispers into my neck. The words blanket my body with warmth and quiet my racing thoughts.

I hum, running my hands over his forearms, which are still wrapped around my waist. "And I love you." I melt into him further.

I feel his dick hardening against my ass, and he pulls his hips back. Clearing his throat, he apologizes. "Trying to be on my best behavior here," he says with a laugh. "Downstairs isn't getting the message."

I take a small step back into him, closing the space between us, his erection hitting me in the lower back. I grip him behind his neck, pulling him closer. "It's been a long time..." I say.

Dom clears his throat as hands tighten around my waist, before he releases me and grabs the body wash off the shelf.

"Did you already wash up?" he asks.

"Not yet," I lie, curious to see where he's going with this.

"You've never been a good liar, Ellie. I can smell it on you."

I smirk, grateful he can't see my face.

"Humor me," I say, looking over my shoulder to catch his heated stare.

"Can I help?" he asks, voice rough as he lathers soap into a washcloth. I nod.

Dom spends the next few minutes cleaning every inch of my body, his movements slow and languid, steady and sure. When he reaches my shoulders, he ditches the washcloth and massages my neck, working at the knots he finds deep in my muscles, before he lathers my hair with shampoo.

"Turn around," he says, voice low.

In doing so, I realize how relaxed every muscle in my body has become. A drunk haze of blissful calm has my mind drifting, a nice break from its usual race.

When I steal a glance at Dom, his face is pulled tight in concentration as he rinses the suds from my hair, careful not to get any in my eyes. He pulls my body flush with his so that my hair is out of the water. He runs his fingers, coated with conditioner, through the ends.

As he finishes rinsing the product away, I close my eyes, enjoying the way his hands tug on the strands and the growing tension on my scalp.

I open my eyes to find his gaze locked on my lips.

"My turn?" I ask.

He smiles and nods. I wash his hair and then lather his body with soap, taking my time. Afterward, I use the handheld showerhead to rinse the suds from his skin.

While we're both tall, I'm more soft curves and he's more hard lines, though in the last year, he's let himself live a little more than he used to. He's less focused on hitting the gym and never says no when I suggest takeout because we're both too tired to cook.

It's moments like this that make me feel silly for worrying so much about my body and how it's changed. Because Dom's has, too, and there isn't an inch of him that I don't want to lick. He's as sexy, if not sexier, now. I don't want him to doubt my attraction to him for a single second.

Is that how he feels about me?

"Are you going to be okay with, uh...that whole situation?" I ask, gesturing to his erection, which hasn't gone down at all. If anything, he's harder.

He flashes me a smile, before saying, "I'll be fine."

Disappointment floods me, surprising me.

Dom's not one to change his mind once he commits to something. But I wonder where this might have gone if we decided to try being physical again. I want to know where this would lead.

"Don't you want better than fine?" I ask.

Don't you want a better than fine sex life?

Don't you want a better than fine marriage?

Because I do.

"Ellie," he says with a sigh. "Really, it's okay. You don't have to worry about me."

I decide on a different approach. We agreed to no sex, but we didn't say anything about...other things.

Did Dom plan this? Did he know my stupid ass would want what I can't have just because we agreed not to have it and now I'm in my fucked-up head trying to figure out how to seduce my *husband* and partner of *years*?

Goddamn it, that's genius.

"I am worried. About you and...about me," I say. I close my eyes before taking a step back under the spray of the water, trying my best to shut down the voices that scream at me to stop embarrassing myself and that there's no way anyone could find me attractive like this.

But when I bring one hand to my breast, gripping firmly while trailing the other toward my center, the focused stare Dom lays on me tells me I should shut my own fucking mind up because he's into this. He's *really* into this.

"I miss you," I say, my voice going a bit breathless as I explore the area surrounding my clit with growing pressure.

"Ellie," Dom says, voice tortured. He slowly moves his hand to the base of his cock, tugging roughly from base to tip.

"This isn't sex," I say. His eyes roam from my hand between my thighs, to the one tugging on my nipple, to my eyes.

"No, it's not," he says with a smirk as his eyes darken.

Fuck, yes. I've got him.

If there's one thing my husband likes, it's a good game.

CHAPTER TWENTY-EIGHT

Dom

"**S**top," I say. My dick would punch me right now if that were possible. He was enjoying the lovely show my wife was putting on two seconds ago.

"I want you to listen to me and do as I say," I murmur with a smile. "And I want you to tell me exactly what you want me to do in return."

If you'd asked me thirty minutes ago if I would prompt my wife to talk me through masturbating while I did the same for her, I'd say you're delusional.

I meant it when I said no sex. The end game of all of this is too important to rush. I need this to work and that can't happen if we do this before she's ready. But like Ellie said, this isn't sex.

I'm not perfect, but my wife's tits are, and they're the ones in charge of my brain right now.

She lifts her chin, clearly intrigued by my challenge.

"Do you want that, Ellie? Do you want to fall apart under your own hands while you control every move I make?"

Her chest is rising and falling quicker now, in rhythm with my own. I take a step closer to her, careful not to touch her anywhere, but not giving her any more space than that.

"Yes, I want that."

"Then drop your hands to your sides," I demand. She gives me a look of frustration, clearly hoping I'd let her pick up right where she left off when I told her to stop, one hand teasing her nipple and the other pushing on her clit.

"You'll go at my pace now, and I'm in no hurry," I say, caught up in the moment before I remember that Luca is napping and the monitor is on the bathroom counter.

Fuck. Maybe I need to hurry a little with an unpredictable sleeper. I wave the thought from my mind. We'll figure it out if he wakes up.

"Back up against the wall." She gasps when her skin hits the cold tile, eyes locked on mine, the look equal parts heat and trust. "Close your eyes." Her breathing continues to quicken, and her nipples are rock hard. "Arms up, Ellie. Hold onto the showerhead."

Okay, admittedly, that one's for me. But fuck, I want to see her back arch and her tits pushed toward me. It's as perfect a sight as I dreamed.

"I want you to listen first, and I'll tell you when to start. I want you to move slowly, and I want you to keep the pressure on your skin light. Understand?"

She nods.

"Say it, baby."

"I understand."

"Start by touching your thighs. I want you to run your fingers over your hips, to your waist, along your breasts, to your collarbone, and around your neck. Do not touch your pussy. Do not touch your nipples."

Her lips quirk in a crooked sort of smile.

"Do it now, Ellie."

She tentatively places her fingertips on her thighs. Slowly dragging them to her hips, where she perfectly traces the faded stretch marks that glow along her skin.

"Slower," I demand, not wanting this to end too soon...or ever, really.

I watch, enraptured as she drags her hands over her body, the touch looking so light it must be driving her as crazy as it's driving me. The animal in me wants to replace her hands with mine, and I don't want to be gentle. Her hands reach her collarbone and neck, and she drops her mouth open with a gasp.

"Now do it again but press down harder this time. I want you to think of me. I want you to imagine it's my fingers tracing up your perfect skin. I want you to envision my hungry touch all over your body, drawing this out and making you wait."

Her grip is desperate, and her brow furrows in frustration, eyes still shut, when I tell her to stop when her touch gets too close to her nipples and clit. *Not yet.*

"Do you trust me, Ellie?" I ask.

"Yes," she confirms immediately.

"Can I try something?"

She swallows. "Please."

My dick is rock hard. *Fuck me.* I'm going to come just from watching and hearing her beg. She's not going to have a chance to reciprocate if I come right now, and I really fucking want to see what she does to me, given the chance.

"Start what you were doing before but using the softest pressure you can. One hand on your clit, one teasing your nipples. Alternate breasts, and when I tell you, increase the pressure," I demand.

Her moan sends a shot of arousal to my groin as she dives her hand between her thighs and starts rubbing small, light circles.

"Fuck, baby. You gotta start telling me what to do now, or you're not going to get the chance."

Her eyes open and lock on my dick with a devilish grin.

Yeah, I'm not going to last.

"Tug on your balls," she says without hesitation, like she's been imagining what she wants this whole time.

I immediately do, the sensation making me practically whimper.

Fucking fuck, I gotta get it together.

"Harder now, Ellie. Just a little," I say, needing her to build with me because I don't know how long I'll last and I want her to come with me.

"Grip your dick at the base, but don't move your hand," she says, breathless as she tugs first on one nipple before moving to the other and squeezing her tit hard in her palm. Her eyes are locked on my dick, and it twitches under her lustful stare.

I follow her instructions, all too eager to give her everything she's asking for. My shaft pulses under my grip. *Holy shit.* I squeeze harder.

She notices and grins. "Naughty boy, Dom."

Fuuuuuck, she's perfect.

"Collar your throat with one hand," I demand. She does, lifting her gaze, eyes hazy. "Faster, harder circles on your clit, baby. Do it for me now."

"Oh fuck," she moans, her head dropping back against the tiled wall, but her eyes stay locked on mine.

"Step closer," she says. "I want you to make a mess of me."

My balls tighten, drawing closer to my body. I don't want this to end, but Ellie isn't playing fair.

I step closer, only inches between us now. If I let go of my dick, it'd hit her stomach.

"Stroke your cock. Slowly," she says before she whimpers, her body giving a small jolt as her fingers fly in hard, small circles between her legs, her other hand gripping her own neck.

We stay like that, touching ourselves, inches separating our lust-driven bodies, hot breaths skimming over each other's skin as we work ourselves into a frenzy.

"Faster," she pants.

"Harder," I growl at the same time.

Her mouth drops open on a moan, and I watch as she starts to shake, the first wave of her orgasm sweeping over her. I drop my palm against the tile beside her head, watching with awe as I pump furiously at my dick. I'm close, but I need this more.

I keep stroking my cock with one hand but use the other to grab the handheld showerhead.

"Still trust me?" I ask with a gasp, wanting her to be sure.

"Yes," she screams, her body convulsing with pleasure.

I turn on the attachment and place the stream of water on her clit.

Her eyes shoot open in shock, and a satisfied grin overtakes my face.

"Fuck, oh my god. Fuck, Dom, oh my..." Ellie's moans don't stop. Her hand that was circling her clit grips my bicep tightly as I keep the water pressure exactly where she needs it. Her hips are thrusting and circling wildly, riding out her pleasure, and it's fucking beautiful to watch. In seconds, I'm coming too. I paint her stomach with my cum and watch her close her eyes and smile, same as I do.

We're both panting, breathless and blissed out. I lean my forearms against the tile on either side of her head, breathing into her neck, our bodies separated until she places her hands on my lower back and leans her head against my collarbone. Unable to live with the distance a moment longer, I put the showerhead back on its hook and pull her body flush with mine. It takes a few minutes before we both come down from the high.

She looks content, and I relax against her.

We both needed that. I know sex isn't everything, but our relationship thrives when both of our intimacy needs are met, and physical needs are a part of that. I know we're getting closer. This is just one step on our way back to each other, and fuck, it sure felt good.

CHAPTER TWENTY-NINE

Dom

Ellie's distracted as she taps away on her laptop at our dining room table, on the opposite end of where her half-completed puzzle lies. The late afternoon sun shines through the window, casting her silhouette in a warm glow. Her hanging plants thrive in this space, soaking up the rays.

Ellie's brows are drawn together in concentration as she looks from her screen back to her notebook, where she jots down notes, returning to type on the keyboard a moment later.

A wave of nostalgia hits me, seeing her at this table deep in concentration. I'm transported back in time. That was always her spot when she would work on the gift registry for Luca's baby shower. She carefully considered each item, weighed the pros and cons of each brand, trying to keep it simple but still making sure we'd have everything we'd need to welcome Luca home.

We spent so many nights sitting together, looking at everything, dreaming about what it'd be like when he was finally here. Eventually, her pregnant body would ache from the unforgiving chairs, and we'd move to the couch. She'd lie lengthways, wedging herself between the arm of the couch, ten pillows, and the back couch cushion.

I'd join her and make sure she put extra pillows underneath her knees and then rub her feet, aching from carrying the two most important pieces of this world around all day.

We'd talk about the seemingly little things—which books we wanted to read to him, which swaddle looked best, what baby monitor we wanted. Then we'd get caught up in lengthy talks about the big things—what parts of parenthood scared us, how unprepared we felt for the unknown, what type of home we wanted to raise our family in, and how we wanted our home to *feel*.

It seemed to be the most important question. What do we want it to *feel* like being a part of this family?

The obvious things, of course; we wanted everyone to feel comfortable and happy, but more than that, we wanted it to feel safe, loving beyond any condition, a place of compassion and understanding for when life was too hard. A place all of us could shelter from any storm. A place our kids would feel comfortable talking to us about anything and asking about everything. One without shame, only growth, without judgment, only acceptance and love.

We dreamed about family traditions we wanted to continue from our own childhoods and ones we wanted to start new, our own little trio forging a new path.

An ache settles into my lungs, my breath cut short, feeling like the hope and optimism we had during that time—the anticipation and excitement—is so far away. Reality stormed into our lives and for a year, we could only focus on the next task, the next hour, the next day—caught up in a circle of survival.

I know it's hard on Ellie when reflecting on the most challenging parts of parenthood. Like she's comparing all of our everyday moments to someone else's best ones.

I know parenthood is more than anyone or anything could have prepared us for. Shit, I had no idea what I was doing—still don't most days. But looking at Ellie reminds me why I'm not scared at all...I'm doing this with *her*.

Luca is finally down for his nap, and god, I hope he takes a good one. It took thirty minutes to get him down, I assume because he was overtired and we missed the good window to get him to sleep.

Ellie startles as I pull out the chair catty-corner to her to sit, relaxing into the seat and crossing one leg over the other, ankle over knee.

"Wow, I didn't hear you come in," she says.

"You seem pretty focused. What are you working on, knockout?"

Her face lights up, and she blushes. "Knockout? That's new."

I shrug, running my eyes over her body. "Seems fitting."

"*Please*," she draws out. "If by fitting, you mean I look like I've been knocked on my ass and this is the best I could pull myself together, then sure."

She's wearing an old pajama set, one I think she got during her pregnancy.

Are those milk stains from nursing? Sure. Maybe a few holes from how often it's been worn and washed? Seems like it. But she could wear anything and I'd still see the same thing I've always seen when I look at her...

"You're perfect, Ellie. But I'm always looking for a reason to get you out of your clothes...want another one?" I raise an eyebrow as I hand her a small gift bag.

"Another one?" she says, failing to hide the surprise and excitement in her voice as she digs into the bag to find the special puzzle piece among the twenty or so regular ones.

"Another one. One week. Next Saturday, if that's okay with you." I was afraid to have Ellie's mom come over today to watch Luca after our last fight about the playoff game where I committed to plans without talking to her first. It made her anxiety peak. I know better now; she needs more notice than that.

"*PJs for days*," she reads, finally finding the piece. "What does it mean?"

"I love these." I lean forward, tugging on the sleeve of her shirt. "But I want to spoil you."

Her face lights up and she leans forward to wrap her arms around my shoulders.

"It's a date," she whispers into my neck.

***

"Okay, ground rules," I say, clapping my hands together.

"Dom," she says, an exasperated laugh escaping her. "Why do we need ground rules to buy pajamas?"

"Ellie." I tsk. "How long have you known me? Since when are things that simple?"

She nods, biting her smile to hide her smart-ass smile from me. "With you? Never. Absolutely never."

"I didn't bring you here so you could pick out pajamas and we'd go home. That's boring and you didn't settle for boring when you married me."

"I knew that boring wouldn't be in my future from our very first date."

"Exactly, and I'm not planning on letting you down now."

"So, what's the catch?" she asks. Good, she's into this. I mean, new pajamas, who wouldn't be? But ever since I've started giving her these puzzle pieces, this voice in my head won't stop nagging that I'm trying too little, too late and it's not enough to repair the damage we've sustained. I want today to prove that little voice is fucking wrong.

We've focused all our attention on becoming parents, trying our best to figure out an impossible task. We've forgotten to do the silly things. We've forgotten to be playful. We've forgotten to let go and have fun.

Sure, I didn't *need* to get a babysitter just to take Ellie shopping, but she can't focus on anything other than Luca when we go out with him. I want her attention on *herself* today, and selfishly, I want a little of that attention too.

Sorry, son, it's date day. Toddler not invited.

"You need at least three new sets, but you're not picking them. I am."

She laughs and rolls up onto the balls of her feet. "Okay, and do I get to help? Do I get the final say?"

"You get the final say on everything we buy today, but do you get to help? Not a chance, you'll be too busy."

"With what?"

"Picking out *my* new pajamas."

"Oh, I like this."

"But remember, ground rules..."

"Afraid I'll come back with assless chaps?"

"I was not aware that this store started selling assless chaps. Please get me three pairs."

Her laugh echoes down the aisle we're standing in. "It's only worth it if they're polar fleece assless chaps. I'll keep my eye out. Okay, rules?" she asks.

"Okay, Momma, it's simple. We pick out three sets for each other. One is for comfort, one for family time, and one for..." I wiggle my eyebrows at her.

"One for sexy time?" she whispers, leaning in close with mischief in her eyes.

"Okay, if you insist." I wink, and she lets out another laugh.

This silly, carefree part of us isn't gone, just lying dormant. I want Luca to see us like this, to see his parents happy together, making each other laugh, enjoying our time together, even if it's doing something as simple as buying clothes.

I want Ellie to feel comfortable enough to let her guard down and know that she can do this all the time. No planning, no permission, no sitter.

This is just the start.

"How much time do I get?" she asks.

"I don't know, thirty minutes sound good?"

"Thirty minutes and no peeking!" she yells as she races away toward the men's section of the store.

I don't need thirty minutes. I spent the last week looking up options, different cuts and styles. I went through Ellie's closet to find the sizes and measurements of the sets she likes best to get the right fit. Now, I just need to make sure the fabric is comfortable since I couldn't tell online.

Once I grab what I need, with everything I picked out ahead of time looking better and feeling more comfortable than I was expecting, I cheat and peek at her progress.

What can I say? I'm an opportunist.

I see her head over the turnstiles and smile to myself as I watch her turn back and forth between different displays, wandering back and forth down the same aisle a few times before she heads to the next.

When she's done, she bounces over to me and places a kiss on my cheek.

"Thank you for this," she says.

"You haven't even seen what I picked."

"I don't need to. This was fun no matter what you put in that cart."

"I'm glad you feel that way, because it's time to swap," I say, grabbing the basket from her hand and rolling the cart toward her.

"You first," she says, keeping her eyes on me.

I bite my lip, failing to hide my smile at her enthusiasm. "One for comfort?" I ask, and she nods. She's picked out a pair of gray sweatpants and a soft, white tee. "I know what you're doing," I say, holding up the sweatpants.

"I have no idea what you're talking about," she says with unconvincing innocence in her tone.

"For family time?" I hold up the next and she nods. "I love them. The long-sleeve Henley and flannel plaid pants are a classic."

I hold up the last with a laugh—a pack of Halloween-themed boxer briefs. "And for sexy time?"

"You love my Halloween pants so much...now we can match! Spooky, sexy time!"

"How did you even find these...it's April?"

"Don't underestimate me with a sales rack."

"I would never underestimate your rack."

"Shut up," she says, shoving my shoulder playfully.

"You did good, Ellie. Tough act to follow," I say, nodding to the cart beside her.

She peeks over the edge, biting her lips together, stifling her gorgeous smile.

"*Oooooo*, I love these," she exclaims, pulling the first from the pile, forest-green waffle jogger pants and a flowy, long-sleeve V-neck shirt.

"I know you like that waffly fabric stuff," I say.

"That is the technical term. And you're right, I really do. One for comfort?"

"Yep, the next is for family time."

"I love these tops for nursing at night," she says, holding up the button-up shirt and pants set. "Should I also expect more Halloween leggings for sexy time?"

I shake my head. "Those leggings are one of a kind. You can't recreate that kind of magic."

She delicately lifts the last, a light purple nightgown with thin straps and lace that will fall right above her knees.

I want to tread lightly here. I know Ellie is still working on her relationship with her body after the changes she went through during pregnancy and birth.

She hums thoughtfully. "I was expecting lingerie."

"Would you rather switch it out? You have the final say."

She looks appreciatingly at the nightgown. "Not necessarily. Why did you pick this one?"

I step into her, keeping my voice low. "I picked this one," I say, drawing my hand along the small of her back to pull her in close while I speak quietly in her ear. "Because I saw this and thought about kissing your cleavage between the lace edges. I thought about running my palm up your thigh to get a peek of what's hiding beneath. I imagined gripping your ass under this soft fabric, before spanking it because you like to mouth off in bed and I like to fight fire with fire.

"You can wear this, or lingerie, or—fuck, Ellie—you could wear a trash bag around the house and I'd still find you sexy as hell. But the sexiest thing to me, is when *you* feel sexy. And when I saw this...I pictured you feeling good in it, and I wanted to see it. I wanted to see it so fucking bad."

She blushes and bites her lip, stealing a glance at my mouth. "I should double-check the sizes. I'm not back to my pre-pregnancy size."

"Same," I say, slapping my stomach."

She rolls her eyes at me and crosses her arms. "Dom, I'm serious."

"Check them, but they should be right. I looked before we left home."

She looks away, something looking awfully close to embarrassment taking over her expression.

"Hey, Ellie. Talk to me. Please."

"Part of me hates buying clothes to fit my body as it is now. It feels like I'm accepting that I'll never look the way I used to again."

"Ellie, look at me." She does and her vulnerability is raw and unfiltered. *Good.* I don't want her hiding from me anymore. "Our bodies change and grow along with the rest of us. It's not about the size on the tag, it's about feeling comfortable in your own skin. The clothes we wear are just the icing on the cake. Why would you feel bad about cake?"

She laughs but tries to take it back. "Dom, it's not just my weight. It's everything. The stretch marks, the saggy boobs. Fuck, even my hair changed, and I swear my feet are bigger now too," she whispers, looking around to make sure no one is listening.

"Ellie, your stretch marks..."

"I swear to god, if you call them tiger stripes..."

"*Grrr*, baby," I growl in her ear, sliding my hands down to her ass.

"I love you, but that's not helping," she says, fighting a smile.

"Austin Powers not doing it for you today?" I ask. She shakes her head.

"Then you'll be relieved to know I wasn't going to call them that," I assure her. "They're more like...strikes of lightning. Every mark like a bolt that came crashing down during a powerful storm, forever changing the landscape with every touch. Powerful. Magical. A force of nature unleashing unrestrained power, creating something unstoppable...like a mother. Someone who would face any threat and come out not unscathed, but unbroken." I pull away to look in her eyes. "You're more perfect today than the day I met you, Ellie. I want you to know it. I want you to *feel* it."

Chapter Thirty

Ellie

Yesterday was...incredible. Dom, Luca, and I had a great morning. It was slow, quiet, and calm.

When my mom arrived to watch Luca so Dom and I could go shopping, it was the first time I didn't consider staying home instead, driven by my anxiety around leaving Luca. Maybe time does make things easier. My heart sings at the thought that this could be one of those things. *God, I hope so.*

Dominic put so much thought into our date yesterday. It felt good to be silly. It felt good to laugh. It felt good to let go with him.

The small voice in my head didn't want to believe that Dom could still find me as attractive as he did when we first met, but his appreciative look when I tried everything on when we got home, made those voices fade away.

He's never looked at me differently. *Why did I stop believing him?*

It's been another slow morning—coffee brewing while I nurse Luca on the sofa. It's mostly for comfort at this point. He's nearly weaned. Afterward, Dom feeds him breakfast while I open all the curtains wide, letting the early spring sunshine brighten every corner of the living room and kitchen. I light my favorite candle on the fireplace mantle, put on some soft music, and sit at the table with my guys.

"Dom, I want to talk to you about something," I say quickly, afraid I won't ever get the words out if I don't do it now.

My tone must tell him it's not something casual, because he gives me his attention, handing Luca some banana to keep him busy for a minute. The kid's a machine when it comes to fruit.

"Do you remember when Abby and Bec asked me to take photos for New Hope and the Center?"

"Yeah, I saw those. They turned out great. Are they online yet? I've been meaning to check the website to see if they've updated everything."

It might seem small to someone else, but the fact that he's been checking their websites—same as me—to see if they've uploaded my photos is so thoughtful, that I melt a little. This giant goof of a husband has no idea how to be unsupportive. He is good and wholesome and giving through and through.

"Not yet. Abby said she heard they should go up sometime next month. But...well, the girls said some things the day I took the photos that got me thinking..."

I hesitate, fear trickling in and...embarrassment? It shouldn't feel embarrassing talking about something I'm passionate about.

"You didn't mention that. What'd they say?" he asks.

"They talked to their manager and got me worked into their budget, so they paid me for the photos I took."

"Wow, Ellie. That's incredible. I'm so proud of you. You always had an eye for that when you were in school. Plus, Aiden can't stop talking about the engagement photos. The guy might like them more than his fiancé."

"Not true." Bec is obsessed with the pictures and already has them framed.

He smirks. "No, not true."

"That's not all they said," I continue, wringing my hands together in my lap beneath the table. "It's probably crazy, but they suggested I try to do something *more* with photography. I guess I looked happy while I was working on the project and they thought I could really do something with it."

"What do you think? Would you like that?" he asks, unfazed but attentive.

"I mean, yeah, I'd like it, but that'd be crazy. I would have to invest so much time and energy to get something like that up and running, plus the cost of equipment and building a portfolio takes time. I'd have to figure out my marketing strategy, what kinds of sessions I'd want to offer, and pricing. I'd need to consider studio space or using space in our home or in public spaces. Plus, that'd be more work for you, solo caretaking while I take on extra work."

He smiles at me, biting his lips. "So just a little bit of thought, huh?"

"I guess more than a little," I say, my nerves skyrocketing just talking about taking a leap like this. "I'm afraid to want it. I'm afraid of what it would mean if I wanted it, tried to make it happen, and failed."

"What would failing look like?" he asks thoughtfully.

"People hate my pictures."

"So, find new clients. What else?"

"I don't make any money."

"We dip into savings until you iron out the details of your pricing and build a client base. Anything else?"

"Well, yeah. I mean, I'm a mom now, and Luca needs me. You and I are a team, and I need to carry my weight. It'd be selfish to leave a stable job for something that could tank so easily."

"Stop." His tone changes and he looks more serious than I've seen him in a long time.

"Don't lessen the importance of your wants because you are a mom and wife. Those are reasons to pursue your dreams, not to bury them. If this is what you want to do, then I want you to do it."

"What do I do about my job? I'm still working there part time and I'm afraid I won't be able to handle both."

"We'll figure out the details. Let's come up with a plan and figure out how we can get you up and running. We'll make it happen." He says it with conviction. Like it's not an *if* scenario, but a *when*.

I'm grateful to have a partner who wants me to chase my dreams so badly that everything *I* need to do becomes something *we* need to do.

"Okay," I whisper with a smile, finally letting the excitement bleed into my tone.

"Okay," he says with a nod, like it's decided. His confidence in me is unmistakable.

CHAPTER THIRTY-ONE

Ellie

I browse the aisle for the third time while Dad meanders around the store with Luca propped on his side. Luca reaches for my dad's beard, pulling as hard as he can whenever he's given the chance. My dad, as patient as ever, always responds to each tug with a deep laugh.

They join me as I look over the pottery options.

"Which will it be?" Dad asks.

"There are too many options. I think you should pick. It's your puzzle piece," I say.

He gives a thoughtful hum. "I was kind of hoping you'd ask for my opinion. I was thinking it could be fun to use...something like this." He gently picks up a clay bowl, more decorative than functional by design, and I consider it.

"Why this one?" I ask, taking it from him and turning the piece over in my hands, looking at it from all angles.

"Do you remember what's on my bookshelf in my office at home?" he asks.

"Uh, not really?" I answer honestly.

"It was Father's Day, and your mother brought you and me somewhere just like this. You know her, always trying to make memories and hold them like keepsakes of the past."

"I don't remember that," I say, my heart stirring at the sweet image of my parents, around my age with a baby, just like Dom, Luca, and me.

"I'd be surprised if you did. I think you were only two or three. She brought us here, picked out a bowl just like this one, and you and I each put our handprint inside, mine first, and then your much smaller one right over top of it. Then we used our thumbs and pressed polka dots around the edges. It's one of my favorites. I thought if you didn't know what you wanted to make, if nothing here stood out to you, that you might want to do the same. Sort of recreate it, with Luca and you this time. I've had mine ever since."

I smile at the sentiment and know that this is something I'll cherish.

"On one condition," I say. "You have to put your handprint down first." I bump his shoulder with mine, and his eyes shine with unspoken emotion.

"You've got yourself a deal."

***

Thirty minutes later, we're all a bit messy, but we have our finished keepsake. We'll leave it here to be glazed and fired and pick it up in a few days.

It's messy and imperfect, and I can't wait to display it at home. All the accidental swipes of paint, strung across the sides as I wrestled a squirmy, but happy, toddler's hand covered in paint into the bowl. Luca loved the entire experience and clapped every time he made his mark. No matter how chaotic the finished product turned out, all those small imperfections are what brought him the most joy. The realization stitches up a tear in my heart I didn't realize he could mend.

"Ready for the finale?" Dad asks, after we clean up.

"Ice cream next door? I think somehow Luca will be on board with that plan."

We settle into a booth in the ice cream shop with Luca on the end strapped into a high chair. I share bits of my ice cream with him, and he plays with the toys the cashier gave him at checkout.

"Thanks, Dad," I say, suddenly embarrassed about how much this is affecting me. "Sometimes it's hard for me to put effort into things like this. I haven't even started Luca's baby book."

The last time I wrote in it, I was pregnant. Guilt creeps along my skin, sinking its way further until it sits heavy in my gut.

Will Luca resent me when he's older? An incomplete baby book. Minimal photographs printed. I can't remember the last time Dom, Luca, and I all took a photo together, the three of us. I know Dom and I collectively have about a billion photos and video clips of Luca on our phones, but I'm no Pinterest mom, that's for sure.

"You say it like there isn't time for all that," Dad says.

"More like I have no motivation for it...or time for that matter."

We sit in silence for a minute or two, Dad seemingly deep in thought, watching as I clean up a massive glob of ice cream Luca managed to fling onto the table when he slapped excitedly at my hand as I offered him a spoonful of dessert.

"Do you think it's hard because you don't have time? Or is it difficult because you don't like what you'd write? What you'd see in the photos? Do you think a baby book has to be perfect? Curated like some kind of prestigious museum? These are memories, Ellie. They're not going to be perfect, and that's okay."

My face falls.

Fuck, is that why?

It makes sense. The last page I completed was the prompt about *Mom and Dad's final thoughts before meeting you*. The next page was *The day you were born*. I opened it once after Luca was born. I shut the book and never opened it again.

"How am I ever going to talk to Luca about the day he was born?" Shame, fear, and remorse threaten to overtake me.

"What do you want Luca to know?" he asks.

I give the question some thought. "I want him to know the important things. How things happened quickly, but that everyone worked hard to bring him safely into my arms. That I've loved him more than anything from that second on."

"Then that's where you start, and you go from there. I'm not saying it'll be easy. Luca will eventually have questions. Some may be painful to talk about. There's no handbook for these conversations or any of the questions he'll shoot your way. In my experience, parenting is ninety percent good intentions and ten percent flying by the seat of your pants. You do the best you can with what you have at the time, Ellie. That's all you can ask of yourself. You love your son, and he knows it. As long as that remains, everything else can be learned along the way."

"You and Mom made it look too easy," I say.

"Being your dad is the best thing I've ever done, and I love you, kiddo. But damn, it was anything but easy...as you've learned." We both laugh and Luca laughs with us like he's in on the joke. "That's why you lean on Dominic, Mom, your friends, and me...you don't have to do this alone. It might feel like failing...asking for help, but that's success in my book."

"Maybe you should take a stab at writing a parenting book. That seems like pretty solid advice to me," I say.

"It would be a short book. Ask for help, adapt to endless change, and do everything with love."

"I'd buy that book," I say with a smile.

We finish our ice cream and Luca sings the whole way home.

When the bowl is ready, Dad offers to pick it up and bring it to our house. I set it carefully on our mantle, wanting to see it every day, reminded of the gift my dad and Luca gave me. Permission to be messy and to own it.

I open Luca's baby book that night and begin.

CHAPTER THIRTY-TWO

Dom

"Do you remember when you used to bribe a librarian for free printing?" Ellie asks, her laugh vibrating against my bare chest as she snuggles closer into my side.

The time we've been sharing before bed, seemingly small conversations, has turned into something more. It's like I'm catching up with a friend I haven't seen in a long time. One of those best friends where you're so compatible that it doesn't matter that it's been too long, the bond hasn't weakened, and you find that talking is as easy as it always was. Like our souls are connected, even when at a distance.

The last few nights have been filled with talks about the future, specifically what we imagine the next year or so will look like. It feels like Luca hits a new growth spurt every other week.

It sounds like Ellie wants to spend tonight talking about the past instead.

"I don't remember it that way," I tease, giving her side a pinch.

She slaps my hand away. "Oh really? Well, how would you describe it?"

"I'd say that dear Ruth was extorting me for free desserts in my hour of need."

"Of course, you were the innocent one in all of this," she teases.

"Exactly. Glad you see things my way. Luckily, I was saved from further harm when this stunning blonde with a perfect ass took on my printing responsibilities. I still had to pay...with coffee dates, dinners, and endless orgasms."

"Seems like such a hardship."

"It was, but I wasn't about to say anything." I lean to whisper in her ear. "I once saw her nearly tear apart a printer with her bare hands. I wasn't going to do anything to risk facing her wrath."

"So, did you stay with this monster?" she asks, pinching my nipple.

"Abso-fucking-lutely. And my life was never boring again." I feel her smile and giggle against my skin. I trace small circles on her back, my other hand behind my head. We both lie quietly for a few minutes. I'm about to doze off when she speaks.

"How did you know you wanted to stay with her?" she asks, unable to hide the vulnerability in her question.

I wrap both arms around her, trying to pull her closer even though we're already as close as we can be.

"From the moment I met this force of nature, I never wanted to leave her side. If I did, she would have taken everything good with her. Every reason to smile would have evaporated. Every breath would have been painful. Every beat of my heart would have felt like daggers digging deep into every muscle. Within moments she became my everything. Without her, I would have lost it all."

She stills before looking up at me, chin resting on my chest, her eyes searching mine for something. I don't know what she sees, but I know what I see. I see the love of my life finding her way home. I'll shine a light so bright she can't miss it, even in this stormy season. I'll do it for as long as it takes for her to find her way safely back to me.

"I love you," she says, sincerity blanketing every word.

"I love you too." I continue rubbing circles on her back. "Do you remember the first time you told me that?" I ask.

As expected, she groans, pulling away from me and burying her face in a pillow. "God, don't remind me. Please, any memory but that."

I laugh and try unsuccessfully to pull her back into my arms. She grips the pillow like a lifeline and keeps her face buried as she whines.

"Come on, Ellie. It was romantic."

"It was not," I think she says. Hard to say with her face still smushed into the pillow.

"Yes, it was."

She lifts her face to glare at me, cheeks pink with embarrassment, hair alive with static from the fabric, framing her face in a halo.

I shrug, feeling brave enough to goad my wife further. "Just because my head was between your legs, doesn't make it any less romantic."

She flops back into the pillow, groaning again before coming back up for air. "You swore you would forget about that and use the PG version of the story for the rest of time. We first said *I love you* to each other at the botanical gardens, *remember*?"

"The PG story is for public." I look around. "No one around, Ellie. The truth is all you'll get from me while we walk down memory lane tonight." I clear my throat, using my presentation voice. "One cloudy evening, on a cold November night in Columbus, a lucky man and a woman *way* out of his league had...*relations*..." She groans again and hides under the blanket. "Of the oral variety," I add, reaching down to smack her ass.

"You're a butthead."

"A butthead?" I laugh. "Can't say I've been called that since grade school."

She laughs. "I'm flustered. Give me a minute and I'll come up with something better than that."

"Nah, I think I like your thoughts unfiltered. You know how I get those?" I ask, raising an eyebrow.

She does the same back to me in a question, but before she can answer, I roll onto her, pressing my front to hers and pushing her back onto the mattress. I take both her wrists in one hand and use the other to grip her ass.

I kiss her neck and run my nose along her chin. "You seem to have an easier time telling me how you really feel when you're distracted." I nip at her neck before trailing kisses down her chest to her cleavage, her thin tank top doing nothing to hide her pebbled nipples from me. "Want me to distract you?" I ask, peeking up at her to find her eyes locked on me, her chest rising and falling quickly. She smiles and nods.

"You sure?" I check in. It's been a while since we've done this, and I want her to enjoy it. We haven't done anything sexual since the shower a few weeks ago, and I want her to feel in control here.

"Yes. I'm sure," she says, rolling her hips into me. I release her wrists, slowly working my way down her body until I'm exactly where I want to be. I slowly peel Ellie's pants down her legs to find she's not wearing any underwear. Perfect.

Before settling between her thighs, I dig my hands underneath her ass, looking up at her only long enough to say, "Dig your hands into my hair and take what you need. Let me hear you."

"Dom," she says, before I sink my tongue into her slit. "Oh fuck," she moans, her body melting into the bed with the exception of her pelvis, which grinds against my face. *Fuck yes.*

I slide my tongue up to her clit, giving it all my attention. Ellie reacts quickly, her hands sliding into my hair like I asked, and she tugs me harder against her center. I groan and she gasps. She's wet and warm and fucking delicious.

I feel her legs shake against my shoulders, and I slide my hands from underneath her ass to her inner thighs, pressing her open wider for me. I find a rhythm, guided by her moans and the involuntary tug of her grip on my hair when I find the right spot.

It's not enough. I want to feel her everywhere. I want her in control.

I slide my palms back underneath her ass and roll onto my back, pulling her along with me until she's propped up on her hands and knees, her thighs on either side of my face. She pushes herself up so she's kneeling over me, her hands gripping the headboard as she stares down at me.

"Dom, what are you doing? I'm too..."

I give her ass a slap, knowing exactly where she's going with this.

"Not another fucking word, Ellie. I want my wife to ride my face and soak my beard. If you say one negative word about your body, I'm going to show you just how hard I want it. Understood?"

Her cheeks blaze and her chest heaves as she nods.

I pull her wet pussy toward me, one hand on her ass and the other on her hip. "I want to make you feel good. Can I do that?"

I remind myself that she might not be ready. I take a deep breath to calm the voice in my mind screaming at me to fuck it all away. To tease her, claim her, and fill her until she can't think about any of the negative shit anymore and all she can think about is how good she feels until she screams out and begs for more.

For a second, I'm scared I went too far. Demanding too much, too soon. But then she smiles at me, adjusts her grip on our bed frame, and slowly lowers her body as she whispers, "Yes."

I don't hesitate. I pull her the rest of the way onto my mouth and lap at her, tasting her perfect pussy and groaning like a starved man eating for the first time in weeks. *Months.*

Her hips slowly grind against me, but I can tell she's holding back. I pull her down harder until she finally lets go, and I circle her clit with my tongue. She gasps and her movements quicken, becoming uneven before she cries out and rides out her release, soaking me just like I asked.

She curses before kneeling, lifting her weight off me. She smiles down at me, lids heavy with lust and satisfaction.

I slap her ass again. "Thatta girl."

"I can't believe we did that."

"It's been a while. You okay?"

"More than okay," she says softly, her expression reassuring me that we didn't take it too far. Relief floods me and any remaining tension in my body releases instantly.

Goddamn, she's beautiful.

Her easy smile morphs into something I can't quite place, until she swings one leg over to shift her body to my side. I expect her to lie down beside me so we can fall asleep, but then her hand confidently wraps around my dick through my briefs, and every thought clears from my mind. I close my eyes, reveling in the feel of her firm grip.

"*Fuuuuck*, Ellie. What are you doing, baby?"

"I'm not tired. And based off this," she says, gripping me tighter and pumping me once, then twice. *Goddammit, I'm going to come in my underwear.* She gives an appreciative hum. "Yeah, based off *this*, I don't think you're tired either."

She positions herself at my side, kneeling beside me as I lie on the bed. Before I can even process what she's doing, she pulls my briefs down, freeing my stiff cock, and sucks me into her mouth.

I mumble something between a curse and a groan, and she takes me deeper, hitting the back of her throat. Her hair tumbles around my groin and I reach down with both hands to gather it all and pull it to the back of her head. My eyes about pop out of my head as I watch her bobbing on my dick, my hands gripping her hair tightly as she works me deeper and deeper.

I know it's been a while since we've done this, but it's still an embarrassingly short amount of time before I'm groaning Ellie's name and warning her that I'm about to come.

I can feel her smile around my dick and that's what does it. Little MILF is getting off on getting me off. *Fuck.*

My vision blurs, my hips stutter, and I still, filling her mouth before she eagerly swallows me down. "Fucking Christ. Shit. You're perfect. That was perfect. Ten outta ten. Holy fuck."

Ellie tries to sit up, but my hands are still gripping her hair and I sit up with her, using my hold to pull her mouth to meet mine halfway in a kiss so needy it's like nothing just happened between us. But something did happen. Another small step in mending another piece of what I was so terrified was broken between us.

We talk for a while longer, reminiscing about all the firsts we've shared, especially in that first year together. I wake the next morning with Ellie's body tangled in mine, and I can't think of anything sweeter.

CHAPTER THIRTY-THREE

Dom

Luca shrieks and giggles, teetering on unstable, chunky legs before tackling Dee and crawling all over as she dramatically plays the weakling, letting him jump on her and have his victory.

"This kid is built like a tank," she says, failing to recover quickly enough to avoid another leap from Luca onto her stomach before he holds her face in both his hands and laughs.

"That's right, baby. You rub it in her face that you won fair and square," Ellie says.

"Fuck, I'm going to be bruised tomorrow. He really got my cheek there," Dee says, sitting up and rubbing her face.

"Shit, I'm sorry. You good?" I ask. Dee nods.

"He's been super into roughhousing lately," Ellie explains. "I'm never worried about him. It's usually Dom and I who need help recovering afterward. Little guy has endless energy and no sense of awareness. He'll clock you right in the eye and then hug you immediately after."

"Lesson learned," Dee says. "At least I can blame Luca for my eyes watering and not be exposed for crying at *Sesame Street* again. Can they take a fucking chill pill? Goddamn, they're not playing fair with these songs."

"Are you crying over a kid's show?" Dylan asks, smirking at Dee as he joins us in the living room.

"Uh, are you *heartless*? Did you not listen to the lyrics of Elmo's song? Anyone with dry cheeks after that is a bigger grouch than Oscar."

"My cheeks are as dry as a desert and I'm an angel," Dylan retorts before reclining on the couch, one arm stretched over the back cushion.

Ellie scrunches her nose. "Ew, this feels weird. Let's not talk about cheeks, wet or dry."

Dee shoves her middle finger in the air, giving Dylan a snarky look.

"Don't flick him off. I don't want Luca to start giving everyone the middle finger," I beg.

Dee furrows her brows and tilts her head, but before she can say anything, Ellie's flying across the room.

"Another point for me! *Flip*, Dom. Dee is *flipping* him off." I hear her yank open the junk drawer to get the notebook.

"You're full of shit. Cheating isn't going to get you anywhere, Ellie. It's most certainly *flicking*."

"Wooooow," Dee says, rolling her eyes. "God forbid I give Dylan the middle finger, but you can tell your wife she's full of shit? I wonder which bad habit Luca will pick up first?"

"Shit. *Fuck*. I mean, yeah, you're right," I say.

Okay, so the *not swearing in front of the toddler who's learning to talk* thing could be going better.

"I hate to break up this party and super important life lesson for Luca, but if we don't want to be late, we need to leave in the next five minutes," Dylan says, checking his watch.

"Dee, you want to join? Dylan planned the next puzzle activity. We're taking Luca to his first music class," Ellie says excitedly as she documents my loss in our commonly fucked-up phrase notebook.

It's good to see her excited about this.

I appreciate the guys all taking this favor seriously. When I asked for their help, it would have been easy for them to brush it off or half-ass plans. But they've each shown up for me and Ellie with thoughtful ideas. As dysfunctional as our small circle can be, everyone showed up when we needed them, and I'll never forget it.

Dee gives Dylan a surprised look. "Huh, didn't peg you for a musical guy. What gives, Dylan?"

"Nothing," he answers quickly. "I mean, you should come...if you want."

"Ooookay, fine. Then I will," Dee says, voice laden with hesitation.

Ellie looks at me, then back at the two of them, then back at me. I can read that look. *What the fuck is going on?*

I give her a look back. *Not a fucking clue, but let's see how far we can push this.* She rolls her eyes.

Dee and Dylan spend the entire class making snarky quips at each other in a battle to outwit one another as usual. But between all that, the four of us have a great time playing music with Luca and watching him try out the drums, tambourines, xylophone, and keyboard.

Ellie watches closely as Luca takes part in this new experience, his eyes glowing with wonder, while hers do the same. My family might not be perfect, but moments like this are.

I want Luca to be anything he wants when he's older, but based on how much he loves this music class, my money is on lead drummer in a rock band. That, or a WWE headliner. Too soon to tell.

CHAPTER THIRTY-FOUR

Ellie

"**O**kay, buddy. Eggs are the last thing on the list. We'll grab them on our way to the register. Then we'll go home, grab some lunch, and take a little nap. What do you think?" I ask Luca as he wiggles in the child's seat of the shopping cart.

He babbles back at me, seemingly in agreement. Luca's vocabulary is slowly growing, but when he's excited, he usually resorts to his two favorite words, *mama* and *dada*. The first time he called us by the right names, we celebrated with a family dance party and brownies because Dom insisted it was a milestone that demanded brownies.

After grabbing a dozen eggs, I sing softly to Luca as I push our cart to the checkout line. My mind always panics a little while I unload the cart onto the conveyor belt and Luca is sitting facing the stranger in line behind us.

I mean, I'm *right here*, but my anxiety never seems to take a day off. My mind races through what I'd do if a stranger ever just grabbed him and tried to make a run for it. The answer? I'd drop everything, turn into an Olympian, and I'd go fucking feral getting him back, probably ending up in jail. Thankfully, my intrusive thoughts stay in my mind and have never become reality.

The woman in line behind me clears her throat loudly as I'm unloading the cart, but I don't pay her much attention. Then I hear, "Um, excuse me. Ma'am?"

My head shoots up to see she's leaning on her cart, one foot propped on the bottom rack as she stares at me with one eyebrow raised. "I was trying to say you need to get that boy off the binkie."

I stare at her for a few seconds, frozen in place, broccoli in my hand halfway to the conveyor belt because...*huh*? My brain tries to make sense of what she's saying, but all I can come up with is, again...*huh*?

Luca looks at me, cooing softly from behind the binkie I gave him before I started unloading the cart to keep him chill while I check out.

Frustrated by my lack of response, she continues, "He getting too old for one. You're setting him up for failure by coddling him. Better to just pull it cold turkey. Here, if I just take it, I'm sure he won't mind." She moves around her cart, approaching Luca, and I see *fucking red*.

Acting on impulse, I step to the side, and as gently as I can so I don't jostle Luca in his seat, pull the cart away from her until I'm standing between her and Luca. My stomach is in my throat and I don't recognize my voice, like my ears are plugged. My heart starts racing, and I swear I can hear its pulsing beat.

"You need to get away from my son and me, right now."

"Excuse me?"

"Yeah, fucking excuse you. Excuse you for inserting yourself into something that's none of your goddamn business. If you ever get the impulse to offer unsolicited parenting advice and then *take a binkie from a toddler*, I strongly encourage you to seek professional help because you've lost your mind worse than I have."

Her expression turns cold, her nose upturned, her hand clutching her honest to god pearls.

But I'm not done.

"Listen, lady, it's the binkie or the tit that'll keep him calm while I pay for my groceries. Which would you rather I pull out, *ma'am*?" My voice has a bite and I let it sharpen, grateful for whatever strength has found its way forward so I can deal with this absolute asshole.

"Wow, still breastfeeding too. Unbelievable. It's just awful, thinking you can speak to someone like that. How crass."

"Crass?" I choke out in disbelief. What a fucking bitch.

"Is there a problem here?" a woman asks me. She appears to be in her forties and is standing alongside the teen cashier who had begun our transaction, I'm assuming his manager.

I angle my body protectively toward Luca, my eyes darting around to see people are staring at me and the mystery bitch behind me. My face heats with embarrassment and my eyes begin to burn.

"I would love to check out as quickly as possible," I say. I do not want to be *that* customer. I need to get out of here without making things difficult for the employees.

"Of course," she replies, helping to finish our transaction without another word from the asshole behind me. *Thank god.* Afterward, the employee walks us to the door.

"I'm so sorry," I sputter nervously. "I shouldn't have gotten so upset."

"Please, if someone said that to me when my son was that age, I would have gotten kicked out of this store. Don't let it ruin your day, okay? You take care." She walks back into the store, the automatic doors closing before I can thank her for being so understanding.

She seems completely unfazed by the entire interaction, but my hands are shaking. I buckle Luca into his car seat, load the groceries as quickly as possible, and then drive us home. My check engine light pops up mid-drive because *of course it fucking does.*

I spend the ten-minute drive ruminating over the entire exchange, my hands still shaking on the steering wheel.

I am safe. We are safe.

My feeble attempt to calm myself down fails. Anger burns again at the thought of that woman passing judgment on a complete stranger and her insane lack of boundaries. *What the fuck is wrong with people?*

She took one look at me and spoke as if she knew my story. She assumed I'm some terrible mother just because I'm doing things differently than she would. I'm already insecure; I sure as fuck don't need strangers vocalizing their disapproval to me in the grocery store of all places.

What is it about being a mom that makes people think they can force their opinions on you like it's some kind of favor, then act like you're the unreasonable one for making your own decisions?

Sure, there are some universal truths to parenting, but I don't think I'm wrong in thinking most of us are doing the best we can. A little bit of empathy would be nice.

My own reaction shocked me. If Luca wasn't there and someone was being critical and confronting me about it, I'd most likely brush it off and not engage.

One step toward my son was all it took, and I finally understood "the momma bear" instinct, because I was ready to rip that woman apart.

We get home and I manage to get Luca inside and set up with his toys in his play area while I unload the groceries and get his lunch ready. I also try to flip the laundry, only to discover that I left the wet clothes in the wash and forgot about them who knows how long ago. I restart the washer and fluff the clothes in the dryer, begging my own brain to remember to flip the laundry at some point tonight to avoid having to do this same thing again tomorrow.

It's Friday and I'm off work today. We normally grocery shop as a family on Saturday mornings, but I thought it'd be a nice surprise for Dom if we had the morning off from errands and we could spend that time together relaxing at home. That plan bit me in the ass quick.

This is the annoying part of anxiety. You have one bad experience and your brain says, *See? I told you. You shouldn't take Luca out on your own. Look what happens.* I want to be able to do things on my own with my son, but one shitty interaction has the power to undo all the confidence I'm trying to build.

Luca's getting another tooth, so he's extra fussy during lunch today. The usual things that make him happy aren't cutting it. He's frustrated and I'm doing my best to hang on as we struggle through mealtime, most of the food ending up on him, the floor, and my shirt—which I just bought and is most likely now ruined by blackberry stains. Do I own clothes that aren't stained anymore?

After I clean up lunch, Luca and I sit in the living room playing with his toys. I can feel myself going through the motions, not totally present but not completely absent either. I smile at Luca, we sing, we play, but my head keeps tossing me back into that moment where that complete stranger made me feel like the shittiest mom in the world...all because of a stupid binkie.

I want to shake it off, but confrontation makes me anxious regardless of context. Confrontation where I feel like my son is in the middle? Fuck, I'm stuck in a destructive loop of thinking worst-case scenarios of how it all could have gone differently.

Bec must have some kind of sense for my impending mental breakdown, because at that moment I get a video chat from her, Hopper curled up into her side.

My face must say it all.

"What happened?" she asks, sitting up and causing Hopper to look alert.

I tell her everything, sounding as detached as I feel. With an emotional hurricane swirling in my chest, I'm always surprised at how I can shut it down and mask up.

Everything's fine. We're fine.

Still, I vent about the stranger, her judgment, and her insane idea to take a binkie out of a kid's mouth.

"That woman has issues. You don't just say shit like that to people, and you sure as fuck don't take a binkie from a stranger's baby."

"Yeah, but I didn't need to react like that, did I? I probably looked like the crazy one. You should have seen how many people were staring."

"I would have stared, too, and given you a standing ovation. You can't let some stranger's opinion ruin your perception of yourself. You're a wonderful mom, Ellie. And hey, at least you didn't have Dee with you. She would have taken that binkie and shoved it up that woman's—"

A sharp cry rings out. I was so distracted venting to Bec, that I didn't see Luca fall. I turned my head for one second...he must have bumped his jaw on the edge of the coffee table. I drop my phone, forgetting the call with Bec completely, especially when I pick up Luca and discover he must have bit down hard when he fell. Blood pools on his tiny split lip.

I'm immediately crying with him. Heaving sobs escape as I let it all go. This shit show of a day just needs to end.

I rock, pat, shush, soothe, and apologize a hundred times to my son, who is incapable of forgiving me at this age.

After a couple minutes of us crying in each other's arms, we both settle down enough for me to take him to his room. As if getting away from where he got hurt will undo the accident. We play in there for a bit before I get him ready for his nap.

I'm nursing him to sleep when another stroke of guilt hits me. The bottom of his chin is bruised from his fall. *Fuck, I can't believe I let this happen.*

This day just keeps getting worse and Luca is the one paying for it.

Maybe that woman was right about me. I am a bad mother.

I sing an extra song and hold Luca a little longer before putting him down for his nap. I grab the baby monitor and plop onto my bed. I hold the screen above me as it comes to life. He looks so peaceful. Tears collect in the corner of my eye, waiting to fall.

How can so many things go wrong in an hour?

Feelings of inadequacy, shame, and guilt all crash around my mind until a notification on my phone interrupts my thoughts.

Bec: Is Luca sleeping?

Ellie: Just got him down. Sorry, I think I hung up on you. Luca fell, and I had to handle it. Call you tomorrow?

Bec: Then I won't knock. Let me in.

Why is she here?

I open the front door, but before I can get a word out, her arms are around me, and I'm sobbing again. Every emotion I tried to bury from the day floods my cheeks.

"I didn't say code red," I hiccup once my tears have slowed, referring to our code we invented in middle school for *get here now, I need you*.

"You didn't have to," Bec says, gripping me tighter.

I lean against my best friend and let her try to hold me together, but I fall to pieces anyway.

Chapter Thirty-Five

Dom

The house is quiet when I get home from work. I caught up with Bec in the driveway before she left. She didn't say much other than that Ellie had a bad day, and she wanted to be here for her.

Why didn't she call me?

No matter how hard I try, how hard I beg Ellie to talk to me, she's still shutting me out. She's still trying to do everything on her own. Why is it so hard for her to include me, lean on me? What's stopping her from asking for help?

I find Ellie in the living room, cup of tea on the coffee table, a book in her hand, but she's not looking at it. Her gaze is fixed out the window, her eyes glassy and far away.

She always feels so fucking far away.

I crouch in front of her before she finally looks at me.

"Hey, how you doing, honey? I ran into Bec. She said you had a rough day. What happened?"

"Just more of the same." She gives a humorless laugh.

"What do you mean?"

Come on, Ellie. Let me in.

She shakes her head, her eyes squeezed shut, and I rub my palms from her knees to her thighs, squeezing once.

"Talk to me, baby. Let me help."

"There's nothing you can do. I'm not good at this, Dom, and it's my problem. I just need to do better."

My heart breaks. She still doesn't see it.

"You don't need to do better. You're incredible just as you are. An amazing wife and a wonderful mom."

"But I'm not," she says, her expression almost empty, haunted. "And even if I was, is that all I can contribute? Who am I outside of that? What's left of me then?"

I pause, not sure how to answer.

"Aren't I more than that?" she asks, her expression full of fear. She looks so lost.

"Those things are only a part of who you are. You're also kind and funny. Empathetic and strong. Protective and silly. Smart and introspective," I say, desperately wanting her to remember who she is, who she's always been.

I feel her slipping away, sensing that we're heading over the edge of the cliff. I'm scared shitless of fucking this up and losing her entirely.

She groans in frustration. "It's like my fucked-up brain never shuts up. Even when I want to be happy, it's like there's this film over everything tainting it. Like my brain is warning me not to get too comfortable because any goddamn second it's all going to fall apart, the worst will happen, and I'll lose *everything*."

"I understand why you feel that way, but we got unlucky once. That doesn't mean it'll happen again."

She stands, my hands falling away from her lap. She walks to the window and stares for a few seconds before facing me again. I stand slowly.

"How do you know that? How does anyone know that? The chances of what happened to us were small, too, and guess what? *They still fucking happened.* I don't believe in taking risks anymore because even when the chances are good, someone still has to lose. The statistics always seem to forget that even when the odds of something terrible happening are low, they still happen to *someone*.

But we're just supposed to forget about them because mostly everyone gets out unscathed."

"You've been doing so well lately; I had no idea you still felt this way." *It's like we're back at the hospital.* "How can I help, Ellie? Please, just tell me what to do."

"What? Like another piece of your puzzle? You really thought you could make up some game to get us out of this? At some point we have to grow up, Dom. These are real fucking problems and we can't escape them with a goddamn *puzzle.*"

A calm, detached emptiness washes over me, so unfamiliar Ellie looks at me like she doesn't recognize me. Gone is my carefree, easygoing demeanor. I take one step toward her and she takes one back. I freeze, afraid she's about to bolt.

"You want to be mad at me, baby? You want to take everything you're feeling out on me by saying shit you don't mean? You need to hurt me so I can feel the way that you do?" I take another step closer. "Do it. Nothing you say could make me believe that we're not stronger than what we're facing."

"What if we're not?" she asks, voice shaking. "We argue over the smallest things. We're at each other's throats half the night, barely together during the day. Do you even have fun when you're with me? Or am I just another chore?"

My heart runs cold. My chest constricts with panic at her words, not liking one fucking bit where she's going with this.

"You've never been a chore, Ellie. You're my wife. You're my best friend and I love you. I love being with you. I just want to help you. I want to help you work through this, push past this. That's all."

"You deserve more than what I can give you," she whispers, not hearing anything I'm saying.

"Don't do this, Ellie," I beg, my voice finally breaking, a sense of dread and cold helplessness rushing over me.

"I'm not doing anything. I'm finally admitting what we've been living in denial of for over a year. Maybe this is it for us. Maybe there's no coming back from this. What if everything that happened broke us? We're different people than we were before."

"Jesus, Ellie. What are you saying?"

"Do you want out?" she asks, voice steady, eyes dry.

I stride toward her, taking her face in my hands, her body melting into mine for a moment, closing her eyes, before she pulls back and returns her stare, empty of everything.

"Never. You are *my wife* and I will never want out. I'm really fucking trying here, but you're still drifting away from me, like you'd rather push me away than let me in. There's not one fucking part of me that doesn't believe we're not meant for each other. And when you're meant for each other, none of the other shit matters. We will get through this. Tell me you still love me. That you still want me. That you still want *us*."

She stares at me, perfectly still. Expression empty of any emotion at all. I can barely breathe.

"Fuck, Ellie, why can't you tell me that?" I plead, barely above a whisper.

"Because I don't want to feel anything!" Her scream echoes through the room. My body is frozen. Her chest heaves, her eyes wide, lost, and fearful. She's seconds from falling apart and I don't think either of us is strong enough to put the pieces back together. "If I let myself feel *anything*...then I have to feel *everything*, and I...I can't do that. Please don't make me do that," she sobs.

"Ellie, you have to. You have to let it all in, baby. But I promise I'll be here for you every step of the way. You're stronger than what happened. You're stronger than you ever believed. I've watched you heal physically. I know you can do the same with your heart. What if we try therapy again—"

"What, so they can confirm all the things I already know? That I'm an awful mom with horrifying thoughts who will never be good enough. Why can't you accept that this is all that's left?"

"Goddammit, Ellie. Stop talking about yourself like you aren't worthy. I *love* you," I yell, losing all control. I take a breath in a feeble attempt to calm myself. I'm backed into a corner and no matter what I say, Ellie's acting like we've already lost. Finally speaking at a normal volume, I plead, "Let me love you."

"I don't know if I can. I'm not the same person I was when we met, when we got married, or even when we decided to start a family. I'm never going to be the person I was before all this shit happened and now I have to live with that and figure out who I am on this side of it all."

"You don't have to figure this out all on your own. You don't have to be that person you used to be to be. Don't you see? The best parts of you are *still here*, Ellie."

"I wish you weren't wrong."

Chapter Thirty-Six

Dom

"Then she left. Went to her parents. Said she needed a couple hours to herself."

"Fuck, man. I'm sorry. I thought things were getting better," Aiden says.

Yeah, me too.

Hopper's snoring on a dog bed in front of a small stack of unpacked moving boxes. Aiden's got enough shit to deal with, what with moving into his new home with Bec, unpacking everything, and being in the thick of his spring season. Thankfully, their place isn't far from ours.

I couldn't stand being in our house after Ellie left the way she did. When Luca woke up from his nap, I packed his stuff and brought him straight here, only calling Aiden on the way to give him a couple minutes' notice. He didn't question it at all and said we were welcome anytime.

"I think you and the guys were right from the start. I was kidding myself thinking I could help with some stupid fucking game."

Aiden's face reads of pity and it makes my stomach turn.

"I'll admit I was worried before, but I think it's helping more than you're giving yourself credit for," Aiden says. "Even Bec has mentioned how good she thinks this is for Ellie. Look, if there's anything David's helped me see, it's that healing works differently for everyone. There's no right way to do it. It's not as if a switch flips and one day you're done doing the work. I know it's probably not what either of you want to hear, but this might just be something Ellie always needs to manage. But I wouldn't give up on your plan. It seems like this is helping her find her footing again. There's bound to be some setbacks."

David's the therapist I started seeing regularly after Luca was born. I gave Aiden his information at the end of last summer, when he found himself at rock bottom and needed a professional to help him work through it. While I know what he's saying is true, it still evokes feelings of defensiveness.

I don't want Ellie to have to *manage* anything. I want her to *thrive*.

"It's impossible to watch her take three steps forward and then fall ten steps back. No warning. Nothing I can do to help. I feel so fucking helpless it makes me want to rip my skin off."

I catch Aiden's grimace before he holds the bridge of his nose.

"It's like with my mom. I feel just as out of control. It's fucking terrifying. But I can't carry it on my shoulders all the time. I tried, and it nearly broke me. If you try to carry this for Ellie, man, you're going to break too. This game...it's thoughtful, but it might not be the final solution. She has to choose to work through the shit on her own."

"Yeah, and what the fuck am I supposed to do? Nothing?"

"No. You do what you always do. You listen, you support her, you lift her up, you challenge her, and you hold her when she falls."

I hear a commotion, and Hopper is up in a flash, zooming past Luca, who claps at the sight and walks—okay, more like waddles—after him, unable to keep up, but damn, it's cute how hard he's trying.

An elated Hopper returns after a minute with Bec in tow, scratching his head and smiling at Aiden, who meets her and kisses her before hugging her, mumbling something in her ear. The carefree smile on her face makes me feel like I'm intruding—and also a little jealous. Things used to feel that easy for Ellie and me too.

I grab Luca and bring him back to the blanket we set up on the floor with the toys I brought over to keep him entertained.

"Hey, Dom," Bec says, voice drenched with sympathy.

I lean back, resting my elbow on the couch cushion from my spot on the floor next to Luca.

"She called you?" I ask.

"Her mom did. Ellie didn't want to talk. She said she just wanted to rest. Carolyn checked on her a little while ago. Said it looked like she had fallen asleep."

Good. I've never believed in the "never go to bed angry" advice that people love to hand out. Sometimes, we all need to go to fucking bed. Everything feels impossible when you're exhausted, and she hasn't slept well since she went into the third trimester of her pregnancy.

I scrub my palm down my face and over my short beard. "I could use some best friend magic here, Bec."

She sits on the floor across from me and Luca. He immediately crawls into her lap and starts babbling. Probably begging her to take him away from his annoying parents and somewhere fun for a change.

Luca sits in Bec's lap with a board book, and she looks absently at the pages as he slowly turns them one by one.

"What if the girls and I made a last-minute change with our puzzle pieces?" she asks, her eyes lighting up, excitement unmistakable in her voice.

"No, I'm done with the games. Ellie needs real help, and it was dumb to think—"

"Hey, it wasn't dumb. You really think I'd let you put my best friend through something like this when she's struggling if I didn't think it'd help? You should have heard her talk about all that she's been doing lately during our last few book clubs. I don't think you realize how special this has made her feel. The way she talks about each piece afterward, I think they're reminding her that it's okay for her to find those buried parts of herself.

"You two are great parents, but that shit is fucking hard, and I'm just an observer. I don't see everything that you two have going on. I don't know what happened today, or what needs to happen next. None of us do. But we're here for you both."

Fuck, don't cry.

"I was kind of hoping you'd just have the silver bullet in your back pocket. The magic ticket I need to fix it all," I say.

Bec makes a show of digging around her pockets, a look of exaggerated frustration every time she comes up empty. "Nope, fresh out of magical fixes, I'm afraid."

Luca giggles at the sight of Bec's theatrics, that deep belly laugh. Hopper, confused by the game, starts sniffing Bec's pockets, purse, and hair, trying to find whatever it is Bec's looking for. Luca screams before his fit of giggles intensifies. He looks around expectantly, and a minute later, Bec, Aiden, and I are all looking into empty pockets and huffing around with cartoon-level reactions to finding nothing there. Luca hiccups from his laughing fit and wraps his arms around Bec's neck. She smiles and holds him close.

Disgruntled at the empty pockets, Hopper trudges back to his dog bed and huffs out a sigh after making a few circles to get in just the right spot, his eyes stay locked on Bec, I assume in case she starts her imaginary search again.

"The girls and I were throwing around a few ideas for our puzzle pieces, but I think we might need to go a different direction."

"What do you mean?"

"Let me call the girls. Give us two days. I think we can make something work."

Aiden and I exchange a look. It's a relief to see confusion written on his face as clear as I'm sure it's written on mine.

"I'd trust her if I were you," Aiden says with a shrug.

"You ladies are in charge. Tell me how I can help."

CHAPTER THIRTY-SEVEN

Ellie

"You're really okay with this?" I ask for the millionth time today. Maybe Dom changed his mind in the last six minutes...you never know.

"*Yes,*" Dom says with conviction. "I know you're nervous about the distance and time away, but I think you'll feel better if you try. Like Bec said on the phone, if you want to leave early, you leave early. Anytime you want to video chat with Luca and me, we'll pause our dance party to hear about how much fun you're having."

I roll my eyes, but a smirk fights its way to my face anyway. I know that Dom and Luca will be fine. I *know* it. But that doesn't stop my hands from sweating or my stomach from rolling with nausea at the thought of my first night away from Luca since he was born almost twenty months ago. And it won't just be one night. The girls are stealing me away for a long weekend. Four nights in the Outer Banks of North Carolina.

Dom's smile fades and he steps closer, his chest a breath away from mine. He holds the back of my neck and his eyes search mine. "I mean it. If you need to come home, say the word. If you need to call me at two in the morning so I can show you the baby monitor to quiet your mind, I want you to do it. I'm here for you, Ellie. Girls vacation or not." His nose brushes mine, his lips so close, a whisper of a kiss between us. "I'm here for you always."

"I love you," I say, squeezing my eyes shut to hold back the tears threatening to escape. "Thank you for loving me back. I know I haven't been myself, but I swear, I'm trying. The other day...I just felt so out of control."

"I love you in every phase, in every shade, in every darkness, in every ray of light. You're in my head and my heart. There's nothing that can change that. Understand?"

Tears streak down my cheeks as I nod, his sweet words stealing my voice. He holds me until I have to go.

I steady myself and prepare to say goodbye to Luca. I sob, naturally, and come back to pick him up "just one more time" at least three times, but then the girls pull into the driveway and it truly is time to go. With one last hug, Luca in my arms, and me in Dom's, I say a final goodbye to my tiny family and roll my carry-on bag down the driveway. Time to catch a flight.

***

"How did you guys find a place for us to stay this weekend? I thought you needed to book months in advance in the Outer Banks? Especially this close to Memorial Day," I say, shoving my last bag into the back of the minivan Dee rented to get us from the airport to the beach house. Our flight from Ohio wasn't long, but stretching my legs before we spend a chunk of time in the car feels like a good investment.

I've never been to North Carolina before, but when the girls told me they had planned a beach trip, it did help lessen my anxiety about leaving home. Hard to say no to sun, sand, and surf with the promise of four nights of uninterrupted sleep. Should make my first overnight trip away from Luca easier. I hope.

"Toby has a timeshare, remember? He's so quiet about it, I swear, even my parents forgot when I told them where we were going," Bec says.

Toby, Bec's oldest brother, is her sibling I know the least. He's soft spoken, reserved, and dedicated to his job. If there's a Miller sibling who could let us all forget he has a timeshare at the beach, it's Toby.

"Nice ride, Dee," Abby says, jumping into the passenger seat as Dee puts a burned CD labeled *Bitches on Beaches: A ~~cum~~ comeback story* into the stereo system.

"Did you seriously burn a CD for this trip?" I ask.

"How did you know we'd get a van with a CD player?" Carissa asks from the backseat. Valid question; aren't those becoming obsolete in newer cars?

"Did I read that title right?" Bec asks as she climbs into the captain's chair next to me.

"Jesus, what's with the interrogation? I need you all to relax. We are on *vacation*. I had a long conversation with Jonah about the accommodations our ride needed to come with. You'll find snacks and drinks in a mini cooler back by Carissa and Evie. We can use the cooler for the beach, but we have to return it with the van; Jonah needs it for his hiking trip on Monday," she says as she puts on her sunglasses and adjusts the mirrors.

"Who the hell is Jonah?" Bec asks.

"Uh, the guy I scheduled our rental with, duh." Dee lowers the passenger seat window and leans over Abby's lap to shout, "Thanks, Jonah! See you Sunday!"

"You ladies have a great time," I hear him shout back as she twiddles her fingers in his direction.

"Pieces of Me" by Ashlee Simpson starts playing and I immediately start laughing. "Oh my god, the ballad of my teen years."

"I thought you would approve. I remember you had a lot of Ashlee on your workout playlists in college. I also thought it was a nice nod to Dom's puzzle and the reason we are gathered here today." Dee turns to face me, pulling her sunglasses down from her head so I can't see her eyes, but her face is completely serious. "Ellie, this is your comeback story. I can't wait to see where it takes us."

"God help us," Bec mumbles.

"I'm your god now, Miller," Dee says in her sexy man voice, quoting our book club pick of the month as she revs the engine, pulling out of the car rental parking lot and merging onto the freeway. It's about a ninety-minute drive from the airport in Virginia to our beach house in North Carolina, where we'll be staying.

"Speaking of our book, who wants to go first?" Abby asks. "Evie, it's your first time in the buddy read. What'd you think?"

"I think I scarred Aiden for life when he walked into my apartment while I was listening to the audiobook," she says with a laugh.

"What is it with your brother and audiobooks?" Bec mutters from her seat next to me.

"What was that?" Evie asks.

"Uh...nothing," Bec says, her cheeks blushing.

"Do we need to stop and get gas before we get too far into the drive?" Carissa asks.

"Nah, Jonah hooked us up. Full tank, and he said he doesn't care how full it is when we drop it off. He did warn me that there's a stretch of road where there's only, like, one gas station and it's super small with only four pumps."

"Ugh, warn a girl before you remind me of my ex like that," Abby says with a groan.

"My condolences. Four pumps are never enough. All that disappointment is in the rearview now, Abby." The two of them cackle.

My muscles relax the farther we drive. We talk about our latest read and scream-sing popular hits from years ago, word for word. Dom sends me pictures every hour or so of him and Luca, always keeping me in the loop without me having to ask, which I appreciate and make sure to tell him so.

Maybe the girls and Dom are right. This trip might be good for me. I dare to hope.

CHAPTER THIRTY-EIGHT

Ellie

We arrived at Toby's beachfront house late yesterday afternoon. I can't believe Bec's never forced him to share this with her before. This is her first time staying as well.

Bec meant it when she told me earlier that the house was *on* the water. We parked the van underneath the covered entryway, which is beside a walking path leading directly to the sandy beach.

I don't care that I'm a married mom of one with a corporate job. Walking into a beachside vacation home with my girls made me feel like we were all a bunch of kids, running through the place, claiming beds, pointing out all the fun beachy décor, and drooling over the stunning views from the main living room on the top floor.

The ground-level exterior has a parking space, an in-ground pool, and an outdoor shower. The interior has a full bathroom, laundry room, and kitchenette. The middle floor has three bedrooms, each with a queen bed and access to the second-floor deck. Bec and I are sharing a room, and we slept with the slider door partially open, screen shut, so we could listen to the waves. It was like a dream. The top floor has a large open-concept living space, a blue and white themed kitchen, a large dining room table, and large living room with a full wall of windows and sliders leading out to the sundeck.

After touring the house, we grabbed some groceries before settling in for the night. We kept it relaxed and shared some drinks on the sundeck, watching and listening to the waves as the sun set.

It's a good thing we decided to go to bed early last night, because this morning, Dee woke us up at the ass crack of dawn and told us to put on clothes that could get dirty. While light on details, she did start talking more like a pirate the closer we got to our mystery destination. It became apparent why when we parked at Coral's Cove Marina.

I followed the girls as they boarded the charter boat before we met its crew.

"Good morning, ladies. Welcome aboard The Veronica. I'm Captain Morgan, and this is my first mate, Taylor."

"Shut the fuck up. His name is Captain Morgan?" Bec hisses quietly beside me, and I giggle at her shocked and impressed tone. "This is going to be amazing. If only this guy knew how many morning classes I missed in college because of his namesake."

Only Dee would choose deep-sea fishing—something that none of us has ever done before nor has any interest in doing—as her puzzle piece for me. And only Dee would be able to find *the* Captain Morgan to lead us on our journey.

The woman is an adventure all on her own. Give her free rein on vacation and she's a menace.

The girls and I stand shoulder to shoulder, swaying as the boat bobs and rocks along the dock while the hot sun bakes our skin. The water slaps against the side of the boat with every ripple. I hope none of us gets sick from the motion because the water looked a lot calmer as we drove along the shore to the docks.

There are twelve massive fishing poles pointed to the sky from a section on the back of the boat. The setup is intimidating, but I push down my hesitation in an attempt to make the most of a new experience. Surrendering fully to the escapade that Dee signed us up for.

"Captain Morgan, I'm Dee. We spoke on the phone."

"Ah, Deanna. Nice to finally meet you." He offers Dee his calloused hand, which she accepts with an aggressive handshake, never to be outdone by a man. I love watching men react to her ever-present need to display dominance. His approving smirk at her tenacity makes me like him instantly.

"We'll be taking off shortly. Taylor here will show you the facilities and get you acclimated."

Captain Morgan heads toward the—fuck, I don't know what it's called. Steering wheel feels like a dumb thing to call it, but I've never been on a boat before, so that's all I've got.

"All right, ladies," Taylor says, clapping her hands together. She's a tall white woman, appearing to be in her mid-thirties or so, with slightly sunburned shoulders, a full tattoo sleeve on her right arm, and her brown hair in a loose bun. "Anyone ever been deep-sea fishing before?"

I don't need to glance at my side to know the six of us are shaking our heads. Her expression turns almost giddy.

"First timers, then," she says, clapping her hand over her fist and rocking on her heels.

"Quick learners," Dee fires back with a smirk, and I turn in time to catch her firing a wink at Taylor.

I bite my lips to keep my smile from turning into a laugh. Seems like Dee has her sights set on catching something more exciting on this trip.

Taylor crosses her arms over her chest, a challenge in her grin, eyes focused solely on Dee. "Guess we'll see."

***

"Do you want some ginger ale?" Carissa asks Bec, whose face is so green I'm shocked her breakfast isn't already overboard.

"If I put anything in my mouth right now, that'll set off a chain reaction I won't be able to stop," Bec says, voice unsteady, leaning her head heavily on Carissa's shoulder as they sit huddled together on the small bench.

Today's been the literal breath of fresh air I needed. And while it's a little unsettling being out on the open water with nothing around, the salty breeze breaks the stifling humidity, the warm sun bakes my skin, and the playlist Evie made is playing over the speakers as we are driven to another fishing spot to try our luck somewhere new.

We haven't caught any fish, but that was never important to me. As I stand here, surrounded by friends who dropped everything for an impromptu long weekend trip for...me, I'm filled with gratitude. I can't believe I actually agreed to this and made it through the long drive and the first night to now with only video chats to dull the ache of missing my family.

The string on my heart pulling me home has been stretched taut since I left my family. I'm enjoying myself, but I'm already eagerly anticipating the moment when that pressure finally slackens, and Luca is in my arms again and Dom holds us both tightly in his.

"Here's the bucket. Your friend won't make it to the edge in time," Taylor says, handing Carissa an old construction bucket with mystery stains along the sides.

Carissa leans forward to place *The Bucket* between Bec's legs. Bec's lips turn down, a face I've only seen her make when she's dancing on the bar after three too many drinks. "Oh god, no. I'm scared of the community puke bucket. This is my nightmare."

"You *cannot* get sick, Bec," Abby says sternly. "I'm serious. *That's* the kind of chain reaction we should be scared of right now. Thankfully we have a nurse on board."

"This is the shit they don't tell you in nursing school. You become everyone's go-to medic," Carissa jokes. She's not wrong; she's put on her nurse hat with us many times over the years. She might be overworked and underappreciated, but when she's needed, nothing ever dampens her compassion and attentive care.

Carissa was incredible with me when I was pregnant. Even though I've never gone into details with the girls about what happened when Luca was born, when I told them the abbreviated version, the one I carry with me and use like armor when people ask about the story, her eyes bore into mine with a knowing of a health care worker who has experienced her share of secondhand medical trauma. She might be the easiest friend to tell someday, but I can never seem to form the words.

"I'm gonna need you guys to get it together. We didn't come all this way to go home without an epic fishing story. I need a picture of my own to rival the gigantic fish pics littering the douchey dating sites. What do you think of this, Chad? Yeah, mine's bigger!"

"Uh, Dee? I think you might get your wish," Evie says from where she's seated on the other side of Bec.

We all look toward the fishing poles, one dipping lower than the others sporadically.

"Buckle up. It's time," Taylor says, a fire lighting up her expression, clearly in her element.

"Fuck, yes," Dee hisses as she hauls ass to the edge of the boat, watching the line drag out into the water.

"Hold tight, we need to let this guy run," Taylor says. I watch, fascinated that this is someone's everyday world. The excitement radiating off Taylor is contagious, clearly overtaking Dee as well, who is leaning off the back of the boat, practically folded in half, watching as the fish runs out the line. "Okay, grab this," Taylor demands, shoving the fishing pole into Dee's eager arms.

"Now, keep your line tight and remember what I said. Lift high, then dip low and reel. Understand?"

"Yes, ma'am," Dee says, completely ignited by the thrill of a challenge. The girl is always two feet into every experience, no hesitation. Simply fearless. Jealousy pangs in my chest, unwelcome. I bury it, and after offering Bec a comforting pat on the shoulder, I join Abby at the back of the boat, her phone held high catching a few pictures of Dee in action.

Dee settles into a rhythm—lift, dip, reel, lift, dip, reel—Taylor coaching her through it.

"Don't give it any slack," Taylor yells as she reaches over the side of the boat with a large hook.

Taylor's muscles flex as she heaves a massive fish with a long, sharp bill onto the deck of the boat, where it begins to thrash around wildly. "Beautiful sailfish. Lively too," she yells, gripping the fucking nose-sword this thing was built with in one hand and grabbing a club out of who-the-fuck-knows-where and then whacking it repeatedly until it finally goes still.

Abby and I both shout in shock, gripping each other's forearms, while Evie's face drops in shock, jaw hanging open.

"Jesus Christ," Carissa murmurs.

Dee's eyes are wide as she watches, hands still gripping the fishing rod tightly. "Brutal, Taylor."

"Holy shit, we're taking fish off the wedding menu," Bec says right before she loses her stomach. Carissa rubs her back while Evie closes her eyes and bites her lips as they press together. "On second thought," Bec says, wiping her mouth with the back of her hand, elbows braced on her knees as she hunches over *The Bucket*. "I'm going vegan. Immediately."

CHAPTER THIRTY-NINE

Dom

"They seriously don't have any bigger chairs?" Jake murmurs, clearly annoyed. He shifts in his miniature chair trying to get comfortable, his knees practically in his chest.

"Something I've learned as a dad will apply to you when you're on uncle duty too. You don't get to be comfortable anymore. Take a seat on the couch? The kid's crawling toward the lamp cord and you're on your feet again. You sit on the floor next to your kid, and they're body slamming you like it's a wrestling match and they're the rookie with something to prove. Close your eyes at night? Instant wake-up call for tiny ears."

"I just don't see why the library can't have more adult-sized chairs, for fuck's sake."

"*Watch your mouth*, man. You're going get us kicked out of story time if these kids start dropping f-bombs because of you," I hiss back at him.

"Shit, sorry. *Shit*," Jake says again, slapping his hand across his mouth, unable to control the profanity word vomit from escaping.

Luca's tottering around the children's play area of the library. There's a young woman reading a book to the large group of kids, who are mostly distracted, while a few of the older ones are paying attention and sitting still.

"So, when are we going to talk about it?" Jake asks quietly from our spot along the edge of the story time circle.

"Oh, you mean you didn't invite yourself to our father-son outing for the young reader literature experience? There's bubble time afterward. Brace yourself. It's about to get wild."

Jake shoots a knowing look straight through me, seeing everything with more clarity than he has any right to.

"I take it *later* isn't an acceptable answer?" I ask, running my hand along my jaw.

"You'd be right. So, let's not waste time. Let me get this straight. You have the biggest fight of your relationship, one where the future of your *marriage* is at stake...and you send your wife states away for four nights. What the fuck are you doing, Dom?" At least he remembers to whisper the swear word this time.

"I don't know. I don't *fucking* know," I whisper back. "Bec suggested it, and I'm not exactly in a position to turn down anyone's help or ideas, since I just seem to make things worse."

"Well, are you and Ellie talking or have things gone silent at this point?"

"Of course we're still talking to each other. We talk all day long."

"You mean texting. You're texting her all day long."

"Yeah? So?"

"Let me see your texts."

"Okay?" I say, before reaching into my pocket and handing him my phone.

"Damn, this is bad."

"You haven't even looked," I say, growing frustrated and earning a weird look from the dad across the circle. I wave him off with an apologetic nod.

"If you were having the right kind of conversations, then you wouldn't let me see your phone," he says.

"Are you serious? I'm not sexting my wife when we've just had a huge fight and she's on vacation with her friends. I'm trying to be a supportive husband."

He scrolls through our messages with the same look of concentration as me. We look a lot alike, broad shouldered, both with dark, messy hair and short beards. His normal appearance and disposition tend to be more serious than mine, but that furrowed brow when we're focused is identical. Luca is starting to make the same face. It's cute on that kid. But seeing it on Jake right now has me feeling defensive.

"These are about Luca," he states plainly.

"Yeah, I don't want Ellie to worry. I've been sending updates so she doesn't have to ask for them. And we're video-chatting before bed so she can say good-night to him. She's actually doing really well…" My voice fades when I catch his stare. "What?"

"I just saw at least fifteen pictures of Luca, ten updates on how much he ate, and unfortunately, more texts about poop than I ever wanted to see in my lifetime. Why do you guys text so much about him pooping?"

"If you think this is a lot of shit talk, you should have seen our messages in the first three months. Trust me, man, you got to know your kid's shit, or the whole family system is in jeopardy. If the kid's not pooping right, everyone's unhappy."

"What I mean is, where is the *romance*? Where is the *affection*? Come on, Dom. This is your bread and butter. You're always telling everyone else—your wife, your friends, your family—how to take care of themselves and the relationships that are important to them. What about you?"

"Are you serious, Jake? I'm fine. I'm not the one who…"

"Not the one who *what*? You and Ellie never talk to any of us about what happened or what's going on with you two when we're not hanging out together. You were obviously there the day Luca was born, too, and you still haven't even talked to me about it."

"Because I'm fine." I can hear the annoyance bleeding into my tone, but I'm helpless to stop it.

"If what Ellie went through caused her to feel the way she feels and struggle the way she has been for *over a year*, there is no way that you are *fine*. If you want to be strong for her, I get it, but you don't have to do that in front of me. I'm your brother and you can talk to me. I thought things were getting better, but shit, you have this massive fight with Ellie, send her states away, and act like everything is fine?"

"I have an appointment with my therapist soon, I'll talk to him," I mumble.

"And then?"

"And then it won't be an issue anymore."

"Just like that, huh? It's that's easy." He shakes his head. "You actually think you made this puzzle for Ellie, don't you? So, she can work through her pain, cope with all the messed-up shit she's going through, but you're *not* paying attention. You also did this for *you*. This is your coping mechanism, Dom. You put the focus on everyone else, all the time. Do you ever stop and think that maybe you need to heal too? In a different way than Ellie? Of course. But this?" He holds up my phone. "This is not the relationship you two used to have. And it's not all on Ellie."

He returns my phone, the weight of it dropping into my palm like a brick. *Fuck, is he right?*

My chest rings hollow and my stomach sours. I shift my gaze to Luca, who's crawling through the bubbles now floating through the group of kids. A huge grin on his face, wheezing giggles and screams roaring out of his tiny body. Story time is over.

Looks like the story I was telling myself is over too.

"By the look on your face, I can see we're finally on the same page," Jake says smugly. "Now, we're getting out of these goddamn chairs because my ass is officially numb, and then we're going to figure this out. You in?"

CHAPTER FORTY

Ellie

"I didn't think anyone else was a morning person," Evie says as she pulls the slider shut behind her, joining me on the sundeck. She plops into the chair next to mine and kicks her feet up on the railing in front of us, wiggling her toes in the humid, salty air.

The sun is about to break over the horizon, but the sky is already painted in color, broad sweeping strokes of orange and yellow waking up with the water and waves as they reflect beauty back to one another.

"I'm not," I say, before sipping my coffee. "But after a year and a half of living with an infant who *repels* sleep, I think my body is operating on autopilot. Couldn't sleep any later if I wanted to."

"Maybe tomorrow. I always have a hard time sleeping in new places. Maybe you just need one more night to get used to it here. That's what I'm hoping for anyway."

"Maybe." I smile at her optimism. "But if not, at least this isn't such a bad view to wake up to."

Evie takes a thoughtful sip out of her own mug before nodding in agreement. "Not bad at all. Carissa didn't move an inch when I wormed my way out of our room. I would say I treaded lightly past Dee and Abby's room, but apparently

Dee snores, so I figured any noise I made wouldn't have done much more damage than that."

I bark a laugh. "Oh god, I completely forgot about that. Did anyone give Abby a heads up?"

"Abby volunteered. Said she sleeps with earplugs anyway."

We sit in comfortable silence. I've known Evie for the least amount of time of any of the girls, but she and Bec have gotten close since she's Aiden's younger sister and soon to be Bec's sister-in-law. I'm glad she was able to join us for the weekend.

"Thank you for coming on this trip," I say. "I know it can be a pain to take time away. Bec mentioned your grad program is competitive."

She sighs. "Even more of a reason to get away. I'm grateful for the invite. I don't have many girl friends. It's nice to be included. When I heard what your husband planned for you, and that everyone was pitching in their own ideas, I was dying to be a part of it."

"Yeah, it's really...something," I say, smiling into my mug, both hands around the warm sides, once again reminded how over-the-top my husband is.

"Does it make you uncomfortable?" she asks without judgment, only curiosity. "The attention?"

"No one's asked me that. Sometimes," I respond honestly. "It's weird that everyone knows I've been...struggling. Everyone planned really thoughtful, unique, and meaningful things for us to do together. Since Luca was born, it's been easier to keep things surface level, you know? But with this stuff..."

"It's like you can't hide from it anymore. Can't run from it either. Not with everyone's attention on you," Evie offers gently.

"Exactly," I say, relieved she seems to get it. "It's not that I'm not grateful, but sometimes it's overwhelming."

"What's the hardest part?" she asks, her eyes on the sunrise.

It's easier to talk like this. Like she's asking the sun questions and I'm answering the ocean. Like I'm writing in a diary, and Evie's just giving me the prompts, letting me air it all out.

"How selfish I feel. It feels like I should be giving my everything, all the time, to everyone else. The fact that all these little moments are being planned for me. It feels wrong."

"We don't know each other well, Ellie, but from an outsider's perspective, I think you should know you're anything but selfish. My parents fall on both ends of that spectrum," she looks at me with a genuinely warm smile, "and you are so much like my mom. Resilient with a gentle, but unmistakable, strength." Her eyes soften with understanding. "You're a really good mom, Ellie. Your friends and your family want you to see what they see. It isn't selfish to be shown how appreciated you are. How loved you are. It's okay to open your heart and receive it."

"For not having had many girl friends, you sure are good at it," I say, emotion stuck in the base of my throat.

"It's easy with the right group of people, I guess."

We cheers to that before we're interrupted by the slider opening again.

Dee pulls the door wide with a loud grunt. "Jesus Christ, why is this so heavy? Morning, dandelions. Carissa is getting some eggs and bacon going. What do you want on your toast? Abby says we'll need our strength for what she's got planned, so we're carb loading."

These girls make it easy to feel loved.

While we sit around the large dining table, the sun rising just outside the large windows, I take what Evie says and wrap it around the broken voice in my gut telling me to feel guilty for needing this, choosing to receive all the good things instead.

***

"Are you still upset? It was not that bad," Dee says, exasperated.

"We watched a fish *murder*," Bec whines.

"What did you think *fishing* was?!" Dee retorts.

"I didn't think we were beating them to death on the boat!"

"Look, I think we should all be grateful we learned something new," Dee says with conviction. "Besides, we got a bunch of fresh fish mailed home for us. *Plus*, we broke a gender stereotype. Six badass bitches, no men, on a fishing adventure? We are hunters. I'm proud of that, Bec Miller. Don't try to take that away from me."

Bec gives up on Dee, who is clearly unfazed by her emotional distress, and pleads with Abby. "Please tell me whatever we're doing today does not involve beating a fish to death."

"I'm with Bec on this. Sorry, Dee. We're going indoors for this next one," Abby says as she turns off the road into a small parking lot.

The building is cute and beachy, otherwise nondescript, except...

"Abby, why are all the windows covered?" Evie asks.

"Time to stretch, ladies. We're pole dancing today," she says, sliding the minivan door open with a heave.

"Oh, fuck yes," Dee cheers, following Abby, the rest of us trailing behind, into the building.

The room is large with mostly open space. Mirrors cover every wall, only interrupted by the occasional window, each covered with bright and bold fabric curtains with sparkly tulle overlays.

"Good morning," a cheerful voice rings out, before a woman joins us from behind a curtain separating the large space from a room in the back. "Welcome to Christy's Beaches. I'm Tessa, and one of you must be Abby?"

"That's me," Abby says with a wave.

"Nice to meet you. Which one of your friends are we celebrating?" Tessa asks.

"This is Ellie," Abby says, sidling up next to me with an arm around my shoulder.

"What are we celebrating?" I ask.

"You getting your spark back. What better way than shaking your ass with your girls to 2000s hits. You up for this?" Abby asks, excitement radiating off her.

I nod. "I'm in." I might not be very coordinated, but I do love to dance. Abby's a great listener, so I'm not surprised she's picked up on that in the short time we've been friends since she started working with Bec at the dog training center last year.

"Perfect, I'll be your instructor today. Let's get started," Tessa says, clapping her hands together.

Forty-five minutes later, we're sweaty and laughing having fumbled our way through learning a few moves on the pole, nothing too difficult. We mostly learned how to move around the pole, attempting to look seductive while we did so. We eventually tried a small spin move, staying safely low to the ground.

It's way fucking harder than it looks.

I've been to several strip clubs in my life, and the dancers always made this look easy, even when in platform stilettos. I'm barefoot and can barely keep from tripping over my feet and crashing into the pole. I narrowly avoid twisting my arms up trying to get the moves done with the right hand in the right place.

Tessa taught us a simple routine, starting on the floor and working our way around the poles. We run through the steps for the first time all together with music, and Dee screams.

"Holy shit, I knew we'd be hot. Fucking look at us. Okay, new plan. We all quit our boring ass jobs and open a burlesque club—we'll be co-owners and headliners."

"This is *not* hot," Carissa calls out over the music as she fumbles the steps. "I don't know what the hell I'm doing."

"Close your eyes, Bambi, and feel the music. It's all about confidence. You'll find your footing," Dee says, going completely off-script and shaking her ass how she wants, eyes closed and arms in the air.

"I'm with Carissa, my hands are too sweaty for this, I'm going to fall on my face," Evie says as she clings to the pole with one hand, wiping the other on her leggings, I'm assuming to give her a better grip.

"*Ugh*, you guys," Dee whines. "When we start performing together, I'm not going to accept this kind of negativity backstage. Now *there* we go. Look at Ellie and do what she's doing."

"I'm not doing anything," I say, cheeks turning red at being called out.

"Uh, wrong, you're showing us exactly how you made that cute kid of yours. Hot damn, Dom isn't going to be ready for the new moves you're bringing home," Abby says, laughing as she drops to her knees and then body rolls back up.

"Someone warn the hubby," Bec yells as she does a shimmy.

I roll my eyes but can't contain my smile because...this is honestly one of the most fun things I've ever done. I might need to find a studio that offers these kinds of classes at home. Or, you know, take Dee up on her offer, quit working in marketing, and become a burlesque headliner. Same thing.

CHAPTER FORTY-ONE

Ellie

After we finish the dance class Abby organized, Carissa takes over with her plans for the group.

She drives us to several incredible local souvenir shops, giving each of us a scavenger hunt card with general prompts that allow us to all be creative and find things we want to bring home, both for us and our families. My favorite finds are a green and brown plush turtle for Luca, who is officially entering his animal obsession phase, the ornament I plan to use next year for our new tradition—thanks to Aiden—and, of course, a puzzle for Dom. The flat, glass Christmas ornament features three sandy crabs walking down the beach. And the puzzle is of a gorgeous beach sunrise over the water.

I haven't missed a sunrise yet on this trip, and I'm sure I'll catch tomorrow's, too, since I seem to be physically incapable of sleeping in anymore. I spend that time mostly thinking of Luca and Dom. Reflecting on Luca's life until now and dreaming of what his future holds. The kinds of interests and personality he'll develop—every day he shows us more and more.

And with Dom...I think of all the cruel things I said in anger, about him and our marriage, and all the things I want to say to make it right. I've thought a lot about what he's said about there still being pieces of myself buried inside. I'm getting closer to finding them, but I still have a lot of work to do.

I need to make a lot of changes before I can build the life I want for myself and my family. I just never imagined how much of that work needed to be done in my own head.

I'm already dreaming of coming back here someday with my husband and my son, sharing this peaceful retreat with them too. I know they'd love it. Luca, so like his dad, would light up with joy and enthusiasm with every new experience. It's been weird being around two effortlessly happy people when I feel the way I've felt. But they make me want to find that again.

We end the day with dinner at one of the more popular seafood spots along the water, much to Bec's chagrin, who orders the *one* vegan option on the menu. Guess her commitment to *no fish* on the menu is going to last a while.

I miss my family, but some time away has helped me reconnect with the more carefree woman I used to be. Today, I'm just someone on vacation with her friends, enjoying the sun, sand, and surf.

After dinner, we return to the beach house for a quiet night. The six of us share a few drinks on the deck while we watch the sunset. We rank who out of the six of us we think can make the most as an entertainer based on the dancing skills we learned none of us have. Carissa makes several pitchers of Moscow mules, and we all inhale the delicious red velvet cake Evie bakes.

The girl can bake. *Maybe she can make Luca's second birthday cake.*

My heart pangs with a stroke of grief. That thought alone is more planning than I did for his first birthday. After the uncomfortable edge of emotion softens, relief and a bit of hope take its place. If I'm already thinking of his next birthday party, maybe it *will* get easier with time.

"Are you having fun?" Bec asks as she falls beside me onto our shared bed. I roll onto my side, trying to see her in the dark, folding my hands under my cheek. I can only see the outline of where she's lying next to me, adjusting the covers.

"I'm better today. The first night away from Luca felt a little like torture. I woke up at three in the morning, panicked because I couldn't hear the white noise from his baby monitor."

"You should have woken me."

"Don't be silly. It was nothing."

"Ellie, please don't do that. It's not *nothing*. Your first night away from Luca is a big deal. Doing it on your first long weekend away from home is *huge*. Thank you for giving us this time."

"Of course, I trust you."

"You're my best friend, but sometimes I don't know if what I say helps or hurts, so if this is the wrong thing to say, please tell me. I want to remind you that Luca is safe. Dom will take care of him, but if at any point you want to leave, I will get your ass to an airport so fast you won't even have your shoes on before we pull up and that boy is in your arms. I swear it."

I giggle at the image. Yeah, I could see it.

"I'm okay. Dom and I hung up right before you finished up in the shower. He showed me the monitor and Luca is sleeping like a dream, thank god. It'd be hard to be away if I knew Luca was struggling. But he's doing really well."

"Then why are you crying, babe?"

I sniffle. I hadn't even realized I'd started.

"I don't know. I want them both to do well while I'm gone, but it also makes me feel like I'm not needed."

"Ellie, I have no doubt when you get back home, Dom will make sure you know just how needed you are."

After a beat, we both break out into a fit of laughter. I know my eccentric, over-the-top husband is doing great, but parenting is a huge job. I'm sure Bec's right, he'll welcome me home with *enthusiasm*, wanting a break and a minute to himself.

"Is any of this helping?" she asks, the hope evident in her tone. For a moment, I imagine what it's like for Bec to watch me go through this. We've been friends since we were in preschool. I never want to see her hurting. What is it like for her to see me struggle like this? Does she wish I'd just get over it?

No, Bec would never expect that from me. I have to stop trying to bury everything. I have to let her in. I have to let them all in. Dom, Bec, my family, my friends.

I can't carry this anymore, but I don't know how to put it down.

"I think it's helping," I say. "Motherhood…isn't what I expected. I don't think I'll ever be the person I was before, which makes me sad. It makes me feel like this huge piece of me is missing, but lately, Dom's game—and everyone's contributions to it—has made me feel like maybe there's more of that version of me buried inside somewhere. I feel like I'm finding pieces of the me I used to be, and she's coming back to life a little bit at a time."

"I'm so relieved. How is being a parent different than you expected?"

"You want kids of your own, Bec. I don't want you to think that my experience will be the same as yours someday." *I don't want to scare you.*

"*Please,* don't worry about me. I want to know." Bec's hand finds mine in the dark and gives me a reassuring squeeze.

"I feel like a failure every single minute of every single day," I spill into the silent space between us.

Once the worst is out there, I can't seem to stop.

"I thought parenting would come naturally. When it didn't, I figured soon enough, it would. But while I wait for this magical maternal instinct to kick in, I'm left waiting, lacking confidence in every small step I take. There's so much pressure to do everything the right way, and everyone has an opinion on what the right way is. How am I supposed to know what to do when there are a thousand voices screaming about every single decision I have to make? They never shut up and they never agree and I'm caught in the middle of information overload with zero confidence in myself.

"Engage with your child and keep his mind busy, but also let him be bored and learn how to play on his own. Get this toy to help with his fine motor skills, but don't have too many toys—that'll overwhelm him. Make sure you're still contributing to the household income, but don't let someone else raise your kid. Don't hover, but also keep him safe at all times because how could you let that happen? Sleep train your baby, but don't make them cry it out. Fed is best, but don't you want to make all-organic homemade baby food? Sacrifice your body for your baby, but make sure you bounce back and don't look like you had a baby at all. Keep in touch with your friends, but don't abandon your child and your partner. Make time for self-care, but make sure the dishes are done. Sleep when the baby sleeps, but don't forget to fold the laundry. Slow down and involve your child in your daily routine, but also make sure your house isn't a mess. Create magical moments, take tons of pictures and videos, but also slow down and live in the present. Make sure you get your kid to all their appointments, but don't make a scene in the waiting room when your kid has a goddamn diaper blowout up his back. Breastfeed, but not in public, for fuck's sake. Keep your kid safe, but don't smother them because they need to learn to be fearless and independent. Help them find their confidence and learn to make decisions for themselves even if you can't do those things yourself. Make sure everyone in your family has what they need, but don't let your sex life suffer or your partner will get bored. And don't complain for a second because you should be grateful for it all because one day you'll wish you savored every minute of this time when your kids are grown and on their own and leave you behind."

I'm so fucking tired.

"Jesus Christ," Bec mutters. "That's a nightmare."

"On top of it all, I'm terrified that all Luca will remember about this time is how stressed out I am. How I can never relax and have fun. I'm caught between nightmares in the past and fear of the future. Somedays feel like a series of one misstep after another."

"I can't pretend to understand what you went through, Ellie, or what it feels like now, but I need you to know that no one is expecting you to be perfect at everything. That's why we have each other. To lean on, to talk things through, and to figure it out together. You'll always have me. I'm not the best at diaper changes, given my track record, but I'll do whatever you need, anytime, Momma.

"From where I'm standing, you're not giving yourself nearly enough credit. I wish you could see what I see. I see a mom who loves her son with her entire heart. I see a mom who plays and laughs, who does her best and learns from her mistakes."

"Thank you," I whisper, tears sinking into my pillow. "It helps to hear that the war I'm fighting in my own mind isn't what you see."

"You don't have to fight this battle alone, Ellie. You have me. You have Dom. You have so many people who will show up for you, no questions asked. We only want you to be happy."

"I want to be happy too," I choke on the words. It's a relief saying the words out loud. "I mean, I am happy, but I'm also so angry. It feels like so many moments of joy have been stolen or ruined by my anxiety."

"Does it feel better doing this? Giving it a voice and letting it go. Letting me carry it with you for a while?"

"Yes." I sigh, noting how much lighter the burden feels. "It's like I can breathe again."

"I've never wanted to push you to talk about it, but I think *you* need to push yourself," Bec says with conviction. "Dom is asking us to open doors for you. We're inviting you in, asking you to share this with us. We want to help, but you need to walk through those doors on your own. We're waiting for you when you're ready."

Chapter Forty-Two

Ellie

I walk along the beach early the next morning, having tiptoed outside, flip-flops in hand, to avoid waking the girls.

When I opened my eyes, there was an immediate pull to come here. To steal this peaceful, secret moment with my toes sinking in the sand, those first morning rays warming my skin, and the warm, salty air filling my lungs.

I take a step into the shoreline. Sand shifts beneath my feet as the waves ebb and flow against my calves and ankles, each time my foundation sinks a little lower, feeling for a moment more unstable, then settling into a stronger, more rooted footing. One after another, the surging waves ripple against my legs, wetting my skin at various heights, leaving my skin exposed and slightly chilled.

The sounding crash of waves farther from the coast is forceful, an echoing reminder of the ocean's strength. For a moment I'm connected to the sand, the ocean, and the breeze.

The burdening weight of everything on my mind comes crashing down so suddenly, I can't fight it. I don't even try, too tired to fight this any longer. I choose to finally let myself feel...I let myself feel it all.

I envision the waves barreling toward me, demolishing the walls I've built around my mind and heart. I let the waves tear them down and relish in the release of everything I've buried, everything I've hidden away from everyone, even myself.

Fear, suffocating and sharp, comes crashing in waves as violent as the ones sounding in the distance, and it pulls me under. I'm drowning in the sudden onslaught of panic; it fills my mouth, my lungs, my soul.

All I can see is the nurse's face. All I can hear is my own agony as I scream, wailing in pain. My last thoughts before they put me under race through my mind, plaguing me with terror: *Is this real? Will I see my family again? Will I ever hold my baby? Will we survive this together?*

My throat constricts and a pit sinks into my stomach, hard and heavy. Every muscle in my body pulls taut; the drive to fight or take flight is overtaken by the instinct to freeze.

I think over and over and over, *I don't want to die. Let us live. Keep us safe. I don't want to die. Let us live. Keep us safe.*

Who I'm talking to, I'm not sure. Religion has never felt like home for me, but I send out the thoughts anyway, into the void of darkness as the anesthesia takes me under into nothingness.

Tears continue rolling silently down my face, the droplets falling from my chin, gently pattering against my chest as they wet my shirt.

Memories flash through my mind again, and again, some more distinct while others remain blurry and unclear. I relieve every brutal moment of birth. Tiny, insignificant details I've buried deep inside come raging to the forefront of my mind. The way the iodine felt on my stomach when they applied it to my skin. The shape of the anesthesiologist's glasses as he stared into my eyes and counted down from ten. The inflection in the voice of the person calling out the baby's—*my baby's*—heart rate.

Eventually the tears stop, my shoulders droop with exhaustion, and my breath heaves out of my chest in a weighted huff.

My body is heavy, but my mind is weightless. My heels sink lower in the sand, but my thoughts are flying, freer than they've been since that day.

That horrible, beautiful, ruined, perfect day.

I wiggle my fingers and they brush my thighs. I sway against the pulse of the water drumming into my legs.

My thoughts begin to shift, melting into a new stream of consciousness, a new narrative I want to believe: I could never be defined by any one moment in my life. I have to believe that I am more than that.

I'm here. We're here.

I'm safe. We're safe.

Maybe the rest of my story will surprise me and hold the joy I wished for with the ease I always imagined I'd feel. The joy that just a few months ago felt out of reach forever.

Maybe the thorns and thistles that barb around my hurting heart have helped root me deeper into who I am.

Trauma buried its thorns so deeply within me, trying to take everything I had. It almost did, but it left me with something precious as well. The freedom to live my life without holding back, because I almost didn't get to see this moment, and neither did my son. Nothing can hurt me as much as when I believed we'd miss out on a life together as a family.

The expectations that stifle me, the judgments that shame me, the comments that rattle me. None of them mean anything. I don't have space to give a shit about any of it.

I didn't ease into motherhood with the beautiful birth I'd envisioned, like the stories people love to share or the ones they show in the media.

I crashed into motherhood at breakneck speed, stumbling out of the wreckage when someone threw a newborn baby into my arms and said *good luck*.

Every day, I'm living and learning through a new kind of failure, not sure when I'll stabilize. Not sure when I'll become the mom I always wanted to be.

That mom would have been great. But maybe...I'm a pretty great mom, too, just as I am, scars and flaws and all. Hurt, but healing.

CHAPTER FORTY-THREE

Dom

"We're going to figure out how to fix my marriage...at the zoo?" I ask as Dylan hands wristbands to the rest of the guys at the ticket booth.

Jake, Chris, Dylan, and Aiden crowd around me and the stroller, where Luca is already clapping, pointing, and making elephant sounds as he points to the exhibit signs.

"No, we're not talking about how you're going to fix anything. We're just going to talk," Jake says, as if it's obvious.

"*Oookay,*" I reply. Jake planned this guys' day after our visit to the library. It's nice to have an extra set of hands around to help with Luca while Ellie's away, so I'm not going to fight them on this.

I pride myself on being a hands-on dad, but it's so much easier to parent as a team. It's all on me right now, minus the visits from friends and family.

Dylan pulls up a map of the zoo on his phone as we walk through the main entrance.

"Have you never been to the zoo?" I ask.

"Uh, no?" Dylan says. "I'm almost thirty, why would I come to the zoo?"

"Dude, you're missing out. You're looking at members over here," I say, pointing a thumb between Luca and me. "One of the gorillas had a baby eight months ago. It's awesome. Ditch the map. Luca and I are your tour guides today."

The guys take turns pushing the stroller, offering Luca snacks, even holding Luca's hand as he teeters from one exhibit to the next. Today is another one of those memories I don't want to forget. I pester the guys into taking one of the group photos the zoo offers and buy the overpriced picture with a rainforest-themed frame.

We talk as we make our way through the zoo. Aiden and I fill the rest of the group in on what the girls have been up to while on their trip. We catch up on Aiden's last game and talk about his schedule for the rest of the season. Jake and Chris share their plans with us for their upcoming two-week trip to Europe, and Dylan refuses to update us on his single guy life, mumbling something about how there's not much to talk about. He ties his longer-than-usual, dark blond hair in a knot at the base of his neck as he denies going on any recent dates.

"You want to talk to someone who's got a good dating life, seems like you've come to the right place," Dylan says, before letting out a long whistle.

"Oh my god, can they—can they show that here?" Chris whispers with an edge of panic in his voice. "Oh my god, the baby. Close your eyes, Luca!" he shouts, running over to stand in front of the stroller. "Shield him, Jake. Shield the youth's eyes."

I turn and see two very enthusiastic gorillas going *at it*.

"Well, how do you think they got the baby?" I ask.

"Jesus Christ, don't they have a privacy curtain or something?" Jake asks.

"Huh, just a couple of exhibitionists. Who knew?" Dylan smirks and shrugs, stuffing both hands in his pockets, his sense of humor returning.

"I think it's making eye contact with me. Let's get out of here," Aiden says, before power walking to the next exhibit, looking over his shoulder to make sure he's not still being watched.

"Maybe he wants an autograph," Dylan taunts.

The whole thing is so ridiculous, I can't stop laughing. Thankfully, Luca leaves the exhibit with no idea what happened, too distracted by the toys attached to the stroller buckle.

I guess I have been feeling stressed lately. It's nice to have this time with the guys without the pressure of talking—

"Okay, ready to talk?" Jake presses.

Fucking hell.

"I thought we weren't doing that today," I grumble in reply.

"I said we weren't talking about how to fix your marriage, and we're not. We're talking about you."

I give him a look. "I don't even know what that means."

"It means that you have spent months trying to decode some mystery quick fix to legitimate marital and mental health struggles. I think we can agree, there is no such thing as a quick fix. So instead, we're going to listen while you get out whatever is stuck in that brain of yours."

"Is it really all I talk about?"

"Uh, were you *not* aware of this?" Aiden asks. "How's work? You've barely mentioned how things have been going this school year."

"You're normally excited about summer break by this time," Chris says. "Are you and Ellie planning a family trip or anything?"

"Have you found any new bands lately? I keep sending you recs and you don't respond," Dylan says.

"Did you see Mom and Dad placed first in the local novice ballroom competition they entered? They're practically begging us to take a class with them," Jake says. "Which you would know if you'd participate in our group chat."

"Okay." I put my hands up in surrender. "Okay." I chuckle. "I guess it was easy to get wrapped up in the puzzle. Point taken."

"Good," Jake says. "Because we won't ever be able to get to the big stuff, little brother, if you aren't even talking to us about the normal stuff."

"When did you get smart?" I ask, ruffling his hair.

He shoves my shoulder, distancing himself and fixing his hair. "Please, I took all the smart genes for myself before you came along. Everyone knows that."

His answering grin is oddly comforting, even though this entire thing is awkward for me.

Time and energy are both in short supply in our house. It's easier for me, and I think Ellie, too, to focus on the next thing that *needs* to be done, forgetting that there's more to life than what fits perfectly into a schedule.

It's also easier for us to focus on what other people need. Her trying to be the perfect wife and mom, me trying to be the perfect husband and father, neither of us ever feeling like we're succeeding. Always falling short of this impossible standard we've seemingly set for ourselves.

So, I do what my brother and friends ask. I talk about…myself.

I talk about how my students this year are some of my brightest yet. How they all show genuine interest in history and its impact on today's world. I leave work feeling inspired because of them and their refreshing and insightful perspective.

I explain that Ellie and I decided to skip out on planning a trip this summer because we want to save up and take Luca to Disney World next year when he's a little older. I've already started researching because planning a trip there feels like a test for a parent on how to maximize your time and budget and still see all your kid's favorite characters. But you can bet your ass we'll have matching shirts and get Mickey ears.

I apologize to Dylan, explaining that I haven't sent him any new bands, because I'm hyperfixated on the one he sent me three months ago.

I confirm that I saw the picture of Mom and Dad holding their trophy but forgot to respond—like an asshole. I can't remember exactly what happened, but I want to say I was getting Luca into his car seat when I got the text, and then I checked it before we pulled out the parking lot. But a nonmoving car and a kid in a car seat is a dangerous recipe for a tantrum, so I put my phone down quickly, forgetting to send my parents a *congratulations* text completely, and therefore never accepted or declined their invite to try out a dance class. I promise him that I will.

But the end of our trip, I do feel better. A little guilty hogging everyone's time and attention with them focused solely on me, but mostly a sense of gratitude.

Maybe I can learn a thing or two from Ellie. She's been open to trying things differently. It's time I do the same.

CHAPTER FORTY-FOUR

Ellie

I tug at the hem of my swim cover that keeps riding up over my ass while we carry our beach gear over the hot sand. I probably should have run to the store to grab a new one, since this is a pre-baby body purchase, but when you have short notice like I did for this weekend, you have to prioritize, and a new swim cover didn't make the cut.

It's a gorgeous day. Hot as fuck? Sure, I'm already sweating, but still, gorgeous.

"Holy shit, Dee. What did you pack in Johnny's cooler?" Bec grunts, using both arms to hold the cooler at her side, heaving it along and letting it drop in the sand with an *umph*. "This feels like a good spot to set up, plus it's as far as I can possibly carry this thing. If you all want to move closer to the water, I'm going to need a hand with this."

"*Jonah's* cooler," Dee corrects.

Bec rolls her eyes, squats, and opens the cooler. She freezes, then stares up at Dee in amused disbelief. "You brought an entire cooler of *frozen margaritas* to the beach? I assumed you'd throw in some seltzers, maybe a few wine coolers and beers, and call it a day.

"Hey, you put me in charge of the drinks. You didn't specify how to do my job. Now you have to deal with the consequences of that decision." She elbows Carissa and nods her head at her. "Only good consequences, I swear."

"I thought I heard the blender this morning," Evie says. "Are those limes? And salt? Nice touch." She bumps Dee's hip with her own and pulls the plastic cups out of the beach bag on her shoulder. "I'll play bartender. Who wants one?"

We spend about twenty minutes perfecting our beach setup for the day. Towels, sunblock, *Jonah's* cooler of frozen lemon-lime deliciousness, Abby's mini Bluetooth speaker, and umbrellas and chairs set up in a U shape so we can all chat.

This might be my favorite part of the weekend yet.

There's something magical that happens on the beach. The sound, the smell, the sunshine, and the breeze feel restorative. I lean back on my elbows, close my eyes, let my head drop back between my shoulders, and take it all in. The call of seagulls ringing out as the waves crash in the distance, the weight of humid air sticking to my skin, the smell of salt, sunblock, and now limes—thanks to Dee.

"Beach day was the perfect pick, Bec," I say, turning to look at my best friend while the rest of the girls continue in a heated debate about the best music video ever made.

"I'm glad to hear it, Momma. I thought we'd want to take advantage at least once since we're only here a few days."

"Dom told me this was your idea," I say. "This whole trip, I mean. Using your pieces to plan things here instead of your original ideas for back home."

Her carefree look morphs into one of empathy with a hint of concern she can't hide from me.

"He came by after you two argued. I know that day was really shitty, and while I know running away from problems is never the answer, I also never had a bad time on the beach with a margarita, either, so I figure the pros outweigh the cons." We both laugh at that.

"Did he seem okay? After our fight?" I ask, guilt gnawing at my stomach. But I need to know.

"He was shaken up, mostly worried about you. He was also worried he might be making things worse by having you participate in his 'shenanigans.'"

"His anxiety is worse than mine sometimes," I say with a shake of my head. "But damn if I don't love the guy more for his shenanigans."

"I know you do. I told him we should keep going, and that's when I called in the girls. You're an incredible mom, Ellie. Everyone can see that. But we wanted you to let your hair down a little this weekend. Thank you for trusting us."

"I never doubted any of you."

"Except on day one, right? The fish murder was a bit much," she jokes.

"Bec, you are going to need to debrief with a professional about this."

"I think you're right. Oh god, things are escalating," Bec says, nodding over to the girls, where Dee has stripped down to her bikini and is acting out Britney Spears's "Stronger" video on a beach chair.

"Oh shit," I say, unable to take my eyes off her, and struggling to hold in my laughter. "She's going to wipe out and eat shit—" but before I can finish the thought, Dee takes a bad step, her foot too close to the hinge of the reclining chair and the entire thing folds in on her as she drops on her ass, legs tangled between the teal blue fabric and metal bars.

She flops onto her belly, rotating the chair with her, and she kicks her legs dreamily behind her, not missing a beat and continuing her lip-syncing of the song until it finally wraps.

We clap and whistle as she untangles herself from the chair, brushes off the sand, and takes a dramatic bow like she's a principal actor on Broadway.

"The performance of a lifetime, babe," I say, tapping my cup against hers as she takes her seat on my other side. Evie starts setting up for her song.

"Spank you very much," she sings in reply. "Hey, Evie. Don't start without me. I need to take a quick dip to cool off, but I don't want to miss a second of the show!" she calls out as she makes her way to the water.

"I could use a minute to cool off too," Evie says. "You guys in?"

"Yes, please. I'm melting," Carissa says. Bec joins them, too, as they head to the water.

Abby packs the speaker in her bag to avoid it getting damaged before she takes off after the girls. Her eyes catch on me as I take out my book under the umbrella.

"You're not coming? Aren't you hot?"

"Scorching, actually," I say.

"Same. Come on then, we need this before Dee starts to recruit us to be her backup dancers."

"God, no. You'd have to drag my ass home. My body would collapse from exhaustion if I tried to do that in the sand," I joke.

"What is it?" Abby presses, adjusting the scarf she's wearing as a headband, her braids wrapped in a bun on her head.

I tug nervously on my cover-up. The girls ditched theirs almost as soon as we sat down, if they even wore one to begin with.

"I haven't exactly been eager to wear a swimsuit since I had Luca. I wasn't expecting an impromptu beach trip with a few days' notice or anything, so I'm not exactly *beach-ready*." I wince, realizing how insecure I sound and hating it.

"My sister went through the same thing when she had my niece six months before our family vacation. Do you know what I told her?" Abby asks. "That her boobs would steal the show, and wouldn't you know it, four guys asked for her number that day...in front of her husband...with a six-month-old on her hip."

"Ah, but she had *six-month* postpartum boobs. Much different from *year-and-half* postpartum boobs. A lot less lift, unfortunately. The ladies have gotten the message that the party is over and they have retired to their new home...way closer to sea level."

"Ellie," Abby says with a laugh. "Okay, I'm not an expert in having a healthy relationship with my body, but I do think that this could be good for you. You don't have to take the cover-up off if you don't want to. Those things are made to get wet anyway. But...I don't want you to wake up someday and feel like kicking your perfectly hot, younger self in the ass for not getting in the ocean with your friends, all because of one small voice convincing you you're not worthy of having the experience. Your body doesn't exist to stay this perfectly preserved thing. We're supposed to live in them. That means a little change, a little wear and tear, and a lot of love."

She steps toward me and reaches her hand for mine. "Don't punish yourself because of some lie your brain is trying to sell you. You in?"

I smile and grab her hand as she helps me stand. Before I can think too much about it, I take off my cover-up and replay Abby's words in my mind, letting them bolster the little self-esteem I have left in this mom bod of mine.

Should I be proud of it for getting me and Luca here safely? I am.

Do I still struggle with the changes? Of course.

But Abby's right. The thought of living with regret scares me more than what others might think or say about my stretch marks, extra rolls, and jiggles. I don't want to be scared of living in this body. Someday, I'd like to feel proud of it.

"I'm in," I say, and we link arms, eventually joining the girls in the waves, gratitude rolling in steady along with the tide.

CHAPTER FORTY-FIVE

Ellie

"I might have gone a little overboard," Evie warns us as we join her in the living room of the beach house.

I clap my hands together at the sight before me and rock onto my tiptoes. "Oh my god, Eves," I yell. "Where did you find all this?"

I have no clue how Evie fit everything in her bag, but this is like a gold mine of nostalgia. Anything I'd have at a sleepover growing up is here. Disposable cameras, a copy of *Goosebumps*, glow sticks, a Tamagotchi, matching tie-dye shirts, Pop Rocks, neon nail polish, toe socks, and a stack of magazines. I hold up an old toy they used to advertise as an easy way to twist hair...they *lied*.

"I can't believe they still make those things," Evie says. "I always wanted one growing up, but my mom said it'd rip out my hair. Then Aiden teased me and said he'd help me with it, and I didn't trust the smart-ass little shit, so I never asked my mom again."

"Ugh, he's the worst," Bec says with a smirk.

"Ugh, right?" Evie laughs.

"I hate to ruin your dream, but yeah, these will ruin your hair," I say. "It took my mom hours to detangle mine when I tried to make cute twists with gemstones in middle school."

Evie plops onto the ground, her back to me, crisscrossing her legs. "Do the honors, Ellie. I won't live forever. It's worth the risk."

An hour later, we've walked down memory lane, filled up on popcorn and candy, and spoiled the shit out of one very happy Tamagotchi. Dom probably doesn't even realize how his selflessness impacts more people than he intended to. He did this for me, but when Evie explains that she never had a sleepover growing up, and watching her recreate what she always wanted, it's clear that this means something to my friends too.

Dominic's thoughtfulness can only take me so far.

It's time I put in the effort too.

I wait and enjoy the activities Evie planned for the night. We play Never Have I Ever and cut up magazines to make up our vision boards of what our "grown-up" lives will look like and who our "dream partners" will be. If there's one thing I learned growing up having sleepovers with Bec, it's the inevitable heart-to-heart at the end of the night. No sleepover is ever complete without it.

When it's my turn, I finally share my story.

***

"Holy shit, Ellie. That is..." For the first time in years of friendship, maybe the first time ever in her life, Dee is speechless.

I attempt to calm my racing heart after finally telling the girls what happened when Luca was born. It's the first time I've told anyone other than Dom what happened, from beginning to end. I couldn't look at any of them; I kept my eyes closed or stared at my hands, folded tightly in my lap.

When I finally gather the courage to look up, I catch Dee's gaze first. She looks at me, her expression...heartbroken? Tears collect at the corners of her eyes. She just sniffs quietly and takes my hand in hers, squeezing tightly.

Sometimes, there aren't words.

"I know. It's a lot. It's been easier to not talk about it. To pretend the worst details were things I made up in my mind. Giving voice to them felt like it would make them real. I didn't want to relieve it all, but clearly holding it in isn't working either."

"I'm really glad you told us," Abby says, her voice kind and reassuring. "You shouldn't have to carry this alone."

"Dom knows everything. I came out of the anesthesia and couldn't hold anything in, it all came spilling out before I was lucid. I'm not sure I would have told him otherwise. He looked traumatized, too, but he still listened to me and held me. Immediately afterward, he asked the nurse for a therapy referral. She told him it was 'just the baby blues.'"

I didn't want to share the story with anyone else after that.

"Are you fucking kidding me?" Carissa asks, rage rolling off her like I've never seen from her before.

"Yeah." I laugh, because, you know…trauma. "I've never seen him so upset. He requested someone new for the rest of the shift, and the next nurse gave us the information we needed. She was amazing."

I duck my head, shame threatening to swallow me whole. "It's felt like that ever since. Other people picking up the pieces. I'm so mad at myself for not being able to do this on my own. It feels like I'm this heavy anchor weighing everyone down."

"No one has ever seen you that way. Parents were *never* meant to do this alone. Besides, what you went through was terrifying. It's not like you could prepare for something like that," Evie says.

"But shouldn't I have been able to do *something*? Every minute of that day has looped in my mind over and over, and every time I wonder, *what if*? What if I did this or that differently? Would it still have happened the way it did? Did the choices I made put us into that situation?"

"Ellie, there isn't always a reason. Sometimes things just go wrong, and there isn't anything anyone could have done to prevent it." Carissa gives me a thoughtful look before asking, "What would happen if you decided to forgive yourself? If you just said, hey, I did the best I could then and I'm doing the best I can now."

"Then I'd be admitting to myself that *nothing* is in my control."

If I can't control everything, then I can't control anything. I know that sounds crazy, but it's just how it feels. How can I expect to function with so much uncertainty?

"Isn't that life?" Bec asks.

"I guess," I say with a shrug. "All I want is to watch my son grow up and see the joy the world can bring him. But the way our lives together started tainted my view of it all. It feels like I can't ever relax, can't ever enjoy anything, because the worst is lurking around the corner, waiting for me to get comfortable before swooping in and stealing everything I ever wanted."

People love to quote statistics to new parents. *The chance of that happening is so low. That rarely happens, don't worry.* But statistics no longer make me feel comfortable, because the chances of something bad happening can be small...but they still happen to *someone.* This time it was us. Being on the receiving end of something that is *rare* or *unlikely* just makes you feel even more isolated when it does happen.

"I used to think the same thing," Evie says with a soft smile. Last year, she and Aiden shared some of the struggles their family faced while they were growing up, and even though she doesn't mention it, I know it's weighing on her mind. "It's easier to get comfortable with the idea that things can't get better, and if they did, then they won't last. It feels like you're doing yourself a favor, saving yourself from a worse fallout when it all goes to shit. But you're also robbing yourself of so much joy. I'm not saying it's going to be easy, but you deserve to be happy."

I want to believe her. I want to *try.*

Chapter Forty-Six

Dom

"How are things at work, Dominic?" my therapist, David, asks during our virtual session. Thankfully, Luca is still napping, so it looks like I'll get to finish the appointment without having to also watch an infant. Hard to focus on adult conversations with a toddler trying to destroy the house.

"Overall, pretty good. The school year's coming to a close, so things will be busy this month. I'm volunteering with prom, after-prom, and the graduation ceremony for the seniors before I finally get to enjoy some overdue family time over summer break."

"And what about at home? Luca's well?"

I can't help the grin that stretches across my face. "His big personality is really shining. He's a happy kid. Thankfully, his sleeping habits are getting better too."

Knock on fucking wood right now, you stupid asshole. He'll probably sleep like shit for a week now that I've opened my mouth.

Never acknowledge the good nights. He'll hear and change the program.

"And with Ellie?"

I pause, nervous to say it out loud. I've been working with David since Luca was born. He won't judge me, but he will be honest with me. Sometimes the truth is fucking scary. Like, *is my marriage failing?*

But I didn't come this far to avoid facing the reality of our situation, and honestly, I could use an impartial opinion on what the fuck I should do right now. I spend a few minutes catching David up on my recent fight with Ellie and the trip she's on with the girls.

"So, Ellie comes home tomorrow," he says carefully.

"Yup," I say, rolling my lips and biting down.

"Tell me if I'm wrong, but you seem anxious."

"Ellie and I had a fight where she questioned the future of our marriage. Who wouldn't be scared of what's next?"

"What do you want to say to her after several days apart?"

"That I love her. That I'm sorry if I pushed her too far. That she doesn't have to do this stupid game anymore if she doesn't want to. That I'll keep trying to find better ways to fix…"

He raises an eyebrow but doesn't say anything. How do therapists always know when to stop talking and let you dig your own grave? The number of times I talk myself in circles while David waits patiently for me to get there is more than I'd like to admit.

"I'll find better ways to fix what's broken," I say, the uncertainty in my voice is clear, even to me. Because I don't know what I'm going to do if Ellie wants to stop this. I'm out of ideas. This was all I had, and if it's not enough…fuck, it has to be enough.

"Do you feel responsible for other people's happiness?" David asks. While I'm stunned into silence, he goes on. "What about Ellie? Do you feel responsible for her healing?"

"This feels like a trap."

"I promise," he says with a good-natured chuckle, "it's not."

"It feels like I'm supposed to say no, but then how do I support her as her husband if I don't see it as my responsibility to help her find happiness? To help her heal?"

"But that's not what you're telling me. What I'm hearing you say is what you're doing isn't working. I'm not hearing anything about what *Ellie* is doing and if *that* is working. Supporting someone, loving someone, helping someone...none of that means you can do the work for them. It's clear you love your wife and Ellie loves you. But what I want to hear from you is an understanding that you can walk with her while she heals, but you can't take the steps for her."

"I don't see the difference."

"Do you feel like you have value, even when you're not helping the people you love? Are you enough as you are, not because of what you give to others."

Fuck. Okay, that one hurts.

"It's easier to take that on, I guess. I don't want to see the people I care about struggling."

"That's perfectly human. But I want to caution you; when you start believing you can take on other people's hurt in hopes of "fixing" it, you risk losing yourself in the process. Have you considered that maybe the best thing you could do for Ellie would be to just love her through it all, without trying to put the entire world on your shoulders? You can be there for her. You can love her and support her. But at the end of the day, she has to find the path forward."

I'm stunned speechless, so he continues, "Have you ever talked to Ellie about the birth from your eyes? What you experienced?"

"What I experienced was nothing compared to what she went through," I respond, I'll admit a bit defensively.

He puts his hands up in surrender, placating me. "I only wonder if you're waiting for her to heal from a wound that you've been avoiding looking at too closely yourself. Maybe it's easier to focus on her healing, because you don't think you need to do your own."

Jesus, David. Not holding anything back today, huh?

"It didn't feel important to share my perspective at the time," I say.

He gives me a look of compassion and empathy, again without judgment.

"If I told you that *her* story didn't feel important, would you agree with me?" he asks, with a knowing look.

Of course not.

Is this why I have this burning need to control everything? To protect Ellie and Luca because the thought of another unpredictable emergency makes me feel painfully vulnerable?

All this time, I've been focused on trying to give Ellie everything she needs to find herself again, but David's words have me questioning if maybe I'm just as lost as she is.

248   JANE HAYES

All this time, I've been focused on trying to give Ellie everything she needs to find herself again, but David's words have me questioning if maybe I'm just as lost as she is.

CHAPTER FORTY-SEVEN

Ellie

It's been two weeks since I came home from my vacation with the girls. Dom and I were quick to fire out our apologies for the things we said during our last argument, but after being together for years, I know that we both need time to process things on our own and work to build trust again before we can truly move on from a fight that big.

I wish the longer you were with someone, the easier it became to forgive one another for being human and making mistakes, but it's a choice every single time. We have to take accountability, and want to change for the better, and I do.

This is me trying.

I owe it to Dom, Luca, and myself.

Therapy didn't work out for me last time, but I have to try again. After telling the girls our birth story, I expected to feel raw and worn down, but I felt lighter than I had in months. That only makes this decision easier.

I sit on the edge of the bed, staring at the business card from Isabel, the woman I met in the park so many months ago. I hope to be like her someday. She seemed so comfortable in who she is and in how she parents. If I want that, I need to make it happen.

Abruptly, I stand, grab my purse, and leave for my appointment before my nerves can get the best of me. Here goes...everything.

***

"Motherfucker," I mumble as my internet connection fluctuates in and out.

Luca laughs as Dom pushes him on the swing set underneath the willow tree in our backyard before demanding to go down the slide another time. I pause, watching them for a moment before fighting with my laptop again.

I'm finally reconnected when I hear a knock on the gate. Bec and Aiden follow as an overzealous yellow lab bounds into our yard and starts doing zoomies around the playset, where Luca claps in celebration, welcoming his best friend.

"You guys know how to make an entrance," I say.

"Who us? No, couldn't be us causing a scene," Bec says, brushing me off. "We come bearing gifts."

"Oh my god, I can smell the garlic. Gimme," I say as Bec and Aiden drop take-out containers on our patio table.

"Uh, you two good for a second? I'd help set up, but I think I need to intervene."

Hopper is climbing with tentative paws onto the playset rock wall, an adorable little whine escaping his muzzle at the sight of Luca so high and out of reach. He lies down and watches Luca intently, silently begging his buddy to join him back on solid ground.

Shit. The last thing I need is to fall in love with how cute Hopper and Luca are together. I'm just coming back to myself in motherhood...let's not add a puppy to this mix.

"You know...Luca looks like a dog baby," Bec sings as she unpacks carryout containers.

I narrow my eyes at her. "If you're reading my thoughts, I hope you heard the rest of them. Cute. Adorable. But that's what we have you for, and why I'm so grateful my best girl and her fancy fiancé and dog only live ten minutes away."

"You and me both."

I run inside to grab dishes and Luca's booster seat before Bec and I spend a few minutes setting up the table for us to eat. The guys are plenty busy entertaining Luca and Hopper.

I smile at the chorus of toddler giggles and excited barks. Spring is slowly fading, and with each warmer June day, I feel the life soaking into my skin with the sunshine.

"Can I ask how it's going, or is that going to stress you out?" Bec asks.

"Despite the cursing you probably heard on your way in, it's actually going...well?"

"Is that a question or an answer?"

"A little bit of both, I guess." I shrug, setting aside a stack of napkins. "It's surprising. Everything is sort of falling into place. I mean, I have no fucking clue what I'm doing, but I already had a few people from my office refer their friends. I booked my first official session."

Bec's jaw drops comically low. "What?" she shouts at me before pulling me in for a too-tight hug. "Ellie, oh my god. Lead with that next time! That's amazing."

I pat her back lightly, my ability hindered by her tight grip around my arms.

"Down girl. It's only one appointment."

"You shut up, Ellie Moretti. This is a big fucking deal. I'm so proud of you. Tell me everything."

I can't contain my smile, a mix of nerves and excitement bubbling up as I explain how I booked my first client ever with my own photography business.

"My coworker's sister is expecting. She's been looking for a photographer for the birth."

Bec's face drops instantly, her expression shifting quickly to one of worry.

"Ellie, are you sure about this? Won't that be triggering?"

I nod. "Honestly, probably. But I've been talking with my new therapist about it. When she first asked me to do the session, I can't explain it, I felt like I had to do it. I figure I'll try it once, and if it's too much, I'll stop booking that type of appointment and focus more on family photos. But there's this part of me that feels like it'll be healing in a way; that no matter what happens in birth, if the mom wants that moment captured, then I'm there to do that. I don't have any pictures from the first few hours Luca was alive. There's a lot that I grieve about our birth experience, and that's one of them. Sometimes it's not possible because the priority is obviously everyone's safety, but if I can give a mom this...then I want to do that for them.

"In therapy we've been talking about the parts of my birthing experience that felt empowering. The choices I was able to make that felt right for me. How strong I felt. How supported Dom made me feel. I think sometimes I forget that I can feel both things. Grief for what went wrong, and joy at what went right."

"Okay, but promise me we can check in afterward. I want to make sure you're okay."

"I promise."

Therapy hasn't been easy and I've only had three appointments. I can barely function afterward I'm so exhausted, especially since my therapist has me doing EMDR, a type of treatment that leaves me feeling emotionally drained but is supposed to help treat my PTSD. We're trying everything and I don't know if it's any one approach or all of them together after over a year of ignoring everything that's making the difference.

I'm committed this time. Regular appointments, EMDR, and I'm starting medication soon too. I'm even making time to sit outside when it's nice to listen to birdsong, because my therapist mentioned it can help with anxiety.

There's no quick fix, but for the first time in a long time, the brain fog has lessened, and in my heart...I have hope.

Hope that I can take pieces of my past and fit them into the mosaic of my future, and it'll be more beautiful than I ever imagined.

CHAPTER FORTY-EIGHT

Dom

I close the door as slowly and quietly as possible, holding my breath until I've completely backed into the hallway and the door is fully latched. I wait, unmoving and eyes wide, listening to see if my exit was a success.

I heave a sigh of relief before heading to the kitchen, grabbing two glasses and a bottle of wine, and rejoining Ellie in our backyard around the firepit. The fire crackles and sparks, casting Ellie in a warm glow as she reclines in the lawn chair.

The willow tree in our backyard sways gently in the breeze. Earlier, when I came home from work, I caught Ellie out here with Luca, her running through the low branches and greenery and Luca laughing and chasing after her as best he could on unsteady feet. I knew when I found this house it would be the home to all of my dreams. I've been lucky enough to watch them come true.

"Seems like it went well?" she asks with a nod to the monitor in my hand.

"It was...too easy," I say with a heavy dose of suspicion, making Ellie laugh.

"I gave up on ever sleeping again. I've been too scared to say anything lately...but it's better, right?" she asks.

"Thank fuck you said it first. Now if it all turns to shit, I'm in the clear." She shoves my hip and I chuckle in my failed attempt to dodge her. I hand her a glass, filling it with wine before doing the same with mine.

"Cheers, to one last decent night of sleep before the next sleep regression, next tooth cuts in, or whatever the fuck else is about to ruin our REM sleep," I say, before tapping my glass to hers.

"Cheers. It was nice while it lasted." She pauses before continuing. "Most of me is ecstatic that he's finally sleeping better, while this small voice is crying out at the fact that he's getting older. More independent. God, I can't think about the day when he doesn't need me anymore."

"Honey, he'll always need you. The way he needs our support and the way we'll show up for him will change for the rest of our lives, but it won't stop. That's the goal, right? Give him everything he needs to grow into the person he wants to be, and then support him the rest of the way."

"Yeah, I guess you're right. Just hard to imagine my little baby all grown up and becoming a dentist or something."

"You mispronounced *teacher*, babe. It's okay. I know you're tired. Just catching up on your sleep for the first time in two years is all," I say, with a small pat on her head, which she swats away with a giggle. "I'm really proud of you."

"For jinxing us and ruining our sleep tonight?"

"For taking care of yourself," I say seriously. "For trying something new."

Her smile softens, sensing the shift in my tone. "Thank you for taking care of me when I couldn't," she says, voice thick with emotion.

"I'm always going to want to take care of you, Ellie. You and Luca both. You two are my entire world. We were meant to do this together. We can't both have it together all the time. There will be days when you have to drive the bus and days where I'm happy to do the same."

"And what about the days when neither of us is capable of driving."

"Then god help us, Luca's in charge."

She laughs and takes another sip of wine. "Do you think he'll remember us like this? I have these memories of my parents in my childhood and they always seemed so confident. So put together."

"I'd like to think even though he won't remember specifics, he'll remember how this time of his life *felt*. Despite all we've struggled with, I've loved getting to learn who he is and watching him grow. And watching you become a mom...it's a gift, Ellie."

"I hope he remembers the way it feels too. I hope he laughs as easily as he does now. I hope he smiles more than he cries. I hope life is kind to him, but he remembers that he can come home when it's not and he needs to heal. I hope he appreciates the small things as much as the big things. I hope he knows nothing is ever broken, just evolving, growing."

Her words soothe fears that linger in my head. "I want all those same things for you too. For us," I say.

"With you, I have it all." She pulls my hand into hers and holds it over her heart. I lean over and kiss her forehead, breathing in the smell of her shampoo and the smoke from the fire, listening to the crickets and the early summer breeze blowing through the trees and the hum of a delightfully calm baby monitor.

***

"We don't have to do this. I haven't talked to my parents about our..." My voice trails off, unsure if I want to bring up the biggest fight we've had in our relationship. "I mean, I wasn't sure if you'd still be up for puzzle pieces after..." I say, hating the unease creeping along my shoulders and into my gut.

Ellie reaches across the car's center console, her hand on my thigh.

"No, we should do this. I want to," Ellie says, voice more confident than I feel.

"We can leave anytime you want," I say as we get out of the car and I take her hand in mine, walking into the building together.

"Please, after the pole dancing classes Abby set up for us, this should be easy."

My brain short-fucking-circuits.

"Hold the fuck up, the *what* now?" I ask, running to catch up with Ellie, who walked ahead of me while my brain froze.

She smirks over her shoulder and gives a shrug. "Maybe you'll get to see some time."

"How about now?" I ask, grabbing her around the waist and trailing through the doorway after her.

"Down, boy," she whispers as my parents spot us from across the room and make their way toward us.

"Unfair, Ellie," I growl in her ear.

"Who said I play fair?" She winks at me. Goddamn winks at me like she was planning on dropping a bomb like this before we have to spend an hour in public and *with my parents*. Ellie in a pole dancing class...*fuck*, I need to think about anything else.

"I'm so glad you're here," my mom exclaims, taking Ellie into her arms for a hug.

"You two are in for a real treat today. The rumba, have you ever done it?" my father asks.

"Dad, you know neither of us has ever ballroom danced before," I say.

"Right, right, of course. Well, it's a good thing you aren't waiting as long as your mother and I did. We had no idea we'd love it as much as we do," he says.

"I heard congratulations are in order," Ellie says excitedly. "Maybe we can make it to your next competition."

"We'd love that," Mom says, linking elbows with my wife and sitting alongside her on one of the long benches surrounding the edges of the open room. "I hope you both enjoy the class today. Maybe you'll even want a repeat." She bumps shoulders with Ellie as she puts on her dance shoes. "The rumba can be very saucy. Keeps the fire lit, if you know what I mean."

"Jesus Christ." I groan.

"Sure does. These steps can be very intimate if you put your passion into them," Dad adds.

Ellie chokes on her own saliva and I'm about to choke on my own vomit.

"We needed something to keep us busy now that we're both retired. Plus, we've got to have something to keep our bodies young so we can keep up with Luca as he grows," Mom says.

"Now that he's walking so confidently, it's like he only has one speed. I think I need to take up running. The future looks...exhausting," Ellie says.

Mom and Dad help us set up and find a spot on the dance floor among other couples while the instructor takes us through the basic steps.

Ellie's a natural. Me, on the other hand...

"They said this was for beginners," I hiss under my breath, nearly tripping over Ellie for the third time.

"Babe, I don't know how much simpler they can break down the steps." She giggles. "Here, follow my lead."

Closing the space between us, she steps into me, aligning our bodies. Her head rests against my chest, and I feel her relax, causing my muscles to do the same.

"I'm pretty sure we're still messing up the steps," I say softly as we melt into less structured movement, abandoning any turns altogether.

"Maybe I like improvising with you," she says, pressing a quick kiss to my neck.

"Doesn't sound so hard when you put it like that," I murmur.

"It might be difficult while we find our footing," she says, pulling back to lock her gaze on mine. "But when you're holding me, even the wrong steps feel safe."

"We'll make our own steps, yeah? Who says what the wrong steps are anyway?"

"You're doing it wrong," the brash instructor interrupts us, forcing Ellie to stifle a snort-laugh. "Horrible, just horrible form. Complete lost cause."

The instructor's critiques draw my parents' attention, who don't seem dismayed or deterred by our apparent lack of talent. Dad throws me an exaggerated thumbs-up and Mom puts a hand over her heart like she's overwhelmed at the sight of Ellie and I, like it's cute and we're not being berated for sucking at this.

I guess the people who love you don't care when you don't do things the right way. They just want to see you try.

Chapter Forty-Nine

Dom

"**D**o you want me to wish you a happy birthday, or would you prefer I ruin it by singing to you instead?" Ellie asks as she cuddles in close, one leg wrapping over my thigh, and her hand snaking around my waist.

I love waking up like this.

I hum, relaxing into a slow stretch of my muscles to shake off the fog of sleep. "You know your husband. I want the fanfare. Give me fireworks, Ellie."

"Fresh out of fireworks, I'm afraid," she says with a giggle, nuzzling her cheek further into my chest.

I reach her hip and pull her closer, catching her surprised gasp in a lazy kiss. She melts in my arms.

"Little liar. It's always fireworks with you."

Her shy smile looks familiar and new all at once. It touches her eyes, and it's like I'm watching the Ellie I met a lifetime ago come back to herself.

"Happy thirtieth," she says. "Now give me the full inventory. How bad is it? Muscle aches? Heel spurs? Did you throw your back out with that stretch a minute ago? What's the damage?"

"Oh, ha-ha. You just wait...two years, and you'll be right here with me."

Her laughter fades and her eyes shine in the early morning sun cutting through the room. "Yeah, I will be."

I hold her jaw and roll her onto her back, taking her in another slow kiss, soaking up every second of her undivided attention. She opens for me—thighs and lips—and moans. Her fingernails drag up my back and I drive my hips between hers.

"I'm curious to see what it's like to drive a vintage car," she says breathless against my lips, barely able to contain her laughter as her hips roll to meet mine. "I'm pretty good with stick shift. Don't worry, I'll be gentle."

"Someone woke up spicy today," I say against her neck, before trailing kisses across her collarbone. Her hands weave into my hair.

"You said you wanted fireworks."

"Is that why I'm being roasted?"

"Precisely."

"Remind me to be careful what I wish for when I blow out the candles this year."

"I didn't get candles," she says with mirth, before rolling me onto my back and straddling my hips. "Can't have a fire hazard like that in the house. We have a child, Dom." The false reprimand in her voice is a relief.

I've missed this so goddamn much. These moments that just feel like...us.

We're still here.

I rub my palms up and down her thighs, and my eyes catch on her nipples, pebbled beneath her soft cotton T-shirt. I reach down and palm her ass before giving one cheek a slap.

"Relentless."

"Consistent," she counters, with a wink. "Lie down on your stomach."

"Baby, I'm all for trying new things in the bedroom, but it's been a while. Maybe we start back up with some vanilla before you go all in, huh?"

She rolls her eyes and slaps my chest. "First of all, I'm disappointed in your seriously lacking sense of adventure and spontaneity. Second, that's not what's happening. Roll over."

I do, and she crawls onto my back, before she starts kneading my shoulders. I unwillingly let out a deep groan as she works my muscles.

"Oh fuck, okay. Maybe I am feeling my age. We might have to cancel any birthday plans so we can do this all day instead."

I can hear the smile in her voice when she says, "Afraid we can't do that, sweetheart. I got us a sitter and plans I can't and won't"—she leans down to kiss my shoulder—"cancel."

My brows hit my hairline in surprise. Ellie got a sitter and planned for us to go out, just the two of us? What the fuck is she up to?

I roll over, careful to keep her braced astride me, and hold her waist tightly.

"What's the plan, Captain?"

"For once, Dominic, that's for me to know and for you to learn as we go. No planning. No interfering. No trying to one-up anything with your exuberant need to be thoughtful. Your job is to enjoy today, okay?" She's clearly put a lot of thought and effort into this, and it's important to her. Fuck if I'll be the one to mess that up for her.

"But before we do anything, you're going to need to open this," she says, handing me a small box with a purple ribbon. I slowly open it and my stomach drops when I see a single puzzle piece inside the packaging.

Turning it over, I read, *Grow with me.*

My eyes search hers, lost in their depths.

"Why did you give me a piece of my own, Ellie?"

"You've spent all this time helping me piece myself back together. But you forgot a really important part of the puzzle. You."

I stroke her cheek and commit this moment to memory. I don't care what the rest of the day looks like, what we do, who we're with, or where we go. I know she's here with me, all the way with me, and I'm never letting go.

CHAPTER FIFTY

Dom

I'm sitting in the passenger seat, waiting for Ellie to join me in the car. She's taking an extra minute saying goodbye to her parents and Luca at our front door before she makes her way down the driveway.

My muscles tense with worry that it's still difficult for her to leave Luca, but my fears vanish when her eyes catch mine, full of excitement as she sits next to me, buckling herself into the driver's seat.

"Okay, before we go, I have something for you," she says, a mix of mischief and glee evident in her demeanor.

"Started my morning with a massage, I'm on my way to a date planned by my wife, and you're telling me there's more?" I pull her close with a firm hand around the back of her neck, brushing her lips with mine. "What more could I want?"

She presses her lips against mine in a quick kiss before I feel her grin. Something falls into my lap and I look down to see an unsealed envelope.

"You'll definitely want these," she says with confidence.

I quickly dump the contents out and laugh when I see a roughly drawn sketch on a piece of paper. There are two horribly drawn stick figures holding hands, with giant shoes on their feet and faces so warped I can't tell their noses from their mouths.

"Honey, you are the most talented woman I know...but maybe we stick to photography, huh?"

She pokes me in the shoulder before I unfold the second paper in the envelope. I quickly scan the text and my mind finally pieces together what Ellie's got up her sleeve.

A lifetime of games with you by my side.
With you, I'm winning every time.
Hold on tight and walk with me,
Rolling back to where we dreamed.

"Ellie," I say, speechless. I swallow and take a few seconds to gather my thoughts, failing. I can only ask, "Is this what I think it is?"

"You took me on the first date to end all first dates when we met," she says with a cheek-splitting grin. She puts the car in reverse before adding, "Now, it's my turn."

The poem and the drawing...both over-the-top, cheesy shit I gave to Ellie every day the week before I took her out on our first date.

She's doing the same for me now.

The pulsing rhythm of my heart is the only thing steadying me as I reach across the console to grip Ellie's thigh.

"I fucking love you, Ellie."

"Let me show you how much I love you back."

***

"I think our first date was the first and last time I ever tried this," Ellie says, clinging to the wall of the roller rink. "Now, I remember why." She's unsteady but in good spirits and joking around as I coax her off the wall, taking her hands in mine.

"Jake and I used to come here every weekend growing up," I say. "Maybe we should start coming as a family. Luca might grow up loving it. Who knows? You might become the best skater in the family."

"I hate the idea of spending more time on unstable footing, but damn, Luca would be so cute wiggling around in tiny roller skates, a helmet, and kneepads."

I laugh and skate backward, pulling Ellie along with me, her hands gripping mine tightly as she fights to keep herself upright.

"Of course he would be."

The lights dim and the announcer comes over the speaker. "Aaaaaaattention," he sings. "We have a very special song request for Dominic from Ellie. "

The slow and steady beat of "Ellie My Love" by Ray Charles fills the venue, and I laugh, remembering when I dedicated this song to her years ago.

Ellie gasps as I pull her into my arms, stealing a kiss and stroking my thumb along her jaw as I thread my hand into her hair.

"I love this song," I whisper in her ear as couples skate past us.

"I tried to find one with your name, since I wanted to put my own spin on things while recreating this date," she says with a laugh. "But all I could find was a song about a Christmas donkey. Didn't quite fit the vibe."

"As much as I would have seriously enjoyed that," I say, skating to position myself at her back, my arms wrapped around her waist. "You made the right call," I whisper into her ear as I push us both forward. Her hands drop to my wrist, gripping tightly as she holds on to me for balance.

"I won't let you fall," I murmur in her ear.

"You never do," she says, chancing a look at me over her shoulder.

We spend the next thirty minutes skating around the rink, Ellie getting more comfortable by the end, before we take a break and grab a drink from the concession stand.

"Have you had your fill?" she asks, unable to mask the hope in her voice.

"This was incredible. I'm ready to go whenever you are."

"Great, then come with me. Wait, let me get these off first." Once we're both back in our regular shoes, Ellie drags me over to the photo booth, just like all those years ago.

I smile at the memory of the first time we were here together.

"Come on, Momma," I say, patting my thigh in the tight booth.

She squats, barely resting her body on my leg. Can't have that.

"Get over here, baby," I say, pulling her flush against me. She turns to me, a look of surprise on her face, and she wraps her arms around my neck when the first flash goes off. I kiss her before I hear the next click. Then she rests her head in the crook of my neck, before the final photo snaps. We stay like that for a moment and it feels like I'm the same man from years before, in disbelief of the gift in my arms. The perfect, sunny woman in my arms.

I can't reconcile the two emotions hitting me. It feels like yesterday that I held this incredible woman in my arms, the future unknown but full of possibility and hope. Almost everything has changed, but not the important things.

I reach around Ellie to grab the photo slip from the printer. She takes my hand in hers and I laugh knowing what's next.

***

"I hope you know none of this embarrasses me. In fact, I love it. I'm going to wear it all the time," I say, pulling the hem of my T-shirt away from my body so I can once again admire the image of me and Ellie in the photo booth. The picture is massive and spans the full width of the T-shirt with a massive red heart around it.

Fun fact: the roller rink has a T-shirt printer. Years ago, when I took Ellie on this very same date, on my insistence, we had shirts made, screen-printed with a photo of us from the roller-rink photo booth. We wore them to dinner at the same restaurant we're sitting in now. The small, family-owned restaurant's Greek food is as incredible as it was years ago.

She rolls her lips, biting them before letting her smile grow. "You know none of this embarrasses me, either, right?"

I roll my eyes. "Please, our friends never let me live down the stories from our first date. Admittedly, it's a miracle I didn't scare you off."

"It was refreshing, actually. To be with a guy who didn't give a shit what anyone thought. Who lived as big as I wanted to. Who didn't let nervousness stop him from enjoying himself and making sure everyone around him felt that way too. I don't think I had ever met anyone who laughed as much as you."

"That had everything to do with the beautiful woman who let me drag her around a roller rink and then wear my face on her chest the rest of the night."

"It's a cute face."

"Okay, if the shirt didn't embarrass you…" I say, voice trailing off.

"Neither did this," she says, standing and reaching a hand out.

I take my hand in hers and join her, standing next to our booth. I lift our joint hands and wrap my other around her waist, pulling her close. She doesn't hesitate, leaning in to rest her cheek on my chest before we start swaying side to side, slowly circling ourselves in the narrow space between tables.

"Do you remember what you said when I asked you to dance with me?" I ask.

"I have no idea," she says with a laugh.

"You said we couldn't because no one else was dancing."

"Because only *you* would insist on dancing mid-meal in a place clearly *not* meant for dancing."

I shrug, continuing to rock us back and forth in small circles, catching the eye of our waiter, who smiles at us as he walks toward the kitchen.

"Some occasions call for dancing, no matter the circumstances. I didn't want to go one more minute without you in my arms. I wanted to feel your hand in mine. Your pulse beating alongside mine. Your smile against my neck."

"How can you tell?"

"I can always tell, Mrs. Moretti."

"Cocky."

"Confident."

She laughs and I hold her tighter against me.

"Does it feel different? Being here with me now?" I ask, curious to know where her head is tonight.

She looks up, resting her chin on my chest, and her smile reaches her eyes. "It feels different, but not in a bad way. I can't stop thinking of the people we were then. How much those two would go through together and how strong they'll make each other."

"What would you say to us, knowing what you know now?" I ask.

"I would tell you to calm down and to stop acting so nervous, because the girl is *into* you."

"I wanted everything to be perfect for you."

"Maybe I liked that it wasn't perfect. Maybe it was perfect for us," she says.

"And what would you have told yourself?" I swallow my nerves, needing to know.

"I would have told her...to grab onto that man by the ridiculous T-shirt he was wearing and never let go. I would have told her that her life with you will be filled with laughter, passion, and understanding. I would have told her that her life was just beginning and that even the hard days she'll face will be easier with you by her side."

"I want you to be happy, Ellie."

"I am. I promise, I am." Her fingers dig into my skin and she leans against me. I welcome it, the closeness a reassurance to my heart that her words are true.

We dance quietly for one more song, holding one another before we split dessert and settle our bill. I think I can safely assume where we're headed to end our night.

***

"This next song is for Dominic from Ellie," the pianist announces into his microphone.

Ellie and I are at the same dueling piano bar from years ago. We haven't been back since and I have no idea why. I forgot how much fun the environment is. Ellie and I spent the last hour throwing out requests with heavy tips for the musicians as they show off their talents, and we scream-sing along to our favorite songs. I have no idea how they perform with this much spontaneity in their set, but I'm as impressed as I was last time.

"What's it going to be, Ellie?" I shout over the noise of the crowd and the two pianists running their fingers over their keys, warming up for the next song.

Ellie smirks over the rim of her glass before taking a sip. "You'll see."

The familiar, upbeat chorus of "Marry You" by Bruno Mars sounds through the bar, and I slide my chair closer to Ellie's so I can tuck her under my arm and kiss her temple. "This is a surprise. I don't remember this one from last time."

"Because it's new. Think of it as an homage to what you told me the last time you brought me here."

This is probably the part of the date I get the most grief over with our friends.

"But it's my turn to say it," she adds.

She must catch the surprise in my expression because she laughs and leans in closer, her lips brushing my ear as she speaks over the noise of the bar.

"Dominic Moretti, I'm going to marry you."

My face explodes into a smile and I wrap Ellie tightly into my side and feel her, more than hear her, laughing against my body.

"I believe this is the part where you asked me how I could possibly know that," I say.

"And you said it was the surest you've ever been about anything in your entire life."

"And then you called me crazy and kissed me stupid."

"Yeah, I think I did," she says, her eyes bouncing between my stare and my lips. I don't hesitate. I take her face in my hands and do the very same thing.

CHAPTER FIFTY-ONE

Dom

"Ready for pillow talk?" Ellie asks, standing next to my side of the bed. I'm sitting against the headboard, reading on my phone, one leg stretched out and the other bent.

Tonight was the most perfect date I've ever been on. Well, since the first time we went on it, I guess.

"Of course. Get over here, gorgeous." She sits between my legs, leaning her back against my chest, I instinctively wrap my arms around her. "Tonight was perfect. I can't think of a better way to end it than like this," I say, nuzzling into the space between her neck and shoulder, her perfume lingering from our night together.

I run my nose up her neck, pulling her hair to the side and placing a kiss on her soft skin.

"I had fun, but I can think of a better way to end it," she says, almost shy.

Her palms press into my inner thighs, fingernails digging into my skin, demanding all my attention.

"Oh, yeah," I say, my voice low. "What's that?" I grip her jaw, gently turning her to face me over her shoulder. "What do you want, Ellie?"

"I lied to you," she says, her voice trembling. "I'm so sorry for everything I said before I left with the girls. I told you I didn't want to feel anything. I was just scared because everything felt too big to handle, except this. Except you. I just want to feel you." She reaches back, pulling my neck down until my lips brush hers, an almost kiss.

I've been waiting to feel Ellie for so long. We've teased and tortured each other for months, trying to rebuild everything else in our relationship before giving ourselves back this part of our relationship. But maybe I was wrong to think we could put our physical connection on the back burner and repair everything else that wasn't working between us. Maybe they all work in tandem, and we need this piece too.

With one last look at her eyes, full of trust, love, and longing, I give her exactly what she's asking for. I kiss her like a silent plea, a desperate call for her to be here with me, to find me again and stay.

If she wants to feel me, then I'll make it so I'm all she can taste, all she can breathe.

The kiss feels familiar, but new all at once. A reawakening.

She threads her fingers in my hair, grazing my scalp with her nails, and drops her knees to the side, resting them against my own, one bent in the air and the other pinning mine against the mattress, causing herself to open for me.

With greedy hands, I grip her knee and throat. Goddamn, I love the feel of her soft lips working over mine, tongues dancing in an increasing rhythm. She bites my bottom lip and moans.

I'm fucking gone.

Her hips start to move as my hand works its way from her knee to her center, but I don't touch her yet. Instead, I feel my way to the hem of her T-shirt, *my* T-shirt, to find nothing underneath.

I chuckle. "Ellie, did you plan on seducing your husband tonight?"

Her lips pull into a smile against my mouth. "I was feeling lucky."

I hum. "Let me show you just how lucky you're going to get, wife." Her nipples pebble beneath the soft cotton as I start to knead her breast. I continue to play with her tits but ignore her nipples as I slide my grip from her throat to weave my fingers through her hair, pulling the strands taut, her eyes meeting mine.

"Are you ready for this, Ellie?"

"Yes, please."

"Fuck, I've missed you." I move quickly, bending both of my legs and draping her legs over my knees. Her ankles fall to the side and she's spread open for me in my lap. Fucking perfect.

I sit up, forcing her to as well, and I tear the T-shirt off her body to feel her warm skin against my bare chest.

"Goddamn, baby." I groan, running my hands all over her body, not wanting to miss an inch of her. "I want to take from you, Ellie. Will you give me what I want?"

"I'm yours. Please. Dom, I need you."

I steal her lips in a needy kiss, sucking, tasting, biting. She meets me with enthusiasm, and I'm rock hard against her lower back.

She's grinding now, working her hips in circles, seeking friction I'm dying to give her.

Our kiss goes on and on, like we've both been starved and we've finally found our survival in each other. I palm her large, supple tits and finally give both nipples a hard pinch. She cries into my mouth. Her hands slap against my outer thighs before her nails dig into my skin where she grips me harder.

Her head falls onto my shoulder, pulling away from my lips while I tease and taunt and play to my heart's content.

"More, Dom. Don't make me wait," she pants.

"No, Ellie, I'm going to make you wait as long as I'd like. I want you to feel it...feel as desperate for me as I am for you so you finally understand." I grip her chin and force her gaze to meet mine. "There is no length of time away from you that would ever lessen my want for you—ever make me need you less. You're the breath in my lungs, you're the blood in my veins, you're the voice in my head, and the only thing I want is for you to let me take care of you tonight."

I sink one hand to her center, and *fuck*, she's soaked. I circle her entrance, gathering her arousal and using it to glide two fingers in small circles over her clit.

She moans and her hips stutter in their movements.

"Fuck, yes," she whispers.

I circle over her clit, alternating between soft and firm pressure, still teasing and kneading one nipple with my other hand.

"I've got you. Let go," I say, thrusting two fingers into her, letting my palm rock over her clit in place of my fingers. She gasps and I bite into her shoulder.

Ellie cries out, arching her back and driving her ass into the length of my hard dick.

"Dom, don't stop," she pleads.

"I'm not stopping. I want you all fucking night. I want you for fucking ever, you got that?"

Her muscles tighten and her back straightens and I feel her rocking desperately against my hand as I seek out that spot inside her.

"Eyes open, Ellie."

She listens and lets out a surprised gasp.

We haven't had sex in months and even then, sex after birth was usually her or me on top, facing one another. We haven't had sex like this since we bought a new dresser with a mirror resting above the drawers...directly across the room from our bed. It's like a front-row seat to our own movie, her dewy skin on mine, legs draped open, baring herself completely to me. *To us.*

I watch her face as she takes in the sight of her body in the mirror, writhing over mine, tits bouncing as I press into her harder and faster in an unrelenting, building rhythm. She tries to close her eyes, but I grip her chin, keeping her head facing forward.

"I said open. What do you see, baby?"

"I see your...your fingers inside me," she gasps.

"Do you like seeing my fingers soaked because of how much you want this?"

"Yes."

"What else do you see?"

"My body," she says. I drop my hand to collar her throat and feel her gulp before she pants as she works herself over my hand.

I hum, running my lips over her ear.

"I see it, too, and I love it. Fucking beautiful. I dream of this body, Ellie. These tits," I say with reverence, gripping one firmly before tugging roughly at her nipple, then move down her stomach. "This body that grew and transformed. *Fuck*, do you feel how hard you're making me?"

She drops her head back again with a whimper when I press another finger into her, her drenched pussy easing the movement.

"Now stop holding back, and fucking give me what I need," I demand.

Her back arches and she drops one hand to the back of my neck, scratching my skin and pulling so hard I let my head fall forward, biting her shoulder again.

Her other hand digs into my thigh and she moans louder this time, riding out her orgasm while my fingers fuck her relentlessly, keeping the pace that pushed her over the edge.

"Fuck, fuck, fuck," she calls.

"That's it, baby. Fucking beautiful," I say, lifting my head to take in the filthy view we're creating in the mirror as she moves.

Her body goes limp, cradled between my legs and against my chest. I catch a small smile before she says, still catching her breath, "There's a situation back there that feels like it needs attention."

"Sounds serious. Might be a two-person job," I say with a smirk.

"God, I hope so," Ellie says with an easy laugh.

"Care to help your husband out with that?"

She smiles at me over her shoulder before turning to the mirror. I follow her gaze, meeting her stare in the glass. She shifts and I follow her lead. She straddles my thighs and I straighten my legs. She rocks her ass back into my cock and my vision tunnels at the feel of her ass cheeks nearly swallowing my dick.

"Fuck, El," I choke out, gripping her hips tightly.

She isn't deterred in the slightest. She rocks hard, grinding up and down, teasing and torturing me, my cock wedged between her ass cheeks, separated only by a layer of cotton.

"Off," she says, tugging at my boxer briefs.

"Yes. Yes, ma'am," I rush out, earning a laugh from her as I awkwardly shimmy them down my legs.

"Jesus Christ, Dom."

"Hey, you said off. You got it." I finally kick them off my feet and pull her hips back in a silent plea for her to continue. She does, and when she leans forward slightly, she gets more room to work her hips in my lap, drenching me with her wet release and smearing my precum all over herself.

Fuck, do not come before you even get inside your wife. Goddammit, don't fuckin' do it.

"Fuck, Ellie, I need you," I beg, before it's too late.

She sits up on her knees, turning her head toward me. With her eyes on mine, she waits.

I wanted to heal our relationship, before we came back to this part of it. We may still be a work in progress, but I know we need this too. We need each other in every way.

I lock eyes with her, gripping the base of my dick and lining it up with her center. She doesn't wait another second before she starts sinking onto my cock, sliding my dick into her hot, wet pussy. Her jaw drops and we moan together at the relief.

Fuck, I missed this. I missed *her*.

I groan, unable to keep my eyes open any longer. I lean my forehead against her shoulder as she slowly works herself up and down, up and down, slowly fucking me out of my mind until she's seated all the way. My cock is drenched in her soaked pussy and my balls are already starting to tighten. I splay my hands on her body, one over her heart and the other crossing over her stomach.

"I love you," I whisper.

"And I love you," she says, tears in her eyes.

We move together, me holding her close and thrusting into her from below, finding a rhythm. When I look in the mirror again, I nearly come from the sight alone. Rising and sinking onto my cock, riding me at a relentless pace, my cock glistening. Her tits sway and bounce with every movement. I never thought I'd be so goddamn grateful for new fucking furniture. A weird thing to be thankful for when I'm balls deep in my wife but *holy shit, what a view.*

"Ride me, Ellie."

Her pace doesn't increase, but she drops harder and lower on my dick with every undulation of her hips. I dig my fingers into her perfectly soft skin before moving one hand back to her clit.

Her mouth drops open and her eyes find mine in the mirror.

"Don't stop," she begs.

"Fuck me, Ellie. Fuck yourself on my cock and take what you need. Take it all."

She breaks apart, taking me over the edge with her. She moans my name, and her body stutters and convulses while I grip her tightly. My release hits me fast and hard. My balls draw up and I'm spilling into her with a groan. The position gives me a vantage point I never knew I needed. I watch my cum running down my dick and from her pussy as she pulses over my cock, her head thrown back as she rides out the waves of pleasure.

When she slumps against me, I lean back along our headboard, our breathing hard and fast as we come down from the high.

"We still got it, huh?" she asks.

I laugh. "Baby, we never lost it. Just a brief intermission. It's always been perfect with you," I say, kissing her swollen lips.

Her eyes glisten as she trails her fingers over my jaw, pulling my lips to hers again, stealing another kiss.

"I love you, Dominic.

"I love you forever, Ellie."

"Is *this* why you voted for this dresser?" she says with a heavy dose of suspicion in her voice.

"Nope. But fuck, what a happy accident." We laugh and I cradle her in my arms while we get to have our first real *pillow talk* in months.

CHAPTER FIFTY-TWO

Ellie

"Jesus, he's getting really good at this," Dom says as he waits for Luca to throw the ball his way.

Luca does a dramatic windup, his arm all the way in the air, before he launches the ball with no sense of direction or amount of force needed. Just pent-up enthusiasm and a will to cause chaos—something I'm thinking he's inherited from his fur-cousin, Hopper.

The ball strikes Dom in the forehead and I stifle a giggle. Apparently not well enough, because he gives me a *you're gonna pay for that* look and it has my body reacting in all the good ways. It's nice to feel that spark growing and flourishing between me and Dom again.

"Maybe he'll take after Aiden and end up going pro," I say with a shrug from my spot on the floor on the opposite end of the living room. Luca races, little bare feet slapping against floor, to retrieve the ball that bounced off his dad's head before he takes his spot between us again and throws it at my head this time.

I duck and deflect with my palm, and Luca giggles before running off again to find the ball before the abuse continues.

Luca is absolutely going through a growth spurt again. His sleep is still miles better than it was a few months ago, but he's needed a little extra help getting down at night. He is much more mobile, wanting to run everywhere and climb on everything. He's adding new words to his vocabulary all the time, surprising us. What's *unsurprising* is that one of those words is *dammit*.

I know I'm not supposed to laugh when my son swears because that'll only encourage the behavior, but, holy shit, it's hilarious the way he pronounces the word and the emphasis he puts on it.

We wrap up our Friday night with a dance party to "Old McDonald Had a Farm." I think you have to really love someone to parent with them. I learned a while ago, I needed to swallow any embarrassment I might have felt when acting stupid to make my kid happy. Because if anyone else watched me cluck like a chicken in my living room, my arms tucked into my side, elbows flapping, and my neck bobbing, I'd die of embarrassment. But with Dom, it's our normal life.

Our amazing, wonderful, silly life.

I'm finally feeling grateful for it. All that this life has given me. Everything was muted before, buried in a haze of weak self-defense mechanisms that had stopped working. I can breathe again.

Dom and I help Luca through his bedtime routine, starting with a bath and ending with Dom reading him a story and me rocking him in my arms for a few minutes.

Those last few moments of the day are always my favorite. Some days I hold him longer than he needs, waiting until he's asleep in my arms, my mind clear and focused on the present and the gift that it is to share these memories with him. Other days I think about how far we've come and how proud I am to be his mom. And then there are days like today, when I dream about what's next. Who Luca will be. What he'll choose to do with his life. How I hope he takes only the best from his father and me.

After settling a nearly asleep Luca in his crib, I tiptoe into the hallway and, as slowly as possible, close and latch his bedroom door.

When I rejoin Dom in the living room, he's already cleaned up the toys and sorted them into the toy bins. He's sitting on one end of the L-shaped sectional, hunched over, elbows resting on his knees, fingers laced together, his attention on his hands.

"Everything okay?" I ask, a thread of anxiousness pulling my spine straight as I cross one arm over my stomach and the other to fidget with the collar of my crew neck sweater.

He startles, but when his eyes find mine, they soften. "Yeah. Can we talk?" he asks, gesturing to the couch. I sit on the other stretch of the couch, our knees almost touching since we're both nearly wedged into the corner cushion.

"What's going on, Dom?"

"I owe you an apology."

"I mean, yeah, you laughed a little too hard at my rendition of 'Five Little Ducks.' I thought I was getting better," I joke in a desperate attempt to avoid whatever serious topic it sounds like he wants to discuss.

"I think that was the most beautiful rendition there ever was...next to mine, of course," he says with a casual shrug, instantly putting me at ease with his playfulness. "No, I want to apologize for not being honest with you when I started this whole puzzle game with you."

"I don't know what you mean. We're almost done, right? I think there's just the one corner left to go."

"I told you when I first introduced the idea that I was doing this to help you. But I didn't realize that I was also doing it to help myself."

"What...?" I question, my voice trailing off in confusion before he takes my hand in his.

"I've been really good at focusing on what *you* were trying to bury. The things you were struggling with that you wanted to hide. I wasn't willing to acknowledge that there were things I was afraid of facing too. Things I was too scared to admit to myself. That wasn't fair to you."

"I would never hold that against you," I reassure him, gently swiping my thumb across his knuckle. "It's not like I was doing a good job facing my own shit either."

"I want to tell you now, though..." his eyes flicker between my own, and my heart breaks at the fear reflected in them.

Has he really been hurting this whole time? How could he bury this all for so long?

"I'm sorry you felt like you couldn't talk about it until now," I say.

"No, it wasn't until recently that I think I was forced—by both a professional and four not-so-professional people in my life—to look more closely at why I was so determined to fix everything. I think I was trying to fix what you were struggling with in hopes that it would fix my problems too."

"Tell me," I plead. "Tell me everything."

Without hesitation, Dom pulls me into his lap and holds me to his chest while he tells me about the day Luca was born...from his perspective. He speaks slowly, and when he pauses, I look up to see tears escaping as he shuts his eyes. He doesn't just tell me what happened, though, he tells me every thought that ran through his mind, every detail of the nurse's expression when she tried to explain to him what was going on with his wife and newborn son post-operation. How it felt staring at his phone when texts poured in from family members and friends asking for updates while he sat next to my body as I slept off the anesthesia. The guilt for being unable to do anything to protect his wife and son. The relief when I opened my eyes and the pain as he watched me fall apart from my own experience. The joy when he held Luca for the first time and the way his heart stuttered watching me become a mother, as unsure and traumatized as I was.

When he's done, he asks me to do the same. To say it all out loud and to not leave one detail out. I've told the people important to me all the same version, giving more of myself than I had since it all happened. But never like this.

I take my time and don't rush. Some things feel too dark, too terrifying, to say out loud, but I do. Dom doesn't interrupt. He holds me, stroking his hand up and down my spine, giving my arm a reassuring squeeze when I have to pause to collect myself or my thoughts.

By the end, we're both crying, and I wrap my arms around his shoulders and hide my face in the crook of his neck and shoulder, finding comfort in the arms that have held me through it all.

"It was easier to focus on you and Luca than to face the hurt and unresolved grief from everything that happened," he says softly, before placing a gentle kiss on the top of my head.

"I don't blame you for anything, Dom. We were delt a card we had no idea how to play, and we both did the best we could. Since Luca was born, I've wondered what type of mom I would be if we didn't experience such a traumatic birth. But every day, that question fades as I ask myself, what kind of mom do I want to be now that we made it through it all? Everything you've done...you've helped me find the answer to that question."

"I felt responsible for putting us back together, because while I was terrified, I knew it couldn't compare to what you went through. I did us both a disservice by not admitting I was struggling too. I thought I could fix it all, but I couldn't even see myself clearly."

I take his face in my hands and make sure I have his full attention when I say, "You helped me more than I can explain. You gave me your confidence when I had none of my own. You gave me space to process and grieve when I needed it. You made me laugh when it felt impossible. You never gave up on me. It's not your fault that what was broken couldn't be fixed."

I kiss him, moving into his lap to straddle him. His hands grip my hips possessively, but travel quickly up and down my sides, to my waist, my back, my shoulders, my ass. After holding in this pain and hurt, we can finally let it go and make room for love instead.

I'm dizzy by the time I pull away, and his lips chase mine for one more soft kiss before he leans his head back along the couch cushion.

"I love you, Dominic. At my most broken, at my most healed, I love you always."

"God, I love you so much, Ellie."

We start to move again, slower this time, savoring every moment.

I trail my fingertips over his skin, and his palms pull and push until I'm grinding in his lap.

"I need you," I whisper into our shared breath.

"I need you more," he growls, pulling my top over my head and tossing it behind the couch.

I stand and slowly push my leggings off. He leans back, admiring the view with hungry eyes. "No underwear?"

I shake my head and smile, kneeling back over him in just my bra. My plain, gray nursing bra. But the look that Dom gives me makes me feel like I'm wearing lacy lingerie as he removes it.

After all these years and everything he's seen my body go through, he makes my entire body hot with just a look.

I run my hands over his abdomen before lifting his shirt off, tossing it with mine, lost somewhere on the floor. I push the band of his pants and boxer briefs down while he raises into me, lifting us both a few inches before his clothes finally fall past his hips, then his knees, before he kicks them away.

Neither of us moves, eyes locked on each other, my hands resting atop his shoulders.

"You're so beautiful, Ellie." He strokes his fingers reverently over my stomach, hips, and thighs, not missing an inch of my stretched, scarred, and dimpled skin. But I believe him. The way his gaze roves over my body, not to mention his hard length between us, I've never felt more cherished or desired than I do in this moment.

"Let me love you?" he half asks, half begs before kissing my neck, sucking and biting gently, causing my head to drop back, eyes closing, overwhelmed at the feel of his warm skin against mine and his kiss lighting a fire inside.

"Yes, yes, please."

He groans against my chest, his face between my breasts, his beard scratching the soft skin, before he pulls me close and shifts us both so I'm lying on the couch and he's pressed along every inch of me.

Dom doesn't wait; he slides home, filling me with a satisfying fullness. We moan together as he slowly slides out, lifting his head to look into my eyes.

With one hand pressed into the cushion next to my head, his other grabs my hip as I wrap my legs around him, pulling him closer with my heels, silently begging him to fill me again.

His fingers tighten, pulling me up and toward him as he sinks in again, starting a relentless rhythm.

His hips grind down as mine roll and rock against his pelvis, desperate for him to be closer, as close as he can be. My hands frantically search along his skin for somewhere to hold on. I settle with one on his back and the other on his shoulder.

"Fuck, Ellie," Dom groans, before kissing me, his tongue dancing with mine.

"God, don't stop," I beg, before pulling his bottom lip between my teeth.

He doesn't. Every muscle in my body is tight, every nerve on fire as our bodies burn hot together. Everything is building and I'm helpless to stop it. I fall over the edge, moaning Dom's name.

His lips find my nipple, sucking and biting as he continues to thrust into me, our bodies slick with sweat.

"I want another one," he demands.

"I don't know if I can," I say, even though I'm nodding.

"You can." His mouth doesn't stop working my nipple, while he rolls his hips into mine with perfect pressure. I scream at the intensity of my second orgasm.

Dom's hips stutter. "Shit, Ellie. Just like that. Fuck, baby, look at you." He throws his head back, eyes squeezed shut as he fills me.

We lie in the afterglow for a while, him pulling me into his side and tossing a blanket over us so we can catch our breath.

"I want to show you something," he says, before standing and pulling on his joggers. He helps me stand and wraps me in the blanket before taking my hand.

"Come here," he says, leading me from the couch and into our dining room. He stops in front of the far end of the table, his focus on the puzzle he made me. He takes a box from the cabinet and hands it to me.

"The last ones?" I ask, and he nods.

My heart is suddenly racing, nerves firing with awareness as my throat tightens. I don't fully understand why this has me emotional; my brain can only quickly rationalize that we've gone through so much and fought so hard to make it this far together. Far from perfect, but stronger every day.

I place the final dozen or so pieces into the last corner of the puzzle. None of them have any writing on them. We're finally done. Dom takes my hand, squeezing it once before sandwiching the puzzle between two poster boards and flipping the entire thing over, finally letting me see the picture on the other side.

"Do you finally see what I see?" he asks. "My wife is so fucking beautiful."

My trembling fingers find my lips as I gaze in shock at the photo of me, laughing and smiling as big as I've ever seen. My hair's a mess, and I'm not wearing any makeup, but I...love it. I look like joy personified.

"When did you take this?" I ask, voice unsteady.

"I took it about a week after Luca was born. We had only been home for a few days. It was about three thirty in the morning and we were delirious. I remember trying to take all these photos in the first few days—I probably have a hundred from the first twenty-four hours of his life—but I found this one later on mixed in with all the other candid shots I grabbed during that time. I honestly don't remember what was happening, I only know the time from the tag on my phone. When I saw this photo, we were in the shit storm of the newborn phase and I thought...there she is. She's still there.

"You were *never* broken, Ellie. You were *never* lost. You were just rearranging the pieces of you that make you whole. The pieces that make you who you are. You've always been beautiful, put together or not. Besides, I like you a little messy. I like our life when it's a little messy. No matter what, I love you every way imaginable."

Epilogue

Ellie

Dom chases after Luca as he makes his way to the playground. We agreed beforehand that Dom would take the first shift while I drink my coffee, then I'm up.

"Isabel, right?" I ask as I join the woman seated on the park bench. You might not remember me. We met here, gosh, almost a year ago. I'm..."

"Ellie, of course! Good to see you again," Isabel says, scooting over to make room for me and draping her arm along the back of the bench to face me. "How are you?"

"Better. Thanks to you in part. I'm sorry I haven't reached out. It's been...a year. But things are going well, and I finally started working with the woman you recommended."

"She's fucking amazing. Oh, I'm so glad," she says, waving off my concern, genuine excitement clear in her expression.

I'm kicking myself for not having reached out to Isabel to get to know her better. It'd be nice to have more mom friends, and clearly, she gets how crazy it can be and doesn't begrudge me for it.

"She really is. I'm finally starting to feel…like myself again."

She smiles and nods. "You seem different. In a good way. I'm happy to see it."

Giggles pull our attention to the playground, where her daughter is holding Luca's hand at his insistence, while he guides her around the playground. Okay, guiding might be a strong word. Luca's dragging her around. She's laughing and pointing her finger this way and that way, trying to teach my rowdy toddler how to conduct himself.

"She's patient, huh?" I ask Isabel.

"Apparently," she says with a laugh. "That's news to me."

Dom gives us a wave and supervises the two new best friends as we enjoy the crisp, fall morning.

"Are you home with him full time?" Isabel asks, her smile growing as the pair make their way to the slide.

"Part time. I recently quit my job in marketing to focus on my photography business," I say, still unable to believe I can say that out loud. It took some planning and a lot of luck. My clientele list grew unbelievably fast, and I couldn't be more grateful to finally be spending my time doing something I'm passionate about. It's also incredibly convenient to make my own hours that best fit what our family needs.

"Oh wow. Any chance you do family sessions? I've been looking to have family photos taken before it's time to order holiday cards."

"That's the majority of what I do. That and newborn photos."

I decided after two bookings that I didn't want to take photos of labor and delivery anymore. The two I did were great, and went well. Mom and baby are happy and healthy. But I decided I needed to set a boundary for my own mental health. I much prefer to focus on families *afterward*. I love working with newborns especially. It's easy for me to see which moms are in need of a little extra love, and I hope that with my experience, I'm able to offer them another level of understanding of what they might be going through.

Postpartum is no fucking joke. I'm grateful to walk with someone as they navigate such a confusing, wonderful, terrifying, and incredible time in their life, while also giving them some special photos to look back on one day.

"You're probably booked," Isabel says, biting her lip. "Right?"

I smile and shrug. "Eh, not too booked for the ultimate mom's mom."

"Seriously, Ellie. That would be amazing."

I hand her one of my cards.

"Let's set something up. Then maybe we could take these two kiddos to the aquarium downtown or something." I nod toward Luca and Isabel's daughter who is still being a great sport and is now teaching Luca how to spin the large tic-tac-toe spindles.

"I'd love to," Isabel says with a smile.

I catch Dominic's eyes on me, my happiness reflected back at me.

***

Dom is leaning against the doorway, watching as I rock Luca, his lanky limbs limp and his body heavy against my torso. I try not to give into the emotion threatening to spill over at the thought of how this little kid used to be such a tiny baby. How gummy smiles have turned into toothy grins. How his cooing has turned into words and short phrases. How this small wonder developed such a huge personality. How someone so small could steal my whole heart.

Instead of his normal bedtime story tonight, I did something my therapist and I have been talking about for a while. I showed Luca his baby book. The one I couldn't touch until long after his birth. It went from empty to chaotically overstuffed. I printed pictures, added small keepsakes, included his earliest crafts, and wrote as much as I possibly could. All the things I want Luca to know.

As I hold my exhausted toddler in my arms, worn out from his two-year birthday party—one I was able to participate in planning...enthusiastically—I decide to take the next step.

I worry that when Luca has questions about the day he was born, I'll freeze and say all the wrong things and inadvertently make him feel terrible about a day that was supposed to be all celebrations and joy.

I've been working on how I want to talk about it, and I figure it's easiest to start now, and start small, and as I grow more comfortable talking about it, it'll be easier to answer Luca's inevitably more difficult questions someday.

I want to be honest while also ensuring that Luca understands that none of my struggles have ever been his fault. He and Dominic gave me the strength I needed to find hope in healing, in overcoming, and in love.

So I begin.

Dom's eyes focused on me, full of compassion and...pride.

I keep my eyes locked on his, drawing strength from his confidence in me, and in us. I brush my hand over the back of Luca's head, placing a kiss on his forehead.

"Years ago, your daddy and I made a wish. We wished that our family would grow. We were so lucky, and when we found out you were on our way, Daddy thought he had to furnish an entire nursery right then and there." I smirk at Dom, who chuckles, crossing his arms, glancing down, quickly trying to stifle the sound.

"When it was time for you to be born, some unexpected things happened, and instead of taking a long time to join us, you were born quickly and with the help of a lot of people. There were a lot of hands and hearts holding us close during that time. When I finally held you, it was like my heart had fallen out of my chest and into my arms. You were so small, but immediately you became our everything. Your first smile took our breath away. Your first laugh gave us life. And the first time you said *Dada* and *Mama*, you changed our world.

"*Everything* changed the day you were born. Thank you for growing with us. Thank you for teaching us. You are safe. You are loved."

Luca, asleep in my arms, sighs and snuggles into my neck. I kiss him once more before laying him in his crib, doing my best to not fall in after him as I bend at the waist over the railing. *Wow, he's really growing.*

I wait, watching for a moment while he adjusts before laying a blanket over him and softly rubbing his back for a moment. "Night, baby boy."

Dom reaches his hand toward me, and I take it, following him out of Luca's room. He holds me in silence as we stand outside his bedroom door in the dark hallway.

One of the best things about my over-the-top, loving, considerate husband is he loves me in the bright, loud moments and in the dark, quiet ones too. I usually need him most somewhere in between. Where I'm lost, and he always helps me feel found.

Dom

It turns out Ellie meant it when she said she was going to marry me. Because months after my birthday and the promise she made at the piano bar, I woke up to a surprise vow renewal ceremony being set up in our backyard and Luca in a white button-up, khaki pants, and suspenders.

Fucking adorable.

I watch as my parents play with Luca in the backyard. He moves from seat to seat, testing each one before running circles underneath the flower archway set up in front of our willow tree at the end of an aisle formed only by rows of folding chairs and two strips of raked leaves and small pumpkins.

"You really had no idea?" Ellie asks, biting her lip and wringing her hands together, drawing my attention away from the window.

She's stunning in a cream sweater dress that hugs every one of her delicious curves with a swooping neckline and brown, leather boots.

"I can honestly say you shocked this husband of yours more than you ever have before," I say before taking her fidgeting hands in one of mine and using the other to lift her chin so I can kiss her.

"Even that time I pulled out the nipple clamps?" she asks, mumbling loudly against my lips, making me laugh.

"Ellie, *please.* I do not want the image of Dom wearing nipple clamps in my mind before I'm expected to perform," Chris chastises.

Chris has been ordained since we got married, having performed our first ceremony and apparently about to perform our second.

"They weren't for *me*, but maybe later…" I say, pulling Ellie flush against me by her hips, digging my fingers in just a little.

She laughs and pulls me down by my neck for another kiss.

"Only if you behave today," she says.

"Okay, I really don't need to hear this," Jake says as he walks in with a simple bouquet of wildflowers, handing them to Ellie.

"Yes, we fucking do. Keep going. Then what's going to happen?" Dee asks, leaning against the kitchen counter, resting her chin on her fists, propped up on her elbows.

"I vote for a blindfold," Abby says, before sipping from her champagne glass.

"Oh yeah, then handcuffs," Bec adds, clinking her glass against Abby's as they lean back against the island.

"What are you guys reading this month?" Aiden asks with mock outrage, but he's not a good actor. It's clear his interest is piqued as he winks at Bec and she winks back before biting her lip.

"I think I just threw up in my mouth," Jake says, dramatically leaning over the kitchen sink.

"Show some compassion, Jake. They've got a kid. It's not like you don't already know they're banging. Besides, the mom and dad of the group deserve some freaky time. You need me to watch little man, so you can go…you know?" Dylan asks, making his eyebrows dance.

"I'm pretty sure this is the second time this year I'm going to ask us all to have better boundaries," Carissa says, fighting a laugh.

"I'm with Carissa," Evie pipes in as she gives Aiden a disgusted look. "Stop eye-fucking Bec in the kitchen, Aiden. You're around people, you know?"

"Ugh, I'm too single for this." Dee sighs.

"Well, when you're ready, baby, I'll be available for your ceremony too," Chris says with a smile.

"You're hired," she says, kissing his cheek before opening the sliding door to our backyard. "All right, you crazy lovebirds, it's time."

The rest of the group files out of the house and into the yard, taking their seats. It's a beautiful, warm fall day. I scan the yard, observing our family and friends that made it today and can't believe how lucky I am that my wife did all of this for me.

"You're perfect, you know that?" I ask, just me and Ellie left standing in the soft, evening light filtering into our home.

Her cheeks are glowing and turn a deep shade of pink with her blush. I stroke my thumb over the rosy color, marveling at how in love with her I am.

"I don't know about that," she says.

"I do. There's no one in the world I'd rather spend my life with. The highs and the lows. I wouldn't want to face any of them without you by my side. You've given me so much in such a short amount of time. I'm going to spend the rest of my life showing you how much I crave you, appreciate you, and love you."

She hums, stepping into my arms and wrapping hers tightly around my middle. Resting her head in the crook of my neck, she whispers, "Maybe you could say that all again in like five minutes when we exchange vows." We both laugh and I brush my lips across her forehead, taking it all in. The feel of her warm, incredible body in my arms. Her breath against my skin. The smell of her shampoo and the earthy, fall breeze. The laughter of our loved ones waiting for us to share this day with them.

She strokes her thumb over the stubborn wrinkle in my forehead, and I poke the solo dimple on her left cheek. I take her hand in mine and lead us into the grass, leaves crunching with every step. Both of us, smiling like two kids in love. I thank the skies for returning the woman in my arms to me, keeping her close to my heart.

Ellie and I will always come back to each other. We will always find each other. We will always find ourselves.

Bonus Epilogue

Ellie

"**S**top being gentle with me. I'm not a mom tonight. I'm your wife. Fuck me like it."

"Okay, *wife*, close your eyes." Dom's command sends shivers down my spine, my core tightens, and my thighs press together in a desperate attempt to ignite the fire that's building. I do as he asks. "You say stop and I do. Understand?"

"Understood," I whisper.

Dom's tongue slides up my neck before he sucks and nibbles on my ear lobe. "Turn around," he murmurs. "Turn around right fucking now."

His strong hands grab my hips, and I shriek before giggling as he forces me to turn around, my palms pressing against the wall of the closet in front of me.

Sue me, sometimes a girl wants to see a guy lose his mind with need. I like when he has to work for it. I haven't seen Dom like this in so long, and it has my heart pounding.

His hands immediately begin to wander, grabbing, pulling, twisting, and teasing. One finds its way into the top of my dress. He dips his hand between my sensitive skin and the soft fabric of my dress before palming my full breast and pinching my nipple. His other hand rests firmly across my lower belly, holding me tightly against him.

"Maybe we shouldn't do this. We're forty feet from Bec and Aiden's wedding reception, Dom. I don't like being quiet, or have you forgotten?"

In an instant, his hand wraps around my throat, pulling me flush against his body, all of his body, enough for me to feel the very distinct outline of his hardness pressed against my ass and lower back. He tilts my chin so I'm forced to look at him. His heady gaze heats me from my core to my throat. I can't find the words; I can't say anything with him looking at me like that. Looking at me like he's about to devour me.

"You say that like I don't want you screaming. You say that like I'm not dying to hear you calling my name as you fall apart. You say that like I give a fuck who hears me taking my wife and giving her everything she needs. Do you want this?"

I nod enthusiastically, at a loss for words.

"Then give me your mouth," he says, before stealing my lips between his.

His hands continue exploring my body, lighting my desire, waking up a deep-rooted need. His grip moves, first to my throat, coasting to my jaw before sliding into my hair, threading his fingers through the strands and gripping, the tug igniting my core in a pulsing fever.

I pull him closer so I can bite his lower lip. He moans into my mouth and I do the same. I'm dizzy with need, his grip on me being the only reason I haven't stumbled to the floor.

Dom drops a hand to my thigh, clawing at my bridesmaid dress like a man undone, scrunching it up in his fist as he works the fabric higher and higher. Then he's pulling my dress even higher, all the way to my waist, revealing my lower half to him.

"Thank fuck," he groans into my neck. "None of that goddamn shapewear in the way tonight."

"I was hoping I'd get lucky."

"Ellie Moretti, you brought me here with every intention of seducing me. Filthy Momma," he murmurs into my ear, before tipping my jaw so I'm forced to meet his eyes. "I'm the lucky one. These panties soaked for me?"

"What are you going to do about it?" I challenge.

He tugs my thong to the side in one swift movement before his other hand comes down hard on my ass cheek. I squeak in shock, then moan at the feel of his fingers entering me, seeking my G-spot, which he finds with ease.

"I haven't decided yet," he says, voice laden with playfulness. "I like feeling you gripping my fingers almost as much as I like to feel you clenching on my tongue. But when neither of those is enough, I dream of you squeezing my cock with this pussy."

We both freeze, hearing voices approach from down the hall. Dom wraps a hand over my mouth and I bring my hands up to hold his forearm, my breaths coming quickly from my nose as I struggle to keep my breathing even with his fingers still inside me.

Is that Dee and Dylan?

The voices and footsteps quiet as they pass the closet we're hiding in. Alone again, Dom starts moving his fingers, his palm pressing firmly against my clit with the perfect amount of pressure. I grip his arm tighter, leaning my head against his shoulder and moaning into his palm.

"Dirty girl, Ellie. Moaning while I finger fuck you in this closet with people just outside. Do I need to keep my hand here so they don't storm in wondering why there's a woman screaming in the coat closet?"

Fuck, oh fuck, I'm going to come.

I nod frantically, not caring who hears because I'm so desperate to come. So close. My hips grind, willing him to increase the pressure of his palm on my clit all while shoving his thick fingers deeper.

"I don't want them to hear you, but I want to see you," he says, pulling my head back so it rests against his chest. My eyes roll back and I'm unable to hold out any longer. My body convulses around his hand. Dom never slows his movements. He helps me through it, singing praises into my ear as I come down from the high.

"Fucking beautiful, Ellie." I watch as Dom brings his fingers up in front of me, the sheen of my release glistening in the dim light of the closet. Then he moans as he sucks them into his mouth. I can't look away as he cleans his fingers, then presents them to me and I do the same. His cock still presses firmly into my ass and I grind back against him, still mindlessly seeking to be filled again. The orgasm was incredible, but not enough to satisfy. I want him to bend me over and take me hard and fast.

"Back against the wall, Ellie."

I move quickly, and he's on me just as fast, drawing one of my legs up and around his hip as he sinks his thick cock into me just like I wanted, hard and fast.

The music from the wedding reception thumps loudly in the background as a more upbeat song plays over the speakers.

"Thank fuck," Dom groans into my neck before he unleashes himself on me, pounding into me in a delicious rhythm before we both come loudly, thankfully drowned out by the bass of the song.

He takes my face in his hands, both of us breathless, before we laugh.

"Great wedding," I say.

"Fucking phenomenal," Dom agrees.

"Let's never tell them."

"Deal."

Then my perfect husband cleans us up, takes my hand lovingly in his, and dances with me all night long.

Acknowledgements

To you, the reader. A truly heartfelt thank-you. I love to write, and sharing love stories with all of you is a dream come true. For those of you here because you loved *Winning the Nightcap*, I appreciate your continued support. I recognize this was a very different story, told through the perspective of two people who were hitting rock bottom both as individuals and as a couple. That can make it difficult to feel the lightness of a love story. I wanted this novel to show the highest of highs, but to do that and still do the source of Ellie and Dom's struggle justice, I needed to also show the lowest of lows. Thank you for sticking with these characters until the end. It healed a piece of me—more than I could ever explain—to see them through their conflicts and eventually finding their way back to each other. I hope you loved the journey as much as I did. If this story resonated with you and your life experience in one way or another, please know that I'm rooting for you to find those pieces of yourself that you're hoping to rediscover. There's beauty in the puzzle of your ever-evolving life, even if it isn't always easy to see from where you're standing.

To my husband. Thank you for never once complaining about the *click-clack* of my keyboard when I wrote into the early morning hours just so I could do so more comfortably from bed while you slept. Thank you for being an incredible father and taking care of our family so that I can follow this dream and get these words out of my head and my heart. Thank you for being my alpha reader, my number one supporter, my everything. Much of what happened to us during the most vulnerable time in our lives as new parents inspired me to write this story. The darkness and the light were equally important for these characters as they were for us. Words are not enough for me to tell you how grateful I am to you for being at my side during the scariest moment of my life, and for staying there every step of the way after as we learned to heal together as a family. In the end, we went through something horrific, but were given the best gift I could ever imagine, our son. We're not perfect, but you're my matching puzzle piece, and we fit no matter what our picture looks like at the end of this life. I love you forever.

To my son. We're here, and for that, I could not be more grateful. Being able to spend my life raising you, learning who you are, and being amazed at all that you do is all I've ever wanted. I used to wish our story had started differently, but after all we went through, there has not been a day that has gone by where I haven't loved you with every beat of my heart and every fiber of my soul. I will always love you so much, sweetheart. Thank you for painting my world with color, laughter, and joy. Being your momma is a gift.

To my two fur babies. Endless cuddles, distractions, and inspiration. You two are the best faithful companions I could ever dream of having by my side. I love you both so very much.

To my family. Thank you for laughing with me, supporting me, and loving me. Thank you for making a fuss over buying my first book, having me sign it, and sending me conveniently timed SNL skits about romance books in math class. Thanks to *almost* all of you for not reading my book. And thank you to those of you who decided to read it for not making it awkward at family get-togethers, for hyping me up about how much you liked it, and for sharing your favorite quotes with me. Writing about fun, healthy, happy families is easy when I've learned from all of you. I love you.

To my friends who journeyed into motherhood with me. Thank you for every late-night text, ridiculous parenting story swap, and shared TikTok videos that reassured me that I was not alone. Thank you for helping me laugh at the insanity of it all; I need that more than I could ever say.

To my therapist. There aren't words to adequately explain my gratitude to you for walking with me the past few years. I was barely holding myself together when we met, but you brought me back. You helped me uncover pieces of my old self I believed I had lost forever. You showed me that I could mold them into a new, more healed me. I can never repay you. You are a treasure in this world, and I'm so lucky to know you.

To Paisley McNab of Perfectly Write Editing Services. Finding a copy editor as a new indie author is a daunting task, but luckily for me, I only had to do it once. Thank you for taking on another novel from me and working your magic. Collaborating with you on this book is something I was looking forward to the entire time I was drafting the manuscript, itching for you to put your touch on things and make it the best story possible. You're a one-in-a-million talent (you know these references will only get more ridiculous in book three). I'm forever grateful this experience brought us together and I was lucky enough to find both an amazing editor and friend.

To Lindsay (@lindsayyandbooks). I'm so grateful you took a chance on a baby indie author and signed up for an ARC of my first book. Thank you for your endless words of encouragement, your incredible edits of *Winning the Nightcap*, and your friendship. Having you beta-read this novel put my mind at ease, knowing you would help elevate this story. Brainstorming with you in countless voice notes got me through some truly difficult edits, and it made a world of difference having you cheer for this story all along the way. If you ever need a monster romance rec, you know where to find me!

To the Beta Reading Team at E&A Editing Services. Thank you for sharing your thoughtful insights on the earliest version of this novel. Your feedback gave me so much to consider and informed so many decisions that led to this final story. I'm so grateful to each of you. And to the one reader who shared your personal experience with me in your feedback, please know how much that meant to me.

To Melissa Doughty of Mel D. Designs. Thank you for creating a beautiful cover for this novel. You made the entire process easy and enjoyable. You designed the perfect snapshot of Ellie and Dom's world, and it feels like home every time I look at it.

I do not personally know Dr. Teela Tomassetti, PsyD (@theteaonbirthtrauma) or Kayleigh Summers, LCSW, PMH-C (@thebirthtrauma_mama), but I have the deepest appreciation for their work. In the early weeks after giving birth, I could barely sleep—not only because of the adorable newborn who needed fed and held, but because my mind was somehow both frozen and racing throughout the day and night. The quiet moments were interrupted by loud flashbacks, and though I was rarely alone, I felt overwhelmingly isolated. I didn't understand what happened to me, and I didn't understand how to recover from it. While I was searching for a therapist who specialized in perinatal mental health, I found your social media accounts, and they were a refuge. The community you were building, the understanding you were showing, and the voices you were bringing to birth trauma were my lifeline so many times. What you are doing is incredibly important, needed, and appreciated. Thank you both.

About the author

Jane Hayes writes sweet and spicy contemporary romance. In her work, you can count on finding witty banter, strong friendships, found family, comedic relief, heart-warming connections, and, of course, a happily ever after.

When she's not writing, Jane's chasing her toddler and two dogs, oversharing very descriptive details from her latest alien or dark romance read with her husband, working part time at the local bookstore, or devouring another romance novel.

Also by Jane Hayes

FOR THE HEART SERIES

Winning the Nightcap